CW01212636

1

Alpha Zander

By V.Turner

Copyright © V.Turner

All rights reserved.

The characters and events in this book are fictitious.

Any resemblance to real persons living or dead is coincidental and not intended by the author.

No part of this book may be reproduced or stored in a retrieval system or transmitted in any form or by any means electronic, mechanical, photocopying, recording or otherwise without express written permission of the publisher.

A little idea can turn into something wondrous and magical.

With a bit of faith, passion, and support, you can accomplish anything.

Always believe in yourself.

Contents

Chapter 1 - ASHLEIGH 10

Chapter 2 - ASHLEIGH 14

Chapter 3 - ASHLEIGH 18

Chapter 4 - ZANDER 21

Chapter 5 - ZANDER 24

Chapter 6 - ASHLEIGH 27

Chapter 7 - ZANDER 31

Chapter 8 - ASHLEIGH 34

Chapter 9 - ASHLEIGH 37

Chapter 10 - ZANDER 41

Chapter 11 - ASHLEIGH 44

Chapter 12 - ZANDER 48

Chapter 13 - ASHLEIGH 53

Chapter 14 - ZANDER 57

Chapter 15 - ASHLEIGH 61

Chapter 16 - ZANDER 67

Chapter 17 - ASHLEIGH 72

Chapter 18 - ZANDER 75

Chapter 19 - ASHLEIGH 77

Chapter 20 - ZANDER 79

Chapter 21 - ASHLEIGH 82

Chapter 22 - ZANDER 85

Chapter 23 - ASHLEIGH 88

Chapter 24 - ASHLEIGH 91
Chapter 25 - ZANDER 94
Chapter 26 - ZANDER 97
Chapter 27 - ASHLEIGH 99
Chapter 28 - ZANDER 102
Chapter 29 - ASHLEIGH 107
Chapter 30 - ASHLEIGH 109
Chapter 31 - ZANDER 113
Chapter 32 - ASHLEIGH 115
Chapter 33 - ZANDER 118
Chapter 34 - ASHLEIGH 121
Chapter 35 - ZANDER 125
Chapter 36 - ZANDER 129
Chapter 37 - ASHELIGH 132
Chapter 38 - KYLIE 136
Chapter 39 - ZANDER 140
Chapter 40 - DANIEL 144
Chapter 41 - ASHLEIGH 147
Chapter 42 - ASHLEIGH 150
Chapter 43 - ZANDER 155
Chapter 44 - ZANDER 162
Chapter 45 - ASHLEIGH 166
Chapter 46 - ZANDER 172
Chapter 47 - ASHLEIGH 177
Chapter 48 - ASHLEIGH 181
Chapter 49 - ZANDER 185

Chapter 50 - ASHLEIGH 191
Chapter 51 - ZANDER 194
Chapter 52 - ASHLEIGH 200
Chapter 53 - OLIVER 206
Chapter 54 - ASHLEIGH 212
Chapter 55 - ZANDER 217
Chapter 56 - ASHLEIGH 220
Chapter 57 - ZANDER 225
Chapter 58 - ASHLEIGH 230
Chapter 59 - ZANDER 234
Chapter 60 - ASHELIGH 239
Chapter 61 - OLIVER 245
Chapter 62 - ZANDER 250
Chapter 63 - ASHLEIGH 255
Chapter 64 - ZANDER 258
Chapter 65 - ASHLEIGH 263
Chapter 66 - ZANDER 268
Epilogue - ASHLEIGH 275
Epilogue - ZANDER 278
Bonus 282
Pack Information 290
Acknowledgements 291
Author Note: 292

Chapter 1 - ASHLEIGH

"Ash, Ash come on! We're gonna be late for school," my best friend and soon-to-be Alpha, Oliver bangs on my bedroom door hurrying me up.

"I'm ready, just give me a few minutes to finish my assignment," I call back.

"Ugh! Stop being such a nerd, Ash. We all know you finished it last week," my younger brother Brent calls out.

I hear a growl come from Ollie followed by a slap. "Ouch! Hey, what was that for?" Brent responds.

"Don't be disrespectful to your sister," Ollie snaps.

"Pfft, if you weren't our cousin, I'd swear you were in love with her," Brent grumbles before making his way down the stairs.

"Come on Ash, we're gonna be late for school," Ollie bangs on the door once more before heading down to breakfast.

I sighed. It's no use trying to finish anything now, both were up and ready to go.

I look around my room admiring the different shades of light pink, silver, and white. In the middle of the room is my king-sized bed with a mountain of pink and cream pillows I love to snuggle into at night, with fairy lights strung behind from floor to ceiling. Flanking the bed are matching bedside tables that have light cream lamps and an alarm clock. Off to the side is a silver dresser with a few knickknacks, including my jewellery box.

There are two other doors in my room, besides the one leading out of my room. The one beside my full-length mirror goes to my wardrobe while the other leads to my ensuite bathroom.

As I make my way to the bedroom door, I stop by the full-length mirror. "Yep, this is as good as it's going to get," I mutter to myself.

'Aww, come on I think we look hot,' my wolf Kia says. *'If you add a little human make-up, do the hair, and maybe show some skin, the boys will be clawing for us,'* she giggles.

I roll my eyes at my wolf and mutter, 'what happened to wanting to find your mate when we turned 18?' I ask her.

'Well, I know you are longing for companionship, so as long as we don't fall in love with him, I don't mind what you do, but it all stops as soon as we meet our mate,' Kia says with a shrug.

Today for school I am wearing my skinny black jeans with white Vans and a beautiful light pink short-sleeve button-down top with puffy sleeves. My light brown curly hair is thrown up with a large hair clip into a half-ponytail-loose, my big brown eyes staring back at me.

Maybe I could ask Meghan for some makeup tips. I will need something for this weekend at least.

Kia starts jumping up and down in my mind, *'Yes, yes, yes, I'm so glad Oliver talked you into having a birthday party, more chances of meeting our mate and meeting more people.'*

I muttered back to her, 'I suppose we are going to be the Beta of this pack, might as well put Dad's and Uncle's training into some use.'

I collect my things for school and make my way down the stairs into the kitchen where everyone is seated in the large dining room table happily clinking away and eating breakfast.

"Ahh, there she is," my dad says, looking up from his conversation with Uncle David, the Alpha of our pack.

"Morning Daddy, Uncle, how are you both?" I chippered as I made my way through the dining room.

"How are you feeling today? Nervous, excited?" He asks with a sceptical glance at my uncle.

"I'm fine, I tried to get more work done before we headed off to school but the boys wouldn't let me, pretty happy with the result so far, let's just hope it's enough," I answer back as I take a seat between him and Meghan.

We are in the final stages of my Bio classes and have just a few assignments and reports to finish up on. I want everything to be perfect before handing them in this morning. Thankfully, I finished everything last Thursday, so it gave me the weekend to proofread everything and make sure it is all perfect.

"Oh, you will be fine," Meghan says as she passes me food from the table, filling my plate. "You worry that pretty little head of yours too much when you should be having fun and relaxing."

"I guess so," I mutter as I eat the food.

Meghan is our Gamma, Alex's mate, and both are three years older than Ollie and me. Meghan came into Alex's life when he turned 18. They found each other when he was out in the clubs celebrating his birthday and have been together since.

We all grew up together in the packhouse. Since are all heirs to pack leadership, it was natural for us to forge friendships and ensure the pack works well together. If the leadership doesn't get along well, how else is the pack supposed to get along?

I looked up at her from my plate of food. I sigh heavily, not believing the favour I'm about to ask her. "Hey, Meg. I want to ask a huge favour, but pleaseeeee don't make a big deal about it, okay?"

She had stops mid-conversation with Alex. Ollie and Brent also become quiet from across the table, obviously listening to our conversation.

"Erm... as you know, Friday is my birthday, and we are having a party Friday night after school. Could you help me with makeup and clothes? You know everything I have is not great for a party."

She lets out a squeal of joy and claps her hands. "Yes, yes, yes, so excited you finally asked me to do a makeover for you! You are going to love this! We will also get something for Friday if you meet your mate; you must look hot and sexy."

She turns to uncle, "Alpha David, can we please use the car and credit cards on Thursday night so I can take Ash for a much-needed shopping trip?"

She bats her eyelashes and asks in a sweet voice, causing her mate Alex to growl in annoyance at the over-affection towards our Alpha. Typical possessive male, I laughed to myself, looked over to Uncle David and dad, who had also stopped what they were doing and are now giving us attention.

"Sure, consider it a 'welcome to adulthood' gift," Uncle David smiles and nods. "But ..."

Meghan lets out an annoyed groan. Everyone around the tables laughs. There is always a 'but' with Uncle.

"Two guards will be with you at all times." Being ranked members of the pack I should expect nothing less.

Meghan nods and looks at me, an annoyed expression on her face. "Sure Alpha, thank you. Ash, I'll pick you up after school on Thursday. The boys have football training, so it works out."

I nod in response while trying to work out my schedule in my head for the rest of the week since Thursday and Friday study time are pretty much cancelled. Whenever possible I do my homework a week ahead in case important pack business comes up that will require my assistance. Personally, I think it is better to be overprepared.

"Okay, are you kiddies ready for school?" Auntie Sarah calls out as she walks through the dining room.

"Yeah ma, just finishing up now," Ollie answers while wolfing down the last of his food.

I quickly finish my breakfast and check the time … we had about 20 minutes to go till first period. Mom and auntie are waiting at the door as we all pile out.

“Have a good day today! Please try not to cause any trouble.” Mum kissed each of us.

“No worries, auntie, we will be on our best behaviour,” Ollie calls back as he waves while walking out the door.

Brent, Ollie, and I pile into Ollie’s shiny black Jeep and head to school.

Chapter 2 - ASHLEIGH

"Do you guys mind if we stop by Victoria's house? I told her I'd pick her up this morning," Ollie asks, looking at Brent and me through the front mirror.

He didn't have to ask; he knows what we think of Victoria. In a nutshell, she's a total psycho bitch. At one point she was so bad I had to tell him about her bullying other pack members and flirting and flaunting with other men. Obviously, she denied everything later.

They stopped seeing each other for a couple of months but then we caught them sneaking around again the other week. He finally came clean and confessed that he and Victoria were dating again.

Being the future Alpha and all, he really doesn't owe us any explanation. But he is our cousin, and it hurts that he would take her word against ours. However, if she doesn't change then sooner or later, she will out herself and he will find out on his own.

"Sure," I respond with a shrug. To be honest, I don't really care anymore. As his Beta I can give him advice. Beyond that, I can't change his mind or opinion. He must do that on his own.

"Why don't you hop up front, Ash, and she can sit in the back with Brent?" he mutters.

I look at him in surprise. "Are you sure?" I ask.

"Of course!" he replies with a frown. "First, you're my best friend. Second, you're my Beta. And third, we just started things back up a few days ago, I just want to see if anything changes in her attitude before we make it official again. And, well, what better way to test it?" He shrugged.

I fold my arms in frustration and look back at him sternly. "I am not going to be part of your girlfriend's attitude experiment."

"Please," he asks, looking back at me pleadingly. "I took in what you and Brent said. I just want to check things out and take it slow."

I sigh guess he really likes this girl. He was depressed for a few weeks when they ended things the first time around, and the parents tried to ask us what happened. Of course, Brent and I kept quiet about the whole thing because it wasn't our place to tell them.

I am only slightly older than Ollie who is turning eighteen in three months and will then be able to sense his mate. Our parents are very particular about us waiting for our mates. Nowadays, a lot of people don't really wait, but I like the idea of my mate being my one and only. I didn't really see the point in dating because we were going to find our fated mates. What was the point in falling for someone if we already had someone destined for us, the heartache and hurt alone would be pointless so I always avoided it. When I was younger, I wanted to have a boyfriend but as I grew older, I realized there wasn't any point.

"Fine," I sigh and move to the front. He grins then steps on the gas, taking off in the direction of Victoria's house.

Victoria was waiting for us on the steps of her front porch. She looks and smiles when she sees Ollie then frowns as soon as she sees me in the front seat then peered behind and sees Brent.

Her frown becomes a frustrated pout. I guess Ollie forgot to mention we were coming along for the ride. I braced myself for the explosion that was going to happen when she reaches the back door.

"Hi baby, I didn't know we were going to have company this morning," Victoria said in her sickly-sweet voice while she hops into the car.

"Sorry, I forgot to mention it," Ollie half-heartedly responds.

The tension in the car is thick and we sit silently for the rest of the trip. Brent shifts around awkwardly in the back seat trying to get away from the whole situation. Victoria just sits there looking at her nails and fiddling with her hair. She looked up at Ollie once or twice as if trying to decide if she should say something but decided against it.

Ollie mind-linked me just as we pull up to the school. 'Are you ok?' he asked, eyes still on the road in front of him trying not to give away that we were having a silent conversation.

'Yep, just stressing about this test and my reports,' I answer back. I quickly grab my schoolbooks and get out of the car as quickly as possible. "See you guys in the cafeteria at lunch," I call out.

As I run up the school stairs lots of people looked at me and nod, muttering "Morning, Beta" out of respect. I nod back and respond with the same "good morning".

As the future Beta of Liverpool, I like to keep the peace, I like to know who's who, and what's what. Not in a bad way, just that it's my job to know if there are any threats old or new, and I need to evaluate them accordingly to protect our pack and future Alpha.

At school Kia likes to keep a low profile and will only stir if she senses a threat of any kind or to anyone. Today seems like a harmless day, so she retreated to the back of my mind and let me get on with the day of schoolwork and teachers. My two closest female friends, Chloe and Skyla, come bounding up to me with big smiles on their faces. It's nice to have some familiar faces around when we first started high school.

Chloe and I belong to the same pack and grew up together. We met Skyla in the second term of our first year and quickly became fast friends. She is from the Westfield pack about 30kms from our pack lands. Visiting her has been hard but we made it work. At least we get to see each other in school. We also made sure to include her in everything.

"Girl, how have you been? How was the weekend? I am so excited about Friday! So happy you decided to throw a party," Chloe babbles on as she reaches my locker.

I smile, "it was good, just study and more training with uncle and dad," I shrug and walk towards my Bio class. "How was both of your weekend?" I asked them both.

There are many people standing around and muttering as we entered the main hallway, which led to the different classrooms and fields. I look up and frown. Kia's restless, pacing back and forth, unsettled. She's never been like this before.

'What's wrong?' I ask her.

'I'm not sure, something just feels off,' she mutters.

'Like a bad thing?' I ask.

'No, just different,' she responds, still pacing in the back of my mind. It is unusual for her to be this restless.

"What's all the commotion?" I wonder out loud.

Chloe and Skyla looked at each other with concern. "Zander Blackwood is back," Skyla mutters.

My body goes stiff, and I quickly mind-link Ollie. 'Ollie, Blackwood is back, how do you want to handle this?'

'Just keep an eye on everything, keep your distance,' Ollie responds.

'Noted,' I reply.

The eyes of some students' glaze as Ollie mind links pack members who are currently in school and makes a formal announcement. 'Zander Blackwood is back at school, keep your distance and watch your back around him and his pack. Do not engage. The North side of the cafeteria is out of bounds while he and his pack are in the area. If any issues arise between our pack and his, link me and Beta Ashleigh.'

'Yes Alpha,' came a wave of responses after the announcement.

Chloe glances at me with a worried expression. "I guess things just got a little harder than we liked," she mutters softly as we walk past humans and other pack members gathering around and gawking at the new arrivals.

I nod and glance around. Blackwood is standing between the massive pillars leading to the English classrooms with his arm around the waist of a she-wolf with long-dark hair. She is wearing a short white cropped top with her boobs spilling out, a black and white striped mini skirt, and black stiletto heels. She has long dark hair and she was wearing black stiletto heels, a black and white striped mini-skirt, and a short white cropped top with her boobs spilling out.

My breathing hitches and my heart races as he runs his hand through his beautiful dark brown hair. His hazel eyes look excited, happy even. Perhaps he is happy to be back in school. Or it could be because of the she-wolf standing next to him presenting herself to him like a prize to be claimed.

“I guess so, yeah. Honestly, I didn’t think they were going to come back. I thought they’d go somewhere closer to their pack.” I shrug as we walk towards the science labs.

“This is me; I’ll catch you guys at lunch? I have three periods this morning,” I wave to my friends as I walk into my science class.

“Sure thing. We will text you when we all finish, and we can meet up,” they chipper back.

We wish each other luck for the morning and go our separate ways until the lunchtime bell.

Chapter 3 - ASHLEIGH

The start of this week has been hell so far, and it's only 12.30pm on a Monday!!

I don't know how much more I can take, I'm not usually this wound up, I suppose maybe because I got up earlier this morning to finish some work and maybe because Kia has been so restless today ... it all just added up.

I just finished two exams and hopefully, I aced them both as I'm aiming to be dux of the school this year. Thank goodness it's lunchtime and I can finally get some food. I'm hungry!

I make my way over to the cafeteria to see that Chloe and Skyla are already lined up. Chloe has her phone out and is tapping away furiously. She looks up as I approach them and smile.

"There you are, I was just texting to see what you wanted for lunch," she says and frowns as she feels my annoyance and frustration.

I may be a Beta but Ollie's dad and mine are brothers which means Alpha blood also runs through my veins. When I get upset, which is rare, I can't hide it. My aura just pushes out and affects the people near me.

"What's wrong, babe?" she asked. "How did the tests and reports go?"

I sigh. Of course, she picked up on it, even Skyla looks worried.

"It's not like you to be this, what's the word ... itchy?"

Skyla laughed, "Itchy?"

"Well, yeah I mean, she's all jumpy and frustrated like she can't reach an itch," Chloe laughs back.

I smile and shake my head at my silly friends. They always know how to make me feel better no matter what. Their mates are going to be so lucky to have them.

"I just had Mr. Trevor for Bio, Miss Libbs for English, and Mr. Dominic for Economics," I sighed.

"Offt damn, I'm sorry gurl that sucks, Trevor and Dominic are dickheads. Libbs isn't too bad, but you have to be on her good side," Chloe says, understanding my frustration.

The cafeteria is a wide-open space that can accommodate well over 150 people, with tables of various sizes that can fit 6, 8, or 10 people. The glass doors all fold out making it nice and fresh in the summer and when closed in the winter, it keeps the warmth in nicely. Today is a beautiful Autumn day so someone opened all the glass doors to let the fresh air flow through.

They usually do a special every day with a variety of different foods you can purchase, if you pre-order in the morning you can get reserve homemade sandwiches, so you don't have to line up for 20 minutes.

I just nod and sigh while waiting in line for food. I look around the cafeteria to see where everyone is sitting today. With Blackwood's pack back there would have been some adjustments made.

When the humans found out about the supernatural world, they adjusted a lot of their lifestyle as did we to accommodate each other. The school we currently attend is one of the most prestigious schools around. Being on neutral ground or human land means that different packs clash as more than one Alpha and Beta are in the school grounds at the same time.

In a way it made sense. All these packs being together in one place means that there are better chances to help each other in case of an attack. It also helps in building relations between packs as well as building a relationship with the humans. However, if something goes wrong between packs because of any pent-up issues that haven't been resolved, then things go sideways quickly.

Luckily there has only been one or two instances where Ollie or I had to step in.

I look around and see Ollie with most of our pack over at one of the far corners, all crammed around a 10-seater table. After we grab our food, the girls and I intend to join them there.

Ollie looks up from his conversation with Brent. Feeling my gaze on him, he grins as he meets my eyes.

He suddenly frowns. Jeez is my agitation really that bad for Ollie to sense it all the way over there. I sigh and shake my head. 'Later,' I tell him in the mind-link. He nods in understanding and continues his conversation with Brent.

Mondays and Thursdays are the worst days to line up at the cafeteria; Thursdays because we get more meal options. I was in such a rush this morning that I wasn't able to pack my lunch.

As we slowly get closer to the pay station my thoughts are derailed as someone slams into me. I look up in surprise and was about to apologize when the girl spoke to me in an annoyingly bitchy voice, "watch where you're going, bitch, I just had to wait 20 minutes in line for that," she growls as she spills her lunch all over the front of my clothes.

Everyone around us gasped and went silent. Kia pushes forward, her aura blazing around me absolutely pissed at the disrespect coming from this stupid she-wolf. Quite frankly I've had enough today, too.

The she-wolf looks up in surprise, her lips open and close like a fish gasping for air.

"Excuse me, you ran into me," I growl with Kia overlapping.

I could see in my peripheral vision that Ollie was starting to get up to come over. I shoot him a look. He frowns then shrugs and sits back down. Chatter started back up with those who don't really care about what happened. But for the people around us, they were already cowering in submission.

“I... I..” she splutters. Kia is getting more and more frustrated with this she-wolf and pushes her aura out more, making her presence felt even more.

I suddenly recognized her. She’s the she-wolf draped all over Blackwood this morning...

“Is there a problem Beta?” a rich husky voice asks behind me.

I slowly turn around and come face to face … with Zander Blackwood.

Chapter 4 - ZANDER

I am going back to my old school today, Summer Vale College, one of the most prestigious high schools in our area. Both males and females attended since this is a coed school. It is also progressive and accepts both human and non-human students. Although mostly it's humans and wolves. Vampires and witches aren't really into mixing cultures.

I argued with my old man for about a week about why I had to go back to school, especially one with Oliver Steward and his little gang in it. Oliver is from Liverpool pack and they're not actually bad folk. It's just that our packs have been in a feud for three generations now. It got so bad at one point that it triggered a war which made humans aware of the existence of the supernatural.

My pack, Charwood, blamed Oliver's pack, Liverpool, because of some witchy voodoo shit his great great grandmother did. At the same time, Oliver's pack blamed us because apparently the witches were on our lands. Our pack gave the most evidence against theirs and the council gave their final verdict. Long story short, we all know it was the witches in the end, but it wasn't until the leaders of Liverpool at the time were sentenced to death did the truth come to light. Charwood and Liverpool have been enemies since.

I shouldn't have to waste my time with this shit. I finished all my studies when I went to Alpha training for two years. I was even already looking into university classes. But my old man decided that my packmates and I had to go back to the same high school as before, even though we clashed with the Liverpool pack the last time we were there.

He says that I still needed my certificate to state that I completed high school. So here I am on a Monday morning in the middle of a cold April day, driving back to the school I thought I had left behind. Personally, I think it's all BS and his stupid way of trying to get me out of the house to "build relationships like the good little Alpha I'm supposed to be".

Thankfully, I have Grace to keep me company. She's a nice enough girl, I suppose, and she's a good shag and fuck anytime I want.

Jace, my wolf, isn't happy with all the women I've been with but, hey, I can do what I want until my mate comes along. He can just sit there being sulky and not enjoy anything in the meantime.

I'm standing near the pillar entrance with Grace all over me kissing my neck trying to look all cute while I catch up with my friends before class. Jace has retreated to the back of my mind sulking because of her.

In the middle of a conversation with Danni, the most beautiful scent of forest wood and fresh water smacks me like a freight train. 'What the heck is that?' I think as my body stiffens and I soak in the smell.

Jace is frantically pacing at the back of my mind salivating at the scent. Before I could grasp what happened the scent had all but disappeared. My eyes dart around trying to figure out where the scent is coming from, but as quickly as it came it vanished.

I sigh and turn to Grace and the guys, "come one, it's time to head to class." I have English and double Maths today, so yeah, not one of my favourite days.

- - -

Lunchtime at the cafeteria is crazy. I'd forgotten how busy it could get here. Grace is in the line with me and the guys, she ordered a warm pumpkin soup while I went for 2 meat pies and a coke. I am paying for the meals when I hear her shrill voice. I groan internally. What shit had she caused now?

I make my way over and to my surprise I find Ashleigh Steward soaked in Grace's soup, her aura blazing around her. As I try to hide my surprise at how powerful her aura was, I give a cocky grin, "Is there a problem Beta?"

My smirk deepens as she turns around to face me with a frustrated look on her face. "Your pack member just deliberately ran into me and insulted me," she growls, her wolf flashing through her eyes.

"I don't believe it was intentional," I reply, making my way over next to Grace. As I pass Ashleigh, I am hit with the same amazing scent of forest wood and freshwater. I frown. What's going on?

"I can sense the malice coming off her, the words that came out of her own mouth were most certainly intentional," she glowers back at me.

Grace just stands there her head bowed down in submission. I try to bring Jace forward in my Alpha power, but he isn't budging. He just sat there smirking in my mind.

'What the actual fuck, dude, she is dominating one of my pack members,' I growl at him.

He smirks at me and says, 'deal with this yourself, I told you a thousand times that girl is bad news'.

'She is still a pack member,' I snapped back.

He finally gives some power as I let out my Alpha aura. Ashleigh didn't even budge, everyone else around us was cowering in submission, afraid to speak up against the stand-off between two ranked wolves. Even the humans were trembling slightly, some of the weaker ones had their eyes cast down and were looking away.

"Do I need to remind you of the peace treaty we have while on neutral grounds, Alpha? It seems not everyone is aware," she states while narrowing her eyes at me.

"Not at all Beta, my pack members are aware, Grace here is new to my pack and doesn't know who everyone is yet." I responded.

“I suggest you teach your new members who everyone is, Alpha, so there isn’t an issue, next time she may not be so lucky.” Her eyes snapped back at Grace, her aura not settling with her wolf blazing furiously in her eyes almost completely in control.

“Change the attitude, otherwise, you won’t get far here,” she snaps. She turns and pays for her order and stomps towards Oliver and her pack members, two females scurrying behind her to catch up.

I sigh, “well that was eventful”.

“The bitch didn’t even apologize or offer to pay for the food she spilled,” Grace pouts.

Jace pushes forward and growls at her, “Don’t be so stupid. They are the second largest pack around. Zander told you not to get mixed up with them. Next time, I won’t allow him to protect you.”

She bowed her head in submission. “Yes, Alpha,” she whispers.

With a sigh I pull out my wallet and give her a $20 bill. “Here, go grab some more lunch and I’ll meet you at the back with the rest of pack.”

She nods and takes the money then scurries to the back of the line.

I glanced over at the table where Liverpool pack sits. I couldn’t spot Ashleigh next to her Alpha or brother. What the fuck just happened?

Chapter 5 - ZANDER

After an eventful lunch hour, the rest of the day went by slowly. I relaxed with my friends and figured out what I was going to do on the weekend. I love a good night out and am no stranger to the night life. Rumour has it that there is a party at the club on Friday night. The guys and I intend to go and check it out.

As I walk into the packhouse after finishing classes I call out, “I’m home!” and wait around for a response. No one’s around. Dad is too busy nowadays to just be hanging around the house and Jake, dad’s beta, is surely with him.

The packhouse is a huge mansion with an open floor plan. As you walk in the door you are invited into a wide-open living dining area. A massive 100-inch plasma TV up on the wall with a 20 seat sunk in lounge, the dining table is behind, fitting about another 25-30 people.

The kitchen is at the back with two massive fridges and two industrial ovens and an island bench with bar stools. We used to hang out here a lot when we were kids. Since growing up we were allowed to venture out to the pack grounds.

Our pack has a variety of different shops and businesses around town. With a gym that most people train in twice a day. And if you can’t get to the gym during the day there are plenty of hiking trails around that many people use.

Danni and I make our way to the kitchen for something to eat.

“Bro, what are you hungry for? Pizza? There are a few frozen ones we can heat up?”

“Yeah, sure, whatever suits you,” he responds, shrugging off his jacket and slumping onto one of the bar stools.

Danni is Jake and Ella’s kid. He is a year younger and a year below me in school. With the age gap just being a year and him being the next beta, he and I grew up together and are close friends. We may have drifted apart a bit while I was on alpha training but since getting back it’s like I never left. No weirdness at all.

“So, what do you think about Friday night?” I ask him while waiting for the pizza to cook.

“What’s happening on Friday?” Danni asks curiously, leaning over the kitchen table planting himself on one of the bar stools.

“Something about a birthday at one of the clubs? Are you keen to go out? Maybe have a sniff around the females?” I ask.

He laughs and shakes his head, “bro, that’s exactly why your old man is the way he is about you becoming Alpha.”

“Come on. Why can’t I have my fun while I’m young and single?” I sigh.

“Ha! You’d better not say that while Grace is around. She’s been clinging to you like a leech lately,” he said.

“Pfft. She knows what we are. I never promised her anything,” I reply, shrugging off the uneasy feelings that linger from that comment.

“Hmmm, maybe you should keep your distance then or tell her again because … today, man. She was all over you like she had claimed you,” Danni warned.

I sigh. I know he’s right. Especially after the incident with Ashleigh. Man, I’m still so confused over that whole thing, I have no idea how Ashleigh didn’t back off even when I used my alpha command. It’s like it just didn’t affect her at all. But I am definitely not saying anything to anyone.

Just as the timer went off for the pizza dad, Jake, and Ellie all came into the packhouse. I scramble to grab some mittens before pulling the pizza out of the oven.

“You guys hungry? I can throw another two or three in the oven,” I called out as they make their way over.

“Sure,” Dad replied.

“How was the first day back? Anything exciting happen?” Ellie asks as she made her way around the counter and grabbed some plates and cutlery.

Danni and I share a glance before responding. “It was ... interesting,” Danni says, chuckling to himself. While I am cutting up the pizza, I shoot him a salty look. I don’t want dad knowing about what happened at lunch. And, of course, he caught on.

“What happened?” he sighs.

I roll my eyes in response. “No big deal, nothing I couldn’t handle.”

He folds his arms across his chest and gives me the ‘I don’t believe you’ look and I sighed in defeat. If I don’t tell him now, it will just get worse later.

“No big deal, Grace got into it with the Liverpool Beta. Although, from what happened she could have used an ass kicking. Grace was being a total bitch and the Beta told her so,” I shrug.

Danni rolls his eyes at my comment. I made sure to leave out the part where Grace soaked her with her lunch and the disrespectful language she used towards Ashleigh. Dad doesn’t need to punish her as she learnt her lesson ... I hoped.

“Oh, Beta Ashleigh?” Ellie asked.

“Umm, yeah, I guess,” I shrug, tucking back into dinner.

“She’s a sweet girl, it’s actually her eighteenth Birthday on Friday.”

I look up and frown. “I guess that’s whose birthday it is at the club Friday night then?”

“Are you still going?” Danni asked curiously.

“Might as well. It’s a club, right? Anyone can go, plus there would be more shifters around because of the birthday.” I look back at dad and ask, “unless it’s not okay with you?”

He nods, “it’s fine, just behave as it’s on neutral grounds. The peace treaty is still in place, maybe take a few of the young ones who haven’t found their mate yet.”

I nod and look at Danni. We already have a few people in mind, I’m still contemplating if I would invite Grace. I know she’s new and it would be good for her to meet people but with what went down today … I’m not sure we need a repeat of that.

Jace is still grumbling at the back of my mind. He agrees with Danni and thinks Dad should punish her, so she learns her lesson. Personally, I think she has. I still don’t think she did what she did intentionally.

“What do you have tomorrow?” I ask Danni as the adults’ chat at the other side of the counter.

“Sports in the morning and then science and maths in the afternoon,” Danni said. “What about you?”

“Study hall first period then history. It’s stupid. I hate history. At least they make it somewhat interesting and put some of our history in the classes now.”

Ever since our worlds merged many adjustments were made so everyone would feel comfortable and accepted. Humans helped put in place schools like Summer Vale where everyone can attend and have no issues or worries. If any arise, then the ranked members of the pack have to deal with it.

Thankfully, there hasn’t been much hate towards our kind. We just needed people to understand that we won’t hurt anyone or harm anyone unless they harm us first. We are very protective over our pack members and mates.

“I’m out for the evening. Going for a run then heading off to bed.” I wave to everyone as I head out.

Chapter 6 - ASHLEIGH

After the lunchtime drama I kept my head down and kept to myself. I didn't enjoy being front and centre like that. I didn't enjoy being questioned by Zander Blackwood of all people. I didn't enjoy the rumours that went around the school after.

In the car ride home, the boys mostly talked about the upcoming dance and football games. Every year the school holds a Valedictorian dinner dance where we can receive our diploma and also have a chance to say goodbye to everyone.

Once we reached the packhouse I head to my room and start on some homework and assignments.

Not long after mum comes up and knocks on my door. "Hi, sweetie, How are you doing today?"

I look up from the work I am completing. "Hmm I'm good, just finishing up a few things."

"Okay, dinner's nearly ready if you want to wash up beforehand. Are you sure you're, okay? Oliver said there was an incident at lunch time, and you've been avoiding him since."

I look back in surprise, "Oh, no it was okay. I was able to sort it all out."

"Okay, sweetie, don't take too long. Dinner will be about 20 minutes."

"Sure ma, I'll be down shortly."

I shower quickly and I finish the last of my homework before mum calls me for dinner. I walked down the stairs and headed for the dining room. Everyone had already taken their seats and started dishing out dinner. I found myself at the end next to Alex and Ollie.

"You all right?" Ollie asks.

I nod. I didn't exactly want to rehash all that happened at lunch time and neither does Kia, who has been quiet this whole time. I've never lost control over her like that and honestly, it's scary. I just hope she doesn't make it a regular thing.

"You definitely gave Blackwood a run for his money," Brent says as he grabs the salad and chicken.

"He deserved it and so did that stupid girl. Kia wanted to rip her head off," I grumble as I glare at him.

Thankfully, the parents were at the other end of the table and too engrossed in their conversation to care what we were talking about.

"What were you thinking of wearing on Friday?" Meghan asks as she leans over from Alex's other side, opposite Brent.

“Hmmm, maybe something light and airy in pink! I do love pink at the moment,” I reply. “Are you going to make me wear heels?” I grumble.

“Of course! You have to show off those sexy legs of yours.”

I shake my head and smile. Maybe an afternoon shopping is exactly what I need after today.

"You're going to wear something fabulous at school on Friday!" Meghan claps excitedly.

"Let me guess, you want to make a huge statement, right," I sigh.

She grins mischievously, “you know I am. Don’t worry, I will make you look hot and sexy for your mate. It won’t be as blingy as the dress I have in mind for the evening.”

I sigh. It’s no use arguing with her. She always gets her way when it comes to fashion. In two days, she will be dragging me around the shopping mall like a mad woman.

“Oh, and don’t forget the sexy lingerie.”

Ollie and Brent cough and splutter over their dinner. Brent slaps Ollie on the back trying to help. “Can we please not speak about my cousin's underwear,” he wheezes out.

“More like please don’t talk about my sister’s underwear.” Brent says with disgust.

Alex just chuckles at his mate making the boys uncomfortable.

“Pfft,” she pouts. “We always have to listen to you boys and your crap. Why can’t we talk about our stuff?”

“You can. Just not around us,” Ollie said, folding his arms across his chest while giving us a frustrated look.

Meghan rolls her eyes and goes back to eating dinner.

“What’s everyone got on tomorrow?” I asked.

“I’ve got English, history, and sport in the morning,” Ollie said.

“Ahh, damn. That means I have history second class. First class I have a study hall.” I pause and take mental notes about what I still had to do before Thursday and Friday.

Wednesday is an easy day, so I just have to make the most of the next two days before crazy Thursday and Friday with Meghan. After that I could focus again on the weekend.

Dad is going to teach me a few tracking skills which I am super keen about. Kia’s always had a good sense of direction and is naturally cautious of new areas so we thought it would be a handy skill to learn. For the last few months, I’ve been studying the different pack lands and their borders. I’m already quite familiar with our pack lands but it isn’t always easy to tell when a border is crossed so it is best to know where they are.

Liverpool is the second largest pack in Australia with allies in Europe and America, which makes us a threat to many packs here and overseas. Thankfully, Liverpool has a good reputation with most packs and our leaders have earned their respect.

I know most of the packs in this state, but other states have hundreds of much smaller packs. We have been lucky that things have been peaceful and any altercations over the last few years have been manageable.

When the time comes, I hope that Ollie and I can live up to the expectations of our parents and grandparents.

Kia has been restless since lunchtime. I'm not sure what is going on. It's like she's hiding something from me and just won't let me in. It's strange since we share the same body and mind, but for some reason, while Kia can access my thoughts, I can't access all of hers.

Kia says it's because they, our wolves, can communicate with each other when one is close by without the human connection and if they are in the same pack. For example, she can communicate to all of my family's wolves that are currently around the table right now. Maybe she is, which is why she's been so silent. I don't really know, to be honest.

A part of me is worried. I just hope she's okay and sorted out before Friday. I can't have her on edge on the biggest day of our life.

After everyone had finished dinner, mum and auntie went to the kitchen to finish cleaning up. Uncle, dad, and Alex all went into uncle's office to continue their talk about pack business while Ollie and Brent said something about video games in the pool room. This left just Meghan and me in the dining room. I'm not as close to Meghan as I am to Chloe and Skyla, but I am hoping that maybe Thursday shopping will help build the friendship even further.

"I'm really excited for Thursday night," I smiled.

It was the truth. I'm excited to dress up for my mate. I'm really excited about the possibility of finding my other half right away. I just hope he won't reject me. Plus, I hadn't been shopping in ages. I would usually ask Chloe and Skyla, but Chloe has cheerleading practice and Skyla is rarely allowed out these days.

"I'm really glad you asked me and I'm so excited for you to find your mate. I know some people don't like to be tied down so early but it's just magical being with your mate from the start," she sighed and looked into the distance, reminiscing.

"I can't wait. Although I am so nervous. I've never even kissed a guy. I just hope he won't be disappointed. I will dread it if he has been with heaps of women. I will always be so self-conscious."

"Oh, honey, it'll be okay. That is what the mate bond is for. It completes you; his wolf wouldn't allow him to reject you, anyway. And even if he had been with others before, nothing will compare with the way it feels with you. The bond amplifies everything. The feeling when you are with your mate is indescribable."

I'm glad I have Meghan to talk to about it. As much as I love my mum it would be hard to have this conversation. I know Ollie has been with others but with Brent, I can't tell, if I'm honest. He's a strange one. I know Alex waited for his mate and I wondered …

"If you don't mind me asking... Did you wait for Alex?" I asked curiously.

Her eyes went wide with guilt. "Umm … no, I didn't. I had a boyfriend in high school. They say you can sometimes tell who your mate is when they are nearby, and I guess I thought he was it at the time." She looked a bit guilty … maybe because she knew Alex had waited for her.

"Sorry I didn't mean anything by it," I quickly said.

"Oh, it's totally okay. You were curious and it's not a secret … Alex knows anyway. I just feel a guilty about it sometimes," she said.

"Thank you, though, I appreciate the advice. I hope my mate and I fall as much in love as you and Alex are." I smile warmly at her.

She chuckled and said, "it's not always sunshine and rainbows, especially being a ranked member. Like everything it has its good days and bad, but I wouldn't change it for the world. I wouldn't even wish rejection on my worst enemy. Now I know what the mate bond is like. I don't know how I ever lived without Alex."

I smiled at the thought of my mate and I having that type of love and relationship. I hope maybe one day we will be at that point of love and happiness.

Chapter 7 - ZANDER

I had to drag myself out of bed this morning. I ran patrol for about 8 hours and didn't get home until 1am so I was mentally and physically exhausted after last night.. I have half a mind to skip my first class because it was study hall, and no one really cared that much about it. But I don't want to get a scolding from dad, so here I am, half-awake, getting ready for school.

Danni practically tackles me to the ground for the keys when he sees how exhausted I am, insisting that he will drive instead. To be honest, I didn't mind letting him drive, it means I get about 30 minutes' extra sleep. By the time we reached school, I managed to get a bit of energy about me. I wouldn't want anyone to think I'm weak now, would I?

After shoving the rest of my stuff in the locker, I made my way to the library. Study Hall was nearly always in the library, mostly because it had access to everything you needed for whatever reasons, so if you forgot something there was no excuse. This week I had two sessions. One today and one on Thursday. I needed to catch up on a few different bits of homework, but honestly, I just wanted to find a nice corner and try to sleep more.

They renovated the library just before I left for Alpha training and now, you'd have to walk up 25 steps to reach the top. Today as I walk in it seems that the library is all booked out. Busy as anything, people were lining up to borrow things or to ask about one thing or another.

Huge double-thick glass windows wrapped around the whole library building bringing in natural light. Double doors lead out to the courtyard and football field. Bookshelves weaved and wrapped around the middle of the library, with little desk nooks with computers and printers next to them.

The library allows students to print what they need, but for a fee, which is deducted from their key card. You always had to carry your key card to print or borrow something. It costs about 20c a page to print. They tend to make a bit of money if you forget an assignment back home.

Besides the main library floor, there are four big rooms - two computer rooms and two study conference rooms. These rooms could be split up or combined as needed. When combined it could hold 100 people easily. Under the stairs is the bag room and restrooms.

The study sessions were always in the conference rooms and today it seemed everyone was taking advantage of the free class because it was full. Only one more table was left at the back of the room. I sighed happily. Thank God, I can finally get some rest by just sitting and relaxing.

I go over to the teacher to confirm I had taken the class and make my way to the back corner. It's not too bad; it has a view of the oval and one of the tennis fields. Not that anyone was doing anything on them, but it was better than nothing.

I bring all my books out to make it seem I was 'doing work' and sit with my back to the teacher and the rest of the class looking out at the view trying to relax my busy mind.

Fifteen minutes into the class, the door to the room flew open, nearly slamming into the back wall.

"Miss Steward, you need to watch yourself and not damage the school property," the teacher scolded.

"My apologies ma'am, here is a note from the office." I hear her sweet voice respond.

I could hear the rustle of the paper and the tapping of the computer. "Very well. As you can see, we are quite full today, but there is one spot left, over next to Mr. Blackwood."

I could feel the tension in the air thicken as she explains the situation about our packs. "I ... but we ... I umm, don't think that would be a good idea ma'am," she finally sputters out.

The teacher sighed and said, "I understand you all have "issues" outside school hours, but there is an agreement that when you are at school it won't be a problem, is this not the case?"

I rolled my eyes at the discussion that was playing out. I could hear her footsteps come closer as she made her way over.

"Yes, ma'am, my apologies. Never mind, I'll take that seat," she replies.

As she takes the seat near me, I turn to her and say, "you know I don't bite, right? Well, only if you want me to," I add, tossing her a wink.

Her cheeks turned bright red upon hearing what I said. "Pig," she muttered softly.

I just laugh and she looks up at me stunned. I shrug, "I've been called worse things."

Now it's her turn to roll her eyes. Ashleigh sits opposite me and starts scribbling furiously in her book.

"Can't get it right?" I ask as she tore out her fourth piece of paper and threw it into the trash.

She looked up startled and I suppose we had been sitting in silence for the last twenty minutes.

My mind is too jumbled to do anything right now, with her sitting across from me smelling the way she does. It's been driving Jace crazy. I'm sitting here trying to control him not to say or do anything stupid.

"Just can't get the start of the report," she replies.

I nodded. I always hated the beginnings of any report or assignment, especially if you didn't get it right the first time since it basically determined where it would go and how it would finish.

"Sorry, I'm not much help with them either."

"You don't have anything to work on?" she asked.

I shrug, “probably.”

She rolls her eyes again and mutters, “typical boys.”

I flashed her another smirk as we sit in silence until the end of the class.

“Till next time, Beta Ashleigh,” I smirk and pick up my stuff.

“Huh,” she says distractedly.

“You know this class is finished now, right?”

“Shit, shit. Ugh, thanks,” she groans.

Her voice suddenly does something to my dick as it twitches in my pants, perking up and getting ready to have some fun. I look back in surprise. I’ve never thought about Ashleigh in a sexual way or any way, for that matter. I guess with our pack's history, it’s just been off limits … taboo. Now I’m here supporting a semi. I will have to get Grace to take care of that for me.

“Later,” I muttered, and left the library as quickly as possible.

Chapter 8 - ASHLEIGH

I hate running late. The boys usually tell me when they are leaving, but they had training this morning so I was on my own.

It is a nightmare. I get too distracted and forget what time it is, especially when I am busy working on my schoolwork or other stuff my dad has given me to look into. Today, unfortunately, was one of those days. I bolt out the door just as I know class had started. I have study hall first, so it isn't as bad as a regular class, but I still hate being late. It gives me major anxiety.

I hadn't spoken to Kia since yesterday's incident, but I know she is still around. I could feel her presence faintly, which concerned me a bit. But the thought of coming of age on Friday helped me settle down a little bit. We usually aren't out of sync like this.

I make my way to the library which seems to be quite busy with many students this morning. I rush to the room where study hall is conducted, and she pointed me to a seat beside Blackwood. I try to explain why I should sit somewhere else but in the end, she reminded me that we are on neutral ground and need to learn to get along.

I honestly don't expect to have much of a conversation with Blackwood. He seems to be the typical alpha male … cocky as anything and without a care to what other people think. I wouldn't want to boost his ego any more than it already is, but damn, he is sexy.

His tall muscular figure, short dark brown hair and brown eyes … with the shadow of a beard growing along his jawline. It should be a crime that someone can look so sexy in just jeans and a button-down shirt.

I surprised myself by even allowing myself to think those things about him. We wouldn't even be able to date, or even be intimate. Sure, our generation doesn't hold the same amount of hate towards each other's packs compared to our parents. But it would still be a strange situation.

I suppose when we were told the stories of what happened to our great great grandparents it was hard to relate to because we haven't had a huge war break out like that since. We've been living in peace even amongst humans.

Is it so strange to think he could maybe be my mate? I am of an Alpha bloodline, so the chances are a bit higher than average. At the same time, any of the other unmated wolves could also be my mate. For all I know, I could have a human mate.

All these new thoughts are driving me crazy and arousing me. I hoped he couldn't smell me; I would be so embarrassed after that stupid remark he made earlier.

When he said that class had ended and it was time to leave, I hadn't gotten anything done. He stood there for about thirty seconds looking like a constipated child trying to figure out something and just said 'laters' and took off.

I mean, I should count myself lucky, right? At least, he said something to me at all. I kinda felt a little like an idiot at the beginning of class when I tried to avoid sitting next to him. It wasn't as bad as I thought.

This weekend was going to be stressful, that's for sure. I at least had Thursday study class left, which made things easier. I'll try to finalize the rest of my work then.

I walk into the classroom for history and see that Ollie and Skyla are already there. Ollie is already seated next to one of the windows and Skyla is beside him, saving the end seat for me. I made my way over with a small smile, waving.

"Hi guys", I chipped.

I miss sharing classes with them. This being our final year, the school split us up into different classes. It was difficult at first. It's not like I don't know anyone … I guess I'm just not used to them being around all the time. You can imagine my surprise at seeing Ollie and Skyla in my class. Thank goodness!

As we take our seats, our teacher, Mrs. Lang, arrives and tries to silence the class. Just as everyone had settled down, Blackwood and his bimbo walk into the room.

He definitely looked a bit more rumpled than he did at study hall where I had just seen him in. His shirt was untucked with one or two button loose and his hair was ruffled. If you weren't a wolf, you wouldn't notice the distinct smell of sex in the air. I rolled my eyes. Really, we only had 10 minutes between each class and these two were off doing that.

I turn to Ollie and start chatting again with him, while Blackwood was having a discussion with the teacher about being on time. Luckily for her, she was a human, so she couldn't smell what they were really up to, but there were a few kids from Riverview snickering in the back seats.

Ollie was telling me about a football game they have in the next few weeks which will be the start to the season. The first game of the season is usually between Liverpool and Charwood. They try to make the teams as even as possible, especially, since us wolves are stronger than humans. They have two teams, the wolves and the supernatural, and then the humans. We don't really compete against each other, but the games are still a huge event, and everyone makes it to the fair with lots of food stalls, a BBQ and a few rides.

The school goes all out and usually each member of every pack attends too. I wondered who the captain of Charwood this year was. I am brought back to reality as our teacher starts the class.

"Today I will be handing out one of the final assignments. This will be a shared assignment between two people. I have already selected the pairs and you will be expected to present your findings together as well as write the report together."

"Oliver Steward and Skyla Long."

"Ashleigh Steward and Zander Blackwood," I groan as she reads out my name paired with Blackwoods.

"Lachlan Kings and Daniel Smar."

"Grace Hicks and Tommy Don."

Listening to all the pairings, it seems that she made a point with not only me but everyone and purposely paired us with someone outside our packs.

Ollie raised his hand just as he was given his assessment paper, "but Ma'am, this is due the week of the first football game, can we please have extensions? We are training nearly every day until the game in 4 weeks."

"Sorry, Mr, Steward, this assignment has already been given plenty of time for you all to finish and I'd taken into consideration other events going on. Any assignments that are late will receive a penalty."

I sigh and look over the assignment. It's not too bad, I would be able to get my part done quickly. The question is if he would do any of the work. I glance over in his direction and see him talking with Grace. She is pouting and trying to lean into him.

Oh, moon goddess. I hope she won't be coming along to the planning sessions we will have to do. As the bell rang to let us know that class has ended, I got up and start to pack my books away.

I look up and see Blackwood making his way over. "So, it seems it's me and you on this assignment Beta," he says with a smirk.

"Yep," I nod. I don't trust myself to say more. Kia was stirring in the back of my mind as Grace walked beside him and linking her arm with his.

"When is your next study hall? I have mine both on Tuesdays and Thursdays," I look up and ask.

“Really? So do I,” he replied. He flashes a cocky smile and says, "it seems we have something to talk about now. See you then."

He gave Ollie a nod and headed out of the class.

"What did he mean by that?" Ollie asked.

"Oh nothing, I was just put on his desk earlier because I was running late." I sigh, not really wanting to go into any details.

"Ahh, we'll let me know if he gives you any trouble."

I nod and look at the rest of my schedule for the day.

Chapter 9 - ASHLEIGH

The rest of my day went by without incident, everything is back to normal. Lately it has been hard to connect so it is nice to be with Ollie and the rest of our pack members for lunch.

Wednesday went by quickly and it is my turn to be on patrol that evening after school. It helps me get into the groove of what my duties will be when Ollie and I someday become Alpha and Beta of the pack. Father and Uncle like to keep us in shape and show us the ropes to what is expected of us when we are leaders.

Being on patrol means Kia gets to come out for a run. With so much pent-up energy a run around the pack grounds for a few hours is just what she needs. She's been a lot quieter than usual and we still haven't spoken about what happened with Grace. I just hope Friday helps her settle down.

Thursday afternoon came around only too quickly. I spot Meghan in one of uncle's vehicles, a black shiny SUV big enough for her shopping endeavours. As I walk towards her, I pass by Blackwood leaning against his sports car with hands groping her ass. I roll my eyes as I walk past.

It's strange ... it is like he has two different personalities. On the one hand he's a decent guy who I could actually have a good conversation with and possibly even be friends with, despite being from different packs. And then he turns around and does something like that and I'm brought back to reality, to what type of person he really is and just doesn't care at all about the consequences or anything.

Upon reaching the car I reach for the door of the front passenger seat and get in. After fastening my seatbelt I turn and greet with a smile.

Our conversation the other night brought us closer together. It's nice that we don't have to be awkward about anything and we can talk about some harsh truths when we need to. It's good to have someone older and a bit more perspective on the different situations.

"So, any thoughts about what you want to wear tomorrow?" Meghan asks.

"Well, I love pink. It's my signature colour. So, I think anything with pink, as long as it's not too revealing," I said.

She nods in agreement, "Well, the shops have lots of different styles so we can have a look around." She starts up the engine and we make our way towards the city's shopping mall.

The city is about a 20-minute drive from our pack lands and about a 10-minute drive from the school. Since we are on neutral ground the peace treaty still applies. This deal was confirmed by the council to protect not only humans but packs and their members.

The treaty applies to everyone who is in a pack, not just Charwood and Liverpool. If someone breaks the treaty, the council can step in at any time and determine the outcome of the pack and its Alpha.

If something was to happen between two or more pack members in the same pack on neutral ground, then the Alpha in charge of that pack would determine their fate. However, if the issue had gotten too out of hand and had also broken the human laws, then the council would have grounds to vote on the outcome.

The main packs that are around the area are Charwood, Liverpool, Riverview, and Westfield. There were a few smaller family packs that didn't want to go rogue but didn't want to join a larger pack, so the council gave them an exemption to create their own pack.

It is hard to start a new pack, you have to have valid reasons and funds to support the members, but Frankton and Shelow have done it so far and have had no issues or problems that we know of.

Charwood is the largest pack in the country, with Liverpool close behind, followed by Riverview and Westfield. We have built up strong relationships with all of the other packs except for Charwood. There is still hate between the packs, especially with the older members.

We help support the smaller packs when they ask. It helps build alliances and businesses in the area. A few packs have joined ours over the years for various reasons. We have just been grateful that they trust us enough out of all the packs to join. It shows true loyalty when we built the alliance.

Over the years, the council has stepped into some situations that have gotten out of hand. Luckily, it was stopped quickly enough before another war started.

Nothing major happened over the last few years since Ollie and I have started to be more involved with leadership and decisions. We pulled up to the shopping mall car park 10 minutes later and made our way to the first set of shops.

The shopping mall is huge with rows and rows of different shops. It has a long hallway that stretched for about 1 kilometre. There are lots of different shops on both sides, you could weave your way around the mall easily. A service desk is at the front and centre for anyone with inquiries or issues. Behind the service desk are pop-up stalls that sell jewellery and a few bits and bobs.

"Didn't we have to bring guards?" I ask Meghan.

She nods and says, "yes, they are on their way now. I just told them the first shop we are going into."

Meghan grabs my hand and leads the way to the nearest shop. I looked up at the sign and could feel my cheeks burning furiously. "I didn't think you were serious about the lingerie shop," I mumble.

"Of course, I was! Alex loves my stuff," she giggles. "Plus, if you didn't want to try anything, I was going to update some of my stuff anyway. Come on, it's not that bad, the lingerie helps you feel sexy and confident. Especially when your mate can't take his eyes off you."

I sigh in response, I guess she did know a thing or two about that. I've never even considered going to a shop like this before, so I guess now I have a reason to. It can't hurt, right?

After browsing for what felt like forever, Meghan threw every single item at me that I seemed remotely interested in and kept telling me 'You won't know unless you try it'.

I swear by the end of the evening that quote will be engraved on my forehead. After trying on several items I chose three: a lacy black one with a cute pattern, a flirty red one had a little bit of sheer mesh and strappy details, the last one was a pink and black warrior glam bodysuit that had trapping details over cut-outs with a mini v back. I also got a black Nicolette Push Up Baby doll nightdress to accompany the new lingerie.

Meghan also got some for herself and paid for them separately. She said she would feel guilty if she bought them with the pack funds. Alex likes to spoil her and keeps an account for funds she's allowed to spend only on shopping and other things she wants. I sometimes wonder if she had previously gone overboard with shopping and that is why there is a bit of a restriction, but that is not my business, and it would be too rude to ask.

After the lingerie store, she insists that we need to get our nails done to help us with the dress selection. I didn't exactly want to get my nails done. They don't stay on when we shift so I don't really see the point. Nevertheless, Meghan insists we get them done.

She drags me to a cute little salon with several people sitting in chairs getting their nails done. I surprisingly enjoyed myself and am happy with the result. I got a short fake nail, with a light pink and creme pattern with a few silver jewels on every second nail.

After doing our nails it was time to shop for dresses and Meghan drags me around like a ragdoll. I don't think I have any energy left to try on more clothes.

"Oh, come on, hun, we only have one more hour until the shops are closed and I know the perfect shop we can go to for the dresses."

I sigh, thank goodness it was only one more shop. We walk into a cute little corner boutique shop. Not many people were in the store, but it is nearly 9.30pm, so nearly everyone had already left.

Meghan went to the first rack of the store, "I was here the other day and thought these dresses would be your style …, nice, simple yet elegant." she smiled. "Ha, here it is!"

She pulls out a beautiful jewelled light pink dress with a sweetheart neckline, thin feather spaghetti straps, with beads and jewels scattered all over the bodice and skirt. "I thought this would be perfect for tomorrow night for dinner and the club. You can either wear flats or a short heel."

I nod as I look at the dress. It is beautiful.

"Perfect, we will quickly try that one on and see if you like it. Oh, what about this one for school?" She had pulled out a dark pink mid-length dress with a straight neckline and long sleeves. I tried on both dresses, and they fit well and were just perfect! They complement my dark hair and olive skin perfectly.

I couldn't wait for tomorrow to come. I am so excited and hope I would get to meet my mate. Meghan must have been energized by our shopping trip as she was still full of energy on the way home.

By the time we reached pack grounds it was 10:30 pm. I linked mom and dad that I was almost home and that I was heading straight for bed. Dad was out on patrol, but mom had already turned in.

'Good night, Kia, I hope you are okay and tomorrow will bring us peace and happiness.'

'Good night Lei, I'm okay, sorry I haven't been chatty much. There's just a lot going on and I'm trying to get advice from the Elders, but yes, hopefully, tomorrow will bring some peace to our foggy minds.'

I could feel peace and excitement from Kia with her words. I was excited and nervous. Who wouldn't be? I could potentially meet my mate.

Chapter 10 - ZANDER

Friday, who doesn't love Fridays? It sucks that we still have to go to school on this boiler of a day, but here I am on a Friday morning in the kitchen trying to get my shit together for school, instead of going to the river.

I hear Danni coming down the stairs wearing just his boxers and hair all tangled. He looks around suspiciously and asks, "Are the parents around?"

I looked up from my phone frowning "huh, nah. Why?"

He quickly sprints back to his room and comes back a few minutes later with Annie. She looks dishevelled with her light brown hair in a mess and her short black tank dress just barely covering her ass and boobs.

I roll my eyes and chuckle, "If your mum found out what you were doing on a school night, she would beat your ass."

He shoves the girl out the door as quickly as he could, while she gave him a quick kiss and said, 'call me'.

"Shut up, you're one to talk. You know ma scolded you for some of your stupid nights," he mumbled.

"Haha, Oh, I know only too well. Grab something to eat before we hit the road, if you like. I need to pick up Grace in 10 minutes."

Danni scrunches up his nose. "It's all good. Maybe next time."

"It's Grace, isn't it?" I sigh.

He just shrugs. "You do you, man. I need to freshen up before school anyway. Are we still going to the clubs tonight?"

I nod in response, "we will head out at around 8.30pm."

"Ok I'll tell Annie. Are you inviting Grace?"

I shrugged, “Still haven't decided."

"No worries. Till then." He salutes and heads back to his room to get ready for school.

I start my car and drive to Grace's house. Jace was grumbling in my mind about picking up Grace today. He didn't want to be around her.

'She isn't that bad', I tried to reason with him.

He snorts. 'You only like her because of her pussy.'

'We had a deal, until I find my mate, I can do what I want. Until that happens either enjoy it with me or shush.' I growl back.

'Fine' he snaps 'but mark my words. As soon as our mate enters the picture, your shenanigans are over. I will not allow you to hurt her.'

He curls himself up at the back of my mind, sulking and giving me a death glare. If looks could kill, I'd be a goner.

Five minutes later, I pulled up to the apartment block Grace lives in and I shoot her a quick text message. The apartment building isn't very big, about five floors with two car parking garages underneath. It has a modern look with white paint and grey and tan trim with a glass stairway leading to the top.

The balcony of each apartment is wide enough for a small table and two chairs.

Grace came bounding down the stairs with an excited little smile. Damn, she dressed fine today, wearing another one of her miniskirts, making it easy for me to grab her ass. My eyes go straight to her boobs as they spill out of her top. We make small talk during our half-hour drive to school. I'm painfully reminded that she isn't as bright as one would hope. I guess that is what her looks make up for.

My mind drifts off to yesterday's conversation with Ashleigh in our study session. It was easy, simple. I enjoyed teasing her, making her annoyed and frustrated in a playful way. I smiled a little to myself. I wished, hoped, being with my mate would be that easy.

We arrive at school a little earlier than usual with fifteen minutes to spare before the bell rings. I hate being the first one in the classroom. I pin Grace against the side of my car and lean my weight against her.

"Someone wants a little fun?" she purrs groping my dick as it twitches in my pants.

I grunt as she squeezes my junk. She starts kissing me needily, wanting more than just playful teasing. She tries to unzip my pants while kissing me furiously.

The breeze suddenly changes direction, and I am smacked with a mouth-watering scent of pine and freshwater.

'*MATE*', Jace screams. I jerk back suddenly, confused about what he said.

'What?' I said.

'MATE, MATE, MATE you dumbass', Jace yells.

'Are you sure?' I asked, looking around frantically. If she's here she may have just seen what I was doing with Grace. Shit, shit, fuck! I would be so screwed if she saw me.

'*Yes, you dumbass, find her now*!' I kept looking around in a craze.

My eyes land on a pair of beautiful brown eyes, locked on me a few cars away, frozen in place. Her eyes widen as she realizes what just happened.

Fuck! How am I going to get out of this? I don't want to be rejected; I have longed for my mate ever since mum told me about mates. Someone to love, someone to cherish, someone to be yours forever.

I wanted the love that mum and dad had. She passed away when I was just ten and it has been hard for us all. I still remember the love she gave everyone, not just her family. She would greet you with a beautiful smile and be the most patient, kind person you would ever know. I want the love of a mate. My mate.

I looked into the beautiful eyes of Ashleigh Steward, pleading silently for her to give me a chance, begging for her forgiveness.

Chapter 11 - ASHLEIGH

"HAPPY BIRTHDAY!"

I hear a chorus of voices waking me up from my peaceful sleep. Mum, dad, Brent, Ollie, Uncle David, and Auntie Sarah were all around my bed with huge goofy smiles and arms stretched wide, each holding a present. I sit up and rub my eyes, taking in the view from my bed.

I smile warmly. "Aww, thank you all so much!" I say as I get out of bed and walk over to mum and dad, giving them a hug first.

"Well, today you officially become an adult, so we wanted to let you enjoy this moment before heading off to school," mum said.

They put the presents on the bed and they each give me a quick hug. "I know we don't have much time before school but quickly get ready and come down to breakfast. Alex is off on patrol this morning and Meghan is just downstairs getting set up," dad said.

"Sure Dad. I won't be too long. I'll just have a quick shower and get ready," I reply as they wave and leave the room.

'Happy birthday Kia,' I whisper to her, hoping she would hear me.

I feel her moving around feeling excited for the day. It's nice she's excited. It's been a while since she has been happy like this.

'*Happy birthday Lei, I hope today is good. I'm so ready to not have any messy bullshit going on.*'

I giggle at her comments. Yep, it seems she is back in full swing.

'*Sorry I've been a bit MIA Lei, but it all should be okay now.*'

I could feel her confidence and happiness radiating through, giving me energy for the day. I'm happy she's sorted herself out. One day I hope she will share it with me.

I shower quickly and get ready for school. I put on one of the new lingerie sets I bought. They are surprisingly comfortable, and Meghan was right. They do make me feel sexy and confident.

I then put on the dress Meghan chose for me. A beautiful dark pink with long sleeves that stops just above my knees, it feels appropriate for school while still a little sexy at the same time. Twenty minutes later, I'm running down the stairs ready for breakfast.

Everyone was sitting around the dining room table; Meghan had really put up a feast this morning. pancakes, sausages, fruit, yogurt, hash browns, toast. So many goodies. It was a mouth-wateringly amazing sight.

We do have Omegas in our pack but mum and auntie love to cook and taught Meghan when she moved in. Now we just take turns at cooking for everyone. Every now and then, the boys help. Mum always said it was a good skill to have, no matter the age or who you are. We get help when we have big functions and parties like tonight. But mostly the Omegas just help out with the cleaning and groceries when needed.

" Ahhh, there she is!" Dad smiled and walked over to give me another hug.

"Happy Birthday!!" Meghan squeals, running over, slamming into me with a tight suffocating hug. "You look amazing in the dress. Oh, didn't we do so well!" She smiled big like a Cheshire cat.

"Haha, yeah, it's perfect thanks so much," I laughed and did a little twirl showing off. "Oh, thank you, Uncle! I really did enjoy yesterday evening", I smiled at my uncle, who is seated at the head of the table with Auntie Sarah next to him.

"It's okay, I'm glad you had a good time and got home safely."

"So how are you feeling sweetie? Nervous, excited, scared?" Mum asked.

I take a seat between mom and dad, across from Ollie and Brent. I guess they want to have me close today, feeling a bit vulnerable because their little girl is all growing up.

"Hmm, oh, I'm a bit of everything if I'm honest. Mostly nervous and excited, Kia has given me a lot of energy for the day, so that has really helped," I respond with a smile.

Dad nodded. "It can be nerve-racking; you don't know if you will meet your mate today or on another day. That is why our actions, how we carry and present ourselves are always important."

I nod in response and looked up to see Ollie and Brent looking a bit guilty. I know Ollie's history, but what has Brent done? As far as I know, he hasn't had any girlfriends or partners. I guess I will have to ask him about that later.

We all chatted and made small talk while eating the glorious feast when one of the bells chimed on someone's phone, announcing that it was time for school.

We said our goodbyes with more hugs from mum and dad and headed out the door into Ollie's car. I sit in the front and Brent in the back.

As we head out to school, I turned around and asked Brent, "what was that about?"

He frowns, "I don't know what you mean."

I rolled my eyes, "you know, the guilty look you both had when dad was giving his little speech this morning? We all know Ollie's history, but what are you guilty of?"

"You might as well tell her, bro, she ain't gonna let it go," Ollie mumbles.

"What the hell?? Have you been keeping secrets from me?!" I practically yell, startling Ollie and making him jerk the steering wheel.

"Great, thanks so much, man. Look, it's no big deal. I've just been seeing someone the last few weeks and Ollie caught me the other day," Brent shrugs.

I looked at him stunned, my mouth opens and closes a few times trying to comprehend what he just said. "You're serious?" I ask.

"Yeah, why, what's the big deal? Ollie sees chicks all the time and you never give him any shit about it."

"That's different," I mumble.

"No, it ain't and you know it," Brent snaps.

"You're my baby brother, it's my ass mum and dad are going to have if you mess up," I said.

Brent just starts laughing hysterically.

"What?" I look back and forth between them, confused.

"Please, you're a princess to mum and dad. You could get away with murder if you wanted." Brent says.

"Nuh-uh," I say, shaking my head furiously. "You heard dad this morning, I'm just trying to live up to his expectations."

Brent rolls his eyes, "Look, it's my life. If they give you crap about it, just tell them it was my choice, I don't have to live in the stone age like everyone else, and I don't want to either."

I sigh in defeat. Obviously, I wasn't going to win this one. "So do I get to meet her?"

"Maybe one day. I'm just trying to figure out feelings and stuff," he mumbles.

Ollie linked me 'It was a complete accident that I caught them. We really didn't mean to hide it from you, we just didn't know how to tell you either.' I look at Ollie trying to study his face, it looked sincere.

I suppose I also have been in my own mind about things lately. I sigh and say to Brent, "okay, I'm sorry I got all grouchy on you."

He shrugs, "It's all good, I get it. I would be pissed if you guys hid something from me. I'm sorry I did."

"Great, now we are all one big happy family again. Can we please discuss tonight," Ollie says demandingly.

"Hmm sure, what is there to discuss?" I ask.

"What time are we going out? And who is going?" Ollie responds.

"Well, we have dinner beforehand. I think mum and dad have invited a few people, so maybe 10pm? Honestly, I'm not sure how many people are coming. I didn't exactly send out invites, it's just word of mouth at this point."

"Perfect. My type of party," Ollie responded, grinning like a damn fool as we pulled up in front of the school.

School is packed as usual, everyone seemed to be running around like crazy trying to get to class on time. It's not like we are late, we still have 10 minutes left. As I stepped out of the car, the breeze swept through, and I smelled a beautiful mouth-watering scent of wildflower and honey.

'*MATE, MATE, MATE*' Kia yells.

'Really! Where?!' I say excitedly, looking around frantically trying to find the source of the delicious scent.

My heart stops suddenly. I'm frozen in place as I discover who the scent belongs to. He's up against his sports car making out with the bitch.

No, no, no. I shook my head. This can't be happening. Why? Why him of all people? My heart clenches as I see him groping her ass as he deepens the kiss.

'*Let me out, let me at her,*' Kia hisses, '*I'll rip the bitch apart, I don't give a shit who sees.*'

He jerks back suddenly and starts to look around crazily. His eyes land on mine widening in fear, begging for forgiveness, but the damage has been done. I'm completely broken, standing there frozen, unable to move my legs. My body feels like it's on fire, the pain shooting through every limb.

Do not cry, do not cry, you will not cry, you are the damn Beta of Liverpool, DO NOT CRY!

Kia is livid, pacing in my mind trying to get out, '*Let me out,*' she growls.

'Kia, we are still on neutral ground, the treaty is in place,' I whisper.

'*I don't give a shit!*' she hisses, '*That is our mate. I'll be damned if I let this bimbo of a bitch be all over him like that!*'

'Kia,' I whisper. 'Even if he wasn't doing that, we still wouldn't have been able to run to him.'

She growls back, frustrated, '*I don't care what uncle thinks, he is MATE!*'

"Ash! Are you coming???" Ollie calls back to me, snapping me out of the trance I was in. I quickly gather myself together, locking Kia in the back of my mind, turn around to face Ollie and head through the school doors.

Chapter 12 - ZANDER

My heart dropped to the pit of my stomach. The look in her eyes absolutely killed me. The pain of betrayal flashed through her eyes. I never wanted to cause her that pain.

Jace was furious, thrashing around inside me as I tried to get him under control. She turns around and walks away and into school, following Oliver and her brother.

"Baby, is everything okay? We can skip first class. I have study hall," Grace's voice rang through my ears as she tries to reach for me.

"Don't," I growl back at her. I know Jace was showing in my eyes with the amount of command that radiated off me.

She looked back at me startled, her eyes blinking up at me wide in fear. "I... I'm sorry, Alpha," she whispered and bowed her head in submission.

I took another step back, closing my eyes and taking a deep breath to try and get Jace under control, and said to Grace. "We're done, you need to find your own way to and from school from now on."

"But, but why? What did I do?" she whispers, her voice barely audible.

"This isn't working anymore," I say as she starts to sob. I moved away and started to walk towards the school gates.

"But I thought you loved me," she murmurs through her sobs.

I stop dead in my tracks and turn back around to face her. I was fucking furious. Fuck, Danni was right.

I completely lost control of Jace. He pushed forward and growled. "Don't be stupid. He has never shown you anything more than a good fuck. If you have caught feelings, then it is on you and you should have backed off. Zander was always clear on his intentions. It is your own stupid fault if you fell in love. You knew the rules."

I sighed, 'Did you have to be an ass to her?'

'*How else will she learn to back off,*' Jace growled. '*We have a mate. I told you time and time again this shit will happen if it's a regular occurence.*'

I roll my eyes internally to Jace and look back at Grace. Yes, I feel guilty doing this to her, she isn't a bad person. But I did also understand where Jace was coming from, and he was somewhat right.

I would rather she hated me and backed off, so I could move on and try to be with Ashleigh. Trying to figure that shit out and not have any more issues with an already messy situation.

After contemplating the situation for about thirty seconds, I decided that my priority is my mate. I'm already in deep shit for what happened. I didn't want to make it worse, so I just turn and walk away, ignoring Grace's hysterical sobs.

All throughout the day, Ashleigh avoided me. We didn't have another class together until Monday and I couldn't wait that long. I'm sick of her avoiding me. I saw her once or twice walking along the hall between my classes only for her to turn around and go the other way.

Jace is constantly pacing in my mind, every time he picked up her scent he would go berserk, pushing forward trying to get me to find her.

'We have to be smart about this, we can't just go up and claim her,' I told him for what seemed like the fifth time today.

'Yes, we can, she is your mate, my mate. I get to claim her.' he grumbles back, frustrated about the whole thing. I sigh again, it's no use explaining the situation, he knew it. He's just being a stubborn ass.

'It could start a war no one wants Jace. I know you want her, but you need to calm down. You are scaring people.' I try to reason with him 'We will see her at lunch, they will sit in their normal place. Just please calm down.'

'Fine, she had better be there, I just need to be in the same room as her.' he mumbles.

I sigh. Ever since our bond snapped into place being away from her weakened us, even without our marking. We can't be away from her for too long, we need her.

The lesson before lunch was running long. My Maths teacher was an old bag, and she just took so long explaining everything and answering everyone's questions. So, of course, it ran ten minutes longer.

Jace was fuming by the end of the lesson. He just wanted to get to the cafeteria where he knew Ashleigh would (hopefully) be. Once the teacher called the class to an end, Jace tried to move forward again, frantically trying to get to the cafeteria.

'Dude please chill out, people are noticing'. I try to calm him down.

'Don't fucking tell me to chill, I will chill when we see our mate!' He growls.

It's useless to try to settle him down until he sees Ashleigh is okay. He'd been pissed off all morning that she somehow managed to avoid us all day.

I arrive at the cafeteria and it was crazy busy as usual, with everyone was already lining up to get the food. This is going to take for ever. I groan to myself.

'Who cares! Find mate. NOW!' Jace growls demandingly.

'Well, is she here? Can you smell her?' I snap back.

He pushes forward, trying to seek her out. As her beautiful scent comes through, Jace immediately settles down.

'*She's here.*' he whispers.

I sigh, 'We need to play it cool, Jace. We need to figure this out without causing suspicion or issues.'

'*I know, I just want to see her, to be close to her*' he mumbles. I can feel his pain. He hates what I did to her. I hate it, too, but I can't take it back. I can only try to fix it, let her know that I'll try to be worthy of her … to be a good mate.

I look around slowly to find her and I see her with Oliver, her brother, two other females, and a few other pack members.

Fuck, she looks amazing in that dress, it fits her perfectly. The colour is amazing and complements her beautifully. And her hair … has she always had them in those gorgeous curls? Fuck, when have I ever noticed this type of stuff?

I must have been staring too long because she looks up from what she was doing and her eyes on land on mine widening, panicking. Shit, why is she panicked?

I give her a small smile, trying to reassure her I wouldn't do anything stupid here, I just wanted to see her.

'*We need to talk to her',* Jace says.

'She probably hates us,' I frowned back, 'How can we talk to her without anyone noticing?'

'*Just anything to be close to her, I need to be close to her,*' he pleaded.

'I'll try to figure it out, I just need to get some food and we'll mull over it, okay?' I try to bargain with him.

We line up for lunch and walk over to the rest of our pack in school. Grace was on the other side with some random people avoiding me also, giving me a few death glares here and there. Honestly, she had better watch herself and how she acts, I'm her damn Alpha.

I sit at the table next to Danni across Eric, Billy, and Annie. Eric and Billy are in the same year as me. Both their parents are warriors and they, too, enlisted to be warriors as well.

We chat amongst ourselves, making small talk about our weekend plans. Jace is getting restless, pacing again. I sigh and ask him, ' what's wrong?'

'*She's gone*' Jace said, frustrated.

'We can't be around her all the time.'

'*Yes, we can, she is our Mate!*' Jace insists.

'What do you want me to do?'

'*Find her, make an excuse, anything!'* he demanded.

I finished up my lunch quickly and told the guys I'm headed off to finish something before the next class. I walk down the hallways trying to find Ashleigh's scent again.

I know I've gone full on stalker mode. Don't blame me, this is all Jace. I'm just about to give up, thinking she must be on the other side of school or in a classroom. Jace suddenly picks up her scent and she comes quickly around the bend, slamming into me and falling backwards on the floor. All of her books fall and scatter on the ground around us. Sparks fly through me like fireworks with our contact.

"Offt, sorry," she mumbles, looking down, trying to gather her things quickly.

I frown, surely, she knows it's me, right? Jace is going crazy with the contact. I can feel him pushing forward again. *'Make sure she's all right dumbass!'*

"Are you okay?" I ask. Bending down to help her I knew it was a loaded question, but I had to ask. My heart is pounding in my chest about to explode from just being so close to her. Shit, is this what it was like with the bond? I feel alive.

Besides the fact that Jace was pissed off at me and the situation, it still feels amazing that I could be near her. It takes all of my strength not to reach out and touch her face, to kiss her, to hold her and be close to her.

People around us stop and watch cautiously. I glare back, making them start walking past quickly with heads down. Good, no one needs to see this interaction between us.

"I'm fine," she whispers.

"Can we talk?" I ask.

Her eyes snap up to mine. "If you want to reject me, just do it here." she says demandingly.

I frown again. "Wait, what? No, can we just talk, please."

She nods and I look around. The hallway we are in is completely deserted.

I guess Jace pushed out more aura than I anticipated. I saw a small supply closet that was on the corner of the hallway, not too far away from where we were. It probably isn't the best place to have this conversation, but we need to have it, and this is the safest option. The bathrooms and classrooms are always occupied. At least there will be minimal interruptions, if any at all, in there.

"Over here," I mumble and reach out to help her up.

"Don't," she replies coldly and moves away. Shit, I wasn't getting out of anything that easily.

'*No, we fucking aren't, you had better pray that she doesn't reject us,'* Jace growled.

I looked around to make sure the coast is clear. Everyone is either already in class or quickly moving to be in class in the next 3 minutes. I guess neither of us are taking the next class.

Chapter 13 - ASHLEIGH

The storage closet?? Does he honestly think this conversation should be in the storage closet? Kia is still fuming and still so pissed off since this morning. 'What do you want to do?' I asked her.

'*I want to be close to our mate, but he is making it hard to be around him right now,'* she mumbles.

Every time we sensed him today, she would have a new-found anger raging through us after this morning's images flashed through our minds. So, I tried my best to just avoid him all day. I didn't want Kia's anger to make us do something we would regret.

I knew he wanted to talk but I wasn't ready. My mind was still trying to grasp that we were mates, I wasn't ready for a conversation that would have to end badly and ruin my birthday, a conversation that would ruin the rest of my life.

I panicked when he showed up in the cafeteria. The thought of him rejecting me right there in front of everyone, in front of Ollie, my brother and best friends, it was just too much. But all he did was smile at me and went about his day like we were nothing.

I was so stuck in my mind trying to calm down Kia I didn't even pick up his scent when I ran into him. Sparks flew through my body when I crashed into him. I didn't want to look up into his beautiful eyes, I feared I would burst into tears.

There is no way we will be able to be mates and happy. The only logical way of this working is rejection. I didn't want to be rejected, but his pack will never accept me as their Luna. My uncle and father will never allow me to leave my current position as Beta to become our enemy's Luna, it just wouldn't work.

I didn't want to have this conversation. I certainly didn't want to have it at school, but right now it was our only option. I sigh internally and take a deep breath as he opened the door, and we walked in.

The storage closet is tiny, it barely fit one person, let alone two, and with his massive size it was an uncomfortable fit. I move back and put space between us but it seems he doesn't want that.

Every step back I take he moves one forward. I put my hand on his chest to stop him moving forward again. Sparks fly through my body; the desire to touch him, the need for him to hold me.

I shake my head and drop my hand, missing his warmth instantly. "You wanted to talk, so talk." I say coldly, looking into his eyes.

I could feel Kia pushing forward. I struggle to keep her at bay around our mate. Now was not the time for her to go on one of her anger rants.

"I just..." he sighs and runshis hand though his hair, his eyes flashing a golden colour as I feel his wolf pushing forward responding to Kia.

"I'm sorry," he mumbles.

"What?" I'm stunned. I even got an apology from him.

"I'm sorry you saw that this morning, and I'm sorry I even did it in the first place. Jace warned me multiple times about being with someone before my mate, but I just didn't listen. I never wanted to cause you that pain, for that I am sorry," he says.

I stare at him, astonished that these words are even coming out of his mouth. Zander Blackwood is apologizing for his activities? He was always proud that he had the hottest girls, that he could get any girl he wanted. He literally said it regularly amongst his friends and usually in front of multiple people. Every week he would have a new girl hanging off him. Everyone knew if you were involved with him you were going to end up holding the short end of the stick.

He looks into my eyes with such sincerity and guilt. It is hard to see if he is lying or not but judging from what he's told me about his wolf so far, I doubt it. It sounds like he is also worried about me rejecting him.

"I'm not going to lie and say it didn't hurt, because it hurts like a bitch seeing you with her, and knowing you have been with her multiple times, as well as others multiple times, it hurts. But it was my choice to wait for my mate. At the end of the day, we all have a past and you chose your path and I chose mine. We can't take anything back."

"Thanks," he mumbles.

"I'm not saying I forgive you; I understand why you did it. Maybe in time I will forgive, but Kia is still pissed."

He smirks and reaches out to touch my face. On instinct, I move back a little and he stops midway, his hand hanging in the air between us. Emotion flashes through his eyes so quickly I nearly didn't catch it.

Crap, he apologized and I kind of accepted it, now I'm hurting him without even realizing it. Kia whimpered at the thought of us hurting our mate, he always seemed so put together and so strong, here he is trying to be vulnerable to me. Trying to make it work. Trying to make us work.

"Sorry, I just... I'm just not used to it yet," I mumble.

He nods in understanding, and drops his hand, letting it fall to his side. His face is back to his usual cocky smirk. "Can I see you tonight? At the club, do you want me to go?" he asks.

I frown and say, "It is on neutral ground. I don't have the right to say whether you can go or not."

He rolls his eyes, " I know that, but I don't want to make you uncomfortable if I go."

'*He already cares about us,'* Kia purred.

"You can come if you want to." I mumble, looking down at my feet. I could feel my cheeks heating up with embarrassment.

He chuckles at my response, leaning in quickly and placing a kiss on my head.

I look up, startled at his gesture, my heart pounding at the contact and him being so close. "Then I'll see you tonight sweetheart, until then stay safe." he said, his voice husky and deep. I nod, my head bobbing up and down on its own. My mind is in such a daze with him being so close.

He chuckles at my silence, my embarrassed face flushed so red I could feel it burning. He leans back, turns the doorknob and slips out backwards, returning to the hallway.

A few minutes after Zander left, I blinked my eyes and shakemy head.

'What just happened?' I mumble to myself.

Kia laughs at my reaction. *'If a small kiss on the head does that to you, then maybe we won't make out with him any time soon. We don't want you passing out,'* she giggles.

I internally roll my eyes at her. 'Go away,' I mumble.

'*At least he didn't want to reject us. If anything, this is moving forward, right?'* Kia asks.

'I guess so. We haven't covered everything but at least, we know he wants to try.'

I poke my head out of the door to check if the hallway is clear. I make my way back to my locker quickly. I needed some perfume or something to mask his scent, I don't need anyone asking why I was around him. Once satisfied, I look at the clock to see we only had 15 minutes left until the next class, so I walk to the bathrooms to freshen up.

While I was in the bathroom waiting around a little longer than usual, I hear the door open and close and footsteps walking in.

The scent of Grace and someone else caught my nose. Kia's anger flares again after being calmed by our talk with Zander. Smelling the bitch who almost ruined us made her angrier.

"Annie, hun, I told you Danni only likes one-night stands." Grace's voice rang through the bathroom.

"But he asked me to go to the club with him and the boys tonight. I just don't understand why he has to be such a jerk around his friends," the girl who is supposed to be Annie sobs.

"Wait, the boys are going to the club?" Grace asks.

"Yes... tonight," Annie sniffles.

"The fucking asshole/ Did he really just dump me so he can get a stupid fling at the club?" Grace growls.

'*I guess that answers what happened between him and Grace,'* Kia mumbles.

"Zander dumped you?" Anni asks.

"Well, sort of, this morning, he just abruptly ended things and said we weren't working anymore while we were making out. I wouldn't have minded having a good time before class, now I'm just pissed." Grace said.

I smirked thinking I know the exact reason why he stopped everything and didn't continue their 'relationship'. It gave me comfort to know that things didn't progress further once he found out we were mates. Hope blossomed in me knowing Zander was more serious about us than I initially realised. I feel a little guilty about judging his intentions so quickly. I guess I always thought he didn't want a mate, given how he always acted around everyone.

"Well, that settles it, I'll go to the club with you tonight and we will try to get our men back!" Grace demanded.

I groaned internally to Kia.

'*It's a good thing our dress looks sexy,'* Kia giggled. '*Don't worry about Zander, Jace will keep him at bay from doing anything stupid and it sounds like he really wants to try. I doubt he will screw it up'.* Kia tried reassuring us both.

'I guess you're right' I mumbled back to her.

The two girls had left the bathroom after chatting a little more. I definitely need to be going now or I was going to be late for my Economics class. I couldn't miss two classes in a row.

Chapter 14 - ZANDER

Jace was so hyped up after our conversation, I had to bargain with him again to get him to leave our mate. Grumbling, he finally gave in. She was so cute when she was all flustered like that. Just when I thought her cheeks couldn't get any redder, I was worried the kiss I gave her froze her in place.

So here I was in English with a grumpy old wolf grumbling about not being around our mate. 'We will see her tonight,' I try to reason with him again. 'We have to be careful, Jace, before anything else happens we have to build a relationship with her and then figure out father and our packs.'

'*We should bring the Luna family heirloom your mother gave you, for her birthday present,*' Jace sighed.

'Oh shit, you're right, it's still her birthday! Isn't that usually given at the Luna ceremony? That's what mum always said.'

'*Yes, but I think in these circumstances it'll be okay. It'll show that you are serious about her being your Luna. We may just have to explain the significance of the heirloom to her, but I think it will be okay. Besides, it's not like we have time after school to go and get her anything either.*' Again, of course, he is right.

A few of us had training after school, then we would be going to the club after. At the end of class, I bolt for my car in anticipation of getting out of school ASAP. Unfortunately, I didn't see Ashleigh for the rest of the day. I tried to hang around a little longer but instead of Ashleigh walking out, I saw Grace.

She starts to make her way towards my car, looking determined ... like she was not going to take no for an answer after this morning's conversation. Instead of waiting around for Ashleigh, I decided to take off.

I don't need any more trouble than I already have and I certainly don't need Grace's stench all over my car or me. A little bit cowardly maybe but I always made my intentions clear to Grace and never promised her anything more. Yet here she is acting like a spoiled little brat. Can't say I'm surprised. It is just another painful reminder that both Jace and Danni were right.

Training went as normal. We are always split up into groups. Our commander in chief, Richie, is Danni's uncle. He and Jake are brothers and since he was raised with the understanding of leadership as well as the physical strength of a Beta, it made sense to put him in a more leadership role.

Of course, we held tryouts, but Richie came out on top anyway. Richie always likes to pair up with me because we are somewhat evenly matched in fighting skills. I have pulled one over on him more than a few times, but he always gives his best and is never afraid to throw a few punches or kicks my way.

I at least learn a new trick, whenever he pulls one on me every now and then. Since coming back from Alpha training, I've picked up a few more fighting techniques that I wouldn't mind using to whoop his ass.

After a few laps around the training center, we all had our blood pumping through and full of energy ready to get going. As usual, Richie pairs up with me. I haven't had training since I got back, so it'll be interesting to see how much he holds against me. After a few rounds at each other, we both have sweat and blood dripping off us.

He has a busted lip and a black eye forming from some of my attacks and I have a bit of road rash and a busted jaw. The bastard hid a few of his moves from me and was able to knock me down a time or two.

I guess by me throwing some new moves, he has to up the ante. In the end, it didn't matter, I was still a lot stronger than some of our top warriors in the pack. We just laughed it off and shook each other's hand as Richie called training to an end.

I take off for the packhouse immediately after. I need to get ready for tonight to see Ashleigh. I called the club earlier to see if they could do something for me and they happily agreed . It is already 8.45pm and Ashleigh said she was going to be there around 9.30ish.

So, I have a little time to get ready and have a bit of dinner beforehand. After I showered, I went to my walk-in wardrobe and pulled out one of my favourite dark navy long sleeve, button-down shirts. Darker colours always looked better on me. I paired it with nice jeans and dress shoes.

Okay, don't judge, yes maybe I am dressing a little fancier for the club tonight, but I don't want to look like a sleaze like the others were going to. I at least wanted tonight to be special for her and wipe away the bad memory of this morning.

I just hope she knows I am trying to make up for the shit I had caused her.

'*Don't forget the gift,*' Jace mumbles.

'Oh, look who decided to show,' I tease him. I am kind of glad he said something. I haven't heard anything from him since we got back to our territory.

'*I've been around,*' Jace mumbled.

'What's wrong? Cat got your tongue?'

'*Nothing's wrong, I just want to see her. I'm getting weak because we haven't seen her in the last few hours.*'

I sigh, I know he was right, I could feel how weak he was getting, and it wasn't from the earlier training session. We become weaker if we are not around our mates after a few hours.

No alpha, no leaders, no rules can stop the bond from happening unless one of the people decides to reject the other. In response, a new law was established between the council and humans alike that if a mate is in another pack or with any other race, they have to move to be with their mate depending on the ranking and other circumstances. If this law is breached at any time, there can be serious consequences and penalties. Without these laws or peace agreements between packs wars would ensue.

This was one of the things I was concerned about when I found out that Ashleigh is my mate. Yes, I can be an asshole and just claim her in front of everyone and take her, but I don't think that would help with our relationship. I want someone to help me rule my pack rather than stand beside me looking pretty and doing nothing.

I don't want there to be a war between our packs either because of our history. I want to try to resolve this peacefully before it comes to that. Especially with both of us in leadership positions.

I searched my drawers for the box my mother gave me. It was a blue box with a white lace ribbon around it. After searching for about ten minutes, I found it in the back of one of the drawers next to my bed. I sit down on the bed trying to prepare myself for opening the box.

I hadn't opened it since mum gave it to me, I'll never forgive myself for that day. If only I was stronger, if only I was older, If only I had Jace, I may have been able to save her. That day, I lost the only woman who had ever loved me unconditionally. I sighed, looking up at the ceiling. I was not going to cry about this. I want to remember the good times I had with Mum.

Thankfully, Jace isn't saying anything stupid. I suppose he was trying to conserve his energy.

I wonder if Ashleigh is feeling weaker, too. if Kia felt the impact at all or if it was just a male thing.

I open the box, trying not to tear it. I don't want to ruin it now. I don't know how old it is. Inside is a letter with a key on it.

What the fuck is this? I open the letter and recognize my mother's handwriting.

Oh, fuck no. I am not ready for this.

'Just take it slow, deep breaths,' Jace tried to encourage me.

'My dearest boy Zander,

I am truly sorry I am not there to see you become the man you are today.

If you have this letter, it means I have not made it to your coronation to become Alpha. I hope by now you have found your Luna and she loves you, respects you and is with you every step of the way during your leadership. Please remember that love takes two. Love is given and received by both people.

I pray that during the time your father and I were together you saw the love we held. My prayer is that my little boy will become strong and bold in all things. My hope is you show your love, friendship and loyalty to all who deserve it.

Please forgive those who are to be forgiven. Life is too short to hold grudges and be angry. So many lives have been lost because of jealousy and hate. I pray you can change the future of our pack and bring peace amongst all.

The key is to grandma's cottage on human land. It is still under her name as Isabella Harper.

Address: 202 Gilbert Ave, Landon 2265

Consider this as a sanctuary when needed. Good luck my son, I wish you all the best.

Lots of love. Mum xoxo

Chapter 15 - ASHLEIGH

The final bell rang through the school ending the week, I was so excited to be out. Don't get me wrong, I usually love school. It just means I get to see Zander soon. I smile at the thought of seeing him tonight. I am excited about seeing him again.

It's a little strange that in the short amount of time I have been around him I've already become so attached. I guess the talk we had this afternoon really helped me relax and find out what he wanted.

He wanted me. He wanted to be mates. Yes, we have a lot of different challenges ahead. I would like to build my relationship with him before anything else. I'm glad he just didn't claim me in front of everyone. I'm glad he understands.

I try to get my thoughts off Zander. Surely it isn't healthy to be thinking about him this much. Kia isn't being helpful, flashing all kinds of images through my mind of him naked and dirty and just looking so damn sexy standing there in the dark closet and so close. I try with all my might to get him off my mind, especially since I am about to get in the car with Ollie and Brent.

'Kia please... now is not the time, the others will smell me,' I hiss at her as she flashes another one of her naughty images through my mind.

'We'd better see our mate tonight,' she mumbles.

'We will just, please, stop dirty thoughts right now while I'm around others.'

'*Fine, fine, fine'* she sighs. She finally stops with the craziness and I am able to settle down until they come over.

"How's your day been?" Ollie asks.

"It was good," I shrug. "I was able to catch up with the girls and just go to classes. I'm excited for tonight though. It will be good. I haven't been to clubs before."

"Oh, yeah, that's right. I forgot about that," Ollie laughs.

"Well, I'm sure Chloe will make sure you have a good time," I rolled my eyes,

"True, she is a bit like you in that sense. She loves the nightlife."

Ollie drove like a maniac on the way home. We need to get ready before people start coming over. There aren't many but there are enough to make me nervous. At least I know I wouldn't find my mate, it is hard to be around everyone now I know Zander is my mate. But we cannot do much about it until I accept him fully. I need to decide what I am going to do.

'We *are not rejecting our mate',* Kia snaps. '*I will only allow you to reject him if he displays any sort of abuse or cheating, not because of our packs or their stupid disagreements that happened nearly a hundred years ago.'*

'Fine, I'll accept those terms, but we still need to be comfortable with him and be okay around him before telling uncle or any family. Do you agree?'

'*Yes, I suppose'* she sighs. '*At least he does understand that. He is trying to make us work and trying to get to know us before anything moves forward.'*

At least both Kia and I have come to an agreement on Zander. I hate being out of sync with her. It's nice she's been more herself lately.

There aren't many people coming tonight, just our head warriors and one or two of our chief leaders. Mum and uncle wanted to invite some single alphas around the area to see if they were my mates, but I asked them to keep dinner small and with some pack members for now.

Maybe in a few weeks we could have something bigger if they still wanted it. I suppose I don't really need anything now that I've found my mate. I certainly wasn't going to tell them it is Zander Blackwood. Maybe later on when we have a more solid relationship, but I'm not going to tell them now.

As we arrived home, mum and auntie hurry us all inside and upstairs to get ready. The boys had to put on nice dress shirts and jeans and I put on the dress that I bought with Meghan.

I decided to put on some of my sexy lingerie to help make me feel confident and comfortable. Zander won't be seeing it tonight, but just for myself, I wanted to feel sexy.

I had to stop myself looking at the clock every minute. I am already counting down the time until I can see him again. It's so weird that I feel this way about him even after this morning.

Yes, I was annoyed about what happened, but I can't hold that against him. People have a past. We wouldn't be able to move forward if I kept bringing it up every time. He stopped instantly when he found out we were mates, and by the sound of things he broke it off with Grace also.

Yes, I wanted to trust him a lot, but a part of me is still hesitant and I think I will always be hesitant until we become one. I hope in time we can trust each other and become one. I don't want to be angry and bitter about it, especially if I am going to be his Luna. I want us to be equals.

People start showing up at around 6.30pm. I let mum know we are heading out at around 9.30pm. About eighteen people show up for our small intimate dinner. We are close with everyone who arrived, and I really enjoy talking to the leaders and going over the work with them.

Usually there will be a big party, but since we are going to the club tonight and we invited everyone to come, I didn't want to bother.

They still call me Beta but deep down I know I am destined to be Zander's Luna. I feel bad about the deception. It hurts a little that I have to keep this secret from my family, from Ollie and Brent, but right now, I'm not ready to tell them. I can't tell them until I figure it out myself.

I could see some disappointment in my mother's and uncles' eyes when they saw that no one they invited was my mate. Would they be disappointed if they knew that Zander was my mate? Would they be angry? Would they disown me? I know dad respected the mate bond, but would he be accepting enough with Zander? Or would our pack's histories outweigh the mate bond entirely?

Chloe arrived towards the end of dinner and was just making casual conversation. So many different possibilities run through my mind that I am startled when Ollie comes up to me and asks if I am ready to head out. Ollie drove the four of us to the club.

Everyone in the car is energised and buzzing with excitement. I hope Skyla is able to come out tonight. I really would love her to come. Once we arrived at the club we noticed the long line of people waiting to be let in. It is a mix of humans and supernaturals.

Either word got around about the party or this is a normal Friday night. Ollie nods to the bouncer who opens the rope and lets us in, followed by annoyed groans and shouts by some of the people in line.

I giggled as we walked through, "Thanks for getting us on the VIP list, Ollie."

"Hmm, oh no worries, they know it's your night, so how could they not allow it?"

I sighed, "Do they know it's my birthday?"

"Yep, you have a few surprises later," he grins and winks.

"Ugh, fine, but can I please have a drink before that starts?"

"Yeah, this way," he motions towards the bar and we all follow in a line.

"Just get me whatever," I shout over the thumping music. He nods in response. I lean against the bar and look out onto the dance floor.

The club is medium-sized with bright coloured lights flashing. A DJ is up in front and a pole dancer in a silver and gold bikini is wrapped around the pole and dancing to the music. Stand-up tables were around the dance floor and tables with seats were down the back. There were two staircases that led up stairs.

One had a rope tied to it with a sign saying, 'Closed private function'. The other staircase was a 'smoking zone'.

An overpowering smell of wildflowers and honey drifted through the unsavoury club's smells of sex, sweat, and smoke.

Kia perks up and starts jumping around. '*Mate, mate is here!*' she shouts.

I smile a little, trying not to let my brother or Ollie know anything was going on. They are too busy chatting and ordering our drinks.

I look around to see if I could find him. I spot him with Danni and two females. Instantly my smile dropped. I feel sick to my stomach, Kia pushes forward, trying to make herself known, her possessive side comes out and she does not like what she is seeing.

One of the females leans towards him and whispered something before walking away. He looks at her once and turns his attention to Danni.

'Relax Kia, He is an Alpha, his pack has females they are going to need to talk to him.' I tried to reassure her.

'Not like that they don't,' she growls.

I sigh. I don't like it either, but I can judge just from that interaction alone. I don't want to always be so insecure of everything he does. It wouldn't be fair to treat him that way.

I shake it off and turn my attention to Ollie and Brent. If Zander wants to see me he is going to have to talk to me himself. Ollie motions to sit at one of the booths across the way. We make our way over and started to chat. I've already finished my drink while Chloe and the boys have yet to finish theirs.

I signal to Ollie that I am running back to the bar for a refill. As I make my way through the crowd of people stumbling up to the bar, I am overwhelmed by his scent. Is he close by? I don't want to look around to just be disappointed again.

"Hello, mate," his husky voice whispers in my ear as I grab my drink.

I shudder at the closeness of his soft breath against my neck. I whip around and see him standing right behind me in a dark navy button-down top, jeans, and dress shoes. Did he dress nicely for me tonight or is this something he always wears out?

I scold myself for thinking negatively again. I don't want my stupid thoughts to ruin tonight.

"Are you free?" he asks.

I look over to the table where my friends are sitting and notice that Skyla arrived while I was away. No one seems to be looking for me so I can quickly escape to spend some time with him now. I nod in agreement.

He grabs my hand. Sparks shoot through me like freaking fireworks, I never want to let go. He leads me towards the staircase that has the closed sign. I frown and pull back a little. We aren't allowed up there. I point to the sign and shake my head instead of explaining myself over the loud thumping music.

He rolls his eyes and points to himself then back at the sign. I cock my head in confusion, looking between him and the sign, trying to understand what he is saying.

'He must have set something up for us,' Kia mumbles. *'Jace won't tell me anything, just that it's a surprise.'*

I widen my eyes in understanding and nod, motioning for him to move forward.

He leads me up the stairs, to an outside balcony. It is beautifully set up with little fairy lights lighting up the area in soft cozy colours unlike the flashing lights downstairs. Against the back wall and sitting under the shade of a tree is a cream and pink loveseat that faces the city views of the river and buildings. The music gets quieter as we close the door behind us on the balcony.

"Happy birthday, sweetheart," he says with a smile.

"It's beautiful," I gasp, looking around at the beautiful space. He just shrugs.

"It was nothing. I wanted to spend some time with you, and this is what they were able to set up. I know it's not the best place or anything, but considering our circumstances, it would be okay."

I nod as I take in the beautiful space. I feel guilty for the earlier thoughts I had about him. I really need to learn not to judge so quickly before making any type of assumptions about him.

"Ohh, here I brought this for you, too. I hope you like it."

He gives me a beautiful small blue velvet box with a lace ribbon around it. I open the box and see a beautiful hairpiece sitting softly on a soft white cloth. The hairpiece is silver with sapphires, diamonds, and white pearls all around. It is so beautiful I don't want to touch it in-case I break it. It look so old and well looked after.

"It was my mother's," he mumbles.

My eyes snapto his. My heart is pounding, is this what I think it is?

"My mother used to wear that when she was Luna, so did my grandmother and all previous Lunas. It's an heirloom passed down by generations."

"Zander... I, it’s beautiful, thank you," I say breathlessly.

"I know we had a rocky start, but I wanted to show you I was serious about us being mates. The only way I would back down is if you rejected me."

Kia pushes forward, making herself known. I know my eyes are probably flashing silver as she tries to talk to Zander. It is hard to control her around him.

"Then who were the two shanks you walked in with?" she demanded.

He frowns then smirks at Kia before answering her ridiculous question. "One was my cousin and the other was the human woman who owns this club with her husband. She actually helped me set this up for you tonight." He waves his hands around with his smirk deepening. "Jealous, sweetheart?"

Kia just growls in annoyance instead of responding. He chuckles back at her, shaking his head.

"Sorry about her, she wouldn't calm down," I mumble in embarrassment.

"It's alright, sweetheart," he laughs and raises his hand to stroke my face. "You do look beautiful tonight. I had to put Jace in his corner too many times when males looked your way."

Chapter 16 - ZANDER

When I walked into the club my eyes immediately tried to seek her out and I immediately knew where she was. Her scent overpowers everything and draws me in. I see her. She looks so fucking beautiful in her dress.

Several men were ogling her, and I pretend as though it doesn't bother me. I have to push Jace to his corner several times and remind him to calm down. She is so beautiful and, obviously, oblivious to her impact on the people around her. I play it cool and chat with my cousin and friends, but Jace would have none of it. He is determined to be with Ashleigh now!

Honestly, I don't think she knows the hold she has on me. She is too perfect and pure for me, and I don't know how I got so damned lucky to be mated to someone like her.

I take her upstairs to the little setup Lydia and her crew made for me. She found me as soon as I entered the club. Kia apparently saw our interaction and assumed she was one of my flings.

Can't say I blame her for feeling like that. I like that she has the same possessive feelings towards me as I do her. At least I know I have something going for me, hoping that it's enough that her wolf won't allow her to reject me.

I brought my mother's hair piece as Jace suggested, and she looks somewhat shocked as she opens the little box. Does she know the significance of the item already? Or was she just shocked I gave her something at all? I try to let her know what it means and I hope that she understood. I hope she knows that I have never been this invested in anyone before.

Everyone else was just to fill the void, just a quick fix. But Ashleigh, she is my other half, my soulmate. I would do anything to keep her as mine, I am not going to fuck it up. I sit on the loveseat while she looks at the gift. I want her to take her time, to love it, and understand what it means to me.

She looks towards me and blushes as she sees me seated on the loveseat.

"Join me?" I ask while patting my hand on the space beside me.

She hesitates and it looks like she is arguing with her wolf. I could see Kia flash through her beautiful eyes a few times. She eventually nods and bites her bottom lip, still blushing furiously as she takes a step forward.

She sits next to me carefully angling her body away from me a little to the side like she isn't sure of what my reaction would be even though I asked her to join me. I could feel Jace relaxing with Ashleigh sitting to close. Her scent of forest wood and freshwater swirling around me.

I inhale as much of it as I could, relaxing my tense body. She's here with me, not downstairs with anyone else. All I want to do now is hold her and kiss her but I know it is a big step for her to just sit down on this couch with me. Hell, it is probably a big thing for her to be up in this space with me.

I don't want to push and scare her or make her reject me. I need to take things slow, I know this, I just didn't realize how hard it was going to be.

"How was the rest of your afternoon?" I asked, trying to spark a conversation and not make things awkward.

"It was alright. Mum and uncle held a dinner tonight to see if my mate was in the pack. I think they were a little disappointed, but I didn't want to tell them about us just yet."

A low growl ran through me at the thought of others seeing her like this, she was fucking beautiful, and I wanted her all to myself. Hell, I fucking hated it when men around the club were watching her.

She rolls her eyes. "Relax," she mumbles and pats my thigh. Sparks shoot through me at her touch. Her breath hitches and her eyes become dark as Kia pushes forward.

Jace wants to push forward, too, in response. 'You need to calm down, I don't want to move too quickly for her,' I warn him.

"What about you, did you get up to?" she asks.

"Hm, yeah good also, we had training today before we came here so it wasn't too bad." She nods in acknowledgment.

"Can I get your number?" I ask her, hoping that if we had a proper line of communication things would be better for talking and I wouldn't have to rely on seeing her at school.

"Sure," she replies.

I pull out my phone and open a new contact address before giving it to her. She quickly types in her name and number before passing my phone back. She grabs her small gold purse and pulls out her phone.

"Here, put in yours," she says as she hands me her phone.

"What are you doing this weekend?" I ask as I typed in my details.

"Hmm, just more stuff with dad and uncle and probably try to catch up on study."

"When can I see you next outside of school?" I didn't know what her duties as Beta looked like during the week. Obviously being from different packs and both packs being so closed lipped on how they function I have no idea what she does outside of school.

"I can probably try to do something Saturday evening or Sunday evening?"

I nod and pull my phone back out, "I'll send you an address we can meet at, it's on neutral ground if anyone questions anything."

"Oh ok," I hear her phone make a little beeping sound as she received the text message. I smile at the thought of this message being the first of many.

"Ahh, crap! Ollie and the others are looking for me. He just linked me, worried where I got to," she mumbles softly.

I nod. "It's probably time we head back before people start to notice both of us are missing and come looking."

"Thank you, Zander, I really didn't expect all of this," she says before we head back down, rewarding me with a quick kiss on the cheek.

I smile, "It was no problem. By the way, you know the rumours about me are just rumours, right?"

She rolls her eyes and scoff. "You are a notorious fuck boy, and you know it. "

"Not anymore," I say with a chuckle and shrug as I open the door back to the club below. As we make our way back down the stairs, she put both her phone and my gift back into her purse for safekeeping. We part ways quickly so no one would catch us together and I make my way back over to Danni, Amber, and the others.

Amber is my cousin. Her mom, Aunt Katherine, is my father's sister and is mated to one of the head warriors of our pack. Since dad did not take a chosen mate after mum passed, she helps out with Luna duties.

Amber is a year older than me and a bit of a wild one. Maybe not as crazy as me, but she enjoys the nightlife and likes to fuck around. She's had a few boyfriends in the past but was disappointed when none of them turned out to be her mate. Since then, she stopped getting into anything serious to avoid heartache.

"So … does anyone want to hit the dance floor with me?" Amber asks, doing a little twirl.

I roll my eyes and look over at the guys. Danni was in the corner of our booth making out intensely with Annie. Eric and Billy, are just sitting there drinking and chatting with each other.

"Sure, babe. I got you," Eric says, shooting up from where he was sitting.

"No, not after last time," she snaps while shaking her head at him.

"What? You fucking enjoyed it, and you know it!" Eric replies.

Amber folds her arms across her chest pushing some of her boobs out and making her skinny dress move up a little bit.

"I was piss drunk, it should never have happened"

"Wait... what the fuck happened?" I demanded.

"Nothing," they say at the same time.

I don't have any siblings so having Amber kind of filled that slot growing up, especially after mum passed away. I look at them and I realise what happened. Fucking son of a bitch "You have got to be fucking kidding me," I growl.

"It was our choice, Zander. Back off," Amber snaps.

"Oh, so now you are defending us," Eric mumbles.

She shoots him a death glare, "and it will never happen again. I'm going to dance," she spins around and leaves for the dance floor.

I round on Eric, pissed off. He is one of my best friends and he slept with my fucking cousin. I haven't ever once looked at his little sister like that.

"Look, bro. It was nothing, okay. We were both just there and it just sort of happened. If you found out you found out, we weren't trying to hide anything from you," he tries to justify his actions.

"So, Stefanie is single, right?" I snap back.

I would never sleep with another woman again now that I know Ashleigh is my mate. I am still pissed, though, that one of my best friends slept with my cousin. Insinuating I would sleep with his sister somewhat makes me feel a bit better because it pissed him off and got a rise out of him.

His eyes go dark as his wolf pushes forward in the protection of his younger sister. "Come on man, it was no biggie," he mumbles as he scrubs a hand over his face trying to settle his wolf down.

"Whatever," I say as I get up and make my way over to the bar. I need a fucking drink to wash this BS down.

While waiting for my drinks, I feel someone's hands move from behind me making their way around my waist linking together and pulling me into a hug. I smell her before she even spoke.

"Hey, baby. Want to get out of here for a bit?" She leans up to my ear and whispers.

Jace pushes forward, pissed off that this fucking woman even considered touching us without our permission. And the fact she did it in the first place after this morning's conversation …

I spin around, almost knocking her over. She stumbles back but regains her balance despite her high heels.

"What the fuck, Grace?" I growl, letting Jace push forward.

I am pissed off. I don't want Ashleigh to think this was something I wanted in case she happens to see it. This bitch is not backing down and I have had enough.

She starts sobbing hysterically and slides to the ground. I link Danni, 'Dude, come over here to the bar. I need you to handle this bitch and get her sorted out.'

As Danni makes his way through the crowd I spot Ashleigh with her two girlfriends whispering in one of the corner booths. Her eyes connect with mine and she gives me a small smile and a little nod before turning back to her friends to join their conversation. Not too obvious but just enough for me to know.

Thank fuck I wasn't in the doghouse for this one tonight. I had already made good progress with her; I didn't want this to screw anything up.

Justin, the club manager, makes his way over. He is a burly-looking bloke with short cropped blonde hair and a cleanshaven face. "Everything alright here, Alpha?" Justin asks giving me a nod.

"Yeah, bro, sorry for the disruption. One of my pack members is just being a bit unsettled, Danni is on his way to sort it out."

He looked at the mess that was on the floor. Grace isn't even drunk enough to not know what is going on, in fact, there isn't even a hint of alcohol on her at all. She knew exactly what she was doing, and she knew exactly where I was which pissed me off even more.

Jace pushes forward just as pissed off with the interaction "you are never to touch Zander again without our permission or say so, is this understood?"

He growls at her using his aura. Several people around us had cower in submission with my aura blazing around me in fury. Most of the people in the club are human so ordinarily they wouldn't react but they are more susceptible with alcohol in them, so they submitted as well, not understanding why.

Danni stopped in front of her waiting for her response. "Yes, Alpha," she says through her fake tears.

I can only hope that finally with this humiliation and the Alpha command she would finally leave me the fuck alone. I grab my drinks that are sitting ready on the bar waiting for me and nod to Danni to deal with that shit, as I walk back over to the table.

Chapter 17 - ASHLEIGH

I roll over to my side as sunlight shines through my windows disturbing my peaceful sleep. My head throbs slightly from the number of drinks I consumed last night. We have shifter healing, yes, but it doesn't help that Chloe drinks like a fish and I'm a lightweight. She had about 3 rounds of tequila shots and too many cocktails to count. I don't want to know what was in the coke she kept on giving me, but it was not just coke. I'm sorely paying for it today.

I groan and stretch across my bed and I slowly sit up trying to get my bearings and see where my headspace was for today's workload. Looking around my room I'm glad to see I wasn't a messy drunk. Everything is still neatly in its rightful place, my dress is draped on the light pink cushioned armchair in the corner, and my shoes are placed next to the door.

I look down and see I am wearing an old bed tee and the same pair of panties from last night.

I feel Kia string around inside me waking up as well. '*What happened last night?*' she mumbles.

I laughed at her, 'we weren't that bad, were we?'

'Honestly, I'm not sure. All I remember is the talk we had with Zander and then spending time with the girls. Oh, speaking of. Where's the gift from Zander? I want to see it!'

I grumble in annoyance trying to get out of bed and find my gold purse. Thankfully it was next to my dress on the seat. I moved the dress off the seat and transfer it to the bed so it isn't damaged.

Opening my gold purse, I see the little blue velvet box that Zander gave me. I smile. I honestly thought at one point it was all a dream and i was going to wake up and still have to live through yesterday.

The hairpiece is beautiful. Little jewels and pearls all around the metal frame formed to make small flowers with fork-like ends to help hold the hairpiece in place while it is worn.

'I wonder what it's made of?' I ask Kia.

'I don't think Zander would have given us anything that would be dangerous. Maybe it's platinum, it would make sense given how old and well maintained it is.' Kia mumbles back.

I nod in understanding. Platinum is rare but if you had connections and knew where to get the raw materials, it wouldn't be too hard to make something like this.

I sigh and put the hairpiece back in its box. I don't want anyone to find it and I don't want to lose it. I put it inside my bedside drawer for safekeeping. I smile hoping I might see Zander again this weekend.

My phone buzzes on my bedside table letting me know I received a text message. I look at the screen and see that it's from Zander. I fumble around quickly trying to see what he had sent, nearly dropping the phone in the process.

Zander: Good morning, sweetheart. I hope you enjoyed yourself last night. Let me know when you are free, and we can organize a time to meet up. xoxo

My breath hitches as I read the message. Inhale, exhale, Inhale, exhale. I chant to myself as I read the message over,

Moon goddess, why was this so scary? Do I answer him? Do I leave it for later?

'A*nswer him now, silly! Pfft who cares about the silly human girls and their stupid games? This is our mate, not some boy toy,'* Kia mumbles, annoyed I was even considering waiting to answer him.

I sigh. She's right, I don't have to worry about wooing someone, he's already mine. I breathe in and start typing trying to figure out what to say.

Ashleigh: Good Morning, Zander. I had a good time, thank you. xx

Zander: Ohh, hey! You're up.

Ashleigh: Yeah, I forgot to close the blinds last night so the morning sun woke me. *Annoyed emoji*

Zander: haha, aww poor diddums. I hope you at least got a good enough sleep.

Ashleigh: Yeah, it wasn't too bad, wait... how come you are up at 5 am?

Zander: I'm usually up this early *boy shrug emoji*

Ashleigh: Really? Why so early? School doesn't usually start until 8.00 am.

Zander: I like to go for a run every morning. It helps to clear my head for the start of the day. I try to catch up on any work or pack work I need to do beforehand if I have time after.

Ashleigh: Sounds fun.

Zander: Hardly.

Ashleigh: To answer your earlier question, I'll have to double-check with my parents but I'm mostly free this evening or Sunday, although I usually keep Sunday evenings reserved for catching up on schoolwork, plus we now have that history assignment to do so that's added on top of everything else. Sorry! I ramble sometimes. *shy blush emoji*

Zander: Haha, it's alright, sweetheart. I like your rambling.

Zander: Ok so it sounds like tonight is more likely ...

Ashleigh: Probably, yeah.

Zander: message me the best time, yeah, and we can meet at the address I sent earlier.

Zander: Have a good day, sweetheart I have to head off now, message me when you are free. xoxo

Ashleigh: You have a good day also!

I sigh and roll on my bed clutching my phone. He messaged; I mean I know he said he would but the fact that he actually did makes all the difference.

Kia is buzzing around with new happy energy, happy with the progress with our mate.

I grab some Panadol from the bedside and take a few before I hop in the shower taking a long warm soak before the day begins.

Chapter 18 - ZANDER

I was surprised to see Ashleigh up at the same time I was. Granted she did say the morning sun woke her up.

I guess she isn't an early riser like I am. After my 10k morning run, I race back up the stairs and to my ensuite shower. Once I was all cleaned up I make my way back to my room and tense up when I see someone lying on my bed, trying to look sexy.

Jace growls. 'W*hat the actual fuck! Can I just say again, I fucking told you so, oh, I soo fucking told you so. If our mate catches wind of this not only will Ashleigh be pissed off but so will Kia. I managed to calm her down earlier, but I can only do so much.*'

"I heard you dumped Grace hard yesterday; I would have come up last night but you guys had gone to the club," Libby tried to say in a sweet sexy voice. Honestly everything just sounded whiny and needy now the bond had snapped between Ashleigh and me.

"Not interested, Libby," I snapped. "Now get off my bed and out of my room and never enter again," I demanded, linking with an Omega to come and change my sheets to try and get rid of her stench. I was not taking any chances; I had half a mind to look for some sort of camera with Libby. She likes all the kinky stuff and that includes recording us while having sex on multiple occasions.

"Aw, come on Zander. You know we always had a good time," she whined.

"Leave now," I said, with Jace flashing in my eyes putting in command.

Yeah, I'm having someone check my room, stat. For goddess sake, how many more will there be? I thought I was finished with these stupid bitches after Grace.

Jace is still grumbling in the back of my mind saying I told you so over and over giving me the death glare, it's frustrating because we used to be in sync. Now he's just grumpy unless we are around Ashleigh.

She finally got the message and scampered out of my room, but not before giving me a sultry look.

I linked Danni also, 'Danni, you up?'

Danni grumbles sleepily, 'What's wrong? I have this wicked hangover, don't think I can come to training today.'

I roll my eyes. Of course, the kid got wasted last night, and by the sound of things, is paying for it today.

'Can you organize someone to come and sweep my room? Libby was here.'

'Ahh, yeah, no worries. Did someone have a good time after the club, hey?' Danni chuckles.

'Nope, she was here this morning after my run, uninvited and unwanted.' I wanted to make it clear that she was not wanted in case rumours start to spread around.

'I'll get someone to do a sweep, don't want anything like last time.' Danni confirms.

I roll my eyes at the last comment. That's exactly why I didn't go back to the crazy bitch. She hid cameras in my room and car. I don't fucking know how she managed to do it in the small amount of time she had.

Dad found out and was crazy angry with the lack of respect towards the future leader of the pack, so he punished her with a month doing community service consisting of helping the Omegas and looking after the children on weekends. He basically stripped her of her rights in the pack for a month.

I know it doesn't sound like much but with someone like Libby who cares about positions and rankings and loathes work it was priceless seeing her try to cook and be bossed around by the head Omega and having the children trample her every weekend.

This was before I had Alpha Training. You would have thought she learned her lesson but I'm taking any chances. I haven't been with her since, it wasn't worth it.

Today, I had training until 3.00, I'll head over to my grandmother's cottage early to make sure everything is okay. I'm not sure if anyone is living in it or if anyone has looked after it so I want to at least see the damage before Ashleigh comes over so it's not so disgusting and dirty.

Training on weekends is different. The warriors and the high school kids train together which means we get to learn a few new moves and see where we rank in the group.

I don't usually get to pair up with Richie on weekends as he is too busy walking around helping others by correcting their positions if needed. Instead I am paired with Mark.

After a few hours, we all finish up and head out. I grab something to eat before heading to grandma's, I haven't been here in years, not since mum passed. I don't even remember when Grandma passed.

I pulled up to the little cottage, and as soon as I did all the memories flooded back. Memories that I thought I buried long ago.

Fuck. Maybe I wasn't as ready as I thought.

Chapter 19 - ASHLEIGH

Around 5 pm I pull up to the address Zander gave me. His sports car is already parked in the driveway on the left side, so I park my pristine white Suzuki Swift next to him.

It's a cute little cottage, a classic English white, and grey old-style cottage, with a white picket fence all around the garden, you can see some of the fence beams have been damaged over the years. There is an archway leading to the front door with a little gate that opens as you walk through.

The cottage has overgrown shrubs and vines running all through and around the front of the house. The flower bushes have gone crazy running along the fence line, and it seems that someone hasn't looked after the place in years. Almost as if it is deserted.

There are a few houses around but you couldn't see them for a few miles. I passed them on my way here. It is a beautiful place to grow up if you had a wolf to run around in the back woodlands.

The sun is starting to set, splashing the sky in pinks and orange.

I was starting to get more nervous about moving forward with Zander. This would be the first time we would be together without any interruptions, the first time to spend some quality time together and not have to worry about anyone else.

I try to psych myself up to get out of the car, Kia was bouncing around all happy we were seeing our mate. '*Come on, it'll be okay. He is waiting, and so is Jace. He can sense us from here.*'

I internally groan Damn her and her logical thinking.

It's too late, I can't turn back now, I'm already here. I slowly get out of the car and make my way through the gate towards the front door. Inhale, exhale, inhale, exhale... I had to remind myself several times.

As soon as I smell his scent, Kia goes crazy, making me even more nervous. I'm not saying we will be mating and marking tonight. No, no. We still have a lot of stuff to sort out before we get to that point. For one thing, I have never been in the same room alone with Zander Blackwood, other than in that tiny closet at school and well, I was a nervous wreck with that.

I want to know I can trust him, and maybe actually get to know him for him rather than knowing what he is like at school or around friends and all the rumours that go around. I close my eyes as I reach the front door and raise my hand to knock.

Tap, tap, tap.

I hear heavy footsteps making their way towards the front door his scent becoming stronger and stronger with each step. The door swings open to reveal him standing there looking like the most beautiful thing I have ever seen. He's in dark jeans with a short-sleeved tee and comfy vans. His dark beautiful hair is slicked back so it doesn't get in the way of his eyes.

My breath hitches and I blink up at him giving a small smile, which is all I can muster with his scent of wildflower and honey surrounding me ... invading my senses. It makes it hard to concentrate to find the right words to speak.

His eyes gaze at me longingly as I stand there, in jeans and a light blue long-sleeved top that reaches down to my bottom. I thought as a nice gesture I would wear the hairpiece he gave me yesterday, so my hair is tied neatly behind and held by the hairpiece.

After about a minute of us both standing there in silence, he finally breaks the awkwardness and speaks first.

"Hey," he mumbles with a smile.

I frown... maybe I wasn't the only nervous one.

"Hey," I smiled back.

"Come on in. Can I get you anything? Have you had dinner? I wasn't sure what was here, so I ran by the shops before I arrived and grabbed a few things." He starts to ramble.

I smile, "ahh, no, I haven't had anything yet. I had a busy day, so no haven't had anything yet"

He nods and steps aside to let me through. As I pass him I feel a wave of tingles shoot through me when my shoulder grazed his rock-hard chest.

'*Mate, mate, mate,'* Kia chants as she bounces around like a little pup. I am 100% sure my eyes are dark and Kia is flashing through making herself present.

I look up to see Zander's eyes had also changed to a dark shade as his wolf tries to push forward in response to Kia.

I sigh. Why couldn't they go in the back of our minds and communicate that way instead of making things harder here?

"Sorry, Kia is a little excited," I say to him.

He grins. "It's all good, , Maybe later on we can introduce them to each other."

Kia pushes forward before I could answer "*I will hold that to you, mate"* she purrs and takes a step closer to Zander making sure the gap between us is smaller than I'd like.

Zander chuckles at her comment, lifts his hand to cup my cheek, and kisses me on the head. I could feel my cheeks flush with embarrassment and pleasure as the fiery tingles fill my body once more.

Chapter 20 - ZANDER

Grandma's place isn't in as bad shape as I had thought. The outside is overgrown with flower bushes, vines, and scattered trees all over, while the inside is just a little dusty and stuffy. I open up all the doors and windows to air the cottage and get it to look somewhat decent for when Ashleigh arrives.

It is a cozy cottage. From the front door is the living room to the left is the living room with a medium 3-seater lounge with a wooden coffee table in front of it and an old TV box near the window next to the door. Straight ahead is a path to the kitchen in dark wood and white and to the right is the staircase leading upstairs.

I haven't been here in years, this cottage belonged to my mother's mother. She was one of the last people in her pack, most of whom had already passed away or moved on to new packs.

I remember a few people in our pack who used to belong to my mother's small pack. Mum was the Alpha's only child and already leading the pack. When she found out she was mated to dad, she chose to be with him and merge the two packs.

I tried to bring up the heritage over the years, but dad didn't ever want to talk about it. I only remember snippets that mum told me when I was younger. I wish I remembered what grandma was like, I guess like all things related to mum I buried that long ago.

I wander around the house trying to get a sense of where everything is before Ashleigh arrives. I still have about two hours. Hopefully she wouldn't be early.

I flick the light switch on and off to see if we had any electricity, I only half expected it to work. I doubt that anyone has been paying the bills to run this place considering how overgrown outside was.

As expected, nothing works so I looks around to see if there are any candles to light for the evening. If not I would have to make a list and head to the shops quickly to grab some things.

Thankfully I find a few candles with a lamp so they can be placed in the living room where the coffee table is and I'll light the small fire stove in the kitchen to warm the place up and provide some more light.

Being wolves, we don't need the light or warmth, but it is still nice to have the ambiance. I know we won't be able to go on many dates outside so this would have to be the way to do things for now. I want to make things special for her, to make her see I'm worth it.

Fuck, I don't have any matches. I groan and shake my head. I guess I really have to go to the store. The local store isn't far from here, but I wanted to avoid having to go so that there wouldn't be more people knowing I'm out here. I make a list in my head. There isn't much around the kitchen either so I'll have to grab some cups, plates, knives, and forks.

I spent about 20 minutes in and out of the shops. I try and think of something simple to cook on the fire stove rather than using the oven or gas cooktops. I need to get the electricity sorted out so this isn't harder later on, and we can be comfortable if this is going to be our regular meeting spot.

After an hour of walking around the cottage, I try to make the place look nice enough with the fire lit and candles burning in the holders. God, I hope she doesn't give me shit about this. I at least hope she knows I'm trying.

Jace chuckles in the back of my mind, snickering about what I put together.

'What, would you rather I go all asshole mode and do nothing? Then she really will reject us,' I mumble.

He grumbles and rolls his eyes at me.

'I didn't think so'.

Tap... tap.. tap.

The knocking at the front door pulls me out of the argument I with Jace. As I move closer to the door the stronger I could sense her. Jace perked up, buzzing around in excitement that she actually came.

I stand at the door for about a second and breath in her mouth-watering scent. I know she wants to take things slowly but fuck this was going to be hard.

I open the door and take in her beautiful figure. I stand there for about a minute, hoping she didn't mind me admiring her fucking sexy body, Ashleigh wore simple tonight, simple but sexy, in tight skinny jeans, a light blue top with a v neckline made its way down to expose some of her boobs, which I appreciate.

I just want to pick her up and devour those pink pouty lips and lick and suck on those beautiful tits of hers. Just thinking about it gave me a semi already.

Her wolf is a spicy one, no wonder Jace likes her. I guess I have to keep my promise to her and go for a run later.

I lead her through the cottage asking about her day and how she's been. I stop behind her suddenly when I see something glittering in her hair.

"You wore it," I say, half-surprised.

She frowns, cocking her head and looking back at me confused. "Wearing what?"

"The heirloom." I nod to her hair.

"Ohh, of course. I hope that's alright; I wasn't exactly sure where I can and can't wear it but I thought if it was just going to be the two of us tonight, it would be a good start."

I smile and nod and move closer to her to kiss her on the lips but instead, she gasps and moves away from me a little. I move quickly towards her again. She doesn't flinch but is just a little bit uncertain of what I was planning.

It's kind of cute, intimidating her considering she was the Beta. Although I guess since we're my mate I have a different effect on her than others. I chuckle and move past her heading for the stove I had put on earlier. I guess she isn't ready for some things just yet.

"Unfortunately, I was only able to get some soup and bread for dinner tonight. We are only able to use the fire stove because the gas stove and electricity aren't working at the moment. I'll look into it this sometime this weekend and hopefully have something set up for our next visits."

She nods and says, "that's okay. Thanks for getting something. I forgot to eat before coming here."

I had put on the soup beforehand knowing it was going to take some time to warm up, I walk over to the fireplace and look in the pot, it is slowly simmering away almost to the boiling point.

"Probably a couple more minutes then it should be good to eat," I mumble looking back towards where Ashleigh was standing in the living room.

"This is a cute place, how'd you find it?" She asks.

I sigh internally. I suppose she's going to ask about my family sooner or later. I sort of hoped it would have been a bit later.

'*Just take it slow and explain the situation to her. No need to go into the big details tonight but you can at least share things you are comfortable with,'* Jace encouraged.

Chapter 21 - ASHLEIGH

He knelt to be level with the fire stove to stir the pot full of our dinner.

I try to make conversation, I thought a nice comment will be ok. Oh, how wrong I was. As soon as I ask about the cottage he is all uncomfortable, squirmy. His eyes flash a gold rim with his wolf peeking through like he was arguing something.

I didn't even consider the history of this place, then it dawns on me... maybe it belonged to his mother.

"I'm sorry. I shouldn't have asked, I didn't mean to make you uncomfortable," I start backtracking quickly.

Things are already somewhat awkward because of earlier when he tried to kiss me. It came so naturally to him to want to do the action. I didn't mean to hesitate when I did, I just wasn't ready yet. I hope when I get to know him more as himself then maybe I'll feel more comfortable doing those things naturally, too.

Kia is fuming that I didn't let our mate kiss us, but I wasn't ready, and she needs to understand that.

"It's alright, you should know anyways. I'm still coming to terms with this place myself if I'm honest," he mumbles.

I frown, not sure where this is going.

"It was my grandmother's cottage, my mother's mother. I guess she moved here to be close to mum when she moved to dad's pack. I hadn't been here in years. I only have a few memories of this place, some of them are snippets of mum with me in the garden but not too many," he says with a shrug, his eyes darting all over the place rather than meet mine.

Damn me and my big mouth. I try to make nice yet I just made him uncomfortable. So, rather than making things worse I just nod my head and smile at him, waiting to see if he will continue.

He is silent for a bit as he peeps into the soup over the fire.

"I think dinner is ready if you would like to eat now?" He says.

"Sure, is there anything I can help with setting up?" I ask looking around. The inside of the cottage is beautiful. I love the little living room and kitchen area. It’s a cosy area, not too small, just big enough for two people or a small family.

He nods in response and grabs some plastic bowls from the bench and starts to unwrap them.

"I wasn't sure what else was around so I just bought a few throw away cutlery and dishes for tonight, I might have to go to the shops properly later and buy a few things if we are going to spend our time here."

I look up to him, a bit startled that he would consider meeting regularly here.

"What's wrong?" he asks while studying my puzzled face.

"I didn't know you'd want to meet regularly." I shrug. I know we are mates but I kind of thought the whole thing with our pack's history and all the girls he likes to be with might turn him off being with me.

Yes, I know he gave me the Luna heirloom and has confirmed he wanted to work things out, but I still had a small bit of doubt lingering in my mind, that maybe one day he would wake up and just not want to be together anymore, especially with his history.

He nods and says, "Yeah, for sure. You are my mate, I want to be with you and you only. Plus, Jace would never let me be with anyone else."

I smile at the reassurance and determination in his voice, it makes me feel a little guilty for having the doubtful thoughts.

He moves closer to me invading my space, cupping my cheek, sensing my unease, "you will always be the one I want, I know it's only been a few days, but the only way you will be getting rid of me is if you reject me."

His scent is making me dizzy and with the feeling of the sparks coursing through us, it's like all time has stopped and I don't want to move away from this feeling, to be here in this moment together forever.

His eyes turned dark with lust as I unconsciously licked my bottom lip soaking in his delicious scent. I said I didn't want to wait to be intimate with him just yet but being alone here in this house with him is harder than I thought.

A sizzling sound startles us bringing me back to reality. The soup had boiled over the top spilling onto the fire stove.

"I think dinner is officially ready," Zander smirks. I swear I see a little glint of mischief flashing through his eyes as he moves back towards the stove.

'He knows exactly what he's doing,' I mumble to Kia.

'O*f course, he does! He wants to jump your bones. I also wouldn't mind getting a taste of our mate,'* Kia responds, licking her chops greedily.

I roll my eyes internally to her. Silly, horny wolf... maybe one day we will be with him, but today is not that day. Kia grumbles about me being silly and retreats to the back of my mind.

As Zander dishes out our meal I could see outside through the kitchen window. The sun has set completely leaving a black sky covered in shining stars. I love running in the evenings. At night, when everyone is asleep, Kia and I could be ourselves without any worries. I wonder if Zander did actually want to go for a run tonight or if he meant next time.

While my thoughts ramble he guides me through to the lounge to sit and eat, I look around and realize there isn't a table for us to dine at.

He must have noticed me looking so he asks, "is the here all right? The dining room is out the back. Here felt a bit more comfortable."

"Ohh yeah, this is okay," I reply with a warm smile. "Let's eat, I'm starved."

He chuckles and rolls his eyes at my exaggeration as he sits on the lounge, placing the things on the table for us to use.

"So, you were thinking of fixing something up?" I ask while stirring my food and taking a sip of the beautiful rich sauce, hoping this line of conversation will be okay to discuss and not make him feel uncomfortable again.

He nods with a mouth full of food. He'd scooped up the soup making the bread all nice and soggy.

"I just need to make a list of a few things and maybe get some updates for a few things. I was surprised Dad didn't have anyone checking in on the place, but then again maybe he also didn't know anything about it." He shrugs.

"I can help out too if you like, the garden looks amazing, I don't mind getting into that if you want some help," I suggest. "Anything you need help with just let me know."

He nods in response, settling down and relaxing back on the sofa.

I am still leaning forward with my bowl placed on the coffee table for support, but I could feel Kia wanting to push back and cuddle into our mate.

Chapter 22 - ZANDER

We sit and talk for about an hour, the sun set long past. It is getting colder in the evenings now being so close to winter. It doesn't bother us shifters much but we could feel the nip in the air.

The more I get to know Ashleigh the more strongly I feel about her. I have never felt love before, not from a girlfriend or any of my fuck girls at least. They may have loved me or my status but I was always explicit in my intentions. Everyone knows that wolves have mates, and I was not going to give mine up for some one night stand or some girlfriend I could barely stand or know.

I try not to make her uncomfortable, she is still sitting so stiffly on the other side of the lounge, not even budging to move closer to me. I am a bit surprised she doesn't lean into me and relax a bit. I've felt the itch to be closer to her all evening.

'*Kia says she wants to know us before doing anything further,'* Jace mumbles, answering my thoughts for me.

'That makes sense I guess,' I reply.

I remember the comment Kia made before about going for a run and meeting Jace, maybe that will help her relax a bit more.

"Would you like to go for a run around the backwoods?" I ask.

"Um, sure, are we allowed to be out there?"

I nodded, "yep, the backwoods are a national park, you need a permit to be in there so it should be ok for us to go for a run for a little while, I saw a stream before heading into town so there might be a watering hole they can swim in if you want."

"Sure, I have to be back home in an hour and a half, if you think that will be enough time then I'd be happy to do that. Kia would love to have a run and meet Jace. Although I don't have a change of clothes to swim this time. Maybe next time if we are going to be meeting here more regularly."

"That's fine, too" I shrug. I jump up and grab her hand helping her up. She seems a bit startled at the action. "Come on, if we don't have much time let's head out now then."

I lead her to the back door next to the kitchen. As we step out we see the moonlight shining through the thick trees.

The backyard was very much the same as the front, all overgrown trees and shrubs you could barely move through except for a little paved pathway leading out towards the backwoods.

I hold onto her hand and move towards the back. I can feel Jace getting all excited to be let out and meet Kia officially. They can communicate now on some level but not huge amounts since we aren't marked, but it would be nice for them to meet in each other's forms.

We pass another gate to the woods, I turn to face her to see if she is ready to shift. She stands there looking a bit confused.

"What's wrong?"

"I, erm, don't have any other clothes..." she mumbles.

I frown, looking at her trying to decipher what she means.

Jace rolls his eyes at me. 'S*he doesn't want you to see her naked.'*

"Ohh, okay. Uhm, I'll turn around and you can shift." Fuck! I wanted to steal a look. I've been dying to know what her tits are like.

'D*on't let her know you're been thinking that,'* Jace teased.

'Just take it easy with Kia. Ashleigh still has to be comfortable with everything you do,' I warn him as his emotions become more prominent, with lust and excitement overpowering.

I turn around to let her strip and shift. Jace pushes forward to shimmer into our black fur, and within seconds I am on all fours.

I could feel Kia moving around behind me. She nips Jace's tail letting him know she's ready. Kia is a bit more playful and relaxed than Ashleigh. I stay at the back of my mind and let Jace take the lead just watching through his eyes as he chases and plays with Kia.

Jace has more control when we are shifted but I still get to retain some control. Wolves are mostly instinct. In the past if the wolf has more control over the body than the human, they can turn feral especially if they don't have a mate to ground them. We've seen this happen when someone's mate passed away or with a rejection. They lose their mind, and the wolf takes over.

It is rare to be rejected, and it is rare to not have a mate, especially more so nowadays since everyone knows about the supernatural and all the rules and laws around mates it makes it a lot easier to find your mate.

Kia and Jace run around for about 40 minutes to an hour. I think both of them enjoy being out in the open and at peace, with no responsibilities, no drama, and no issues.

It's just us.

At times like this I wish I wasn't the Alpha Heir, that I could just be a kid and be myself, and maybe our situation won't be as complicated. But at the end of the day, I'm still the Alpha. I have responsibilities, I have a pack, my dad, and everyone relying on me.

I have no idea how we are going to bring up the subject of moving forward when the time comes. I just hope my father won't make me reject her, I already like her so much and so does Jace. He would never choose someone else to replace Ashleigh, especially now that he has met Kia.

After a while of playing around in the trees, I tell Jace we need to head back so she can go home to her family. He grumbles but gives in, heading back in the direction of the house.

Ashleigh hides behind a tree and quickly gets changed while I just stand there getting changed in the open.

"Thanks for that, Kia loved it," she replies with a smile.

"Any time, so did Jace. Maybe next time it can be longer." I reply happily.

I lead her back through the cottage and to the front door.; "Don't you need any help cleaning up?" she asks.

"It's all good, all throw away, so it won't take any time at all."

She nods, opening the front door and turning around to face me. "Thanks for tonight. It was nice to just sit and chat."

I nod in response, agreeing with her. I move my hand closer to her testing the waters. Will she be comfortable with a goodnight kiss?

Her eyes keep darting to my lips as she moves her tongue along her bottom lip. This girl will be the death of me! I'm already supporting a semi and I am definitely going to have blue balls again tonight.

Or ... was she going to hesitate again? Her cheeks blushed furious pink as my hand softly stroke her cheek. I love that I have that effect on her. Moving in slowly to kiss her I could feel the hesitation as I get closer.. As I am just about to reach her lips but she turns her head just enough for my lips to land on her cheek.

I could hear Jace chuckling, '*smooth.*'

'Shut up,' I snap back. Damn, I guess she still isn't ready.

"I'll see you Monday!" She says, stepping out into the night.

Chapter 23 - ASHLEIGH

Monday morning rolls around, but all too quickly. The weekend is never long enough.

It was great to see Zander on Saturday evening. I loved the little cottage and could imagine us maybe living there or in something similar if we had to be on the pack lands.

It felt somewhat familiar being there. I couldn't quite put my figure on it, but I had a few weird flashbacks and a strange feeling of deja vu. After a while, I brushed away the odd feelings and enjoyed his company. It was nice to get to know him a bit and try to understand him and put aside all the rumours and previous encounters we have had. As hard as some of them were, I was still going to be mindful that he had a past. I didn't want to hold it against him, but I still had to keep it in mind.

Kia loved running around with Jace. She is a bit more of a free spirit than I am, but we are always in sync, epically more so, now we have found our mate. While I am still getting to know Zander, Kia has already decided she wants Jace and only Jace. So even if something happened it would have to be a lot for her to allow me to reject him, she won't have it any other way.

Monday is my day to help helpwith cooking and cleaning, so here I am, up at 6 am on a Monday morning helping Mum get everything ready. I quickly shower and get ready for school. I kind of wish our school had a uniform so it wouldn't be so hard to choose what to wear. We were told, however, that in most workplace environments a uniform is not worn , so they are preparing us more for adulthood and responsibility.

I check my appearance in the mirror one last time before running downstairs, ready to help with the cooking. Mum is already in the kitchen cooking away on the stove. I hear a timer go off as I stop at the Island bench.

"Morning. sweetie! Could you please grab the plates and set the table," mum asked with her back turned as she focuses on what she's cooking.

"Sure, mama", I nod automatically even though she couldn't see me.

I reach up and grab the glasses from the shelf above the stove and then turn around and grab the plates and cutlery out of the drawers on the island bench.

I hear a gasp behind me. Frowning, I turn to see what happened. Mum is standing behind me her face pale, looking at me like she had seen a ghost.

She stands as still as a statue like she couldn't comprehend what was going on. The tea towel in her hand is crumpled as she holds it tightly.

"What's wrong?" I ask, confused.

She quickly pulls herself together as though nothing happened in the last 30 seconds.

"Nothing sweetie, don't worry about it," she waves a hand dismissively and goes back to cooking the rest of the food.

"So how was your weekend? Did you enjoy yourself?" she asks trying to start a conversation to forget the awkward encounter.

I nod again, a frown on my face although this time she could see me.

I really want to tell them about Zander. I hate keeping secrets from everyone but I am wary of the repercussions once I do. I don't want to have any drama if it can be avoided while I'm still trying to figure out my feelings.

"It was good, I enjoyed the training with dad and uncle, and hopefully, I will get better at tracking. Kia definitely enjoyed it." I keep it short and simple, with a little bit of detail but not too much for her to ask more questions... hopefully, it would be enough to not pry any further.

Mum nodded in response while cooking, I could hear everyone starting to wake up now, there were a few showers that turned on upstairs and down the corridor where Meg and Alex live.

I quickly go around and help set everything up. Everyone is usually up and downstairs by 6.45 am or 7.00 am. We have to make sure we are ready to leave by 7.30 am, at least, to be at school on time.

In the next 15 minutes, everyone's buzzing around downstairs seated at the table ready to start the day.

Ollie and Brent look exhausted. I wonder what they got up to last night? Or maybe they're just exhausted from the warrior training they had last night. I honestly didn't think it was too bad. Last night we got to train with our wolves instead of in our human forms as we usually do so I really enjoyed it. It was a nice change.

Afterbreakfast we pile into Ollie's car and take off for school. I'm looking forward to going today and I'm willing to admit that I miss Zander. I wish we'd had more time last Saturday night but I needed to get back when I did to be ready for Sunday training.

As we arrived at the school parking lot I see him get out of his car with Daniel, I feel butterflies form in my belly as I watch him.

'Ugh, I feel such a creeper right now.' I mumbled to Kia.

'Hehe, *I don't. I like our sexy mate, I want to go over there and jump him right now, stuff what everyone else thinks.'*

I rolled my eyes. Silly horny wolf.

'I will only wait for so long, Lei, he is our mate whether you are okay with that or not. I won't reject him, not now.' she tells me with such determination and confidence it makes me wonder what I am actually waiting for.

I meet Chloe and Skyla at the lockers to catch up on the weekend. As we chat by the lockers I smell him before he has even walked past. My breath hitches and everything is buzzing around me. Feeling a little numb with power, Kia is bouncing up and down happily just being near him. It's a different feeling from Saturday evening. I feel energized and more alive now than I did before.

I wonder at the new power I feel, 'What's going on?' I ask Kia.

'Sometimes I get a little weak from being away from Zander and Jace for so long. Being near each other helps us both,' Kia answers my confusing question.

It's weird since I didn't feel any difference on Saturday night. I didn't even notice we had gotten weaker. This worries me a little bit, but we will see Zander here at school and will probably meet him regularly throughout the week, it helps me settle and feel that we will be able to manage it.

I hope he noticed me wearing his hairpiece, I really love it and want him to know I am all in with him. I want to make this work. As I think this his beautiful eyes move up to lock with mine. I give a small smile as he passes through chatting with Daniel and one of his other friends.

It is so hard not to go up to him and talk to him. For now we have to ignore each other, only allowing our eyes to talk, hoping no one notices .

Chapter 24 - ASHLEIGH

It was a very frustrating start to the day. Every time I smelt him, I had to act as though it was nothing. Every time he walked passed it killed me that I couldn't speak to him.

I didn't realize how hard this was going to be, is it hard for him, too?

It seems he is just moving along casually without any care for the world.

'*Remember this is what you wanted, I'm 100% sure Zander would have loved to mate and mark Saturday night when we saw him,'* Kia oh so helpfully reminded me every time I pined for him.

'I know, Kia, I just wish it wasn't so hard. I wanted to, at least, be able to speak to him a little bit. But even then, I don't know what we could discuss.'

I wait for the girls at the steps by my locker. We always have lunch at the cafeteria and today is no different.

I feel a pull towards the football grounds, I walk towards the windows that open up all through the hallways to provide sunlight through the dark corridors.

I see Zander in a sports outfit with a red rugby top, black shorts, and black shoes. He is running around being a bit silly and stupid with his friends. Some of the cheerleaders are on the steps watching the boys. A pang of jealousy courses through me as the twins from Westfield sit there giggling at Zander.

Brooke and Mia, the identical twin wolves from Westfield are tall, stunning blondes. They always wear matching outfits. Today they are wearing white jeans, red heels , and red crop tops with leather jackets. Their parents are the Gammas of the Westfield pack, making them Gamma heirs.

Would I always feel this insecure with him being around others?

I must have been watching him too long, as he stopped a tackle from one of his friends he looked up in my direction, his eyes locking with mine. They were different from the other night, not a cold glare but not a friendly happy one either. I wasn't sure what happened between us. I tilted my head questioning what was wrong. He just completely ignored me and looked away coldly.

Kia whimpers at the thought of him being angry at us, I am confused and getting upset myself. I wasn't sure what I did, even if I did anything at all.

'Can you contact Jace?' I ask her.

'*No, I don't know what's happened,'* she mumbles .

I try to fight the tears that threaten to fall. What did I do? I only wanted to figure things out. I didn't want to ever make him angry or hurt. I thought we left on good terms last Saturday.

As I stand there thinking of ways to try and contact him Chloe came up behind me startling me. "Hey, girl. You ready?" She asks, linking her arm with mine.

"Oh, hey! Yeah, sure. Lunch at the usual spot, right?" I respond.

"Yep. Is everything ok? You look distracted?"

"Yeah, I'm all good. Let's go," I mumble back and turn around walking through the doors tothe cafeteria.

"So, I hooked up with Bobby on the weekend," Chloe blurts out as we walked.

I had to hold back a giggle, Bobby Enderson has been trying to get in Chloe's pants since she started cheerleading. He is the Alpha heir of the Riverview and has the same arrogance and cocky demeanour as most Alphas.

"Really?" I ask while trying not to sound so amused.

She looks at me and pouts. "I know I always said I didn't want to, but he asked me on Friday, we had study hall together and he isn't a bad guy," she continues her rant as we walk into the cafeteria.

I hadn't had much to do with Bobby, just that he is in our year and not a bad guy. He also sleeps around from what I have heard. I'm a little surprised Chloe gave in to going out with him, though. I guess we all have that one weakness.

I've had my fair share of guys asking me out but back in 10th Grade, it got out that I was waiting for my mate so everyone kind of stopped asking me since. It didn't exactly bother me much, I was true, after all. I was waiting for my mate, I just wanted to be the one to tell people rather than being in the rumour mill.

We make our way over to the table where Ollie and Brent are already sitting with Sam and Don. some of Ollie's buddies who he hangs out with and who are part of the football team this year with them.

I am somewhat surprised Chloe didn't say anything when we sat down, She and Don had a fling going last year. It seems that is well and truly over if she is going to go out with Bobby now.

We sit down and start chatting. The boys were being boys with their stupid talks and discussions about the football game and what girl was the flavour of the month. I see Skyla over with her pack. I guess they were sticking close together today, I smile and wave at her.

Just as I do Zander and some of the others who were on the football ground file into the cafeteria making all sorts of noise while lining up to get lunch. Thankfully, I had packed mine this morning and need notwith the crazy lines today.

As I dig into my lunch I felt a course of pain shoots through me so unexpectedly. It hurts like nothing I have ever experienced before. I could barely move.

'Kia, what's happening?' I whimper.

'*Where's Zander,'* she asked quietly.

I look around and see the twins all over him, one of them is kissing him on the lips moving her hands all over his body and the other is whispering something in his ear while playing with his collar.

My eyes blur with tears fighting to release the hurt and anger that flow through me, I tried to keep everything under control. This time Kia remained silent rather than the usual thrashing around trying to be let out.

I have never felt so weak, so humiliated. Even though no one knows we are mates, but we knew, and I thought it meant something to him. I guess I was wrong. I was so very wrong.

I don't know what to do so I just get up and leave without a word to anyone.

Chapter 25 - ZANDER

Mia launched herself at me while her sister whispered things in my ear while playing with my collar. The kiss feels like sandpaper scratching against my mouth, it is the most horrible thing I have ever felt. I hate hated this. all I want is my mate, but right now she doesn't want to tell anyone so I have to still act like my old self before.

Jace is pissed at me as usual. 'She *didn't mean flaunt yourself around with other women, you dumbass.'*

'Honestly, I'm confused as to what she wants.' I snap back at him.

'Just *because you had a shitty weekend after she left on Saturday does not give you the right to hurt her like this. She can fucking see us! Do you know the pain you are causing her? The pain you are causing us by going against the bond?'* Jace growls.

No, no I didn't know the pain I was causing her, I didn't want to look at her and see the brokenness I caused.

I hear Oliver call her name, snapping me out of my funk. I look up just in time to see her leave the cafeteria and head toward the school gates. My stomach churned as I see the hairpiece tightly tucked away in her hair holding all of her beautiful locks together. The one little item that makes all the fucking difference.

Fuck! I screwed up big time. I want to follow her so badly, but I also didn't want to cause any unwanted attention.

'Follow *her,'* Jace says demandingly.

'I can't,' I mumble back, scrubbing my hand over my face in defeat, and of course, he is more furious at that response.

'Yes, *you fucking will. You will fix this I will not lose my mate over this.'*

The twins had since stopped their assault on me and moved back towards the line waiting for the food mingling with their friends. What the fuck! was that just to make a fucking point?

I was more than pissed, I was fucking furious, I have just probably lost my mate and these stupid girls are now acting as though nothing happened.

I don't want to follow her because I don't want to know the outcome of the conversation we had to have. There was always going to be a conversation whether I wanted it or not, especially more so now after my actions that just happened in the last five minutes.

While I was having my internal debate with myself Jace had taken control and made me move in the same direction as Ashleigh.

'Jace, give me back control now!'

This is the first time he has ever done this and locked me in the back seat not giving me any control, even in his wolf form he at least gave me half of the control, we always made decisions together, but this time was different he had something to lose.

'No, I am fixing your fucking mess,' he growls at me.

'You know what she wanted Jace, I can't go after her right now. At least give her a ten to fifteen minute head start.'

He whimpers in pain knowing I'm right. People around me are already cowering in submission from our aura.. He reluctantly gives me back control as I step out of the line and head toward the bathrooms.

Fuck how am I going to fix this?

Going to the bathrooms I go straight to the sink. Two younger kids scurry out straight away I guess me being pissed off they could feel my anger still radiating through.

I go to the far sink and turn on the cold water and filled the basin. I splashed my face with the water trying to get my shit together as I prepare myself for what I must do.

My eyes close as I try to calm myself, letting everything flow through all the different emotions, taking deep breaths. A newfound emotion flowed through me; one I haven't felt in a very long time.

'Because *we have something to lose now,'* Jace whispers.

Fear was evident in my eyes as they snapped open staring in front of me through the bathroom mirror.

'What do I do, Jace?' I mumble.

'You *find her, you fix this,'* he says, curling up and putting his head between his paws sulking.

'I, at least want our mate at the end of all this, that is the goal. To let her be comfortable in telling everyone about us so we can be together fully. Even if she does not want others to know yet you need to be mindful of her. You can't keep on doing what you use to do, it physically hurts her, the pain of someone else with our mate, going against the bond. It's something no one should ever experience.'

'I want her, too, I'm just not used to this.' I sighed, trying to get him to understand my point.

'I get you aren't, but this is something we both have wanted for a very long time, we can't lose our mate.'

I know he's right. For as long as I can remember, I have always wanted a mate yet here I am fucking it all up.

'We've *waited long enough now, go and find her.'*

I sigh, letting the water out of the basin making a slow gurgling sound as I make my way back to the cafeteria.

Everyone seems to be minding their own business as I slip out, walking towards the parking lot. I check to see if there are any cars missing. Maybe she ended up driving somewhere.

'We *can still smell her, so that means she ran.'*

'Where do we check first?'

'Try the house. Maybe she went there hoping we would follow,' Jace replies.

God, I hoped she did. As much as I didn't want to confront the shit storm that was going to happen, I at least wanted to be in the same room as her. It has been so fucking hard to not talk to her today.

I grab the keys and make my way to the car taking off in the direction of the little cottage hoping, praying that she will be there.

Chapter 26 - ZANDER

From school, the drive is only tab out 20 minutes. Yesterday I took the time to set up the electricity and water. I also made a key cut in case she ever needed to go to the house and I placed it in a hiding spot last night and messaged her so she would at least know where that is to get in.

As I drive, I think about how to explain away my actions. Hell, I bet she'll be pissed off considering the way she left, but at the same time, that is how I always acted even before. I can't go out of character, can I?

Jace stayed quiet on the drive there. He purposely blocked me from his thoughts and feelings. Before he did that, I could sense that he was filled with anger and hurt so it's probably best I didn't get those feelings right now. I needed to figure this out on my own.

When I pull up to the cottage there's no car in the driveway or any lights on in the house.

'*it's in the middle of the day,'* Jace mutters softly to me. .

I sigh. Of course he is right again. I park in the middle of the driveway and kill the engine. I sit in the car for a few seconds before gathering up the courage to go in and deal with the fallout of my stupidity.

Let's face it, usually when things get hard, I just take off. But right now I need to go in there and face the music. I try to gather my thoughts, trying to make sense of my reasoning. I honestly don't know what my reasoning is but I couldn't let her know that, could I?

Slowly making my way out of the car, I catch her strong scent in the air.

'Did you know she was going to be here?' I ask Jace.*'No, but I had a hunch she wanted us to follow,'* he replies.

Seems his mood still isn't changing even though we know where our mate is.

I knock softly at the door before letting myself in. I know it's probably a little stupid but I wanted to give her a heads up that I was coming in.

I take a deep breath and walk into her scent filling the room, forest wood and freshwater. Another scent grabs my attention, stopping me in my tracks, making me numb and forget all of my stupid reasons for being such an asshole.

Salty tears.

She's curled up on the couch crying silently, some of her sniffles come through as she sits there. Her legs were held tightly together with her arms wrapped around them, and her head buried into her knees.

My chest clenches as I see her in this state.

Fuck! I promised her I would never make her feel like this. I promised her I would try to be worthy of her, to be her mate.

Closing the door behind me I slowly make my way toward her.

"Ashleigh, sweetheart," I softly murmur as I drop to my knees to be level with her. She hasn't said anything, she hasn't moved since I arrived, and even her sniffles and crying haven't stopped. She knows I'm here, right?

Jace hasn't said anything to me since walked in the front door, opting to give me the silent treatment. I hope he could try and contact Kia while I try to talk with Ashleigh.

"I'm sorry, I'm so sorry that happened, I'm sorry I didn't stop it."

Still nothing, her crying stopped that much I could tell, but no other movement or gesture towards me. I move my hand slowly to touch her arm and she flinches away before I could even touch her.

Fuck, that hurt! She doesn't even want me to touch her.

"Fuck, sweetheart, please say something," I beg.

This time she looks up and stares straight into my eyes. Hers are all puffy from crying and her cheeks are red and swollen. The light grey shirt she is wearing has her tear stains all down the front.

Seeing her like this fucking kills me.

"I, Beta Ashleigh Steward, reject you…"

Oh, hell no! I was not letting that happen! I did the one thing I could think of to stop her from saying those words. I lunged forward and kissed her.

For a brief moment, she melts into the kiss, her lips moving with mine. The mate bond pulses through me, alive with the need to complete the process.

It is the best fucking kiss of my life. Her lips are soft and tender, trembling a little as she tries to calm herself, I could taste her tears as I try to deepen the kiss but she has other plans.

She pulls back suddenly. I feel her aura pulsing through, it seems Kia is also present.

"You don't deserve to be my first," she growls, pushing me away as she gets up and walks towards the back door.

Chapter 27 - ASHLEIGH

Anger.

That is all I feel right now. The pain from his actions is long gone and now just a memory of what happened. He doesn't deserve to be my first kiss, he doesn't deserve to be my mate. Not with how he was flaunting himself around everyone.

Kia didn't say anything while my mind was in this mess, we agreed if he cheated or did something of the same vein he could be rejected.

I didn't think he would, especially after what he said on the evening of my birthday. Was none of it true?

I'm surprised she didn't stop me when I tried to reject him. She stayed silent letting me make the decisions on our mate.

I know she was hurt by his actions, probably even more so because Jace allowed him to do such a thing. But she hasn't said anything to me since arriving at the cottage, even on our run here she was silent lost in her own thoughts and emotions.

I honestly wasn't expecting him to come after me, but Kia chose to come here while running. To our surprise he arrived shortly after, of course. I was still a blubbering mess when he arrived and then he goes and says stupid things that make me do the one thing I feared he would do to me.

For him to think it was okay to just kiss me like that, I am beyond furious. I get up and storm towards the back door where I came in through.

"Sweetheart, please wait." I hear him beg behind me as he scrambles up off the floor.

I am too far gone. Kia bubbles to the surface and my anger swells around me.

I grab the door handle nearly breaking it off its hinges as I pulled it open, storming out to the back garden heading for the forest line.

Just as I go to shift again he grabs my hand and spins me back around to face him. He pulls me so powerfully that I slam into him hitting his hard chest.

"Just one minute, please," he softly whispers, dipping his head into my hair and holding me tightly.

I try to wriggle free, hitting his chest as hard as I could but he won't let go. He didn't even flinch or move against my struggle.

"Zander, let me go now," I growl at him.

"No."

Struggling against him for a few more seconds I slowly give up and relax in his hold leaning my head against his chest. Being this close to him is affecting my emotions. Whether it is the bond helping me calm down or him just holding me, I am slowly beginning to lose the feeling of anger and melting into him, not wanting to let go.

"I'm sorry," he whispers again, still holding me tightly. We haven't moved in the last 5 minutes.

I am not going to be the first to talk. I close my eyes and breathe in his scent. I don't want to remember the pain, I don't want to ever experience it again.

"Do you understand the pain that caused me, you going against our bond?" I ask him.

I open my eyes and look up into his beautiful hazel eyes seeing a swirl of emotions ... guilt, hurt, and a little bit of uncertainty.

"It felt like my entire body was on fire, Everything ached and burned I never want to feel that pain again, I can't ever go through that and that was only a kiss. So you need to decide right now if this is something you can commit to or if we need to part ways." I tell him sternly looking into his beautiful eyes.

I feel him tense up at the last part. I already tried to reject him, clearly he didn't want that so he needs to make a choice right now ... his past life with flings and one-night stands or me, us, a future that could be.

"I never wanted to hurt you, I'm sorry I caused that. She just came onto me so quickly that I didn't have time to react. I didn't know it was going to happen. I will never let it happen again," he promises.

"Don't make promises you can't keep," I mumble as I look away, looking anywhere but at his confused eyes.

"Look at me," he grabs my chin, lifting my eyes up to look at him.

"You are the only one I want. When she kissed me, it felt like sandpaper. Everything hurt and I never want to experience that again either, especially when I hadn't even kissed you yet. You are all I want Ashleigh, you are my Luna and mate, no one will ever replace you."

I sigh and nod, closing my eyes and leaning back into him.

"Where do we go from here?" I mumble, feeling slightly embarrassed about my behaviour.

"Back inside? I can show you around properly if you like, maybe we can clean a few things up or chill out? I got the electricity working so the TV and stove should now work. I don't know about you, but I do not want to go back to school."

"Sure, that sounds nice," I smile.

He asks me hesitantly, If I let go, you promise you will stay?"

"Yes," I mumble.

He chuckles and slowly releases me from his tight embrace.

Chapter 28 - ZANDER

As soon as she let go and moved away, my body felt numb and cold, and the incredible sensation of tingles left my body.

All I want is for her to be back in my arms and her scent all around me.

"What do you want to do then?" She asks, blinking up at me shyly.

This girl will be the death of me... one minute, she's all angry and annoyed. Then the next minute, she's all blushing and shy. I stop suddenly before moving forward to grab her hand. I hadn't realized she was only wearing the grey shirt.

'*Because she ran here stupid,*' Jace grumbles.

'Nice of you to join,' I grumble back.

'*Don't give me attitude. You're* lucky it wasn't worse; I had to calm Kia down *a lot, and half the time, I couldn't get to her because she blocked me,*' Jace mumbles.

'She almost rejected me,' I reply, protesting.

'*Yes, thank goodness you knew to kiss her, or we would be mateless, and our pack wouldn't have a Luna.*"

I block Jace as he continues his rant and takes in her figure while she's waiting for my answer.

The grey shirt just covers her thigh, her hair is messy and windblown from her run here.

I breathe in deeply. I know I can't do anything until she's ready but, fuck, she's making it hard not to take her right here, right now. At least before, I had a little bit more self-control. There's a fine line that I'm willing to cross for some hot make-up sex.

"Come on, I'll show you around," I say, grabbing her hand and leading her back towards the house before I do anything I would regret later.

"Do we have to call the school to let them know I left?" she wonders.

I choke back a laugh at her confused frown.

"I guess you've never played hooky before?" I said, still trying to hold my laughter in.

She shakes her head 'no.'

"It's fine, don't worry about it. Danni will text or link me if anything is wrong; I'm sure Oliver will also try to link you if something happens."

She sighs and nods in response, "Yes, I suppose Ollie or Brent will try to link me if something was wrong."

I toss her a grin making her blush red again; it's starting to be one of my favourite colors on her.

I lead her towards the back door of the house. As we enter the kitchen, off to the left, and through a door leading into the dining room.

"This is the dining room I mentioned the other day," I tell her as she moves further into the room, letting go of my hand.

It's a small room with an old chandelier hanging over the dark wooden table. The table is round with six chairs fitted nice and snug. The creamy flower wallpaper has slowly started to peel, showing the old original off-white colour that was the same as the lounge room and kitchen. With the dark navy curtains draped over the windows, you could see a few bits of dust that had settled over the years of neglectful cleaning. The fireplace was old and run down, and some of the steel in the bottom pit had rusted; I don't think we would be able to use it until it was cleaned up, at least.

"It's cute, I don't mind the wallpaper, but we will probably have to pull it all down if we were to try and get someone to rent this place when I move to your pack. I doubt we would need to come here much later on," Ashleigh states.

I look at her, stunned and a bit taken aback by the statement.

"What's wrong?" she asks, tilting her head back towards me and studying my expression.

"Nothing. I'm glad you are still keeping an open mind about us being together and in my pack." I shrug.

"I'm sorry I tried to reject you before, I was just hurt and didn't understand," Ashleigh mumbles, looking down at her feet as though they were the most important thing in the room.

"It's okay, I understand why you wanted to, but now we are in the right direction," I assured her, grabbing her hand again and leading her back towards the kitchen. Right now, I know she isn't ready for me to hold her or do much else, so I'll take what I can get, and at the moment, she seems willing enough to let me hold her hand.

We make our way towards the old staircase leading up to the bedrooms and bathroom. She hesitated for a second; it was so quick that I wouldn't have noticed if I weren't holding her hand.

"You okay?" I ask.

"Yeah, it's nothing."

'S*he's nervous about the bedroom,'* Jace mumbles.

'Oh.' I knew he had finished his rant because I was receiving death glares while he was curled up in the corner, so I let the block down again, only to be hit with his feelings of annoyance and frustration.

"I just wanted to show you the upstairs and bathroom if you ever needed it," I explain carefully, trying not to scare her.

"Yeah, that's okay."

I grip her hand tighter and tug her up the staircase. She carefully walks behind me. I could feel her uncertainty.

As we reached the top, she lets go and moves forward to the middle of the medium-sized open lounge room that had an old yellow one-seat couch with a bookshelf against the wall next to the window.

Next to the bookshelf are two bedrooms with a bathroom to the right of the stairs.

"This is nice, a little dusty, but still will work perfectly," she smiles, looking around.

I nodded, agreeing with her, " It may need a little work but not too much; a vacuum and fresh paint should be ok, I'm not sure what the plumbing will be like, but it seems ok for now."

Ashleigh moves forward to the main bedroom, drawn to the little sun seat underneath the windows that looked out to the forest.

The two bedrooms are simple, both with a double bed and a closet The only difference is the main bedroom Is a bit bigger than the spare. It even has a bigger window with a seat.

She sits on the window seat, bringing her knees to her chest and cuddling herself again.

"Are you cold?" I don't want to disturb her. She looked so peaceful and content, but at the same time, it was a bit cooler up here where there wasn't much sunlight shining through.

"Hmm, no, I'm okay. I just find it comfortable. This reminds me of my bedroom back home. I like the windows and how big they are. I enjoy sitting in my chair and reading or doing my homework."

I nod and move back out of the room towards the bookshelf. It was filled with old novels, history books about my mother's old pack, and photo albums.

One of the larger photo albums catches my attention. I reach for it as it says "Blackwood Family" in gold writing on the spine. Since this was my grandmother's place, I wondered if there would be any photos or homemade videos of the time she had here, or maybe some photos of my mother.

My hands are clammy, and my breathing hitched as the nerves kicked in. I want to know more about my mother. Maybe this is a good start, and with my mate here, we can go through this together.

Grabbing the book on the front, it also had "Blackwood Family" printed in gold writing with our family crest engraved on the bottom. Yep, this was one of ours.

"I found this," I mumble as I walk back into the room where she was still sits peacefully.

"What is it?" she asks, curiosity drawn to the dark book in my hands.

"An old family photo album, I think. Not sure this is the first time I have seen it,"

Ashleigh slides off the window seat, walking toward me, "Do you want to go through it together?"

She must feel my nerves. She puts her hand on my arm, gently looking up at me ... concern and encouragement shining through her eyes.

"Sure," I mumble.

I walk back to sit on the window seat with my mind in a jumbled mess. I lean my back against the wall and bring my leg up, so I'm facing sideways. I look up at Ashleigh as she walks over slowly. I can see Kia trying to come through with the silver rims of her eyes flashing every so often.

Ah fuck, I've just taken her spot. I go to leave and give her space again, but Jace interrupts my movements.

'Give her a moment to decide, see what happens. She might be drawn to sit with us.'

She sits down, moves close to me, and leans her back against my chest. Her ass just misses my crotch as she snuggles against me, tilting her head underneath my chin.

I suck in a quick breath, not expecting this from her. Sparks fly through my body on the contact. I craved this feeling ever since I let her go an hour ago.

I put the photo album on her lap as we read it together. As expected, many of them were of my mother and me when I was younger; I flick through a few more pages just toward the end one of them caught Ashleigh's eye.

"Wait, can you go back one," she requests.

"Hmm," I grumble, not trusting myself with words right now. I'm barely holding on as it is. All I want to do right now is fuck and kiss her senseless.

"I think I just saw one of my mum."

Frowning, I flick back to the page she saw, "Why is my mum in one of these photos with yours?" she asks.

"Your guess is as good as mine, sweetheart."

I could feel Ashleigh starting to panic as she flicked through a few more pages. "Why are there photos of us when we were kids? It looks like it was all taken here in this house or the back garden. We look to be about 3 or 4 years old here."

"Hey, it's okay. We will figure this out." I try to calm her down as she flicks through the book. "Would it be such a bad thing if she knew?" I ask.

Her eyes snap to mine at the question. "Um, no, but I'm just nervous because I haven't said anything to anyone, and this morning she freaked out about something, and now it makes sense because she recognized the hairpiece."

Ashleigh reached out to the photo and pulled it out of the plastic sleeve. On the back, it had written 'Kyle and Ashleigh Steward, Mollie and Zander Blackwood. The year 2007.'

"We were four years old," she mumbles, "if this was taken in 2007, we were four, and that means mum knows I'm your mate because she knew the meaning of the hairpiece."

Chapter 29 - ASHLEIGH

Tingles fill my body as I snuggle against Zander. Kia is practically purring with happiness being so close to our mate.

The sun has moved over to this side of the house, slowly setting into the evening, warming up the bedrooms upstairs as we sit here, flicking through the photos and talking.

I have to give him credit. I half thought he would make a move, something sexual or another kiss. I was hoping he would lean in for another kiss just a little bit, but I guess he didn't want to push his luck.

It worries me a little bit that Mum knows Zander is my mate. It explains what happened this morning. The weird thing is I couldn't even remember anything from back then.

He was so cute when he was a baby. It seems his hair sprouted as he got older and he has the same eyes as his mother. I wish I remembered her or knew her. She and mum looked like they were great friends, like Chloe and me.

A pang of guilt washes over me as I think about my friends and family not knowing about Zander yet. I wish I could tell them. I want to get to know him more before everyone else was knows of our relationship. I hope soon I can have the courage to tell people I found my mate. I don't know how I will control myself around him now that I know what his kisses are like.

'*I vote we just strip naked right now and take him here on the bed ... guarantee he will follow suit quickly,'* Kia mumbles at my thoughts.

'I'm just not ready yet, Kia,' I sigh.

I understand he is my mate, but I also want to be comfortable with him before doing anything intimate.

"It's getting late. Did you want to stay for dinner?" Zander asks, pulling me away from my thoughts while giving me a small kiss on the top of my head as he closes the photo album making a motion to move from the seat we had been sitting at for the last few hours.

"I should probably get going. If the school calls my parents, I'll most likely be in trouble for skipping." I sigh, not wanting to leave his warm embrace. I have gotten used to all the little tingles, giving in to the bond and letting it consume me.

'Stuff *school and parents. Let's stay the night here with our mate,'* Kia perks up excitedly.

'Kia,' I mumble, rolling my eyes.

"Is everything okay?" he asks.

"Oh yes, Kia is just being Kia," I shrug, not wanting to give him too many details about her dirty mind and the dirty images she is currently flashing through mine.

He chuckles at my comment as he quickly lifts me off the seat, placing my feet on the ground, steadying me by placing his hand on my back to make sure I don't fall.

"How will you get home?"

"Oh, I hadn't thought about that. I guess it's past school hours, so everyone would have gone home already. I guess I'll just run."

"Would you like me to drive you?" he asks.

It's sweet of him to want to, but I don't think my family or pack members would appreciate that.

"I would love for you to but, it’s okay. I don't think they will be happy with you dropping me off at home."

He pushes himself off the seat and makes his way towards the door. I step in front of him to block his path. He raises an eyebrow in question.

I stand on my toes to reach his cheek and kiss him quickly. "Thank you for offering."

He stands there stunned. I giggle and head back towards the door. I like that I have the same effect on him that he does on me.

He regains his composure and follows me back downstairs. As I reach the door handle, he quickly closes it before I can pull it open.

I spin around, about to question why. As soon as I do, he slams his lips down on mine making me gasp in surprise. His movements are soft and gentle, unlike before when they were hot and desperate.

His lips dance around mine, moving in deeper, and his hands started to make their way down my body sending pleasurable sparks flying everywhere. Not breaking away from the kiss, he grabs my ass and lifts me to be level with him, pushing me against the door for support. I wrap my legs around him and pull him in closer. He groans and pulls out of the kiss.

"If you don't leave now, I don't know how much longer I can control Jace," his husky voice grumbles.

I look into his eyes. They have gone entirely black with lust. A little bit of gold flicks through every now and then. I can see the struggle he is having with his wolf.

I sigh and nod, unwrapping myself from his warmth. Tingles no longer wrap around me in comfort. A flush of cold washes over me as I pull myself away from him.

I enjoyed his kisses, but I wasn't sure how much further I was willing to take this. I feel a little bit bad leaving him like this but at the same time, I’m glad he went in for another kiss.

Chapter 30 - ASHLEIGH

We finished our classes for the day and caught up and chatted on the football stands, waiting for the guys to finish training. The sun is still out so we are in no rush to head home.

I got home not too late yesterday evening, just as everyone finished dinner and went to do their own thing. I thankfully didn't get into any trouble with my parents for skipping out on school. I know I had a valid reason, but I didn't want to tell them just yet.

It was hard to leave Zander last night. I missed him instantly, and Kia wanted to return to our mate every moment. It was harder than I thought.

"Earth to Ashleigh," Chloe called, waving her hands in my face, pulling me out of my daydream.

"Huh?" I asked, blinking away my daze.

"You know we have been talking about tonight for the last 5 mins," Chloe says.

"What's happening tonight?" I asked stupidly.

"What or who has you in the daydream?" Chloe asks.

Crap, I hate it when she calls me out on stuff.

"Umm, no one." I shake my head furiously, trying to hide the red tinge I could feel showing. She cannot know about the kiss I shared with Zander just yet.

I turn back to look at the guys at the field. The football field is the size of a standard oval and is used for all sports, including hockey, soccer, rugby, and many more.

The pool is just behind the field opposite the library, with an underground car park, a gym, and a basketball center off to the side. The stands surround the field and is massive, it ca easily fit 2,000 people on a big day. The girls and I are currently sitting on the library side of the stands.

During the season's opening, they hold a game that is always huge, and the stands are always packed out. This is what the boys are training for now. The first game is between Liverpool and Charwood.

I can't help but steal glances at Zander as he runs around, all hot and sexy. Once or twice, I swear I felt his burning gaze on me. *'We could just tell them,'* Kia mumbles.

'Not happening, not yet.'

'*Why not? Why can't I be with my mate? I'm getting sick of all this hiding around,*' she whines.

'Because I want some time together for us to just be us. As soon as everyone knows all the pressure of being Luna and Alpha comes, and I don't want that right now. Can't we be in our bubble for a bit longer?' I beg.

It's true. I didn't want people to know yet so I could spend more time getting to know Zander. Yes, I hated that we had to hide it from people, and maybe girls would be less flirty with him knowing he was taken. But I also want to make sure he is ready, too. He's never had a relationship that lasted. As far as I know, he has never had a girlfriend, so jumping into this is risky.

"Hmmm, I don't believe you," Chloe scolded, shaking a finger in my face.

"It's no one, I swear," I grumble, putting up my hands in defense. I have never been a good liar.right now, I am doing everything I could to not look over at Zander and give us away.

She rolls her eyes and starts making plans for tonight, "So my parents are away for the next few days until the following Monday. I was thinking maybe a little party on Saturday night. And if you guys want to stay over tonight, so I'm not alone, that would be awesome."

"I'm kind of surprised you didn't invite Bobby over?" Skyla giggled, shoving Chloe a little bit.

"Well, I was going to... but dad said no to having boys over, so kinda annoyed about that, and well, I want to have a party. I'll live with the consequences later," Chloe says, waving her hand dismissively.

Skyla and I chuckle at her response.

"So who is going to the party?" I ask, trying to keep the conversation going, so it doesn't lead back to me.

"Well, I was just going to invite everyone, and have a big house party, I know it's on pack lands, but will Oliver allow the other pack members to come?" She asks, turning to face me.

"Hmm, it should be okay," I say, nodding. "We have a peace agreement with all packs, so it shouldn't be a problem. I'm sure Ollie will stop by to check it out anyway."

"Fabulous," Chloe cheered, clapping her hands together and turning back to face the field. "Ohh, it looks like the boys are finishing just in time. Do you guys want to come over to my place now?"

"Sure," Skyla and I say together.

"I drove here today because the guys did have to practice. I wasn't planning on hanging around. So, I'm happy to drive us," I tell the girls as we gather our things to leave. "I have to run back to my locker for some things, but I'll only be 5 minutes. You guys can wait for me at the car if you want. I toss my car keys to Chloe as I say this so they could wait in the car instead of hanging around.

"I'll be back in a bit," I call out, heading down the steps toward the field. I need to let Ollie and Brent know I am going to be out tonight and tomorrow, plus tell Ollie about Chloe's plans for this weekend's party.

I look towards the feel to find Ollie and I wave my hands above my head to get his attention. Ollie is at the bench down the bottom of the stand, grabbing his bags and water bottle and talking to Brent.

"Hey, Ollie! I'm going to stay at Chloe's place tonight because her parents are away. I'll text mum and let her know, too," I called out.

He nods as he lifts his water to his mouth, squirting it in and wiping the excess off with his arm.

I walk closer so I don't have to shout. "Also, Chloe wants to have a house party this weekend. Would it be okay if the other packs come over, too? She didn't want to invite everyone without asking first."

A flash of blue quickly pass through his eyes as his wolf makes himself known. Ace is nice enough but can also sometimes be a hard ass, so I'm hoping Ollie will be on my side with her having a party. It would be an excellent opportunity to build relationships with the other packs and Alpha heirs.

"It could be a good opportunity to show the other packs we are open to them," I add. Chloe was set on having this party and would be half-annoyed if Ollie didn't allow it. "It won't be anywhere near the packhouse, just at her house."

"Why didn't she ask herself? Does she really need this party?" Ace pushes forward, clearly frustrated about this. I could feel tiny beads of sweat forming on my forehead and clammy hands forming into a tight fist as I struggled against his aura. Brent was already in submission. Being the Beta, I withstand him sometimes. I guess this was one of those times.

"She was going to, but I offered to ask instead. Please, it would be nice to blow off some steam after this week," I reply.

I could see the fight between Ace and Ollie. Ace finally gave back control to Ollie as his eyes changed to his chocolate brown colour, and his aura settled down.

"Sorry about that. You know how he gets with other packs," Ollie mumbles, rubbing the back of his neck and looking over to Brent as he lifts his head, stretching his neck. "Look, I don't mind, but they need to promise to be decent and respectful, and I'm not sure if that is possible."

"Why don't we try this once and see how it goes? If it doesn't work out, then we never have to do it again?"

Ollie heaves a heavy sigh, "Chloe is okay with this?"

I nod 'yes.'

"I'll ask Dad if it is ok with him and let you know."

"Okay, thanks, I'll head off now. See you both tomorrow," I wave, heading towards my locker.

I make my way quickly across the school grounds. The halls are eerily quiet without the usual chatter and talks of the students.

I reach my locker and start to input my code when I feel a hand grab my arm spin me, pushing my back against the lockers. Zander lifts a hand and fiddles with a loose strand of hair. Sparks instantly fly through me with his contact.

Kia is bouncing around, all happy having contact with our mate.

"You have been very distracting to me this afternoon, sweetheart, " Zander's husky voice enters my left ear.

His warm breath on my neck sends shivers through me, making me feel things I have never felt before.

I blink up into his dark eyes, biting my bottom lip. "I don't know what you mean," I whisper.

Chapter 31 - ZANDER

As soon as Ashleigh left the field, I was on high alert. I knew she was here to be with her friends and brother, but I couldn't help but feel a little smug every time she looked my way. I could feel her eyes on me every damn time. Ashleigh was sitting there all beautiful in skinny white jeans and a red singlet top with a leather jacket. She had taken off the jacket as her back faced the sun to capture the warmth. The struggle to want to go and claim her was so very real, especially when she was there teasing me the way she was.

I saw some guys from both sides looking at her and talking. They were definitely interested in her, but all of them knew she was waiting for her mate, and now she had turned of age, the race was on to see who would claim her first.

Little do they know I already have.

Every day I preen when I see that shiny little item tucked away in her hair, so fucking satisfied even though no one knows yet.

It's always worth it.

I let Danni and the others know I needed to take a piss and head in the direction of the school, following her scent.

I find her at her locker. She's in a daze as I stalk up to her, startling her as I pin her against it.

"You have been very distracting to me this afternoon, sweetheart," I growl.

"Huh, I don't know what you mean," she whispers, blinking at me like a deer in headlights, her eyes wide with confusion.

She can play innocent all she wants. I know the bond affects her also.

"Sending me dirty looks and being there in general," I grumble, picking up a strand of hair and toying with it.

"Did you not want me to come?"

"Not when others look at you the way they do." My possessive side starts to show as Jace pushes forward in his need to claim our mate.

I try to focus on our conversation and keep Jace at bay. I don't want to scare her off by being too aggressive, but at the same time, I can smell her arousal. She's fucking enjoying this as much as I am.

I take my chance and close the gap between us. She lets out a small gasp as my lips clash with hers.

I have wanted to do this all fucking day. I just haven't had the chance to get her alone.

Her hand moves up the back of my head, grabbing a fist full of my hair and tugging at it as I guide her, deepening the kiss. Out of all the kisses I have had in my lifetime, kissing her is like nothing I have ever experienced. Tingles flew around our bodies. Jace kept pushing forward and wanting to claim her. I thought at least if I was able to have some contact with her, he would calm the fuck down. I guess I was wrong. It just makes him to want her more.

I groan as she hitches one of her legs around my waist, looking to be lifted again. Fuck my luck. This will be the second time I'll get blue balls in the last 24 hours.

She groans and pulls away as her eyes glaze over. "I'm sorry, I forgot the girls were waiting," she mumbles, a bit out of breath.

"What are you doing tonight," I ask, leaning in to kiss her neck where I would mark her. I feel her shiver as I did that.

She sighs and moves back to collect her things from the locker. I couldn't help the smug smile on my face seeing how flustered she is.

"I'm staying at Chloe's tonight. Oh, she is having a party on Saturday, and Ollie said he would check, but you guys should come. It would be good to see how things go in a not-so-formal environment."

I tilt my head, "you want me on your pack land?"

Her eyes snap back to mine. "Of course, why wouldn't I? I understand our pack history, but at the end of the day, you are my mate." she replies with a shrug.

'She's *finally admitted it out loud,'* Jace yelled, prancing around in the back of my mind like a love-sick puppy. I couldn't help but grin at the admission.

Her eyes roll as she sees my grin. She throws her bag full of schoolwork over one shoulder and turns to head back to the parking lot.

"Excuse me?" I say, folding my arms across my chest and raising an eyebrow.

"What?" She asks, putting the innocent face on again, batting her eyelashes.

"I should at least get a kiss if I can't be with you for a few more days," I demand, tapping my cheek. I have no intention of letting her go that easily.

She blushes furiously, and the smell of her arousal starts to become prominent again.

My voice is husky as I lean into her. I know my eyes are dark as Jace pushed forward, wanting to claim her. " I don't know what you are thinking about, sweetheart, but if you don't want me to take you right here at school, I would suggest you stop while you are ahead."

Ashleigh lets out a small giggle, quickly kisses me on the cheek and takes off for the school parking lot.

Chapter 32 - ASHLEIGH

The sun shines shone through the window shutters, landing on the king-sized bed with the three of us sprawled across it.

"Turn the damn thing off," Chloe groans, hitting me on the side as alarm sounds ring through the early morning. It was well and truly the next morning when we fell asleep. It was nice to catch up with the girls. I felt like it had been ages since everything had moved quickly with Zander.

Chloe's room is cream, mint green, with a few gold highlights. She has mint green covers and pillows, and her chair in the corner next to her massive walk-in wardrobe is also mint green with cream and gold pillows.

Yes, we see each other at school, but that talk is usually about school and other bits and bobs since there are so many unwanted ears around. It's hard to have meaningful conversations without people listening.

It was so hard trying to keep Zander a secret last night. I nearly slipped up once or twice. Chloe was too engrossed in babbling about her and Bobby to notice. I'm not sure about Skyla. That girl is still a mystery to me sometimes. She just sat silently, listening to our conversation. I hoped everything at home was okay. We don't know much, but we try to include her in many things, like last night.

I look at the clock ... it's 7.15 am, and groan internally. There isn't time to go home and grab some clothes for school.

Chloe and I are similar in height and build but she is bigger around the chest. Thankfully we have similar taste in clothes although she has more dresses than I do. Skyla is slightly shorter. I hope Chloe has some clothes we could borrow.

By 7.30, Skyla and I had already gotten up, washed our faces, and tried to prepare for school. While Chloe slept through the alarms and us getting ready. She was not a morning person.

“Come on, babe, or we will be late. Skyla and I still need to borrow some clothes for today.” I shake her for the third time this morning.

Chloe groans and slowly tries to get up. We weren't drinking last night. We just had a late-night chat, did our nails, went through magazines, and chatted about our future possibilities. But we all need our sleep. Chloe more so than Skyla and me.

“You guys need clothes?” She asks, running her eyes over us with a questioning look. We both nod in confirmation.

"Ohh, I know, we can all dress up super nicely! We did our nails last night. Let's find something to wear with them."

Chloe claps her hands happily, doing a little dance in bed. Skyla and I roll our eyes in annoyance.

"Ohh pleaseeeee, just this once, I promise. It'll be fun."

"We are only going to school," Skyla mumbles.

Chloe jumps out of bed and runs to her walk-in closet. The closet was beautiful. It was cream with beautiful markings on the ceiling. I am always in awe when I see her wardrobe. It's nearly as big as my bedroom.

She goes to one of the sides that is filled with her dresses. On the left of the dresses is a full floor-to-ceiling shoe rack with heels, flats, and Vans sneakers that she always wears. Her handbags with all the different accessories in the drawers are on the back wall behind us.

Most of the items had some gold or mint, her signature colours, but it all worked well together.

Her father is a partner in a well-known law firm in the city, and her mother is a surgeon, so they are swimming in cash. They have busy lives, so one child was enough. Fortunately, that child is the sweetest girl and my best friend.

Chloe pulled out two dresses. One is light pink with puffy arms and a skirt reaching just above the knees. The second is an ocean blue spaghetti strap pencil dress similar in length.

"Chloe, we are going to school! Not the club," Skyla says, folding her arms in annoyance. I somewhat agreed with her but at the same time I am curious about what Zander would do if I wore that dress to school.

"It might not be a bad idea?" I mumble. Both sets of eyes snap up to mine surprised that I commented.

"Really?" Skyla asks, tilting her head curiously.

I shrug, trying to hide the blush that was creeping up my cheeks. "Could be fun."

Chloe grins triumphantly when Skyla groans and snatches the blue dress out of her hands. I grab the pink dress, quickly strip, and wear it.

We head off to school. We're running about 5 minutes late but with the way Chloe's drives we might make it on time.

We soon pull into the school parking lot just as most students are, too. I take a deep breath before opening the car door. I don't know what reactions to expect. I hope I at least get one reaction from the one person I wanted.

Kia is all excited about being at school, bouncing around happily. She's excited to see Zander's reaction. She wants to jump him every time we catch his scent. I am nearly ready. I feel comfortable being around him now. I don't know how to tell him or our family members about our situation.

As we get out of the car, a few whistles go our way. One person called out, "Damn, you look fine."

Chloe let out a little squeal behind Skyla and me as we make our way toward the lockers. We both spin around to see what's wrong only to find Bobby Enderson wrapping his hands around her, bringing her into a deep kiss.

'*I want that with our mate,'* Kia whines.

'We will soon, I promise.'

Skyla rolls her eyes and continues to walk through the school gates. I follow and stop when I catch his scent in the breeze. My eyes dart around and I see him standing next to his car with Danni and his other friends. His eyes snap to mine. They turn dark and feral, flicks of gold flashing through as Jace shows himself.

Kia was still bouncing around all excited; now she had seen Zander.

'*Mate, Mate, Mate,*' she chants.

Skyla turns around, giving me a questioning look, "are you all good?" she asks, snapping me out of my daze.

"Perfect," I breathed, smiling at her and following her into school. .

Chapter 33 - ZANDER

Fuck me. This girl is making it harder and harder for me to keep the promise I made her. As soon as she stepped out of that car, Jace completely took over and wanted to claim her right there and then.

That innocent, sweet smile of hers draws me in every damn time, but today, it was filled with lust and longing. I could smell her arousal from here. I'm sure every other male wolf could as well. Others are starting to circle, making Jace even more possessive and harder to control, our mate so close yet so far away. It was starting to piss me off.

'*Let me go to her,' Jace* growls, frustrated with our situation. We want to respect her wishes, but fuck, when she dresses like that, she knows what she's going to get.

'We can't, Jace, but I have an idea.'

She has no idea what she has got herself into. Play with fire, and you will get burned, sweetheart. I smirk as she turns and walks into school with her friends.

Jace chuckles at my idea as I show him what I plan on doing. Jace then goes into full-on passive stalker mode, trying to find her scent and moving around the students so swiftly and quickly that by the time they turn around to see who is there, I've already disappeared.

We only have about 5 minutes left until the first class, and I don't want to wait until study hall to see her next.

I pick up her scent around the science labs. Most of the students are already in the classroom by now, and I'm hoping that because Ashleigh and her friends arrived late, she doesn't have her books and things, so she'll be a little late for class.

Her scent is stronger as I move around the hallway. I hear her footsteps hurrying in my direction. Smirking, I slip into the bathroom next to me, waiting, listening as she comes closer. I reach out and grab her to pull her in with me.

"Hello, mate," My voice rumbles, overlapping with Jace's. I know my eyes are a dark haze with Jace showing through.

Sparks fly around us with the contact of our skin, making me even wilder and Jace more possessive.

She gasped as her hand flies to her chest, breathing heavily, trying to calm herself when she realizes that it's me.

"Zander?" she says, tilting her head in question, her eyes sparkling with mischief and a hint of longing.

"You are playing a very dangerous game, sweetheart," I growl, nuzzling the side of her neck and kissing her softly on the spot where she would one day bear my mark. I don't usually do soft and gentle, but right now, I'll do anything for her.

"Oh? Am I going to be punished, Alpha?" Her sweet voice whispers in my ear.

I growl into her neck as the last word leaves her lips, her soft moans start filling the bathroom as my hands move around her body. Her hands move over my shoulders and into my hair, and she tugs on my hair each time I kiss her neck, egging me on to go further.

I lean in to kiss her on the lips, but a naughty thought passes my mind. I hover over only inches apart from her lips. She groans in frustration when my lips don't meet hers. Her eyes snap back open and stare into mine as we wait.

I smirk. "You've started something you might not be able to finish."

"Try me," she whispers, leaning in, closing the gap between us, and deepening the kiss.

The last bit of self-control snaps. A growl rumbles through the bathroom as I pick her up and carry her towards the stall. We may be in the bathroom, but I do not want every damn person to see her.

She lets out a little giggle as I carry her and I silence it with another kiss. I don't want her first time to be in the bathroom, but I can at least make sure one of us is satisfied. I don't usually care what the girl wants. Usually, sex is all about me, but right now, I only care about her having a good time and enjoying herself.

The door slams against the concrete walls as I push it open, my hands already making their way down her body. Her moans are becoming louder and louder the closer I get to her pussy, teasing her as I run my hands down her back, groping her ass.

She stands on tiptoe on one leg while the other is raised to hook on my waist. She tries to deepen the kiss and her neediness is driving Jace and me crazy.

I slowly make my way to the end of her dress, fiddling with the hem, giving her a chance to pull out or stop if she wants. Ashleigh doesn't even hesitate. She leans into my touch, wanting more. My hands slip under, feeling the sparks and goosebumps rising on her soft flesh. I suddenly stopped expecting there to be soft fabric to be in the way of her entrance.

"No panties," I choke, pulling away from the kiss.

Her eyes arecompletely black, and I'm sure so are mine. "They seemed like an inconvenience," she mumbles, leaning back into the kiss.

I let out a sharp breath as she leans forward, my hand moving on her body. Jace has utterly lost his mind as I have.

My finger is met by her dripping wet pussy. I move at a rhythm for her to get used to the sensation. Her moans become louder and more desperate than before. "Zander, Zander," she chants my name as I pick up speed, her hips thrusting in rhythm every time to move deeper.

I place my hand over her mouth to muffle the sounds. That only seems to make her more excited. As much as I want her screaming my name, letting everyone know she's mine, I don't know if she is ready yet.

Her breathing gets heavier, her head leaning against the bathroom stall for balance as she comes crashing down from her orgasm. Seeing her like this and knowing I caused it makes me fucking ecstatic.

She moans one last time as I remove my hand from her and lick her sweet nectar off. Kia seems to enjoy that as I see her push forward, trying to gain control.

"Meet us at the cottage tomorrow night." Kia's voice rings through.

“Sure, sweetheart.” I bring my other hand to her face and let her lean into the sensation of the bond, hoping it would help Ashleigh regain control.

Chapter 34 - ASHLEIGH

After the most incredible experience of my life, it was hard not to keep my hands off Zander for the rest of the day. Whenever I am near him or see him, Kia perked up, egging me to go and be with him, to claim him … to show everyone that he is mine.

By now I feel like I know him. I feel like he completes me.

Friday afternoon couldn't come fast enough. I want to finish what we started in the bathroom, as did Kia.

I made sure I packed a few little things and took my car today so I wouldn't have to go home and get bombarded with questions from my parents and family about what I would be doing on a Friday night. If tonight goes well, maybe tomorrow before the party I can announce to my family that I have a mate. I couldn't wait to tell him. I didn't want to tell him yesterday in case any unwanted ears were listening.

I got weird looks all day after our activity in the bathroom, probably because this time I didn't hide his scent, although I was surprised Brent or Olly didn't ask on the way home. I could tell they wanted to, but they both decided to keep their mouths shut. Hopefully, I will be able to clear the air tomorrow afternoon before going to Chloe's.

I was sitting in my car in the driveway of our little hideaway house, full of nerves and deciding when to go inside. I know Zander isn't here yet. His car would be out front unless he ran. Either way I couldn't sense him here yet. Kia is happily buzzing around, excited for tonight.

'Come on. It's going to be ten times better than yesterday's excitement. At least we would have some privacy and can do what we wanted.' She then flashes images of our mate in the bedroom and us doing all sorts of things to encourage me further. If anything, the images make me more nervous than excited.

'Stop over-thinking and over-analyzing everything. Just go with the flow, and everything will be fine,' Kia says encouragingly.

I grab the bag I packed this morning and my school bag from the front seat and climb out of the driver's seat, heading for the front door. I pick up the key in the little hideaway rock Zander had left for me and go inside.

The place looks beautiful in the afternoons. The sun shines through the kitchen windows brightening everything up, making it warm and welcoming.

I take a deep breath and started moving about the house, first putting my stuff in the upstairs bedroom. However tonight turns out, I know I will stay the night.

Looking around the bedroom, I notice that the bed hadn't been made or slept in for years, so I found some sheets and made the bed. Then moved to the spare room and made the bed there too. I try to keep myself busy, so I don't stress about what will possibly happen tonight.

After cleaning and taking a shower, I felt a little more relaxed, less busy and flustered. I grab my school bag and head downstairs to do homework. An hour passes and I start to wonder where he is. My mind scrambles again, nervous.

After a few minutes of debating, I get up and to move to the kitchen to get something ready for dinner. Outside has turned to dusk, the sun slowly setting into the evening.

I hear something rustling around outside as I walk into the kitchen. My head snaps to the back door as it opens; Kia at the ready to attack the invader.

Relief washes over me when Zander steps through the door. With his beautiful naked body fully displayed in front of me, I suddenly find it much harder to breathe. My eyes travel over his magnificent body of their own accord … over his shoulders, his chest, and six-pack abs, his cock springing to life. I can feel the blush forming on my cheeks as I sneak a look.

He stops suddenly, taken aback. His eyes turn dark with lust, a predatory look on his face like he is ready to pounce. Stalking up to me, he grabs my waist and pulls me in for a deep kiss. Sparks fly everywhere on contact; his kiss is frantic, desperate. Before I could think of what was happening, he pulls back but not before nipping my bottom lip, making me want him more.

"You are testing my strength and patience wearing something like that, sweetheart. You have no idea how much I've wanted you in the last twenty-four hours."

I giggle, I could feel the blush rising over my cheeks. Even though I planned to take things further tonight, I'm still nervous.

"I wanted to show you what yesterday meant to me. I want to take the next step and thought this was the best way of showing you."

I fiddle with the hemline of the black Nicolette Push-Up Baby doll night dress I bought a few weeks back. Underneath, I wore the red lingerie set, hoping that what I was wearing would give him an indication of what I wanted to do tonight.

Jace pushes forward at those words, trying to gain control. Kia is rattling around in my mind, eager to get to the bedroom. Zander pulls me forward again, tightening his grip around my waist and lifting me to meet him at eye level, kissing me frantically and hungrily. I wrapped my legs around his waist and my arms around his neck for support as he makes his way towards the stairs to the bedroom.

"Are you sure?" he asks, pulling out our kiss for a second and settling me on the bed.

I nod and I lay back on the covers, relaxing against the soft bed. My voice has deserted me and I don't want to ruin the mood with the bundles of nerves fluttering around in my stomach.

A growl of approval rumbles through his chest. The bed dips as he climbs over me, cupping my breasts through the lingerie. I involuntary moan as he flicks his finger over my hard nipples.

"As much as I love this little outfit, if you don't want it ruined, it needs to be off in the next five seconds, or I'm going to rip it off."

'Rip it off, rip it off,' Kia yells, bouncing around, happy with our progress.

I half sit up, pull the dress over my head and toss it to the side. He groans painfully when my panties and bra are revealed.

He reaches behind and unclips my bra, letting my breasts spill out him to see. He sucks in a hard breath as his eyes go straight to my boobs before leaning in and sucking one of them while still playing with the other.

"So fucking perfect," his husky voice makes my entire body shiver with excitement as his breath meets my skin.

Zander slides one hand down my side while keeping the other focused on my breast. His fingers reach my sensitive area, and I gasp on contact, turning into a low moan, wanting him to move inside me.

"Stop with the teasing," I demanded. "Just, just ..."

I'm so caught up with the sensations, our bodies feel like they are exploding with fireworks. He pushes his finger inside me, making me gasp and arch my back.

"Is this what you want, sweetheart," he rumbles, playing with my clit, making me feel things I've never felt before. Even compared to yesterday, this is next level.

"I want you, all of you," I say, opening my eyes and looking at him, his eyes completely black, nearly feral.

He rolls over to the side on the nightstand opening the top drawer and grabbing a black packet. Wait, when did he put the condoms there? He must have picked up on my silent question because he answers it for me.

"I put these here the first day I found this place, I wasn't sure if we would be needing them or not, but I'd rather have a stash, just to be safe," he mumbles, grabbing one out of the packet and tearing it open. He rolls the latex on quickly and moves back to the bed, he leans over me, kissing and massaging my boobs, and within seconds I've forgotten the questions and worries, focusing on him and his movements.

I feel his hard cock pushing against my entrance as I open my legs for him. He slowly moves in, letting me adjust to his size, it's a little painful at first, but his kisses and wandering hands help me forget the pain and turn it into pleasure.

He brings me into a deep kiss as he plunges the rest of his hard cock in, my scream swallowed by kisses as he pushes in deeper.

"How does that feel?" he whispers, adjusting himself against me, one hand on the wall and the other holding tightly against me.

"So ... good ..." I moan my back arches again. I feel my eyes roll back a bit as he grinds against me. I appreciate him taking it slow, but right now, I'm all built up, and I need fast. "Just fuck me, stop thinking I'm fragile," I gasp. " I... I need more."

I see Jace push forward at those words. It's like newfound strength pulsed through his body. He grabs one of my legs and throws it over his shoulders as he moves faster, harder, thrusting into me deeper. The feeling of him finally being inside of me is incomparable with any other experience I've ever had. I'm chanting his name like a prayer over and over, wanting him to keep going. I scream out as I reach my climax, my eyes roll back, and I'm clinging on to the sheets for dear life.

"I'm gonna ..." he growls before I feel his warm seed fill the condom.

"So fucking perfect," he says before crashing his lips to mine and sliding onto the space next to me.

I'm completely spent. We lay there intertwined on the bed. I snuggle against his warm chest, not wanting this moment to end, not wanting to go back to reality, just wanting to be with him. I always want to be with him, and only him.

The realization hits me like it's the most obvious thing I've been missing. Yes, I wanted to take things to this level, but now I have, I don't think I could go back to how we were. I don't think I could do the sneaking around here or at school. I only want to be with him and him only.

"I want to tell people," I blurt out, pushing up against his chest to look into his eyes.

Zander looks back at me curiously and chuckles. "Tell people what exactly, sweetheart?"

"Us, about us, I love you, and I don't think I could go back to how things were. It would be too much for me to be away from you now."

He smiles and brings me into another deep kiss, making me moan at the sensation.

"We have the school dinner next week? Why don't I pick you up then, and we can go together, that'll also give us a chance to tell our family beforehand."

"Okay," I nod, smiling and settling back down.

Chapter 35 - ZANDER

The best fucking sex of my life. No matter how many I have been with, the pure pleasure of the bond flowed through us, making it a hundred times better than any experience I have ever had.

Lying here in the middle of the night, my mind wanders, thinking of all the possibilities that could go wrong when we tell our families. That's part of why I suggested one more week so we can mentally prepare for all the different outcomes.

But holding her here at this moment makes me want to forget all the problems and mark and claim her fully. Jace has finally settled in the back of my mind, but his possessiveness still flows through. He doesn't want to leave this place without her or without marking her. I don't blame him because there is a party tonight with more people than we would like.

I'm so used to getting up and leaving in the middle of the night. I never hang around and always make sure I go to their place instead of mine. No one has ever been in my bed. No one has ever stayed the night with me.

This newfound feeling rolls through me as I lay here, considering, struggling with my flight response … to stay, convincing myself that this time it's different. It's not just a one-night fling. She's it, she's my mate.

'*Don't you fucking dare leave our mate.*' Jace growls, pissed off by my thoughts that woke him from his slumber.

'I wasn't going to,' I mumble. He gives me a death stare. He and I both know I was.

'I know in the past when others have said they love you, you flee. This is different. She is our mate and already loves us unconditionally. Even with all the shit, you have put her through. Do not fuck up now by leaving in the middle of the night.'

'I'm not going to. I was just thinking.' I sigh.

'*Thinking and getting ready to bolt!' His* rant is interrupted when Ashleigh stirs and moves around, making me freeze, and panic a little.

She snuggles further onto me. Her head is resting on my chest, hair falling around me as she wrapped her arms tighter like I was a cuddly teddy. I dipped my head into her hair, smelling her beautiful scent of forest wood and fresh water, calming my crazed thoughts, and holding her tightly until I finally drift off to sleep.

I'm woken by soft kisses on my lips, leading down to my chest, followed by her hands, leaving a tingling sensation.

"Good morning, handsome," she purrs, planting another kiss quickly on my lips. Her voice is all husky, different from last night. My eyes fly open, and I'm met with her beautiful dark ones with silver rims of Kia pushing through. I suppose she's the one in control this morning.

"Morning," I rumble, my throat dry, voice tight as she reaches down, grabs my cock, and starts stroking it.

I hiss at the impact of her hands, sinking back into the pillow, closing my eyes and enjoying the motion. Jace pushes forward, trying to take control as a response to Kia being let out.

'Only if you don't mark her or do anything stupid that will upset her?' I bargained with him.

'Fine,' he grumbles, excited to have a little control in human form. I relinquish control and let him take over for a little bit so he and Kia can enjoy each other's company. I was a little surprised they wanted time in our human forms instead of theirs but I shrugged it off, sat back, and let them do their thing.

By the time they finished their antics, it was nearly lunchtime. Considering we didn't end up with any dinner last night, I'll bet she's as hungry as I am. I pushed forward to regain control. I could see Ashleigh trying to do the same as her eyes flashed her colour, pulling Kia back into her place. Thankfully, Jace didn't put up much of a fight. I leaned into her, giving her a little kiss on her pouty lips. A blush crept over her cheeks. I smirked, lifted her, and placed her on my lap. She let out a little squeal, not expecting the motion.

"Morning, sweetheart," I murmur in her ear. I feel a shiver travel through her body, and her scent of arousal fills the air around us.

"Hmm, morning," she moans, leaning back onto me, closing her eyes, enjoying the movements. I nip at her earlobe and kiss her neck.

If I don't stop now, we will be missing lunch, too. Between last night's time together and Jace and Kia's time this morning, I'm sure she would want a little break, but she was made for me. When she goes into heat after we mark her, we will be rumbling around all day, every day for a week, and I couldn't fucking wait.

"Would you like some breakfast, or I guess lunch? It's nearly midday now, " I ask, kissing her one more time before moving to leave the bed.

"Sure, what were you thinking?" Her eyes flew open, excited at the possibility of food.

"I bought most things: eggs, bacon, hash browns. Take your pick." I shrug.

"Well, I'm famished and would be able to eat anything at the moment. Happy to cook a few breakfast things."

I nod, push off the bed, and head to the closet to grab shorts and a top, throwing them on quickly.

Ashleigh scampers around, grabbing her clothes from the bag she must have brought beforehand. "I'm just going to the bathroom to freshen up," she says, rushing through to the bathroom. I nod and head downstairs to get breakfast ready.

As I cook breakfast, my mind wanders again, and feelings of uncertainty and doubt rise. I enjoyed waking up next to her this morning, so I'm pretty taken aback as to why I am feeling these. Maybe the trial we have to go through with our family and packs?

That is probably most of it, but now I've experienced what the mate bond is like I wouldn't even dare to think of rejecting her. I couldn't, and I don't think Jace would survive if she rejected us. I don't think I would survive without her.

Would she choose her family and pack over us if it came to it? There are rules in place, but sometimes manipulation and threats can cause someone to go against the mate bond.

'*Stop over-thinking. She is a strong woman. She can do what she wants without anyone manipulating or questioning her actions,'* Jace tries to reassure me. '*Ashleigh has already told us how much she cares; why is this such a hard thing for you to accept?'*

'I get that she cares. I'm just more concerned about what her family will be like. I'm always going to be uneasy about everything until the dust has settled and we have told people.' I mumble back.

"You seem to be concentrating awfully hard on the bacon and eggs?"

Her sweet voice snaps me out of my debate with Jace. I look up and see her walking toward me with a cute smile. She's wearing jeans, and a low-cut long-sleeve top, exposing half her boobs in the best way possible.

I let out a possessive growl when I see what she is wearing. There ain't no fucking way she is leaving here with that on. Ashleigh just laughs at my annoyance and rolls her eyes.

"Down, boy," she says, walking around the bench and kissing me on the cheek. "How's it all going?" Ashleigh asks.

"Good, food is nearly ready in about 10 minutes if you want to grab some plates and things," I huff, still half-annoyed.

She nods, moves around, and grabs the plates and cutlery. "Any sauce?" she asks.

"Yeah, there should be some in the fridge." I tilt my head to the left, motioning to the fridge.

Fifteen minutes later, we sit down on the lounge in the living room, tucking into the food.

"Hmm, so good," Ashleigh moans, tilting her head back and leaning into the sofa.

"Careful, sweetheart, or I'll take you back upstairs and have my way with you again," I growl, unable to concentrate with this beauty next to me. I swear she put this shirt on just for a distraction to fucking toucher me, cause its fucking working, my eyes zero in on her boobs every time and don't want to leave.

She blinks slyly at me, a smirk pulling on her lips. Oh yeah, she knows exactly what she's fucking doing.

Silver rims flash through her eyes as Kia tries to look on and see what is happening. I'm about to lean in and kiss her when her phone starts ringing, startling us both.

Ashleigh groans when she sees who is calling.

"Who is it?" I ask.

"Chloe, I'm supposed to be helping her set up for tonight," she mumbles. "I'll just ignore her for now and send a quick text."

She waits for the phone to stop ringing before sending off a few messages while I finish the rest of my food.

"Crap, she wants me to be there in an hour," she mumbles, looking back up at me. I know it takes around half an hour to get to her place from here.

"It's ok. I can finish up here if you want to head off now," I say.

She tilts her head and asks, " Are you sure? You cooked and will also be cleaning?"

I shrug, "It's ok, you have to head off and see your friends. I've probably already taken more of your time than is date before someone notices anyway." It fucking kills me to say it. However, I still want her to maintain her friendships and current responsibilities outside of us trying to work out our own shit.

She leans in and pulls me in for a deep kiss. "Thankyou, you are still coming tonight, right? come around nine o'clock if you are."

"Yeah, if that's okay," I reply while cleaning everything up.

Ashleigh nods excitedly, smiling. "Can't wait," she breathes as she picks up her phone and runs to grab her bag.

I sigh inwardly. Damn, I thought I would have had more time with her today. Jace is also grumbling in my mind wanting our mate to stay longer. I put the things in the kitchen before I hear her coming back down the stairs. I head over and open the door for her before she heads out.

"Thank you for last night," she smiles, standing on her toes to reach me. I lean down, kissing her possessively, not wanting her to go.

"Anytime, sweetheart," I mumble, pulling her in for a deep kiss. "I'll see you tonight."

Chapter 36 - ZANDER

I'm on edge as we drive out of our territory in Danni's jeep and head for Liverpool. Danni is driving, I'm in the front seat while Eric and Billy are sitting in the back. We picked up a couple of cases of beer and ice to contribute to the party.

I never go empty-handed, even if it is a house party. The guys and I always drink a considerable amount.

Driving through the city to get to the other side isn't a long drive, maybe 45 minutes to Liverpool territory, far enough for us to be a little bit on edge. Ashleigh assured me that the other Alpha heirs and pack members would be attending, so I suggested we take a few cars and pile up as best we could.

As we roll up to the house at around 9.30 pm, cars are all parked along the street, fairy lights on the front fence flickering on and off to the beat of the music. The place is nice enough, a two-story white colonial with a dark roof, four pillars out the front to hold the porch, and a few steps leading up to the house.

People are gathered all around the front and back; one or two girls are already throwing up in the front gardens, with their friends holding their hair back, trying to comfort them. I could sense a few others from other packs around the area, which relaxed me a little more. Dad wasn't thrilled that I was going, but I convinced him it was the best way to build relationships. I could at least make an appearance for a few hours, then come home if he was that uneasy about it.

Considering Ashleigh was my mate, I wanted to try and make an effort to be around her in her natural space.

Danni parked on the curb, and we all pile out, grabbing the stuff from the boot. I sling a case of beer over my shoulder, steadying it with one arm to get a good grip on it before we head towards the thumping music and the with the boys following behind.

I walk through the front door, not even bothering to knock or ring the bell, the door already half ajar as people came and go. The house already wreaked of sweat, alcohol, and a slight tinge of smoke.

I scan my surroundings. It's a nice enough place. Open floor plan with the kitchen on the right and a massive lounge room on the front left. Big double glass doors opened to the back patio and stairs on the right-hand side before the kitchen leading up. I notice that most of the people here are from school. A chick I recognize as one of Ashleigh's friends who follows her around the school. She walks up to us and starts talking, waving her hands around and pointing to where everything was.

"Hi, I'm Chloe. Welcome to my home, few ground rules. Firstly. If you are gonna throw up, do it outside. Secondly. No sex in the bedrooms, or anywhere else in this house for that matter. I mean it. I will kick you out even if you are halfway through or finished. I don't give a shit who you are, do it somewhere else. And lastly. Have fun! Just don't break anything in the process. Alcohol is in the outside bar. And bathrooms are to the left of the living room." She smiled and headed toward the kitchen without waiting for me to respond.

Danni chuckles at her rules. "If she thinks people ain't gonna have sex, she's delusional."

I roll my eyes. "Just don't do it in the house. Don't give them a reason to be pissed at us," I mumble, making my way through the busy people outside to the backyard. I spot a DJ playing music on a stand in a corner. People are dancing in front of him on what looked like a plastic mat. Guess they put it down so the girls can wear heels and not sink into the grass.

I scan the area. It is a huge backyard. A pool was further out the back with a seating area off to the right with a large table in the middle. A fire pit is off to the left of that with people already gathered around warming themselves in the crisp winter evening.

I make my way over to the bar next to the DJ. People had already flocked around, lingering and chatting. I try not to be so eager to be near my mate, but I want her and hate that I am around other people who aren't her. Just as that thought entered my mind I caught her scent. I frantically start looking around, trying to spot her in the crowd.

I nearly choke when I saw her talking with another chick next to the fire pit. She's fucking hot! It's taking all of my willpower not to march over to her, throw her over my shoulder, and take her home with me tonight.

After last night I want her more than ever. This afternoon made it quite clear that I couldn't be without her without going fucking crazy, and Jace was just a dick to control.

Wearing knee-high heel boots, her dress only just went past her thigh, the front crossed over, making easy access for her boobs. Gold chains ran across her back and shoulders, keeping everything in place. She is a total knockout, and it is fucking killing me that I'm not the only one seeing her in it and not marching her out of here to have my way with her.

She completely changed her hair. It wasn't curly and crazy as usual. Tonight, she changed it to flowy and wavey as she had straightened it. She looked like a completely different person. I was pissed off this morning with what she wore, fuck, if I knew she was going to wear this tonight, I wouldn't have let her out of my sight.

My heart thumps in my chest as she looks up at me, giving me a small smile. Kia flashes through her eyes, making herself known.

I look next to her at the other girl. I recognize her as Samantha Jane, Westfield's Beta heir. I guess the two ranked females are mingling.

"You want a drink, Alpha?" Danni asks.

"Huh?" Snapping out of my trance, I spin around to face him and the guys grabbing their drinks.

Danni smirks at my uneasiness and hands me a beer. I roll my eyes at his stupid behaviour. I look back over to see Ashleigh and Samantha had been joined by Lachlan King. I never did like the guy. He always gave me the creeps. Out of the four Alpha heirs, he is the worst. His father is the Alpha of Westfield and just a weasel to deal with. His son isn't much better.

He moves closer and goes between the two girls sliding a hand around Samantha, pulling her in close. It seems these two are more than just business. Ashleigh excused herself from the group and starts to head towards me, looking directly at me and giving me major fuck me eyes.

She'd only taken a step towards me when a slap was heard. Ashleigh stops in her tracks and spins back around to face them with Kia's aura pulsing through so strong that the music stopped and everyone was baring their necks, submitting to the Beta of Liverpool.

Lachlan King was smirking like the smug bastard he is, flashed her a smile, and shrugged. I didn't even have time to register what happened when she swung back and smacked him right in the middle of the face making a sickening cracking sound of his nose breaking as he cries out like a baby.

"If you ever touch me again like that, it won't just be your nose that is broken. Now get the fuck off my territory!" Kia snarled.

A few people around her snickered at him as he whimpers like a pup. Samantha tries to comfort him but at the same time seems pissed off at what he did. Considering they are probably fucking, Lachlan looking at another girl for his next fix probably wasn't what she needed to see.

Broken bones hurt like a bitch. You have to reset them before they heal, or there will be problems later on. Shifter healing can only do so much.

Jace sits up, all proud of what our mate did. Honestly, if she didn't beat the shit out of him, I would have. I don't give a shit, who found out we were mates.

I would have killed the bastard for touching what's mine.

Chapter 37 - ASHELIGH

My knuckles still sting after punching Lachlan. What a dickhead for trying to pull something like that in front of everyone, on my territory, and in front of my mate.

I could see Zander tense and Jace flash through his eyes as he registered what happened. I'll say props to him for keeping his cool. Honestly, I was surprised he didn't finish him off after.

'*Because he knows we can look after ourselves, we just proved that to him,*' Kia snorts.

'I suppose,' I mumble back and head for the bar where Zander and his friends are currently posted.

Everyone starts talking, and the music starts back up again, forgetting the incident that had just happened 5 minutes ago.

I nod to Lui, who is looking after the bar. "What can I get you, Beta?"

"Shots, it's been a long night." I don't mind drinking, and tonight is one of those nights where I needed something a bit stronger than the average drink.

Zander leans into Dani and says something before the three boys scampered off to mingle. He moves closer to me as Lui serves me two shots of a dark amber liquor before disappearing over to the other end of the table to serve others.

"Wanna do a shot with me?" I ask, pushing one closer towards him.

He raises a questioning eyebrow and shrugs, "Sure, I'm no stranger to whisky shots."

I grab the other shot, raise it to him, down it quickly, and slap it back on the table. A sweet burn moves down my throat quickly as I shake my head, trying to get used to the taste.

"Are you okay?" Zander asks.

"Hmm, I'm a lot better now you're here," I respond, giving him a sweet smile. I've been drinking for a few hours now, and that shot just gave me back the buzz I lost when Lachlan showed up.

Zander moves a little closer to where he was nearly touching my arm. The tension in the air is so thick you could cut it with a knife. His scent all around us, drawing me in and making Kia go crazy. After this morning and last night, it frustrates me that I can't claim him as mine just yet. I am so nervous about him coming here tonight, nervous about us being around other people that isn't in a school setting.

Zander smirks and lifts his hand to touch my arm as if he could feel the nerves rolling off me. Tingles dance on my skin where he touched me. I see his eyes go dark, and a gold rim formed as Jace pushes forward. I feel Kia moving forward in response to her mate.

Jace leansin and growls, "You have no idea how much I wanted to rip that fuckers head off when I realized what he did. If you didn't tell him to piss off or punched the shit out of him, I would have killed the little shit for touching what is mine."

Kia is purring with happiness as Jace claimed us as his. I see the struggle between him and Zander, trying to regain control.

It doesn't help that Kia pushes forward to respond to him, bringing our hand up to his cheek to calm him down.

"We can take care of ourselves, my mate. You don't need to worry about us," she purrs.

I jump a little as someone squealed in the background with a loud splash as they were thrown into the pool.

"Pool Party!" someone yells while others around him cheer and run towards the pool.

I look around to see a few guys from my pack taking off their shirts and pants before jumping into the pool. I wonder if they realize how cold it is? I chuckle and shake my head when a few squeal and someone yells it is fucking freezing and moves to try to get back out.

I smile back at Zander, who is watching me curiously. He has regained control. There still a light rim of Jace in his eyes, just as I'm sure Kia is still present in mine.

"You look great, by the way, really great," he says, raking his eyes over my body, letting them linger on my boobs and the hem of my dress.

"Ash!" Someone calls out to me just as I am about to respond. I look over to see Ollie marching toward me with a pissed-off look on his face. Now, this could be because of one or two things. One because I'm here talking to Zander. Or two because he found out about what happened with Lachlan, or maybe a third, why Zander's pack was invited and is here in the first place.

"What's up?" I ask.

"Care to explain why Lachlan King just left with a bloodied nose?"

Next to me, Zander snorts and says, "no one told you yet?"

Ollie narrows his eyes and looks over to Zander, "I wasn't asking you," he growls.

Zander crosses his arms over his chest in defense with Jace flashing in his eyes. I can feel his aura pulsing. Not wanting any more bad blood between the two, I quickly jump into my explanation. "He slapped my ass when I stood up to leave when he rudely interrupted my conversation with Samantha so I turned around and punched the dickhead."

Ollie relaxes a little when he understood the disrespect that Lachlan showed.

"You're seriously questioning your Beta? How the fuck do you know she even did anything in the first place?" Zander growls.

While it is sweet and all for Zander to be pissed off at Ollie's questions, I understood why, plus Zander shouldn't really be questioning him. This is his land and territory, after all.

"Watch it, you're on my territory. I have a right to know what the fuck is going on, especially if someone just attacked an Alpha heir that could lead to a war or issues we will have with their pack. You have dealt with Westfield yourself. You know what assholes they can be like." Ollie snarls back.

'*Stop them before this escalates. Oliver doesn't know Zander is our mate. This doesn't need to go further,'* Kia mumbles.

"Guys, it's fine. Lachlan was in the wrong anyway, and if anything does happen, we will deal with it then."

Both of their eyes snap back to me, relaxing a little bit.

"Get a drink, Ollie. It'll be okay," I encourage him.

Ollie watches Zander side-stepped around him to move next to me on the other side as he goes up to the bar. I feel Zander's hands move next to me, itching to hold me. I know he's on edge, and I can't comfort him.

He moves a finger across the hem of my dress around my thigh. A shiver goes through me even at his slightest touch. I could feel his eyes lingering on me as I look around, trying not to get myself so worked up around Oliver. Was he crazy trying something like this? As much as I want him, now is not the best time for teasing.

While I scan the crowd, I see a girl and her friend making a b-line directly for us.

Grace.

Hurt blooms in my chest and my eyes snap to Zander. Did he really bring her here, too? I relax when I see confusion in his eyes as he watches Grace. She isn't wearing her usual skimpy outfits. Tonight, she wore skinny jeans and a low-cut top that barely covers her boobs.

"Baby, you haven't been answering my calls or texts when I try to reach you!" She half-shrieks and seems slightly pissed off as she approaches us.

"Firstly, I am not your baby. It's Alpha to you. Secondly, I have nothing else to say, or I would have said it."

"Well, I need to talk to you," she huffed, folding her arms across her chest and pushing out her boobs to make them look bigger.

"Talk here. I'm not going anywhere with you," he shrugs, grabbing his beer from behind him, and starts to drink it.

Her eyes land on me next to Zander, "Do you mind giving us some privacy?"

Kia snarls in my mind. '*I am not leaving this bitch with our mate.*' I'm sure my eyes flash, making her known.

Zander replies before I could answer. "Beta Ashleigh does not need to leave. If you want to talk, Grace, talk."

"Fine, have it your way; I'm pregnant."

I feel the blood drain from my face. Numb. All I feel is numb. An uneasy feeling settles in my stomach. Zander's body stiffens beside me, coughing up the beer he was drinking. Ollie chuckles next to me, hearing the predicament that Zander is in.

I looked up at Zander to see his face pale. What does this mean for us? My mind spins with so many unanswered questions that I am afraid to know the answer to. For once, Kia remains silent. No smart-ass comment, no pushing forward to claim Zander as hers. This time there is silence, only silence. It worried me that if she is silent this is bad.

"What?" he mumbles, slowly processing what Grace had said.

"Pregnant, Zander, pregnant. It happens when two people fuck, which we did nearly every day. I tried to call you and get a hold of you for the last few days, but you haven't returned any of my calls or texts, and you were avoiding me at school." She says, waving her hands around dramatically.

My mind is spinning. I feel like I'm going to be sick. My heart aches. I thought we had moved past all of his exes and these problems. I understand that everyone has a history. I don't want to hate him for that. Instead, I focused on something we could build together. But now that feels like it would never happen.

It's probably a good thing we haven't told anyone we are mates. I already feel humiliated enough right now, and no one knows.

I don't want to leave him at this moment, but I have to, I have to get out of here. It is all just too much. It's still early, only 11.00 pm, but I can't be here right now. I need to process this myself and figure out what to do. I don't even know the rules on all of this regarding mates.

So, I move between him and Grace and walk away without saying a word.

I feel his eyes boring into me. I can't look back. I don't want to look back and let him see the hurt he caused me once again.

Chapter 38 - KYLIE

* Liverpool Beta Female Kyile Steward (Ashleigh and Brent's Mother) *

The packhouse door slams shut, I hear footsteps making their way towards the living room.

"I'm home," Ashleigh calls out, her voice strained. She sounds upset. Shit, what happened at that party?

I looked at the clock on the wall. It was only 11.20 pm. We aren't expecting the kids home until well after midnight.

"In the living room, honey," I call back, pausing the TV show Robert and I were watching.

"How was the party?" I ask as she makes her way toward us.

She looks a little shaken, paler than usual. I frown at my daughter's appearance. Something happened.

My mate groans as I move off the lounge away from his comfort. I send him an apologetic look. We'd set up a date night for tonight so we could reconnect and not worry about the kids since they would be out for most of the night.

"What happened?" I ask. I'm beginning to feel uneasy with the lack of words from my daughter.

Usually, Ashleigh likes to debrief and chat my ear off for at least half an hour after an event like this. Tonight though, nothing.

She shakes her head as she moves closer to us. Her eyes are glassy, her hair is windblown and messy, and she is holding her heels in one hand. I look down, frowning, and see her feet dirty and covered in dust.

Did she walk home? Not that it's far, only a few blocks away, but she also knows she could have called one of us, or Oliver and her brother were also there to drive her if needed.

I half-expected her to stay at Chloe's tonight, since Chloe's parents are away.

"Ok, hun, why don't you go up and shower, and I'll bring you some hot cocoa and a cheese toastie?" I coax her.

She sighs, nods, and heads for her bedroom.

"I wonder what that was about," Robert mumbles, rubbing the back of his neck and frowning as he watches our daughter head to her bedroom.

"I'm not sure, but I'll figure it out," I reply, leaning in and planting a kiss on his cheek. "I won't be too long."

It only took about 10 minutes to prepare the snack for Ashleigh. Right now, it looks like she just needs some love and no questions asked, so that's what I'll give her.

I have a funny feeling. This is going to be about that boy of hers, if my suspicions are correct, which I know they are.

She is Zander Blackwood's mate, and I swear if that boy hurt my baby I will quite happily knock some sense into him. I haven't even told my mate or Alpha about this news. It isn't my place to say anything. I feel that Ashleigh will let people know when she is ready. I understand why she has kept it a secret, so I'll help my daughter in any way I can.

I lightly tap on the door before opening it to let her know I'm coming in. I open the door and see her sitting on her couch by the window in her pajamas, staring out at the night sky.

"Here you go, honey," I say before passing her the plate of food and hot chocolate.

She jumps, startled that I entered her room. Okay, something is definitely wrong here. She is not usually so spaced out.

"Thanks, mummy," she whispers, taking the food and turning to look back outside. She slowly sips the hot chocolate, closing her eyes in comfort with each sip, the plate balanced on her legs.

I sit next to her on the couch, leaning in and stroking her hair, comforting her, and letting her know I am here for her.

I look curiously at her hairpiece, running my fingers around it each time I stroke her hair. It was exactly as I remembered it, so beautiful and elegant. I was proud that Ashleigh wore it. Proud she has a mate, that she accepted him.

"I told him I loved him after we mated last night, and tonight, one of his exes announced she is pregnant with his baby," Ashleigh whispers so softly I nearly missed it. My heart clenches at the pain she's in. Lola whines in my mind, wanting to comfort our pup.

"I don't know what to do, mum. I tried... I tried so hard, but one thing after another thing just comes up every time we are going well. Something always tears us apart. I don't know how many more things I can handle. Do I forgive everything because that's what mates are supposed to do? Why should I forgive everything he did when he didn't even consider the impact beforehand. Why should I continue to forgive when he didn't even think about me before this. I have been the most forgiving with him, and I don't know how much more I can handle."

I try to wrack my brain for something to say that would help. With so many unanswered questions, and the most challenging thing was that I didn't know. Before giving my daughter the answer, she needed to hear, there were too many variables.

"I'm sorry, honey," I said, kissing her on her forehead. "Before anything else you should talk to him. I'm sure he is also freaked out and doesn't know what to do either"

"I just left him standing there with her. I felt him wanting me to stay. I knew he wanted to follow me to talk, but too many people were around. I wanted to comfort himbut at the same time, I just wanted to leave and process everything without anyone being around. It hurt so much, but now I feel numb."

I frown as I could feel her slightly shake next to me. I grab one of the blankets off her bed, lift the plate of food, and place the blanket over her legs. She grabs the plate and starts eating alternately sipping the hot chocolate again. Her shaking slows as she calms down.

I see her wolf peek through her eyes as she sits, trying to calm herself. It made sense when I saw Kia, her wolf wants to kill the girl, and Ashleigh is trying to control Kia. I can feel her aura rolling off her in waves of frustration and anger. She considers the pregnant girl a threat to her mate, a threat to her and Ashleigh.

'Lola, can you speak with Kia, try to calm her down? Even if Ashleigh is Zander's mate, we don't want to start a war with Kia trying to take control,' I ask.

'Sure, I'll see what I can do.' Lola goes to the depths of my mind to reach out to Kia and see if she could help calm her down.

"Honey, you two have been through a lot already, and while you may think you forgave him if you are still hurting over all of this, he needs to redeem himself before anything further happens. You should try to talk to him and figure this out together."

Ashleigh nods and silently sits there looking into the night sky, holding her mug. I give her one more kiss on the cheek before heading out. Her shaking has stopped, and Kia has settled down. I could see her natural colour coming back. I am more comfortable leaving her in this state than when she arrived home.

"How did you know he was my mate?" she asks softly as she finishes her drink.

I tilt my head, sitting back down, looking back at her moving one of her wet curls out of her eyes.

"His mother and I were best friends. She was from a neighbouring pack. Granny and Pa were a part of an old country pack back in the day until I found out I was mated to your father. They decided to move closer to the city because I was mated to the pack's Beta and wanted to be around you kids. Molly found out she was mated to Zander's father when she visited me one weekend. We promised to keep in touch no matter what, even though the boys still had bad blood with what happened. I asked your uncle if I could still see her because I knew her before I was mated to your father."

She nods in understanding, taking in more information about her mate, "We found old photos in the cottage. Some were of you and his mum."

I smile sadly. "I miss Molly every day. She was my best friend. You cried every night for two weeks when I told you that you couldn't see Zander anymore. It was almost as though the bond was already working in a way. "

She smiles softly. " I don't remember the cottage or even visiting it when I was younger."

"We tried to go as often as possible, but with more attacks that were happening at the time, it was getting harder to be safer. Then when your brother was born, your father felt uncomfortable every time we left the pack land."

She stretches and yawns her body relaxing after Kia stopped putting up a fight. I hoped she would understand and help process this with her. Ashleigh needs Kia now more than ever.

"Why don't you head to bed, honey? Try to get some sleep. Maybe tomorrow you can try to speak to him."

I picked up the plate and mug off the couch and headed towards the door. Putting my hand on the door, I turned back to my daughter, "I understand why you didn't tell anyone, and I'll keep your secret for now, but until you decide, I just want you to know that you are my daughter, and your father and I love you very much, we only want you to be happy. Everyone will understand, you do not need to worry about you and Zander if that is what you choose."

I blow her a kiss one more time before heading back downstairs to be with my mate, who is sitting patiently waiting for my return.

Chapter 39 - ZANDER

I stood in front of Grace, completely stunned as she said she was pregnant. All I want to do right now is beg for my mate's forgiveness. I try not to look at her, but I can feel her hurt through Jace. Since Jace and Kia have mated, our bond has gotten stronger. All we need to do to complete the bond is mark each other, allowing us to link and her be a part of my pack. Our scents will also combine so everyone would know she is mine and I am hers. But I hurt her again. And it makes me feel even more of an ass who isn't worthy of being her mate. Jace is fuming, angry that I hurt her again.

For once though he is silent. I can feel his anger and pain. It makes me wonder if he would ever speak to me again ... if this were the final straw. Then suddenly, while I'm processing everything, Ashleigh leaves. She walks away without even saying anything at all, without looking back at me. I look over and see Oliver watching his cousin in confusion. I wonderif he felt her pain?

Guilt consumes me. I'm so confused. I was always careful and wore protection, and Grace said she was on the pill. Thankfully these days, they have altered medication to accommodate for supernaturals, so the balance worked out. Even so, I can't blame my mate for leaving me with this confusing mess. I stood there for a good ten minutes in silence.

Oliver chuckles again before leaving and returning to the party, leaving me alone with Grace and Anni. I wonder if he knew what I had done to Ashleigh. I'm sure if he did, he wouldn't be laughing. Instead, I would have his fist planted in my face.

"Anni give us a minute," I say, looking at her friend standing behind her.

"Ohh, now you want privacy?" Grace shrieks, throwing her hands up in a huff.

"Calm the fuck down, Grace. Do not speak to me like that." I growl, yanking her hands down so she doesn't draw attention. I can feel Jace push forward as I give the command. She pales and hangs her head in submission.

Finally, some fucking quiet where I can think. I look back to Anni, still standing there, and raise an eyebrow. She quickly gets the hint and scampers off.

"How long have you known?" I hiss.

"Nearly a week," she whispers.

"And during that week, you didn't think to try and contact me to sort this shit out!"

"I tried to. You must have blocked me. I tried calling and texting, but you didn't return anything," she says, crying. I roll my eyes at her exaggeration.

Yes, I may have been a little busy and preoccupied with Ashleigh. But if she outright said she was pregnant in a message, I wouldn't have ignored that. Jace paces in the back of my mind. His anger bubbles to the surface every now and then and it was putting me on edge. I may have just lost my mate, and now I have to deal with this bitch which I don't want to. I pinch my thumb and index finger on the bridge of my nose, trying to concentrate and figure this shit out, where to go from here.

Firstly, she shouldn't be anywhere near alcohol or drugs. Anger rose again, pissed off that she would be endangering the pup by coming here. Secondly, she wouldn't be able to live in her apartment by herself, so she would have to move into the packhouse, which makes me even more fucking furious because I don't want her anywhere near me.

I need to speak to Ashleigh. I don't know what the fuck I'm going to say. But with Jace being the way he is, he won't calm down until he is close to her again. At least he hasn't said anything to make me feel even worse than I already do. Maybe he is just trying to let me think and figure this out before giving me a lecture on how much I failed my mate again because I just wanted to fuck around.

The look on her face, she was utterly devastated. Granted, no one else knew why but I did. How the fuck am I supposed to face her now? What the fuck am I supposed to say to her? 'I'm sorry' won't cut it this time.

She nearly tried to reject me when the twins were all over me before. Will she try to do it again? My mind is spinning with all of these problems. Why the fuck couldn't this be simple? Fuck this shit. I need a drink.

"Go home, Grace," I grumble, waving down the bartender again, getting ready for another drink.

"Wait, what?" Her eyes snap back up to meet mine.

"Go home and start packing. You will have to move into the packhouse. I'll book an appointment with the doctor as soon as possible."

Her eyes widen as I mention her moving into the packhouse. "Why do I have to move in?" she asks.

Jeez, how stupid can this girl be? I sigh, scrubbing a hand over my face, frustrated I have to explain. "Well, you can't do this alone, can you?" I mumble, my hand waving towards her.

A sickening feeling pounds in the pit of my stomach. I want pups, but I want them later on with my mate. I close my eyes, trying to think clearly. What about Ashleigh? How the hell am I going to talk to her about all of this? What am I going to tell my father? Will Ashleigh still accept me after this? Will she still love me unconditionally? It seems Jace is fed up with me already. Would she be, too?

"Okay, I'll get Anni to drive me back," Grace says, turning around, and walks back towards the house to search for Anni.

"What can I get you," the bartender asks.

"More shots, it's been a long fucking night."

~

For the next few hours, I drink myself stupid. By the time the crowd has thinned out I can barely walk and talk. The lightbulb is still flickering in the back of my mind, so I somewhat know what I am doing. I haven't seen Ashleigh since she left.

Oliver is still around. He's been keeping an eye on me, looking at me every fifteen minutes, the paranoid fuckwhit. I have too much shit on my mind to worry about than do something stupid tonight.

Danni and the boys are still around, probably trying to get their dicks wet.

It's about 2 am when I feel my phone buzz in my back pocket. Honestly, I'm surprised I haven't received a call from my father or Beta demanding I get home and clean up my mess.

My heart stops in my chest for a second when I see the message from Ashleigh.

At our place if you want to talk.

I stare at the phone, rereading it for about the fifth time before it registers. I close my eyes taking a deep breath before trying to get my shit together, deciding whether I should go and see her.

Jace doesn't say a thing. He hasn't said anything to me since Ashleigh left.

I begged him once or twice to talk to me. Instead, I was met with a glare filled with his pure anger.

Sighing, I put my phone back in my pocket and searched for Danni and the boys before heading off. I found them by the fire pit with a few very drunken-looking girls. One was a little shaky, leaning on Billy, and the other was trying to get her balance on Danni.

"Yo, I'm heading out," I say, grasping a hand on Danni's shoulder to grab his attention.

"Leaving alone?" Eric snickers. I flick him the bird as I turn around and walk towards the house.

I see Oliver sitting on the lounge in the living room with a few girls as I head towards the door. Sighing, I should probably thank him and let him know the guys are still around. I make my way toward him. He lifts his head and nods.

"I'm headed out. Is it alright if the guys still hang out for a bit longer? Danni is still here. Once he clears out, the rest of my pack will follow," I say, folding my arms across my chest, trying to compose myself so I don't look so fucked.

Oliver frowns and nods, "Yeah, no worries, they know the rules. As long as no one does anything stupid, they are fine."

I nod back, "Yeah, all good. Thanks for the invite, appreciate it," I grind out. He and I have never seen eye to eye, but right now, I'm already in a hot mess with my mate. I don't need to make things worse with her Alpha. I turn around and head out the door.

Stripping down to my briefs, I shift into Jace. Thankfully he didn't put up much of a fight. Knowing where we are going seems to have calmed him. It takes me about 40 minutes to run there, 40 minutes to ponder what to say to Ashleigh.

Each time I try to think it out I come up blank. I see the light in the bedroom flicker on as I reach the house. I wait in the woods behind the trees out of sight as I watch her move across the bedroom to the little window seat. She's wearing one of my shirts that I left there last time. My heart pounds as I watch my mate sit there waiting for me, looking out to the night sky.

What was I going to say when I walked through that door? What would I say to the woman who forgave me after everything I had done? Will she forgive me for this mistake?

Will she be ok with another woman being in the house with us? Will she be ok with another woman having my child?

My foggy brain cleared up as I ran which means that now I can think ... and I'm thinking I made the wrong fucking choice in coming here to see her. I don't want to give her the chance to reject me.

She freaked out at what happened at school only a few days ago. I can honestly say I am not looking forward to this fight, or discussion, or argument, or whatever the fuck it will be. I slowly back away from the cottage, away from my mate.

'*Don't,*' Jace growls.

All night he has listened to my turmoil and problems, and he fucking chooses now to say something.

'*If you leave her now, I will never forgive you. She is here, still waiting for you.*' Jace tries to reason with me.

Unfortunately, my mind is so chaotic going over and over everything that I don't even hear him anymore.

'I can't allow her to reject us. We won't survive that,' I mumble. At least if I don't give her the chance to be able to reject me, she will have to be still bonded to me.

I do the one thing I have always been good at in these situations: I turn and run, run away from everything.

Chapter 40 - DANIEL

*Charwood Beta Heir Daniel Richmond (Danni) *

I got home just as the sun rose, stumbling through the door. Billy managed to give us all a ride home because he stopped drinking a while ago. Thankfully I didn't drive in the state I was in, half-wasted, and wouldn't remember where the fuck I was going.

I start making my way to my room when I hear a thud and crashing sounds from upstairs.

'You should *probably see if everything is alright,'* Sam tells me. Grumbling because I know he's right, I head up the stairs towards Zander's room. As I get closer, I hear a second thud and a groan.

I couldn't smell anything different in the hallways, just Zander's scent and our Alpha, who was down the hallway at the other end. I knock on Zander's door to see if he was okay. He groaned again, sounding in pain.

Opening the door, the foul stench of stale alcohol and vomit reaches my nose. Zander's lying in the middle of his bedroom floor like he's passed out from trying to get out of bed. A few bottles are scattered around the floor. Some still had liquor in them as it spilled while he tried to move.

I sigh and move over to him, trying to help him up. "Come on, big guy, let's get you in the shower." I bend down, grabbing one of his arms and pulling it over my shoulder for support as I lift him.

I bring him to his bathroom and he starts babbling incoherent words while I try to put him in the shower. Some of what he says make sense but not a huge amount. I shove him into the shower with his clothes still on, I'm barely in my right mind to look after him, so I try to do the best I can right now.

After about 15 minutes of sitting in the shower, he looks better. His eyes focus and he recognizes where he is.

"I fucked up Danni. Grace pregnant, my mate, fuck my mate, she probably hates me," Zander starts rambling.

He found his mate, and he's been keeping it a secret. How the fuck has he been doing that? I sit there silently as he continues to babble. What's the saying … a drunk man's word is a sober man's thoughts?

"Ashleigh, fuck, she looked devastated when Grace said …" he mumbles.

That one gets my attention. Beta Ashleigh is Zander's, mate? I sit up a little straighter and lean in, feeling the water, making sure it's not too hot or cold. Trying not to seem too surprised or interested by his words.

"I tried to go to her, tried to talk to her, but I couldn't. What was I supposed to say to her? 'I'm sorry' won't be enough."

So, he chose Grace over his mate? Is he fucking stupid? He chose that bitch over our Luna. Anni told me she had to head home early to help Grace pack. I was confused at first, but now it all makes fucking sense. I told him a thousand times she's a crazy bitch, but he never listened to me.

"You need to talk to Ashleigh. Tell her you are trying to figure this out, so she doesn't reject you. At least by going to her, she knows you are still in this with her and that you choose her instead of Grace."

"I love her, man, and I fucked up. I can't face Ashleigh right now," Zander sighs, scrubbing his hand over his face. I roll my eyes and slump back against the basin, he won't listen to me in this state.

"Come on, let's get you cleaned up," I grumble, trying to help him out of the shower.

He stands and strips out of his clothes and throws them over to the laundry hamper. "I'll stay a bit longer, still stink," he mumbles.

I nod and head back to his room. I gag as the stench hits me again. I move to the two windows opposite his bed and yank them open, trying to get some fresh air in.

The sun is halfway in the sky, slowly rising to start the day. I look at his bedside clock and see it's about 6.40 am. Damn, I hate winter. The sun always rises later.

Moving back around the room, I start collecting the empty bottles to throw them out. I'll have to get one of the maids to come in later and clean the floors to get rid of the stench.

Zander comes out of the bathroom a few minutes later, towel wrapped around his waist and hair wet. At least he can stand on his own now.

"Just leave them, don't worry about it," Zander mumbles, seeing me holding the bottles.

I nod, setting them up on his dresser. "You good?"

"Yeah, man, thanks." he nods back. "I can manage from here."

"Don't tell anyone," he says as I'm about to head out. I turn around, frowning in confusion.

"What do you mean?" I ask.

"Don't say anything to anyone about Ashleigh," he demands.

I sigh. He's still set on no one knowing. "It is a good thing, man. She will be good for you. She's your mate, our Luna. You can't hide from her forever. She might have some good input on this situation."

"I know, just until this shit is over, I just have to figure out what to do about Grace, then we'll talk," he says.

I shake my head, disagreeing with everything he has done in this situation. I mean, I would have freaked out as well, but I wouldn't have walked away from my mate. I would have asked for her help and advice.

"Your choice, man." I shrug, reaching for the door.

"What else could I have done?" he asks, sounding defeated.

I look up, meeting his eyes. He looks drained, exhausted from lack of sleep and too much alcohol. I can tell he's been beating himself up over this.

Sighing, I fold my arms across my chest and say, "Look, before jumping into anything, make sure Grace is pregnant, and make sure it is yours, don't throw away your Luna for something that might not be true in the first place."

He wouldn't listen to anything I was saying before, so maybe this will help him. "Talk to Ashleigh. She is reasonable and understanding, and as far as I can tell, obviously very forgiving with all the shit you have done." I smirk, trying to make things a little lighter and less stressful.

He sighs, looking completely defeated, scrubbing a hand over his face and closing his eyes, trying to gain some sense in all of this mess.

"I'll get going so I can get a few hours' sleep before mum starts calling me for duties," I mumble, grabbing the door handle and heading out.

"Yeah, thanks, I appreciate it," he nods as I leave his room.

I send a little prayer to the moon goddess, praying that he will sort his shit out and that we will have our rightful Luna standing by him.

Chapter 41 - ASHLEIGH

I waited for him that night, I've waited for him the last few nights, and I still haven't heard anything from him.

I can feel him close by through Kia who is fuming that he won't come to us. He lurks in the woods, somewhere out there, instead of coming closer. At least he keeps a close distance, so he knows neither of us will become weak from not seeing each other.

I'm confused and hurt. I feel used and cheapened, like he's just got what he wanted and ran. I've tried to do what mum suggested and work things out. Every night for the last few nights, I have been waiting at our place. I've only sent him one message. I don't think he needs more from me until he makes the next move. I won't seek him out because he needs to come to me and sort this out. It is his mess. He needs to take responsibility.

Part of me understands why he is confused, but at the same time, I am annoyed he won’t talk to me about it. He won’t let me help him.

I told my parents I wasn’t going to school the next few days, so I have just been training with the pack warriors and studying most of the day. Unfortunately, it’s in the evenings when Kia gets weaker. I know I have to go back to our place and have some connection to him, so I won’t be completely useless.

I can last a few days without being around him for now because we haven’t marked each other, but Kia still gets weak because she and Jace have mated and accepted each other. They are just waiting for Zander and me to accept each other, too, and complete the bond. I don’t want to put that strain on her despite how much I am hurt by his actions. I know I need to do this to stay strong/

Kia hasn’t said much to me since the party. I think she is mad and frustrated, and considering we haven’t told anyone we are mates; she is finding it hard not to speak to her elders. She has blocked her feelings from me for now. I feel them when she can’t hold her wall up anymore, which is usually in the evenings, and I know when I need to go to the cottage.

It hurts that he quickly jumped into helping Grace or doing whatever he needed to do but forgot about me in the process. After all of our progress, I at least thought he trusted me enough to be ok to speak to me instead of ignoring me. So here I am on another evening, sitting on the window seat of the main bedroom, waiting for him again.

Tonight feels different, his pull usually is a light tug, making me want to go to him every time. But I have been strong, I have been firm, I know, he knows I’m here waiting for him. I sit by the window so he can see me. I look out into the woods surrounding the area and see a pair of gold eyes behind one of the trees, staring straight at me, waiting, watching.

My heart breaks as he just stands there, not wanting to be close to me, not wanting to feel my touch or hold me. I stare back at him. I am waiting for him to make a choice. He told me I was his. He gave me the heirloom. He told me I was his Luna. He needs to choose because I can’t keep on doing this anymore. I don't know how much longer I can. I don't even know if I can reject him.

He doesn't do anything. He just stands there waiting. After a little while, he drops to the floor and puts his snout on his front paws, stretching out. It makes me wonder if Jace is in more control tonight which is why he is closer? It still hurts knowing that if that was Jace, he didn't want to come to me either. Maybe he is trying to help clear Zander's mind.

A stray tear rolls down as I watch him sitting there. I debate with myself if I should go to him or not. Part of me screams yes, run to him. Make him see I am trying to help. But my more rational and diplomatic side is saying this is his choice. He needs to decide. I can't do this for him. I can't force him to be here with me.

I break eye contact with him as my phone buzzes beside me, startling me. I can feel Kia becoming stronger quicker because we are closer to him tonight. Taking a deep breath, I look down to see who sent me a message.

***Mum: hi, honey . I'm just checking in. Do you need me to contact the school tomorrow and the next day that you won't be there?**

***Ashleigh: Hi, mum. Yes, please I might skip for the rest of the week if that is okay.**

***Mum: Sure, honey, that is ok. Dad and uncle have a few things they need to do for the other packs, so I'll ask if you and Oliver can do them instead. Get you introduced to everyone.**

***Ashleigh: Sure. Sounds good.**

***Mum: Will you be home tonight?**

***Ashleigh: I'm not sure. I will let you know if I am.**

***Mum: ok, honey. Love you. Be safe.**

I shut off my phone after the last message mum sends. I look back to where Zander was and see he disappeared again. I can still feel him through our bond. He is just not in sight anymore. I guess the human side won.

~

It's about 2 am by the time I head home. I can feel he is no longer around. I wonder how Jace allowed him to leave us alone, how he has allowed him to not come to us. My mind is so messy with this situation. I wouldn't even know what to say to him. But at least I am willing to try and work this out. Willing to still be together if he'd just come and talk to me.

As I run through the woods, I can scent him all around. I wondered if it was his way of marking the territory or letting me know he was here. Either way, I'm still pissed at him. If I am to forgive him after all of this, he needs to show me he will never do this again, that he will never choose another over me.

My mind scrambles as I get home and into my bed. I crave his touch. I miss him like crazy, but I know he needs to choose. I have shown him that I still accept our bond, that I am willing.

As my head hits my pillow, my thoughts still ramble on and on. I can feel Kia stir in the back of my mind. She feels stronger than the other nights, most likely because he was closer to us tonight.

I send a prayer to the moon goddess before my tired eyes close, praying that everything will be ok. Praying that soon, I will no longer have this gaping hole in my chest.

Chapter 42 - ASHLEIGH

“Hey, you ready to go?” Ollie asks as I head down the stairs.

“Going where?” I ask back, looking back at him.

“We have a few things to do around the other packs. We have to head to Riverview and Westfield this morning then Charwood later this afternoon,” Ollie states.

“Charwood?” I choked out.

I nearly stumble down the last two steps as he mentions Charwood. I don’t want to see him in his territory. This is not how I imagined a conversation would go if I see him today.

Ollie raised an eyebrow, questioning, “yeah, is that ok?”

I hesitate before answering, “I guess.”

I shrug. I can’t do much about it if Dad and Uncle have asked us to go out.

I grab a bagel off the kitchen counter before heading to the front door to wait for Ollie. Before long, we are in his car heading out to our first two meetings. I hoped Westfield wouldn't give us crap for last weekend. I was so busy thinking about everything else that I totally forgot about the little incident with Lachlan.

I was curious why the Alpha from Charwood wanted to meet with uncle. Usually, they stick to their side of the city, and we stick to ours. Riverview and Westfield need our alliance to keep the businesses going, as some of theirs are on our land. We take a small percentage of their yearly make as compensation.

As much as humans like to think, they run the city with their rules and laws. I don't think they realize how big our population is and how many businesses we have. We have everything from transport and shipping to law firms, police, schools, hospitals, supermarkets, and many more. Between Liverpool and Charwood, wolves own the majority of the city. Hence why, uncle and dad are always out as often as they are. They do have advisors and accountants to help keep everything in check and ensure everything is up to code.

I remember I was about thirteen years old when I heard them talking to each other about these different businesses. I was so engrossed in their conversation that, after a while, I picked up on what they were talking about and started asking all the questions about the rules, restrictions, and different businesses they owned.

That was truly the first time I was interested in my father's position as Beta. Until then, I never really knew what he did every day. I just knew he would be home to have dinner at the end of the day, and we would still have a roof over our heads and money to buy things.

Over the last few years, as my interest piqued and I started to figure out what I wanted to do after school, it was good to get the bearings of my role until Oliver and I took over as leaders, so here we were stepping up to fill our future positions. As far as I knew, I wouldn't necessarily need to be doing any more of these trips as Zander is my mate. However, I still have a duty to my pack and Ollie until I switch to his pack, which, at the moment, seems like a lifetime away.

The first two meetings went as well as they could. Of course, Westfield was pissed we raised the percentage again. I think they were lucky it was only by the usual amount and nothing higher considering the current inflation rate.

If they continued with their bullshit and with what happened on Saturday night. I would have bumped it up even higher and not taken their shit, but the first lesson Dad taught me was relationship building, making a point on moving past it all. You don't have to forget but use it to your advantage. So that's what I did. I bit my tongue and let Ollie do the talking before I said anything damaging to the pack's relationship.

Riverview was easy going. We shared most of the transport and freight lines with them as most of their border was along the coastline, and we each shared a percentage of any shipments and transportation that moved through. We have always had an easy-going relationship with them. Hopefully, it'll stay that way for a long time.

I am a nervous wreck as we move through the other side to Charwood. I'd never met Zander's father before. I was never allowed to attend yearly council meetings, and he had never shown interest in coming to our territory. It made me a bit uneasy that we were going into his territory without any backup. But as much as Zander and I have our issues at the moment, I would like to think he wouldn't allow anything to happen to Ollie or me.

Ollie keeps glancing at me every five seconds like he knows something is up. As if on cue, he asks, "You ok? I can feel your nervous energy from here."

"Huh? ahh yeah," I nod, looking out to the city passing by.

I see his eyes roll in my peripheral vision, "What's up, Ash? You have been all distant and weird lately."

"It's nothing, I promise," I mumble. I don't want to discuss the mate topic with him, especially considering it is Zander.

"Ash..." Ugh, he is not going to let this go, I mean, I did want to tell people, right, but that was before the humiliation.

I sigh heavily before trying to figure out what to tell Ollie. Either way, he would be pissed that I didn't tell him I had found my mate.

"Just, please don't be mad. I was trying to figure stuff out first. I... I found my mate," I mumbled the last bit softly.

Ollie swerved the car slightly before looking back at me with wide eyes before facing the road again.

"And he is from Charwood." I cringeat the last bit. Honestly, the pack he came from didn't matter to me, but I knew Ollie's history with them.

He sighs and scrubs a hand over his face. "Who?"

"Aww, come on, please don't make me tell you. Just not until I have figured some stuff out, okay?"

He gives me a look and sighs in defeat. " Okay, is everything okay. Do you wanna talk about it?"

I guess my distant look didn't fool anybody.

"I suppose everything isn't okay just yet, maybe one day," I smile sadly. I still had a little hope. That was the hope of the bond. He hadn't destroyed that as much as he had destroyed me. I hoped we could rebuild and that this isn't beyond repair.

I am still willing to repair the relationship if that is what he wants. I still care for him. He's my mate. I haven't ever felt so connected with anyone until him.

He nods as we sit in silence for the rest of the trip. I feel weird as we pull up to the border of Charwood. It's a bittersweet moment, One I had hoped I would get to do with Zander, not Ollie.

"Ready?" Ollie asked as we pull up to the packhouse, shutting off the engine and getting ready to head out.

I look over to Ollie and respond, "as I'll ever be." I close my eyes and take a deep breath opening the car door and following Ollie to the front of the packhouse.

I know he's here. I feel him through our bond. Kia stirred in the depth of my mind. I'm glad I could still feel her after all of this. I don't know if there had been any damage to our bond with us not being close to our mate. But I can still sense her feelings and her movements. I didn't shifted yet. I don't want that to cause more strain than there already is.

Some part of me doesn't want to be here, but I have a duty to my pack. So, I tuck away all my emotions and hold myself confidently as we wait by the front door.

Daniel opens the front door with a big cheeky grin. "Good afternoon, Alpha Oliver and Beta Ashleigh."

I hear someone coughing in the house as Daniel opens the door wide enough to let us enter the front room.

It is a beautiful packhouse, very modern with an open floor plan. The open and spacious foyer led to the kitchen on the left with a lovely glass staircase leading upstairs to the first floor. There was a 30 to 40-seat solid wooden table running in the middle of the kitchen with white seats. Behind the table, two sets of double glass doors open to the backyard, with a magnificent infinity pool and spa looking out to the cliffs. The crisp white flowing curtains matched the Hampton-style foyer and kitchen that flow through to the upstairs living area.

I looked around in awe. I love this place. It is absolutely breathtaking. It breaks my heart a little more that Zander doesn't want to share this with me.

As I look around, my eyes collide with intense hazel ones, staring at me in disbelief. His scent engulfs meand it is suddenly harder to breathe. I fidget, a little uneasy with his gaze. I didn't realize he wouldn't want me to be here. I at least thought he would be somewhat happy that I was here. I could feel Kia stirring. She is already ten times stronger than she had been all week, nearly back to her full strength.

"Can I get either of you something to drink or eat before the meeting starts?" Daniel asks, still grinning like a damn fool looking between Ollie and me as if there is some inside joke only he knew about.

I'm suddenly brought back to reality that it's not just Zander and me in this room. Ollie knows I have a mate, just not who, and right now, if he knew it was Zander, that would probably not be the best thing.

"I'm fine for now, thank you," I turn back to Daniel and respond with a forced smile. I could feel Zander's gaze still on me as we stood there waiting.

"Yeah, me too. I'm all good," Ollie says, nodding.

"All righty then, Alpha Wyatt will be with you shortly," Daniel says, his eyes glazed over as he shoves his hands in his pockets and walks over to the kitchen, joining Zander behind the counter.

After what felt like the most awkward five minutes of my life, we hear voices coming from the corridor on the right. I try to compose myself again. I know Zander hasn't taken his eyes off me. I can still feel his intense gaze. Some part of me just wants to forget this stupid problem and just run to him and kiss him and claim him as mine, but he hasn't made any move that he wants me here, and honestly, that hurt more.

Thankfully, I have enough common sense not to wear the heirloom he gave me. I didn't want to freak anyone out today by parading that around. I wasn't wearing anything too fancy, just a nice light grey pantsuit with a long-sleeved white top and black heels. Ollie was wearing a black pantsuit matched with a crisp white top. We needed to look professional today, not only for Charwood but all the packs. If Ollie and I were going to be doing more of our duties to help our parents, we needed to make an excellent first impression.

Two men emerged from the corridor. They were older gentlemen. One looked very similar to Zander, and the other was similar to Daniel. I figured these must be Alpha Wyatt and Beta Jake.

"Alpha Oliver and Beta Ashleigh, Welcome to Charwood, I am Alpha Wyatt, and this is Beta Jake. Shall we step into my conference room and start the meeting?"

Alpha Wyatt's introduction was interrupted by someone thundering down the stairs behind him. They both turn around and part a little for Ollie and me to see who the person was.

"Ahh, Grace, how did you find the guest room next to Zanders? Was it to your liking?" Alpha Wyatt asks.

I swear heart stopped for a second. I feel the blood drain from my face. Did he just say what I think he said? My eyes snap to Zander to confirm. I chant a silent prayer, please, please don't be true.

Zander's eyes are closed. I'm unsure if it is in frustration, if he is trying to calm himself down or if it is to avoid my gaze.

"Oh yes, it's perfect. Thank you, Alpha. I think it will do nicely for me and the little one." She smiles sweetly while rubbing her tummy, moving closer to Zander and Daniel in the kitchen. "We have an appointment with the doctor this afternoon, and I've nearly finished packing up my apartment so I can move in this weekend."

Kia whines in the back of my mind. I feel her pain. I feel my pain. It is agonizing. I am trying my best not to let everything show. First and foremost, I am Liverpool's Beta, and right now, personal issues could not stand in the way of this meeting.

"Sure, I'm sure Zander and Daniel can lend a hand with moving your things."

Alpha Wyatt gestures towards the boys in the kitchen. Daniel is looking at Zander with a frown on his face. It seems his happy-go-lucky mood is gone. That's a shame because we could probably use some of that right now.

Daniel suddenly moved back around the front of the kitchen. He heads towards us, "Anyways, as much fun as it has been to see you both, I have training to do." Without any warning, he walks up to me and places a kiss on my cheek.

"Thanks for the party last weekend, doll. Next time just call me for one-on-one time, okay?" He tosses me a wink and is out the door before I could say anything or do anything.

I stand there, completely stunned at what had just happened. I quickly darted my eyes to Zander only to see that he is furious, with Jace flickering in his eyes. His glare fixed on the door behind Ollie and me.

"My apologies for my son. He gets a bit more friendly than necessary. Completely harmless of course but sometimes he doesn't know boundaries," Beta Jake says, rubbing his hand on the back of his neck, looking confused at his sons sudden behaviour.

I nod in confusion over what just happened and try to shake it off and move on with the meeting.

Alpha Wyatt claps his hands together and gestures toward the corridor they emerged from earlier. "Shall we move into the conference room to begin then?"

Ollie responds with “sure” and we follow them down the hall.

Chapter 43 - ZANDER

Last night Jace took control. He'd had enough of my moping and ignoring our mate. In my defense, I wasn't ignoring her. I was trying to figure everything out before going to her about it so that I would know the answers to her questions. Is that so wrong? To want to be prepared?

But of course, Jace didn't agree with me at all. He wanted her comfort and wanted to comfort her. I didn't realize the pain I was putting her in. Seeing her there last night felt so vulnerable. I felt like such an ass not talking to her all week, I hadn't realized I was treating her like every other ex, but I should have. She is my mate. She's it, and I treated her like crap. I love her and don't even have the guts to tell her.

I was so taken back when she walked into my packhouse. I tried not to stare at her, but she looks so fucking amazing. My mind tries to scramble for what to say to her as they stood there. I went over and over everything and anything that wouldn't give away that we were mates. I guess I was thinking too long because Dad and Jake showed up and started talking to them.

As if my day couldn't get any fucking worse, Grace walks down the stairs like she owns the fucking place and starts blabbering.

My heart stops when she says she is moving in, which I hadn't officially confirmed yet. she went to Dad before anything else and asked for permission to move into the packhouse. And of course, the bitch told him she was pregnant, something which I should have told him. I carefully look at Ashleigh's reaction. She looks surprised and hurt, then as quickly as her emotions showed, she covered them.

Jace is pissed. I could feel him thrashing around. I try to calm him down, but he doesn't care. He wants his mate, and he nearly took control and went to her. I couldn't let that happen, not yet.

Pain shoots through my body as Danni kisses Ashleigh on the cheek. Fucking prick thinks he's so smug. I will beat him later for touching what's mine, and he'd better fucking watch it because I am not in the mood for his bullshit.

"Shall we move into the conference room to begin then?" Dad claps his hands together and gestures toward the corridor they emerged from earlier.

Oliver responds with "sure" and they turn to make their way to the conference room.

"Dad, isn't this something I should be a part of?" I blurt out, not wanting to move away from my mate.

The four of them stop suddenly and turn around to face me. Ashleigh avoids my gaze and moves her eyes around the packhouse while Oliver watches her curiously. I hate that I have made her hate me that much. I hate that I know this is my fucking fault.

"Babe, we have the appointment remember, silly," Grace giggles and tries to step closer to me, invading my space.

Jace let out a warning snarl telling her to back the fuck up. She stops, startled, her eyes lowering to the floor in submission.

"No, it's okay. I will fill you in when you get back. We were going to show them a few things around the pack and discuss some specifics. It shouldn't take too long," Dad says.

I see Oliver's eyes glaze over as he links Ashleigh. She looks at him, taken aback, but forces a small smile as Oliver turns to me with a glare.

I desperately try to find an excuse to be with my mate. "Danni can take Grace. I don't exactly need to."

"It's fine, Zander. You need to make sure all the tests and everything is done correctly anyway," Dad said, waving a dismissive hand.

I sigh in defeat. As much as I want to be with her right now, I couldn't. Jace is pissed we have to leave.

This is the most I've felt him all week. It feels good to feel him again, but at the same time, I knew how pissed off he is so part of me slightly worried if he would ever actually speak with me again.

They turn around and walk down the corridor to the conference room. Ashleigh darts one last look at me, our eyes locking. I could see her pain, whether she wanted to show me or not, she did, and it fucking broke my heart, seeing her hurt and knowing I caused that, her own fucking mate.

Scrubbing a hand over my face, I sighed to myself. Let's get this shit over with.

I walked towards the door without sparing Grace a glance or telling her we were going. I could hear her scramble behind me to try and catch up.

The drive to the clinic wasn't too far, maybe ten minutes without any traffic. However, considering this was a Thursday afternoon, school had finished, and late-night shopping is swinging into gear, it is noticeable that peak hour has started. I am stuck in traffic for the next fifteen minutes and Grace took that as an opportunity to talk.

"So, what should we call this little guy? I was told to do three girl names and three boy names. Do you want to know what the baby is? Like a boy or girl? I'm not sure yet. Maybe we will wait and see." She continues to babble as I sit there silently.

I want to talk about this stuff with Ashleigh, not Grace. I want my mate to be the one sitting in that seat talking about names and driving her to the clinic.

'Well, that's not going to happen any time soon now, is it?' Jace growls.

'You're back?' I could feel my face splitting into a stupid ass grin as I hear my wolf. Relief washes over me as I hear Jace's voice. I was going stir crazy for a little bit. I miss him.

'I was never gone dumbass, just pissed at you. I'm still pissed, by the way,' Jace mumbles.

'How do I fix this? I need my mate. We need our mate. I need you not to be mad at me anymore,' I beg.

'Build *a time machine to take you to when you met Grace, and don't meet her. Better yet, go back to as far as your first hook-up and don't hook up with anyone until our mate,'* Jace grumbles, glaring at me.

'I can't change my past, Jace,' I say, frustrated.

I glance over at Grace. She still hasn't noticed that I hadn't said anything. She is now scrolling through baby stores and making a list of things we would need.

'Let's get through today and see where this goes first. Then we can figure out how to speak to Ashleigh. You know if you just did that in the first place, we wouldn't be in this situation with her.' Jace says.

'I know, I know. I just couldn't face her disappointment or rejection,' I mumbles, leaning my head against the head seat for support.

We finally arrive at the clinic after being stuck in traffic for a brief time. Grace still hadn't asked me to repeat anything. She is still babbling away. I've just learned to tune her out.

Grace goes to the receptionist to confirm that she has arrived for her appointment. We didn't have to stay in the waiting room long as traffic took up most of the time before our 3.30 appointment. The first step is for the nurse to draw her blood to confirm the pregnancy. The second step is an ultrasound which is conducted while waiting for the lab results on the blood test.

Grace sits there chatting with the nurse, all bubbly and excited, while they took her blood. I sit silently staring at the ceiling.

"How long have you two been together?" the nurse asks, bringing me back to reality for a short moment.

"Nearly a year now," Grace answers happily.

"We're not together," I snap, glaring at her, "It was a casual hook-up, nothing more."

I see Grace bite her bottom lip, and tears start showing in her eyes. I roll my eyes at her exaggeration. She knew all of this, just trying to play the victim like she was the good one and I was the bad guy for ending things with her.

"My apologies," the nurse mutters as we sit silently for the rest of the time.

'Stupid humans,' I grumble to Jace as he paces at the back of my mind. Being too far away from our mate on our territory doesn't sit well with him.

"If you don't mind waiting here for a moment, someone will be in shortly to take you to the ultrasound labs," the nurse says, collecting everything before leaving.

"Thank you," Grace says softly as she left.

I am pissed off that I have to be here. It makes me angry that this isn't with Ashleigh. I should have been the one to show her around my pack grounds, not my father. And I should have been the one to introduce her to my father, not her cousin.

So many things went wrong today, and it fucking kills me that I'm not with my mate in that room with her. She barely showed any emotion when Grace was there, only a few flicks, but she stood there so gracefully, waiting.

'*She's our true Luna. what else did you expect?'* Jace mumbles.

'I don't know, maybe some sort of outburst, she couldn't leave that time, I guess, just something.' I sigh.

'*She is Liverpool's Beta. Her pack is her priority right now. Even if you are mates, you haven't accepted her as yours yet.'* Jace says.

'Yes, I have. I accepted her the moment I knew she was my mate. I gave her mum's heirloom,' I protested.

'If you accepted her as your mate and Luna, you would have gone to her about Grace instead of ignoring her. What do you expect Ashleigh to do when she comes to our pack, sit back and do nothing? She will have her duties, and she will help lead and make decisions for the pack. A Luna and Alpha are equals, not only you decide.'

"Fuck," I say out loud, accidentally banging my head against the wall. I hate that he is fucking right. I hate that I fucked up.

Grace looks up from her phone and turns to me with a frown.

“Everything okay?” She asks stupidly, blinking at me.

“No,” I growl. I am pissed that she even said anything to ruin the quiet.

"Wanna talk about it?"

"No," I repeat, closing my eyes and leaning on the back wall for support as a dull ache started in the back of my head.

"I'm here if you want to talk, Zander. We will be spending time together, so we might as well be friendly, right?"

I could feel Jace pushing forward, pissed off that she wanted to have some type of 'relationship or friendship' with me. Even after all of his warnings, she still keeps going. I just sit there silently waiting. Hopefully, she will get the hint that I'm not in a chatty mood today.

A few moments later, another nurse walks in with a clipboard and a few other items.

"Hi, I'm Sally. Let's get you two ready for an ultrasound, shall we?" She smiles and looks between us, waiting for someone to make the first move to get up. I sigh heavily, get up, and walk towards the door as Grace stands, rubbing her tummy. I try so hard not to roll my eyes at the way she is using this baby and it is starting to piss me off.

"So, we have taken your blood and are waiting on results. Your vitals are okay. Are there any concerns we should know about before the delivery and moving forward?" The nurse starts chatting as we walk into the next room.

This room isn't too bad, about the same size as the one before. It has different machines and probes I had never seen before. The lights are dimmed so you could see the screens. A bed is in the middle of the room, with a monitor and a few seats off to the side. I grab one of the seats leaning against the wall and sit back down again.

"Umm, well, our species is a bit different to humans, I guess, so It'll be a quicker process than the average nine months," Grace responds, darting over to me as I rest my head back against the wall. I didn't want to be a part of this, so I didn't have to sit here and answer all these damn questions.

"Ok perfect. Yes, I can see that you both are wolves here on the paperwork. That will be considered when the due date is. Jump up onto this bed for me, and we will get started," She motions to the bed as Grace takes off her shoes, climbs up, and lifts her top to show her belly.

"Okay, so this might be a little cold at first," The nurse nods as she put gel on the probe and lowered it to her stomach.

I frown as I hear Grace's heart race accelerates, and her breathing quickens like she's panicking. I look at her reaction as the nurse starts moving around her stomach. Beads of sweat form on her brow and her eyes dart around, avoiding eye contact. Something is fucking wrong here.

"May I ask why you decided to book the appointment today?" The nurse asks.

"Umm, I took a few pregnancy tests the other week, and they all returned positive," Grace squeaks.

"I'm sorry to say, Miss Hicks, but it seems those tests were incorrect. We have drawn blood with this visit today, so we will double check, but at this point, you are currently not pregnant according to the ultrasound."

"What," I growl, looking between Grace and the nurse. Grace has her head down, and silent tears are streaming down her cheeks. I feel Jace move, his anger pulsing through. "Give us a moment, please," I ask the nurse before turning back to Grace.

I am royally pissed, and I didn't give a shit. I nearly lost my mate over this, all for what? So, she could be Luna? Are you fucking kidding me? Her father is the fucking Alpha of her pack.

I try to calm down as the nurse left us in the room, "Sure, I'll give you guys a few moments. Let me know if you need anything. I will be back shortly with the blood results."

I close my eyes and take a deep breath before talking because as much as I am pissed off right now, I don't need to be provoked.

"Why?" I ask, trying to keep my cool, so Jace doesn't take control and rip her head off.

"I don't know," she whispers. My eyes snap open, glaring at her, furious with her answer, which we both fucking know is a lie.

"Don't give me that bullshit, Grace," I snarl, leaning forward and making her flinch away. I try to reel Jace in and not use his power against her, but right now, I am pissed off, and the more she lied, the more pissed I was getting and the more he showed.

"Do you even understand the damage you have caused?" I ask quietly, thinking about my beautiful mate and how much I hurt her over this.

She looks at me with teary eyes, trying to blink them away.

"Damage?" She asked, "I told you I loved you, and you broke up with me," she shrieks. "You asked me to come with you after training, so I did. I left my family's pack and came here."

"Let's get this through your head once and for all," I snapped. "We were never 'Official' as you women like to call it. You knew that, and you agreed to the terms. As for your family, your father asked if there was room in my pack for you to move so you could have a better future, graduate from a decent school, and maybe go to university and get a good job. It was not my doing bringing you here to be with me. And if you ever pull something like this again that will strain my mate and me, you will not get off so easily. I am only letting you off with a warning this one time because of the relationship with your parents and you being their daughter." I growl dangerously, some of my command slipping through on specific points.

She sits there opening and closing her mouth like a fish out of water. I couldn't be in this room with her anymore. I was visibly shaking and only just managing to have control over Jace.

"I will talk to my father about this. He will not agree to merge with you because of this," she snaps.

I shrug. I don't care if Alpha Samuel merges with us or not. His is a small pack of only about a hundred people. We were the ones doing him a favour.

"This was your fault, and your doing, Grace. You are lucky I don't throw you in the dungeon for this."

'Danni, you need to come and pick up Grace. I can't drive her home. Jace wants to kill her." I link him before heading out, leaving her sitting on the bed, looking at her lap with tears flowing down her face.

'What happened?' Danni's voice rang through.

'She fucking faked the whole thing. I can't be in the same room as her or anywhere near her now. Jace wants to kill the bitch,' I growl.

'Ahh, shit! I'll call her father and tell him she needs to go home. Probably best if she doesn't stick around. Her stuff is already packed anyways. I will be there in fifteen.'

'Thanks. Ahh, are Ashleigh and Oliver still around?' I ask. I know I would probably get shit from him asking that question, but I need to know if she is still there.

'Na, they left around thirty mins ago,'

'Fuck, ok, thanks.'

Sighing as I shut off the link and walk to the waiting room, going up to the desk and letting the receptionist know someone else is coming to pick up Grace. They frown at me and nod but don’t say anything, thankfully.

I need to find Ashleigh. I need to make it right with my mate like I should have done from the fucking beginning.

Chapter 44 - ZANDER

Frustrated with everything, I try to think over and over again what the fuck I'm going to say to Ashleigh as I pull up to Liverpool's border. I don't have an appointment they know of. Considering Oliver and Ashleigh had a little over an hour's head start, I hoped that this was where she would be instead of the cottage.

"What is your purpose for being here?" The warrior asked, eyeing me down and looking around in my car for any signs of danger. He could sense I was Charwood just as I could sense he was Liverpool, even if they didn't know who I was.

I could see one or two pairs of eyes back in the woods surrounding the border before opening into the clearing where the main homes and packhouse were. It wasn't just us out here. There were a few of them around but hidden amongst the trees.

"I'm here to see Beta Ashleigh," I respond, looking at him directly in the eye, using only a little of my command, so he knows I am a ranked wolf.

"Beta Ashleigh does not have any appointments with Charwood."

"Something came up," I say.

"Something came up?" he mimics back, almost mockingly.

I pull back my snarl at the disrespect. He is starting to piss me off, and with the day I've had, you do not want to be on my wrong side. I take a deep breath and try to explain without giving anything away. "Alpha Oliver and Beta Ashleigh were just in my territory. I still had a few things to discuss with them before I left for an appointment. I, unfortunately, didn't make it back in time before they left." I try to sway this prick, reasoning with him to let me cross the border.

His eyes glaze as he links someone to check out my story and hopefully confirm if I would be allowed to cross.

"Beta Kylie is at the packhouse. You can speak with her," he states before stepping aside and letting me through.

I opened my mouth to protest, but he had already turned around and headed back towards the tree line, shifting and running another border check. I sit there stunned at the interaction I just had with their warrior. I wonder if that is normal behaviour or because I was Charwood?

Her mother is the last person I want to see right now, especially if she knows we are mates. I'm sure Ashleigh would have told her what happened. I did not want to face an angry mother right now.

I guess I didn't have much of a choice as they left me there. I know they were still around, following me carefully but giving me space as I drove. It is different from the other weekend. Going through now is more eerie. It is quiet, not the usual hustle and bustle. A few people are still around, the number slowly building up as I drove through the suburb.

It was different from the night-time. You could see the houses more prominently. There is a park in the middle of the square with some children running around, and a small soccer game had started. I smile at the innocence. As much as I had the Alpha blood, I sometimes just wanted to be a normal kid and not have any responsibility, but I didn't have that choice. I learned to love and enjoy it over time and gain respect from my pack members. Now I am happyish...

I've been sitting in the car in front of the Liverpool packhouse for about three minutes now. I don't know what to say to Ashleigh, let alone her mother. I sigh and eventually open the door and get out. I don't think I've ever been this nervous. Even when taking my final exams in training, I wasn't this fucking nervous. I walked up to the packhouse door and tapped on it twice.

"Alpha Zander, Welcome. I'm Beta Kylie," She smiled warmly, opens the door, and holds an arm out, allowing me to enter the packhouse.

"Would you like anything to drink? Coffee? Tea? Cookies?" she rattled off a few things as she walks me towards the kitchen. I smile at the similar trait Ashleigh shares with her mother.

Their packhouse has an older unique style compared to ours. We had ours redone when mum died. I guess Dad wanted new memories rather than reliving the old ones. Liverpool still has some excellent modern finishes but a few nice old touches to complement.

"Umm... Coffee would be great, actually," I say, sliding onto one of the bar stools.

Kylie nods and starts running around the kitchen, getting some things together. I couldn't help but glance up the stairs and down the hall every few seconds, waiting if someone would come out any minute now.

"They are all out this afternoon, so it's just you and me," she smiles, passing the coffeeand putting a plate of biscuits and cake on the counter.

"Ashleigh?" I ask, feeling my cheeks burn with embarrassment as I wonder about my mate.

"Also out, said something about going for a run or training. Probably both knowing her," she responds, sipping her coffee and watching my reaction carefully. I nod, sighing as I take a sip of the warm beverage, trying to think with my scrambled brain what to talk to her mother about.

"I'm sorry for what I put her through. I just didn't know how to speak to her about it. If anything, I was worried she would reject me," I say after what seemed like forever. I'm sorry was a better start than any. It felt like a huge weight had lifted as I exposed my greatest fear to someone.

She nods, "I know, or you wouldn't be here. Tell me something, though. Do you expect my daughter just to stand around waiting for you while you have a child with this other girl?"

"She's not pregnant," I respond quickly, not wanting her mother to get any more wrong ideas. "And either way, if she were or weren't pregnant, I would have tried to speak with her today about it all. I know my wolf wasn't allowing it any longer, and I had a few more answers I was more comfortable giving after today's appointment."

"You really think Ashleigh cared about answers?" She asked, tilting her head slightly and looking at me.

"I don't know what she wanted, but I at least wanted to be prepared for something, to give her some answers for peace of mind instead of stressing about the situation."

Kylie laughs softly at my response and sips her coffee.

"What?" I ask, confused.

"She didn't want answers, Zander. She just wanted her mate. Answers would have come in time. But she just wanted you to choose her."

"I chose Ashleigh. Why is everyone saying I didn't," I snap.

Kylie raises an eyebrow at my outburst. I sigh, scrubbing my hand over my face in defeat. "I'll buy her stuff, clothes, handbags, jewellery, whatever she wants or needs. She can have it."

"You really don't know my daughter if that is your line of thinking on how to get her back," Kylie says, shaking her head and sipping more of her coffee.

"Then what am I supposed to do?" I sigh, frustrated with this conversation. Before, women used to be easy for me. When they were pissed at me, I'd buy them something pretty or shiny, or I'd move on to the next one. With her, though, with Ashleigh, there was no next one. She was it. I know in my heart, in my mind. She is everything.

"Be there for her," Kylie responds so fucking casually as if it was the most obvious thing to do.

I open my mouth to protest, to explain I know her and was there for her, but my train of thought was disrupted by voices outside getting closer to the packhouse.

"I should get going. Thanks for the coffee," I sigh before putting down my empty mug.

"Would you like to stay for dinner?" she asks as I move towards the door.

"Ahh, I think I should probably speak with Ashleigh before family dinners. I don't know if she wants people to know she is my mate. Thanks for the invite, though, but maybe next time." I nod before opening the door.

As I head out the door, Oliver, and Brent are walking towards the front of the packhouse in gym gear. I feel everything accelerate as I look around frantically to see if she is nearby.

'We *would have felt her or scented her if she was near,'* Jace mumbles at my stupidity.

"You have some fucking nerve showing up here," Oliver growls, his wolf flashing though projecting dominance.

Frowning, I started walking down the stairs and head towards my car, which is, unfortunately, behind Oliver. Brent is cautiously looking between us, waiting for something to happen.

"Look, man, I don't know what you are talking about," I mumble, knowing that was a fucking lie. He either found out I was his cousin's mate or that I fucked his girl a few years back, or maybe a few other things, too, but those two were my top pick.

I move closer to my car, but he blocks my path as I try to move around him and Brent.

"Fine then. Are we gonna hash this out, or are you gonna bitch like a little girl?" I sigh, folding my arms across my chest, frustrated with this stupid schoolyard play.

As if on cue, he swings back, clocks me right in the jaw, and shoves me into the car. Surprised by the action, I grab onto the hood for balance as my mouth pools with blood.

Oliver leans in and whispers lowly, so Brent couldn't hear, "If you ever hurt her again like you have this past week, your jaw won't be the only thing you have to worry about." His eyes flash dangerously as his wolf pushes forward, delivering the threat.

Jace growls and shoves forward at the challenge, but I pulled him back down because I know I fucking deserve that, and if that's all it took for me to get on Oliver's good side, then I'll take that any fucking day. Because for her, anything is worth it.

He backs away and walks up the stairs and into the packhouse as if nothing fucking happened. Brent stood there looking stunned and a bit out of place.

I get off the hood, spit the blood out of my mouth, and wipe the excess off with my sleeve. The pain had already stopped, and I could feel it healing. By the time I get home, there would be no evidence that he sucker punched me.

I give Brent a small salute as I backed out of the driveway. He shrugs and goes into the packhouse.

I lean my head against the headrest and sigh as I drive away from Liverpool. I know I didn't see her today, but it feels like her family is slowly accepting that she is mine.

Chapter 45 - ASHLEIGH

Exhausted after everything, I didn't want to go to the cottage last night. I knew Kia had enough strength to last me one more night. As much as I hated the interaction with him yesterday, even if he said nothing, it was good to be in the same room as him. I needed to see his decision which he so clearly made. Whether he knew it or not, he chose her, and I am officially finished with him. I tried everything, I gave him a choice, and he chose her.

So here I am on what is supposed to be the happiest day of our school year, sulking in my bedroom on my bed while Chloe is in the bathroom getting ready for our school formal. Every girl looks forward to the formal in their senior year. Every girl looks forward to being asked out by their crush and hopes they like them back, or my mate. A part of me wants him to show up tonight and pick me up, but the other half doesn't want to face the embarrassment of my family. Only two people know that he's my mate. And for now, I'd like to keep it that way.

“What do you think?” Chloe comes out of my bathroom and does a little spin, letting her beautiful golden hair flow down around her. She looked stunning in her maxi mint green gown and golden accessories. The front has a sweetheart neckline, off the shoulders, and no straps with a light white lace pattern of flowers embedded on some of the front and around half the waist.

“You look amazing, babe, truly.” I smile.

She looks at me and frowns, seeing me still in my comfy tracksuit and shirt. “Why haven't you gotten ready yet?”

I sigh and lay back in my bed, staring at the ceiling. “I don't think I'm going,” I mumble. I don't want to see him with her, the one he chose over me. I don't want to see him at all tonight. As much as I cared for him before, it was just Kia's feelings for Jace or the mate bond at work. He destroyed the last bit of love I had for him yesterday. I came back home, and mum knew instantly something was wrong. I still haven't spoken with her yet. I don't know if I can.

So, after my run, I snuck through the back door without dinner last night and went straight to my room, thankfully avoiding everyone. Ollie knew something was wrong on the way home. He asked if Zander is my mate when we were back at Charwood's packhouse. I

t's annoying how observant he is sometimes. Of course, he caught my reaction and realized what happened before I could confirm. He didn't press for any answers on the way home, as much as I could tell he wanted to. But I also didn't want to talk about it. During the meeting, there were parts where I should have spoken up but remained quiet. I was mulling over what happened. It probably hasn't helped anything, but I can't just switch it off. That's why I went for a run yesterday until my body ached, and Kia let all of her anger out. Today I tried to keep my mind busy and study for most of the day because I missed a fair bit this week since I stayed home, so I wanted to catch up.

“Ok, who is he?” She asks as I look up at her and see her arms folded across her chest and a stern look on her face.

“Who is who?” I ask, trying to sound offended, but my voice came out as a small squeak.

“Come on, babe, you haven’t ever been this sad or depressed before, and well, if it’s not a guy, then what?”

I sigh. If I can’t share my problems with my best friend, what’s the point of having one?

“Please don’t make this a big deal, ok? I’m just trying to figure out a lot of stuff.”

She frowns and steps forward, sinking into the space beside me on the bed. “Babe, I’m here for you if you need me. What’s up?”

I suck in a sharp breath before telling her. I know I might get a bit of backlash for not telling her weeks ago when I found out he was my mate.

“I found my mate, and right now, it’s just a bit complicated. I’m just trying to figure stuff out before letting people know. So far, only you, mum, and Ollie know.”

Her eyes fly wide at my statement, knowing I had found my mate. A massive wave of relief washes over me, not having to keep the most important secret from my best friend anymore.

“Are you okay?” She asked, gently rubbing one of my legs in comfort.

“Hopefully I will be one day. But right now, it’s just a bit messy, and I can’t see him tonight. I just don’t want to face any more humiliation,” I say softly.

Kia had gone back into hibernation after the run last night, trying to preserve her strength. She knows I don’t want to see him for a few days. I feel her move around a bit. And yesterday, she talked to me about a few things, but she’s hurting and trying not to let me feel that hurt, or it might completely destroy me. If this is what it feels like to not be around him without a rejection, I can only imagine what it'll be like when he rejects me.

“Come on,” Chloe tugs at me. I frown at her. Did I not tell her I wasn’t going tonight?

She sighs and says, “you are not letting some ass hat of a guy ruin the best day of our senior year. You get up and wear that beautiful gown we bought months ago. You show him that you are not bothered by him being a stupid dick, that you are a strong independent woman, and if he is going to make things difficult for you, then you are going to make things difficult for him and live your life, show him what he is missing.” She encourages, tugging on me again.

“But...” I begin to protest.

“No buts, babe, this will be good for you, you haven’t been at school all week, and it’ll be nice to see some of our friends. We are sitting at a table with everyone else, away from everything. It might not be as bad as you think.”

I sighed and looked over at the beautiful flowing dusty pink gown hanging on the closet door. It really would be a waste if I didn’t wear it tonight. I had already bought my graduation dress, so one of them wouldn’t be worn if I didn’t go tonight. It was a beautiful dress with embedded flowers woven all through it. The shoulders would be halfway down, just resting on my arms.

"Fine," I sigh heavily and scramble off my bed.

Chloe grins, clapping in triumph, and starts rambling about what I need to do in the next hour to get ready.

"First, we should do your hair, that takes the longest, and then we will do makeup."

Over an hour passed by the time she had fixed my hair and makeup. I am standing in front of my dress before putting it on. When I chose it, I had hoped I would have met my mate by now. I so wanted to be with him tonight. As much as I hate to admit it, I still wish I had tonight. Even after everything, I still wish he is picking me up and that I could be with him one more time.

The chatter grew louder as I open my bedroom door and head down the stairs into the room full of our family and friends.

Victoria is hanging off Ollie as he talks with Brent and some of his mates. I see Chloe and Skyla by the kitchen, getting a few drinks and I make my way to them. They turn around and smile when I got closer. I lean in and hug Skyla as she moves forward. I was sad she couldn't get ready with us, but it’s nice she was able to come over for drinks beforehand.

Skyla is wearing a beautiful flowing blue dress, a lace-up corset bodice held by delicate shoulder straps, and flairs dramatically at the bottom, letting it all flow around her. She looked stunning.

Mum and dad make their way through the crowd holding a camera and waving it in the air. "We need to get a few photos of you kiddies before you head off," she calls, smiling between the girls and me, leaning in to give me a big hug.

"You're not wearing it?" she asks quietly, pulling back and putting a stray hair back in its place.

I suck in a sharp breath, knowing exactly what she was referring to, "I can't, not after yesterday," I whisper softly, shaking my head. I debated for hours whether I should wear the gift he gave me on my birthday, and after yesterday, as much as it broke my heart, I can't wear it, knowing it means something so significant. I won't stand around and wait for him anymore, not after the choice he made.

She smiles sadly and squeezes my hand, "Maybe just put it in your purse, in case you change your mind?"

I frown but nod. Our purses and coats are in my room, so I would have to remember to get it before heading out.

"Photo time?" Mum called around, getting everyone's attention.

We all make our way toward the center of the room, trying to scramble around each other for a photo. We took one with all of us, then just the girls and guys separately, and then a couple with the three of us. Mum also wanted a few with Ollie, me, and Brent.

After what seemed like forever with the photos, someone announces that the hummer is here to pick us up and take us to the hall.

We pull up to a beautiful-looking venue, a loop driveway with a massive fountain in the middle spraying out water continuously, a beautiful stone staircase leading up to magnificent double doors already wide open, allowing everyone access.

We all wait in line to go through the double doors. It was magnificent and rich with character, some other students are looking around in amazement. A marble staircase with gold trim on the banister leads up. A 'do not enter' sign is fixed across a red rope with a guard in a black suit standing off to the side, not allowing access to anyone.

A large board on the side of another double door entrance leads into a room filled with tables covered with white , tablecloths with flower centrepieces. The board had a list of names with table numbers. Each table has 10-15 people sitting around.

Walking into the next room, there is a massive stage in the middle with a wooden floor one would assume is for dancing. You could see outside the tall glass floor-to-ceiling windows all around this second room. The outside looks beautiful, with a fresh white gazebo beautifully lit with fairy lights and climbing roses. The lake behind the gazebo shimmers in the moonlight and lights.

It was such a chaotic moment, getting seated and ensuring we had the right seats. Thankfully, Chloe was on the committee that put this all together for us, so she knows where everything is. She grabs one of my hands and one of Skyla's and leads the way to our table. It is in a lovely spot, just in the corner, where we had a beautiful outside view. I could look out there all evening if I were allowed.

"I was able to grab the best seats in the venue," She smiled happily. "Look how gorgeous this view is!"

Ollie and some of his friends joined our table and started chatting about the final few weeks of our year leading up to the graduation ceremony.

I was chatting with Skyla and a girl named Harper when Kia moved around slightly and murmured, '*Mate*,'

My eyes darted all around, looking for him, and my heart accelerated as I got a wave of his scent of sweet honey and wildflowers.

These few days have been hard, and as much as I have made up my mind, it's hard to resist the mate bond.

I look at the doors we have just entered and see his beautiful hazel eyes staring straight at me. He moves closer, trying to close the gap between us, but one of his friends next to him grabbed his attention and pointed to the other side of the room. He turned back, nodded, and followed his friends to their table. He looked so handsome in his dark tux, with a fresh white top, so alluring I couldn't help but allow my eyes to follow him to his table.

Throughout the evening, my eyes kept darting over to Zander. He caught me once or twice, our eyes locking in a few seconds before one of us was pulled away into a conversation we were having around the table.

How is it that even though this one person has hurt me so much, all I want to do right now is to let him hold me, to feel the sparks and electricity through us once more?

I fiddle with the heirloom he gave me under the table. I haven't put it in my hair yet. I don't know if I will but having it in my hands makes me want to re-think everything and question if I was making the right choice in letting him go.

Ollie darts his eyes over to me now and then, a silent question asking if I am all right. I guess he can sense the internal struggle I am having right now. I send him a small smile to try to reassure him.

After our three-course meal, the DJ starts up the music and tries to encourage everyone to dance. After one or two failed attempts, he puts on Head and Heart by Joel Corry, and a few girls squeal and run to the center and start swaying to the music. Before long, the dancefloor was filled with some students dancing and getting into the swing of things.

Bobby dragged Chloe off to dance with him. She looked so happy and at peace with him. It would be interesting to see if they ended up being mates in a few weeks on her birthday.

"Are you ok, hun," Skyla asked, pulling me out of my daydream.

"Yeah, hun, I'm fine. I might go for a walk and get some fresh air. I feel a bit stuffy in here," I smiled back and started to get up, making my way towards the exit to the waterfront.

"Ok, we will be here when you get back," Skyla called out before turning back to Harper and some others on our table.

I stood in front of the shimmering lake. It was beautiful this evening. Even though it was a cold winter evening, being a wolf helped, but Kia was slightly weaker, so I felt the chill in the air more than I usually would.

The cold helped the pain that consumed me as I stood in front of the water, fiddling with the heirloom, sucking in the fresh air, feeling more at peace than I had all week. My mind was clear, and my heart was clear.

'Mate,' Kia whispers, and I'm smacked with his scent engulfing all around me. I try not to let him affect me as I feel him move closer to me, closing the gap between us.

I don't need to turn around to know when he is standing only a few feet away.

He couldn't just let me have this one night where I tried to enjoy myself without dealing with our problems.

Chapter 46 - ZANDER

When I left Liverpool after speaking with her mother, I went straight to the cottage to see if that's where she was. I even stayed a few hours into the night. But she never showed. I knew it was because of Grace. For the last few days, she would come to the cottage, but after the interaction at the packhouse, nothing.

I debated for hours during the night and this morning whether I should pick her up or not. I even went to the car and got in once or twice, but I convinced myself that she wouldn't want that, that she was already pissed off enough as it is. And throwing gasoline on the fire would only end up with me getting burnt or worse.

Danni watched me running back and forth like a mad man with a stupid smirk on his face. He knows I'm still pissed at him for pulling the stunt he did. But I guess it fucking worked because now I'm more territorial over her and more wound up.

I've had to shove Jace down a few times when Danni was around, so he doesn't rip his head off. He should have known doing something like that would only aggravate my wolf.

A few guys, including Eric and Billy, came into the packhouse carrying a case of beer and started drinking and chatting before it was time to go. Only one or two had dates looking a bit out of place with the lack of girls around. The guys wanted a night to blow off steam and chill without drama. Unfortunately for me, my mind was spinning like a mad house, wondering if my mate would show.

My head was still spinning, my heart was thumping, my hands were all clammy, and my breathing accelerated as the hummer pulled up to the venue. I was fucking worse than I was yesterday pulling up to Liverpool packhouse . Even now, the alcohol didn't help numb the nerves.

It was a nice enough place. Half the chicks had their phones out taking photos or some poor bloke escorting them was trying to take a not-so-posed photo for their Instagram account. I smirked at some of the suckers who were already whipped, not even by their mates.

Jace scoffed and snickered. '*Don't you laugh. You were like a lost little puppy today without Ashleigh.*'

'Was not,' I mumbled back.

We lined up, waiting to get our names marked off and heading into the area to have our dinner. As soon as I enter, I'm smacked with her scent. Jace is up, pacing around in an instant. I spot her at the far table in the corner closest to the outside windows. She looks amazing. Her beauty completely captives me. The flowing pink gown is fucking amazing on her.

I can feel Jace push forward possessively, wanting to claim her. She must have caught my scent or realized I was watching her as her eyes dart around looking for me. She goes rigid when her eyes land on me. I see a flash of hurt move through her eyes.

Jace whines when he sees the pain I caused my mate. He wants to comfort her, to be with her. I move closer toward her, letting the tugging sensation of the bond guide me, but Billy grabs my attention and points to the other side of the room where our table is. Reluctantly I follow them to the table.

All night my eyes seem to gaze over to her, seeing her chatting with her friends. Thankfully, she is seated between her two girlfriends, or that would have been a bigger problem. Once or twice, I caught her looking at me, seemingly having difficulty herself in resisting the pull of the mate bond.

I guess not seeing her last night made it harder on us both. I'm sitting here fidgeting, distracted most of the night, just wanting to be close to her. It's harder to control Jace when she is in the same room as me. I can scent her. I can feel her.

At least before, I could only feel her. Jace was going crazy, but not this crazy. I could at least control him before.

The guys haven't caught on to my unusual behaviour. They are too piss drunk to notice.

For what seems like the nth time tonight, I look over at Ashleigh's table only to find her spot empty. I get annoyed realizing that I didn't notice her leave or see where she went to.

'*Use the bond,'* Jace internally rolls his eyes at me. He's anxious to be near our mate, egging me to go to her.

"Bathroom," I mumble to one of the guys next to me as I get up and leave the table, allowing myself to feel her completely, to open to our bond fully.

I find her outside, standing in front of the lake. What the fuck is she doing out here? It's fucking freezing this time of the year. Most people are out the front near the fountain because they have gas burners for warmth. Being close to the water is colder.

No one else is around us. It's eerie but nice at the same time. We at least have a little bit of privacy. She's moved to the side away from the light, so no one can see her through the windows unless you really tried. Even then, if you were to look, you would only see two people standing out in the night.

I see her shiver a little as I move silently closer, my hands all clammy, my ears ringing, and my heart is thumping loudly against my chest.

I don't want to spook her, but I just want to be closer to her. Hearing her suck in the cold night air, I cautiously step forward. I haven't said anything to her, and she hasn't acknowledged me yet, so I'm unsure if she knows I'm here. Surely, she would, though, right? She's just ignoring me, punishing me for the shit I've put her through this week.

"Are you cold?" I asked softly as I began to shrug off my jacket wanting to give it to her. I scold myself as soon as the words left my mouth. 'Are you cold?' Is that really the first fucking thing I say after not talking to her for an entire week?

She turns her head slowly to glance at me, her arms crossed, rubbing her arms to keep warm, one hand clutching something in her fingers. Annoyance flashes through her eyes as she glances at me.

"I'm fine," she mumbles but tightens her arms around her as she shivers again in the breeze.

"Here," I step forward one more time, closing the gap between us so she is right in front of me. I tuck the jacket around her softly. She flinches a little when our skin connects, erupting with sparks of the bond. All the fucking progress we've made, and now she doesn't even want to be around me.

I haven't been this close to her since that night. It takes everything in me not to pull her in and hold her right there. I think I'm fucking lucky she didn't just push me away. I inhale her scent once more as I finished putting the jacket around her, wanting more than anything to hold her. But right now, I know she was mad or upset. Maybe both. I don't want to push my luck tonight, but I have to try something.

I reluctantly take a step back, giving her some space. Even though every fiber of my being screams to hold her, I know I would have to earn that privilege.

"What do you want, Zander?" She sighs, looking up at me, sounding so defeated. It fucking killed me that I made her feel that way. After everything we went through, I made her feel that.

"I... dance with me?" I stammered, hoping that she would accept. I know I don't deserve it, but anything to be close to her. I wanted to give her a choice. Instead of forcing myself to hold her, I didn't want to make things any worse.

She looks at me, surprised and confused at my request. I just wanted to have this one moment before everything went to shit. I want to make her feel safe and loved again. Even though we were close to her, Jace was pacing in my mind again, agitated.

I knew we have a lot of shit to talk about and figure out, but I didn't want to ruin tonight for her. I hoped maybe she wants the same thing.

"I don't think that's a good idea," she mumbles and starts taking off my jacket.

Now I frown, confused. Not confused because she didn't want to be close to me. No, I knew that was a long shot, but why is she holding out the jacket in the gap between us? It's fucking freezing out. She is clearly cold.

"You're cold," I say, frustrated that she won't just leave the jacket on, folding my arms across my chest instinctively.

"Yes, well, I don't want anyone to smell your scent on me, especially Ollie or your girlfriend," she snaps, tossing me the jacket, and starts walking along the path that wraps around the water.

I stand there stunned for a second, looking at the jacket in my hand. I honestly hadn't even considered it was marking her or putting my scent on her. I just wanted her to be warm, nothing more, nothing less.

Wait, did she say, girlfriend? Oh, fuck! I didn't want to bring up Grace just yet. And, fuck, I haven't even apologized to her about that yet. Guilt consumes me as I jog to catch up to her. She hadn't gone far. Despite the heels she could still walk pretty fast.

"Sweetheart, please..." I start reaching out to her, but she cuts me off abruptly and moves her arm away out of my reach.

"Don't call me that," she grinds out.

"What …" I ask, frowning, spinning around to face her while walking backwoods, quickly trying to keep up with her and not stumble at the same time.

"You lost that privilege when you chose her. It's Beta Ashleigh to you," she growls and pushes me slightly to the side, trying to move around me.

“I didn’t choose her. I chose you,” I call out, stopping where she pushed past.

She suddenly stops and turns back to face me, walking a few steps toward me.

“You chose her the moment you turned around the first night. The moment you went to her instead of me, you chose her, so finish your choice and reject me,” she snaps, Kia flashing through pulsing her aura.

'Can’t you speak with Kia? Help me out a bit here, please,' I plead with Jace. He growls and glares at me. Great, he fucking hates me again.

“No, I can’t, and I won’t. I know I did it all the wrong way. I tried to do right by Grace and the baby but not right by you. For that, I am truly sorry, sweetheart. I didn’t do it knowingly. I was trying to get answers for you if you wanted any. I was trying to be prepared. It fucking killed me every night I was away from you. But I didn’t want you, of all people, to see me as a disappointment like my father. Like everyone who is supposed to care about me, I am a disappointment, I couldn’t be that to you. I can't lose you, too.”

I shook my head, and told her my greatest fear … of being a disappointment to her and losing her.

I am always surrounded by lot of people. Of the girls, half wanted a one-night stand with an Alpha while the other half want to become Luna. That was never going to happen. That title was always meant for my mate and was never ever going to be given to anyone else.

The guys, well, Danni and Eric, are the only two I can really trust. Billy only came into the fold at the start of high school. Sometimes I even have reservations about him. And then there's my father, now that's a big fucking can of worms I don't want to open tonight.

She stood there for a moment, just staring at me with a blank expression. I can see the gears turning in her mind, trying to figure out if I am telling the truth and if I got the chance.

“None of it matters. You are still having a child with another. I won’t stand by and be the other woman. I won’t be the one pushed aside,” she said, shaking her head, staring at me with glassy eyes, and starts to move away.

Fuck I should have started with Grace not being pregnant. Then maybe the pain would have been less if I had told her that from the start.

“She’s not pregnant. She faked the whole fucking thing to get to me. She’s gone now and she won’t ever be allowed back,” I say quickly, trying to move closer to her.

Her beautiful eyes blink at me. Her brow formed into a frown. "Then why the fuck did it take so long?" she snapped, folding her arms back across her body, frustrated.

I felt my mouth gape open. Did she just swear? I don't think I have ever heard her swear before. I quickly gathered myself together again, trying to dismiss that she looks fucking hot when she’s pissed off.

"I couldn't get an appointment until yesterday, and I was going to see you last night with all the information. I am so sorry I waited so long to tell you. I'm sorry I didn't go to you first. Just, please let me try to make it up to you. Let me take you out."

This I can do. This is what I am good at. Just give me a second chance, I plead. I can feel Jace's annoyance and frustration over the whole thing. Hell, I'm frustrated, but I need to show her that I can be with her and no one else. I need to show her how much I love her.

"I'll think about it," she mumbles, looking down at her hands, holding something. I frown, wanting to see what she’s holding. Before I even get a glimpse of it, she curls her fingers around it and tucks it away again.

"That's all I ask," I nod, letting out a sigh of relief.

"I should go back in. I only said I'd be out for a bit," she says softly, moving past me and making her way back to the venue.

I sigh, standing there for a moment, scrubbing my hand over my face. It's a start. I just fucking hope she says yes because, at this point, I don't care who knows. She's my mate, and I need her. I don't think I would survive if she rejected me.

Chapter 47 - ASHLEIGH

My head is still spinning as I lay in my bed staring up at the ceiling, thinking about everything that has happened last night and over the last few weeks, going over and over them in my mind. I haven't slept a wink. Everything is just replaying in my mind. It's hard to switch it off.

A part of me understands why he did what he did, but the other part that shares the bond with him hurts so much. It feels like our bond is a little bit broken because of it. At least before, it could have been mended, but now, even if he tried, I'm not so sure.

He was so quick to jump and help Grace, so quick to jump and help her, yet forgot me in the process of everything, even after we mated, even after he promised I was everything to him. He didn't show that to me last week.

Who's to say that will not happen again. He admitted he did wrong, but did he only realize it because he lost Grace in the process? Was I just a backup option to him?

I hope I made it clear to him last night that I wouldn't be on the sidelines and wouldn't be the one pushed aside because of all of this. If we mark and mate later, I won't ever be able to leave him. Our wolves will die, and we, along with them if I did want to leave him.

I shouldn't ever have been second, no matter the reason. We had overcome so much. I was ready to tell people he was mine and prepared to accept him fully. And he hurt us.

Kia quieted down a bit once we left the venue. I needed some time alone, time to process, so I headed home while the rest decided to go somewhere else. My thoughts were spinning and I just wanted peace and quiet.

Chloe begged me to go along with them for a little bit, but even after my chat with Zander, it was still hard to see him around other people and be around everyone. I just wanted to keep my distance for the rest of the evening.

I know he wanted to come to me once or twice, and he nearly did, but something stopped him. Whether it was his wolf or his own jumbled mind, he at least respected my space and just let me have the evening with the girls.

A ringing sound blasts around me, making me sit in my bed and frantically look around. Oh no, is it already 6 am? I sigh as I reach over and slap the alarm off, making the screeching sound come to an automatic halt.

Thankfully, it's Saturday, but I still have so much work to catch up on, and I usually help around the pack with training and other things if dad and uncle need me to.

'Mum, I'm going for a run if that's okay?' I quickly link her while I jump out of bed and start to get changed. There's nothing better than starting the morning with a nice cool winter air run. After being around Zander for an extended period last night, I could feel Kia's strength is back to normal.

'Sure, honey , just be careful because it's still dark out. Don't go too far west, stay in the city line, and don't go too far out to the countryside, please. There are a few issues your father and uncle haven't sorted out yet,' Mum linked back.

'Oh, is it anything I can help with? Anything major?' I ask curiously, wondering why no one had mentioned anything about this before.

'Not at this point. They are presenting some information to the council today. Hopefully, things will be resolved, but if not, we will bring you, kids in.'

Sighing, I say 'okay' to mum and end the link.

I try to run around the pack grounds a few times a week, either for patrol or for pleasure. It helps keep the fitness up and also helps me deal with whatever stress or frustration I am going through.

I get into my leggings, a loose top, and my old runners, so if Kia wants to transform into her wolf, I won't waste any good clothing or shoes.

I run and run for ages. I can sense the patrol team is around. I assume they can also sense me, so it helps me feel safer after what mum said. I guess that's why dad and uncle couldn't go to the meetings earlier this week and most likely why they have been a bit busy lately.

'*I want to run, please,'* Kia begged. She has been pacing in my mind to be let out for a while now. I just needed some time to think.

'You mean overthink everything,' she mumbles back.

'Fine, but remember what mum said, stay in the areas that are safe for now.' I sigh before starting to strip down to my underwear and hanging my clothes on a nearby tree. This is precisely why I wear old clothes or cheaper ones because if I can't find them later on, I'm sure someone else will have some use for them.

'*I have a place in mind,'* I can feel her excitement pulsing through. What the hell does she have planned? I try to access her side of my mind, but she has put her block up.

'*Nuh uhh, it's going to be a surprise,'* she says excitedly as I shift into her beautiful fur. I love being in my wolf form. These last few days have been hard on us, so it's nice to feel connected again with her. To feel free.

The snapping and rearranging of bones ends quickly. While it hurts at first, the shift becomes less painful and easier over time.

Some can turn so quickly that you will miss it if you blink. This is often with higher ranked wolves like an Alpha or a Beta. I can shift quickly, but nothing like Ollie or uncle or even dad, who are really quick. I always loved seeing their wolf form when I was younger.

I sit back and let Kia explore and run around our land, the sun slowly starts to rise, and I can feel some of her excitement as she moves off the land into neutral ground.

'Kia,' I warn her, fighting to get back control.

'*Come on, I promise it isn't anything bad,'* she sighs, putting up a fight to keep control over where we are going. In our wolf form Kia has more control, just as I do when we are in our human form. We usually agree on most things before doing anything but today she doesn't even want to discuss it. She is in control.

'Where are you going?' I ask as we run by houses and busy streets starting to pick up with the start of the day. We go by some excited children and early risers. Some of the older generations still haven't gotten used to the idea of shifters being in their world, so they are still hesitant, but the little ones are always curious and excited.

As I see through her eyes, I recognize some of the streets and buildings, 'Please don't tell me you are going there. You know I am struggling with Zander right now,' I beg her.

'*But I want to see my mate, and he is here. I can feel him. You can punish Zander all you want, but please don't punish Jace and me for something he couldn't control,'* she pleads her case to me as she slowly pushes open the garden gate with her nose that led into the cottage I had grown to adore these last few weeks.

It's been my sanctuary. We have built memories here together. Despite those memories being few, I didn't want to ruin them memories by creating bad ones. At the same time, she is right. She needs to be around Jace. They already accepted each other. I can't be the one holding them back for something Zander did.

'Fine, but only if you see him in your form, I'm not shifting back, and I'm not talking to him,' I grumble as I relinquish any control I had, not happy at all that this is where she brought me.

'Deal!' Kia barks out happily, wagging her tail, waiting for Zander to come to her since I refuse to shift back.

I can feel him moving closer toward us as he reaches the back door, I don't know if he stayed the night or got here this morning, but he looks like crap as he opens the door. He is wearing a black shirt and checked boxers. His hair is a mess, his shoulders are slumped, and he looks exhausted. Dark shadows are under his eyes, and he looks like he had the worst night's sleep. He rubs his hand over his face before holding it over his eyes to look out.

'Maybe this was a bad idea,' I mumble to her. Seeing him in this state makes me second guess her decision, making me nervous to be around him.

'*It's fine. He didn't sleep much last night,'* she tries to reassure me.

"Kia?" He asks cautiously, taking a step towards us.

She lets out another bark, happily wagging her tail and moving toward him. It didn't take long for him to move in front of us. Zander bent down so he is level with Kia and stretches his hand to pet her. He hesitates a little before slowly sinking his fingers into her fur. Sparks erupt where he pet her, leaving a trail of tingles, making me want to push forward and be with him, but I know this is what she needs. She needs to be with Jace.

"You want Jace to go for a run, too?" he asks as he finishes rubbing her.

She nods and gives him a lick of encouragement, making the side of his face wet with her saliva.

"Ashleigh?" he asks, looking a bit defeated. Kia tilts her head to the side a little bit in a playful manner. I guess trying not to tell him how I feel about being here.

He heaves a sigh of exhaustion and strips off his shirt as Kia moves back to give him space to shift into Jace.

I try not to get overwhelmed by everything around me. His scent makes me giddy and our bond feels so alive in our animal form, making it hard to remember why I was angry at him. It makes it hard to remember why I hurt so much.

'*Because Jace and I have accepted each other,'* Kia whispered, answering my thoughts.

'Why should that matter?' I asked

In my form the bond is stronger because Jace and I have already accepted each other and mated. It makes your bond with Zander stronger as well. I hoped this would help you see what we could have and help build on what we already have,' she tries to explain these new overwhelming feelings I have.

'I just... he needs to earn our forgiveness Kia,' I sigh as she and Jace run around playing together. I can see how happy and free she is with him.

'*I know he does, and I'm not saying discard that. I'm just trying to help clear your mind and show you what we can have.'*

'Meaning you want me to give him a chance to prove himself?'

'*Yes, I think the moon goddess doesn't make mistakes. We do, though, and I believe he regrets how he handled things. I just ask that before you reject him, which will hurt all of us, by the way, please let him earn your love and forgiveness.'*

I sigh and sit deeper in the back of our mind as she runs around more, playing with Jace. As much as I understand why she wanted to come here, it was still hard for me to accept everything.

I have always been the person who accepts everything, including mistakes, but this choice he made hurt so much, and he needs to earn back my trust.

Chapter 48 - ASHLEIGH

I close my eyes and breathe in the scent of comfort before I step out into the wild ways of Monday morning. Ollie had just stopped the soft murmur of his car, and Brent had already jumped out and made a be-line directly to some of his school friends.

"How are you holding up?" Ollie asks, carefully studying me.

I can feel his unease. Neither of us like keeping that I am mates with Zander a secret from Brent or the rest of our family, but I am so grateful that he has. "I'm okay," I reply with a shrug. "Kia kind of took things into her own hands last Saturday, but I managed."

I'm not upset at Kia for the little stunt she pulled on Saturday morning. It was kind of nice not having these feelings of anger and hurt flowing all around me for once, and right now, I feel somewhat oddly calm and peaceful.

I knew he wanted to talk more but I just wasn't ready yet. It still hurt too much, and I need more time to heal. My mind is a mess and I can't simply make a quick decision that could potentially hurt us all in the long run.

But on Sunday, I made sure she didn't pull anything like that again. I just needed time to think and process everything before seeing him today.

"Are you okay going to school today?" He asks.

I laughed at the question. He didn't think of asking me that before we got into the car. In fact, he and mum ganged up on me and said I had to go to school today and not sulk for another week.

So here I am at school, trying to figure out how to avoid the one person I might not be able to. "Let's get going, I have double maths, and I don't want to be in trouble with Ms. Hanagin. You know what she's like even if you are two minutes late after the bell." I sigh as I get out, trying to avoid the question.

I tried not to look around the parking lot to find him, but my eye caught his sports car parked up front. I take in a deep breath as I reach my locker to get what I need for the first two periods.

Punching in the combination of my locker and opened it up only to find a beautiful bunch of wild daisies. My most absolute favourite flower, excitement, washes over me as I drop my school bag on the floor and pick up the delicate bouquet, trying not to break anything in the process. I bring the flowers up to my face breathing in the beautiful scent that reminds me of him.

Kia stirs around in the back of my mind, letting me know he's behind me, waiting for me to look up and give him permission to come closer. I sigh and look over to the window in the corridor where I know he is. He's there leaning against one of the pillars with a stupid grin on his face watching me like he knew this was going to be my reaction.

Now I know that it's a small gesture. I certainly have not forgotten or forgiven what he has put me through, but with small things like this, hope blossoms through me of the possibility that he could be trying.

I'd like to know how he knew the combination to my locker and how he knew daisies were my favourite. By the time I've finished that thought, he's standing in front of me, leaning against the locker next to me.

"Morning, sweetheart," he leans in and whispers only so I can hear. People around us were hurrying to get to class, not noticing us talking.

"Hi," I squeak back. How is it that I am always nervous around him? Even with everything we have been through, nerves still flutter around in my tummy. His scent surrounded me, mixing in with the smell of the daisies in my hands. I have no idea how he managed to get them considering that it's winter.

"How are you?"

I roll my eyes at the question. I hate this small talk between us. It's like we are walking on eggshells, waiting for the other to crack. And yes, part of it may be my fault for ignoring him, but it's also partly his fault for doing the same thing to me. I guess we just need to talk or yell or whatever we need to do to learn to communicate with each other, so this weirdness isn't around anymore.

My brain hurt so much on Sunday, all my thoughts in a jumbled cycle until I was numb. In the end, I decided to just to let it all go because I can't keep this anger or hurt all bottled up, or I'll snap every time something happens.

There is no point in trying to avoid him, he clearly had other plans, so here I am waiting to see what he would do to try and work things out.

"Let me take you out tonight?" He asks softly, not letting the bystanders listen in on our conversation. Even though they are only human, gossip moves around here quickly, and if anyone ever found out we were dating or together, I'm sure a lot of people would have opinions about that.

I blink up at him, dragging my eyes away from the flowers in my hands, "How'd you know?" I ask, curious to know the answers to my questions.

"Hmm, know what exactly, sweetheart?" He asks back, tilting his head and observing me, smirking a little bit.

Damn him. He knows my questions. He's just going to make me say it. "My combination, The daisies? How did you know?"

He leans in a little bit, so he is at eye level with me, and reaches up to brush a loose curl away. Tingles shot through with the slight contact of skin, "Now, where's the fun in that if you know all of my secrets?"

His lips were so close that I would kiss him if I moved forward just a little, his breath soft on my face. Fighting the urge to kiss him, I step back a little bit because as much fun as this is, he needs to earn that kiss. The only reason I haven't given him the cold shoulder or yelled at him is that we are at school, I don't need whispers about us while we are sorting through this.

He smirks and straightens back up, leaning against the locker, satisfied that he has officially made me a permanent shade of light pink.

"So tonight, can I see you?"

"Umm... maybe, I'll see," I mumble, looking away, trying to gather my books quickly before the final bell is about to go. I don't need detention for being late today.

He sighs heavily. "Come on, please. I know you probably hate me right now, but won't you let me try to make it up to you?"

"Zander... I don't think," I start, even with all the thinking I've been doing. I'm not sure that being in the same space without any disturbances is a good idea.

"Just give me tonight."

I turn a little to face him, seeing him leaning against the locker, looking slightly defeated and drained.

Part of me feels a little sorry for him. But honestly, he is only feeling a little bit of what he put me through last week. At least he gets to be around me at school. Last week, he didn't even have the guts to be in the same room as me, and now he's scrambling. Yes, he apologized, but he also blamed other people. He didn't even own his mistakes.

"Let me think about it?" I mumble, closing my locker door, and start heading towards class.

"Okay, I'll message you with details," he nods, following me silently, letting my mind wander. Thankfully my Maths class isn't too far from this building, so in about three minutes, the final bell is about to go, and I hopefully won't be late.

I'm about to walk into the classroom and find him still following behind me.

Spinning around to face him, I put my hand in front of his chest to stop him from walking and slightly stumble at my impulse movement. I ignore the tingles moving through my body because right now, I can't concentrate with his scent and everything else going on. Adding the tingles of the bond is just making things harder for me.

"What do you think you are doing, I have double maths, and you most certainly are not in this class." I hiss.

I did not need anyone catching this, especially the teacher. She is the worst at calling people out on their stuff and embarrassing them. He shuffles around uneasy, rubbing the back of his neck, trying to avoid my eye contact like he knows he will get into trouble for the next words that he says.

"Umm, well before everything happened, I had some of my classes changed to match your schedule," he mumbles.

"What? How?" I ask, my eyes widening as I recall the only way of changing a class is if you confirm you have found your mate, they try to put you together, so neither one gets too out of control. I hope he didn't tell anyone. I don't need the whole world knowing right now. Or if you get moved up a class because of your grades, and he hasn't been here for a little bit, I doubt they would just let him change anything unless it was a valid reason.

He shrugged and said, "I did Physics and extension maths the last few years, I guess they were happy enough with my grades to let me bump up and do extension one maths this year, but with Bio, I had to talk my way into letting them change over because they weren't too happy losing another Art major."

"And the rest? What about Economics and English?"

He shook his head, "You get to keep those to yourself. I couldn't change anymore unless I told them, and well, I didn't exactly want to give up my sport, if I'm honest, but they didn't want to change my English class around without a valid reason."

"Wonderful, just so I have this right, I have Study Hall, History, Extension maths, and my Bio classes with you? You realize that is about 80% of my time at school, right?" I start counting the classes in my mind, trying to remember where they all are in the two-week cycle the school gives us.

He flashes one of his grins and chuckles, "well, sweetheart, considering that is the whole point, I guess so, yeah."

I roll my eyes at him and sigh, "Fine, but you have to wait out here for at least 5 Mississippi before going in."

"You realize a few people have already seen us walking together, right?"

I shrug. It wasn't fair he got to move all his classes around to make it harder for me. Granted, it was supposed to make things easier, and maybe it would have if we hadn't been through so much already, but I still needed him to respect my space.

He sighs and leans against the locker next to the classroom and starts counting down. Telling me it's now or never, before he walks into that room.

Chapter 49 - ZANDER

I loved watching her reaction as she found the flowers. She loved them. As much as she tried to hide, it was nice to see that she at least appreciated the gesture.

The frustrating thing is, we were in such a good place before, and even then, I should have been doing this stuff for her, but I wasn't. Honestly, I was so focused on other things that I didn't even think to give her small things like this, to at least make her feel comfortable enough to show she had someone, to let her feel loved and free.

It made me feel like an ass that I wasn't treating her like the queen she is rather than taking everything for granted and thinking that she would just accept the bond a hundred percent because, the truth is, she had accepted me, but until I knew I could lose her, I hadn't accepted her completely.

I had to call all around to see if anyone knew someone with a flower greenhouse. But I needed specific flowers. Thankfully, someone had some in my territory, so getting the flowers wasn't as hard as I thought it would be.

I'm not going to tell her that, though. I have put an account with the supplier, and I will regularly purchase flowers for her just to see that shade of pink every time she gets something special.

I have already set up everything for this evening. Actually, everything was already set up since Sunday. If she'd come over again, I would've tried to talk her into letting me take her out.

I knew that it was a long shot that she might come over on Sunday, but I just wanted to be prepared because I missed her, I fucking missed her so much, and it killed me that she didn't want to talk to me at all. I understood why; I was a total jackass to her, and I am honestly grateful she just hasn't rejected me yet.

So here I am, following her around like those whipped blokes you see all the time. I never thought I'd turn into one of them, but fuck it, here I am trying to get her back. I'll be dammed if I don't at least try, and I don't think Jace would ever forgive me if we lost her.

My brain is too chaotic to concentrate in my last period of English. This is precisely why they allow us to change to match our mate's classes, or we would be distracted wondering where the other one is, or just frustrated we couldn't be with them. On the bright side, I have most of my classes with her now, so that will settle Jace for the most part.

My phone buzzes in my back pocket as I look out the windows, wondering what she is doing now.

***Ashleigh: Fine, I'll be there.**

I frown at the screen. What does she mean by that? Usually, Fine is bad, right? I had texted her the info for tonight but hadn't heard a response, and it's been driving me crazy.

I am slightly worried at the response. At least she was coming, that was the main thing.

I just needed to be around her.

I sigh and put my phone away as I try to focus on the teacher rather than her still being pissed off with me.

'I'd be pissed at you for weeks,' Jace mumbles. I can feel his frustration, mostly with me and not being around our mate.

I scoff and say, 'No, you wouldn't cause you are as horny as I am half the time. You want Ashleigh and need her as much as I do.'

'*If you honestly think you are getting that far with her tonight, you are more delusional than I thought,'* Jace mutters, curling in the corner of my mind and sulking because he knows I'm right.

He knows we both need her just as much. But at the same time, I don't just want the intimate side with her. I want all of her; I want her to know she can trust me and love me unconditionally because I almost had that with her, and I went and fucked it all up. I need to show her that I love her and that she can feel safe with me … that I won't ever choose another over her, and that I won't ever make her feel that same way again.

~

School finished about an hour ago, and I'm here in the living room, pacing back and forth, waiting for her to get here.

'*Considering you made her wait for days until you decided to talk to her, I think your impatience is childish.'* Jace reminds me again of how long I made her wait and how long I made her suffer.

'Will you ever forgive me for what I did? I can't have both of you pissed at me. I can only work with what I've got right now. Can't you see I was trying to do the right thing?' I try to reason with him again, even though it feels like the same old talk over and over.

'I will forever be angry at you for going against me, going against our mate. When she feels safe and is with us because she wants to be, maybe I will forgive you … but not until she does.'

I sigh and pace again because I know he's fucking right.

I hear her car pulling up out front an hour later. Thank the goddess because I've been going completely stir crazy here. I've had to catch myself whenever I take out my phone to call her because I didn't want to freak her out even more.

But at the same time, I just wanted to see and be around her. Jace was becoming increasingly impatient, which added to my frustrations.

When she opened the door and stepped into the house, I swear my heart stopped for a few seconds. I stood there gaping at her, probably looking like a fucking creep.

She looks fucking stunning! With her hair down and flowing loosely around her, she looks up and smirks at me, satisfied with my reaction. She's a fucking tease and she knows it. She is dressed simply yet sexily in skinny white tight jeans, a red low-cut top that shows of all her curves beautifully, a black leather jacket, and black heels.

I try to regain my composure, so I don't look like a damn fool.

"Hey, you came?" I feel a grin form on my face as she stood there. I almost lost hope that she would come. Two hours, two fucking hours, I was already going crazy.

"Yeah, sorry I was running late. I had to deal with a few family things before coming,"

I nod and, honestly, I did not hear a word she said. I'm just so fucking happy she's here right now, her scent around me, making everything ten times harder. After not being around her for a while, I almost forgot what it was like to be in a room with her and only her.

"I, umm… I didn't know what we were doing, so I hope this is ok," Ashleigh gestures to herself, worrying about her clothes.

Honestly, it doesn't matter to me; she looks stunning in everything and anything, but I so appreciate her dressing up in these sexy outfits because later, I'll be the one ripping it off her.

"You look perfect." I say quickly, glancing over her.

I have to push Jace down a few times. I know he wants to have time with Kia, but he already had that last Saturday. Today, it is my turn with Ashleigh.

"Shall we head off?" I ask as I look outside to see the sun had already set, the start of the evening; it was a bit warmer tonight, which was nice, so I had hoped my plan would be ok.

I'm not sure if she wants to be around people together yet, so I set a nice little intimate date for us, hoping this would help us move forward.

"Sure." She nods and steps to the side, giving me room to walk past. I want to reach out and kiss her, hold her, do anything to have her because I hate this awkwardness. It's like we are back at square one, and maybe we should be, but we've had sex and have been together for a few weeks now, and it all went to shit. One wrong move and all that trust just dissolved so fucking quickly.

The drive isn't too long. If she had arrived a bit earlier, I would have suggested running and letting Kia and Jace out, but I didn't want them to take over tonight. I don't know how much longer I would get with her. We need to sort some things out, and right now, this silence is killing me.

I keep glancing over at her, but she's just looking out the window, not giving me any indication that she wants to talk or that she's mad at me or anything at all. It's like she shut down to the point where I can only feel her nerves. It's like the first time she was at the cottage when we found out we were mates. Even Jace is uncomfortable, shifting around in my mind. He won't talk to me, but this weird feeling I'm getting from both of them makes me uncomfortable.

I hate that I made her feel this uncomfortable. I hate that I caused this.

I pull off to the side of the road where a narrow pathway leads into the woods. There aren't any houses or anyone else around. I had to make a bit of the path myself, so I knew how to find this place again. It was about a 15-minute drive from the cottage. I'm ashamed to say I found this place when I was away those nights, roaming around when I should have been with her.

It was one of my favourite places to come. I hoped that once everything settled, I could bring her here. Since this is a new stage of our relationship, maybe this would be the perfect fit for us to have a fresh start.

"We just have to walk a bit from here. The car won't be able to make it through, unfortunately." I say quickly, cutting the engine and pocketing the keys.

"Not planning on killing me, are you?" she laughs softly, darting her eyes over to me.

I roll my eyes. "Not quite," I chuckle, jumping out quickly to run around to open the door for her, only for her to be out already and closing the door by the time I get there.

I head over to the boot, grab the basket I made earlier, and lock the car while she's there, shifting nervously. I don't know how to make this easier. I don't know how to make this less weird for her.

"Come on, this way." I move closer and grab her hand, leading her toward the pathway.

Thankfully this time, she didn't flinch away or not want to be close to me. She just accepted that she was following me.

As we walk along the pathway, it opens to a small clearing that leads to a view of the mountains and a river down below that would lead out to the river near the cottage.

I had gotten a few solar lights and fairy lights putting them around the trees and rocks, so everything was lit. There are a few plush blankets and soft pillows with bunches of daisies and other wildflowers scattered around, making the area look nice and soft.

"Zander, it's beautiful," she whispers as she moves next to me, taking in her new surroundings.

"I wasn't sure if you wanted to go out and be around people, so I thought this would be a nice option." I smile, hoping that this is what she needs.

Ashleigh relaxes as I move forward, placing the basket in the middle of the blanket.

"Come on, let's sit." I gesture towards the pillows, slowly sinking into one of them.

Sitting down on the pillows, I can feel her settle, nerves slowly lifting. Maybe it was the not knowing part that got her all nervous.

"Was everything okay with your family?" I ask as I get things out of the basket, trying not to make it as uncomfortable as the ride here.

"Hmm, oh yes, we have a catch-up every two weeks, so Ollie and I know what's going on and if we need to change anything around with patrols or training." She nods and smiles when she talks about her family.

I can feel the envy rise as I listen to her talk about her family. She and Oliver have what I want. Hell, they are already going around and being the main contact for their pack. My father doesn't even know I do training or patrol, and I usually have to convince the lead command into giving me duties and not pass it on to dad or Jake. I fucking hate that he doesn't want me involved with anything. I try to express my interest, but even after Alpha training, he still doesn't realize I'm ready for more than just being a school kid.

I shake off this frustrated feeling because right now, it's about Ashleigh. I can't focus on being jealous when I should be proud that she gets a chance to serve her pack.

"It's nice they want you to start some of your responsibilities." I try to be encouraging and supportive because that's what I should be.

"Yeah, especially more so since mum knows about us. It's nice she hasn't said anything to dad or uncle, and even Ollie hasn't said anything to anyone." she smiles at me.

This is good. I feel the awkwardness slowly lifting as she talks about her family and pack.

"They want you to be more involved?" I ask, trying to keep the conversation moving as I empty the basket full of food.

"Yeah, from time to time, they allow us to go to meetings, and I've already been doing training since I shifted at 16. Ollie will do more this year until he goes off to Alpha Training. I don't know if I'll go yet, but I guess I will have to see what universities I can get into." She shrugs, settling into the pillows next to me and taking off her heels to be more comfortable.

I knew she wanted to go to uni and get a degree, but I wasn't sure which one she wanted. "What do you want to do at uni?" I ask.

"Psychology or teaching, maybe a psychologist for students or young adults, something like that, I would like to help people." She smiled.

"You know I'll support you in anything you want to do, right?" I say, reaching across and putting my hand on her leg as encouragement. She doesn't flinch. She leaves my hand there, closing her eyes and accepting the feeling of the bond moving through our bodies.

I take a deep breath before I start explaining myself again because I feel like I still owe her an explanation. Friday night was in an environment we just didn't get time to talk properly, and as much as I don't want to kill this peaceful mood, I'd rather get it all out in the open now.

“I know I explained some things the other night, but I guess while we're discussing the future, I just want to apologize again. I was so caught up in everything and afraid of my emotions and our relationship being in jeopardy that I just didn’t stop and think or listen to Jace. I guess it was just a rollercoaster of emotions that I didn’t realize I was hurting you in the process while trying to do right by Grace.”

“It was all my actions, and I have to take responsibility for everything, including what I did to you. For that, I am truly sorry and hope that one day you can forgive me while I still try to be the best mate deserving of you. I guess out of everything, this would be the first real relationship I have ever had, and I’m still trying to learn. While I know some things, I don’t know how to be open and explain things just yet. I hope that in time I will learn that while I’m with you.”

This is the first time I have ever been so raw, and fuck, it feels so foreign to be this vulnerable. But this is what she needs … she needs to know how I feel right now so we can move forward with our relationship. I hope one day this will help her trust me completely.

Her eyes stay closed as I finished my explanation. I just hope she would understand or realize that I didn’t want or mean to hurt her. I was just a jumbled mess that made some bad decisions.

Her eyes open as she reaches behind her getting out her purse and rummaging through it.

I frown, confused at what she is doing. I didn’t want her to give me anything. I certainly didn't deserve it. If anything, she was the one who deserved everything.

Ashleigh finds what she is looking for and puts her bag back behind her, clutching the item in her hands. She opens her fingers slowly, and I feel the blood drain from my face as I’m presented with the little blue box that I gave her a few weeks ago.

Chapter 50 - ASHLEIGH

His apology is understandable and scary at the same time.

We were intimate, and I trusted him completely. I felt ready to tell people he was my mate and prepared to have strained relationships with my family over him. I gave him all of me; he was my first in everything.

While I understand his reasoning, it also hurts that he didn't think he could trust me enough to realize that I wasn't going to reject him, that I was there for support.

I feel the bond moving through us as he speaks to me, explaining his actions. How was he was able to keep away from me for so long if this is how I feel right now?

I see his confused face as I rummage through my bag. I had already packed the little blue box and was going to give it back to him tonight either way. I didn't want to hurt him, but I also think it's the right choice to give it back to him for now.

I watch the colour drain from his face as I try to give back the little blue box. Taking a deep breath, I hope he hears what I have to say before freaking out completely.

"Thank you for being honest with me. I know that it was hard for you to be so open. While I appreciate the explanation, as much as I still care for you, I also don't want to feel like an obligation to you because it's not fair to either of us if you can't trust me."

"I understand this is new for you, but the fact that you wanted to fight the bond every night to keep away from me showed me that you don't trust me as a mate should. I want you to feel like you can come to me with anything and not have all these unsettling feelings. When you gave me this, you told me the significance of it, and right now, I don't believe we are at the point where we have accepted each other entirely."

"Maybe one day you can give this back to me and be one hundred percent sure that I am your other half and that you accept me entirely, but until then, I think you should have it back."

I feel a huge weight lift as I explain my reason for giving back the hairpiece. I loved that he gave it to me, I loved that it was mine, but he didn't see me as his other half. He sees me as an obligation, and until those changes for him, we can't be together.

Zander stares at the blue box in my hands, confusion written all over his face. Maybe he thought that if he apologized, we would be ok, and yes, the apology helped immensely, but we still have a lot to work on.

When he gave me this, he said it was his mothers, that his father and mother were equals, and they loved each other dearly. Right now, it didn't feel like Zander loved me. It felt like he was just with me because he had to be because of the bond of our wolves.

He stepped up today, but what happens after I forgive him? Will everything just go back to what it was? We need to build some foundation and trust before he gives me something so significant.

"So, what do you want then?" he asks carefully. I can hear the hurt in his voice he tries to hide as he looks up, his confused expression wiped away, leaving me with a completely blank face. I can see his walls thrown up as he stares at me, waiting for me to decide our future.

Part of me knew this might happen, but I had a small hope he would understand how much he hurt me. I'd hoped this would help him grow.

"I think we should date, get to know each other a bit more." I bite my bottom lip looking at him, hoping he would be okay with this as I drop the box into his hand.

"I didn't think you wanted that until we accepted each other, so are you saying you want everyone to know now?" he asks, posture still tense, he removes his hand from my leg, and the warmth and tingles leave along with it, I almost let out a small whimper missing his comfort.

"I just think we need a bit more time together to build the trust so we can come to each other with anything. I want to apologize, too, I know before I have tried to reject you, and maybe things would have been different if we knew how to talk to one another. But I am here, trying to be a better person for you and support you in anything and everything."

I move closer to him, putting my hand on his chest. I can feel him tense as I try to move closer. I know it hurt him to get something like that back, and I just hoped that he would understand.

I see gold rims in his eyes flash forward every so often, letting me know that Jace is present. I hope Jace would help him understand my point.

Zander heaves a sigh, closing his eyes and trying to regain control. It seems there is a struggle between the two at the moment. Kia shifts around in my mind in response to Jace. I know she wants to be with him right now, but Zander and I need to sort us out before they get intimate again.

"It's okay, sweetheart, I appreciate the apology, but it was all mostly my fault." He leans in, grabs my waist, and pulls me in further, so I sit on his lap, breathing in my scent to calm Jace down.

I feel the bond sparks dancing around me as I lean into him, and he wraps his arms around me tightly, kissing me on the cheek. I know we have just spoken about some heavy stuff, and I am so grateful we have sorted it out for the most part.

"I love what you did here. Thank you for making it special," I whisper after an hour of chatting and finishing our dinner. We are now sitting in comfortable silence, holding each other, making up for lost time.

“I’m glad you like it, I should have done stuff like this sooner, treated you better, and now I have realized that I’ll never stop trying,” he says, voice all gruff as he mumbles in my hair, kissing the top of my head.

I nod gently, trying not to disturb the peace, before slowly drifting off to sleep.

I hear him whisper so softly I wouldn’t hear it if it weren’t for my wolf hearing. “I love you so much, and I will strive to show you how much every day.”

Chapter 51 - ZANDER

“I want to tell people about us,” I announce as we’re sitting on the couch watching TV. I’m holding her tightly, not wanting to let her go home or anywhere else but be here with me. It’s been a few days since our chat on Monday, and honestly, I want to be with her this weekend and not worry about sneaking around. As exciting as this has been, I can’t show her how much I love her with only small gestures and walks in the woods.

I want to take her to dinner and show her off to my friends. Announce to everyone I have my mate, and my pack has their Luna.

I think we have grown so much these last few days alone. Imagine what we could be if we told people.

No more sneaking around.

I feel so fucking stupid for the time we lost last week, and my stupidity cost us time together and nearly cost me her. I will never make that mistake again. If I did, it might actually kill me.

“Zander… are you sure you’re ready for that type of commitment?” She asks, pushing slightly away from me and turning around to face me.

“Yes, I want to take you out tomorrow and be around people instead of sneaking around. I wouldn’t mind doing stuff in public, but I think our families should know from us instead of hearing it from someone else.”

She bites her bottom lip as she thinks. Fuck, I have tried so hard not to kiss her all week, tried to let her take the lead on most things so she doesn't feel uncomfortable, and honestly, I know I don’t deserve it just yet. Still, every time I see her, all I want to do is kiss her senseless. But as much as I fucking want to, I know I need to earn her trust again before having that privilege.

At least with all of our talks, I know she wouldn’t ever reject me, and because we have gotten to this point of trust, I want to take things to the next step if she lets me so that we can build our trust more. I don’t want to hide her anymore.

I can see her thinking it over as she tries to decide. After a short moment, she nods before saying, “Ok, Let's tell our families. I would like to go out and do things with you as well,” she beams at me before leaning back into me and snuggling into my chest.

I let out a sigh of relief as she’s leans against me, feeling the bond sparks dance along our skin, holding her at this moment. I know people say you shouldn’t have regrets, but oh, I so fucking do. I don’t even understand how I allowed myself to be away from her for so fucking long, but I was, and now I can’t stand the thought of being away from her for an evening, let alone a whole week.

‘*Because you didn’t fucking listen to me, and now she has given the heirloom back, and you have to earn that trust again,’* Jace mumbles in my mind.

He was so pissed she gave it back on Monday. In his eyes, no matter our situation, she was always getting the heirloom. It was never going to be anyone else's, so she should have kept it, but I understand why she wanted to give it back. Jace is still just pissed about the whole thing.

"We can tell everyone tonight, and I'll pick you up tomorrow morning so we can spend the whole day together?" I confirm as I start to plan out our Saturday.

It would be good to show her around some of the pack lands and take her to a few of my favourite places. Maybe one day we can call them our places.

She looks a bit anxious as she nods, confirming the weekend plans.

"I will tell them all tonight around dinner. Usually, they will be there." Ashleigh sighs, fidgeting with one of her curly hair locks.

"Do you know how you're going to tell your father?" she asks curiously.

"No, I'm honestly considering not telling him until tomorrow and just showing up with you at the packhouse. Part of me thinks that might go down a bit better." I sigh, rubbing the back of my neck, trying to think of something to tell dad tonight. I know exactly where he will be tonight, in his office doing paperwork. Friday nights, he is always in his office till hours in the morning.

Ellie and Jake go out for dinner every Friday night like clockwork. It used to be a family thing they would always bring along Danni and me but as we got older, we sort of phased out of it.

Dad was always invited, but those times reminded him of mum being around. I just used those times to keep her memory alive rather than dwell on her being gone.

"You should tell him it could be good for you guys to talk," Ashleigh encouraged, rubbing the side of my leg.

I tried so hard not to roll my eyes at her suggestion. I know she is only trying to help. There have been too many times when I have wanted to talk with Dad only to get shut down … or one of us gets pissed off and leaves, or it's another screaming match.

Maybe telling him, I found my mate could be different. I doubt he'd be ecstatic. A part of me hopes he would be, but I highly doubt that. He was so quick to enrol me to Alpha training the moment I turned 16 and just shipped me off for two years. I didn't have a choice in the matter, I was going, and that was final.

He didn't come and visit once. He didn't want me to come home at all.

He didn't send any letters or phone calls. Fuck, I wouldn't have known if he was still alive if it weren't for Ellie calling me every fortnight to check in.

Only for me to come home and be thrown back into school where I have already done most of these classes and passed everything, I'll bet if we didn't live in the city, he would have shipped me off to boarding school for another year if anyone would take me.

So many conversations about so many different things always came to the same ending. Dad uses his Alpha command as the final say, and we don't talk for a long time. It's gotten to a point where we barely say anything to each other unless someone else is in the room as a buffer.

Even with the situation with Grace, he barely said anything to me, didn't give any advice, just grumbled something and went about doing business.

This year has been a little different. I can fight against his command, which only seems to piss him off even more. We still haven't recovered from the last blow up, which was me returning to school. Now I do my own thing and avoid him.

"Okay, well, we should get going then, it's nearly 5 pm, and it'll take us both longer to get home with the traffic." Ashleigh sighs, pushing against my chest, trying to get away from me.

I tighten my arms around her as she goes to leave. She groans and falls back into my chest with force, not expecting to be locked in.

"Offt, Zander..." she mumbles, half annoyed. Turning around to face me, I can see the amusement dancing in her eyes as she tosses her hair to one side.

"You want to play it that way, huh, big guy?" Ashleigh asks sweetly, leaning into me and swinging her legs around, so she's straddling me.

Her top is a little revealing which I one hundred percent appreciate. My eyes go directly to her boobs as she leans in and starts kissing my neck, her lips soft against my skin, leaving explosions of tingles. My dick is already rock hard from her grinding against me, and one of my hands is on her ass, kneading it.

I can feel Jace push forward, wanting more with her. I know she started this. I didn't think I would get anything until I was at least forgiven but fuck I want more. My heart rate quickens, and my breathing increases as she kisses me, teasing me while putting me in a trance.

Closing my eyes as I enjoy this moment, I go to grab her hair, sliding my hand up her back from her ass, but she pulls back and jumps off quickly. My eyes fly open only to see her smirking at me and moving toward the door.

"Such a fucking tease", I grumble, folding my arms across my chest and giving her a playful pout.

"Are you going to stay here tonight? Or at home?" She asks while opening the door.

She looks like a fucking dream with what she's wearing right now. Her top shows off just the right spots and her jeans. I couldn't help myself but run my eyes over her body, memorising her for a trip to the bathroom later.

"Probably back here. Jace doesn't settle at home anymore because you haven't been there yet." I shrug, trying to adjust my dick in my pants as I swing around to sit up properly.

'You don't like it either', he grumbles.

He's right. I hate it at home. I'd rather be here where I at least can still be around her presence.

"Ok, I'll message you and let you know how everything goes," she nods and blows a little kiss to me before leaving, "I'll see you tomorrow!" she calls out while heading out to her car.

I groan and lean back on the couch. Fuck! Now I've got this hard-on.

~

Pulling up to the packhouse , I can only see a few lights on. The front porch lights automatically turn on as I step out of the car closing the door behind me. I don't see Jake and Ellie's car around or Danni's. I guess it's just dad and me tonight; hopefully, we don't kill each other this time.

I almost do a double back and move towards the car to get the fuck out before it's too late. I can feel Jace being just as on edge as I am. I know this is supposed to be a good fucking thing finding my mate, but with our history, even the good things somehow turn out worse than the bad things.

I hesitate before opening the packhouse door as I do. Of course, I'm met with silence, and only a kitchen light is on, offering some guidance, only to be expected. Everyone is always out on a Friday night, including me these days.

I sigh, running my clammy hands through my hair before walking down the hallway where dad's office is. I can see light streaming through the door's cracks as I walk down. I know I'm delaying but, fuck, I don't want this to be another problem.

It should be a good thing that I found my mate. I shouldn't have to be so fucking worked up over telling my father about it. I stand in front of the door, trying to come up with what I'm going to say to him.

Jace is unsettled, pacing in the back of my mind, giving me a fucking headache from being away from Ashleigh for so long.

I muster up enough courage to reach for the doorknob and open the door slowly. I haven't set foot in this office for years. Too many memories of mum. I'm honestly surprised dad didn't demolish it or move his office into another room. It would have reminded me too much of mum if I had to be in here every day. This was one of the only rooms that didn't get remodelled a few years back.

The door opens into a spacious room, two skylights in the ceiling offering sunlight during the days as there were no other windows around. Dad is sitting against the back wall with a big oak wooden desk, two computer screens, and a few piles of paperwork. A tall, long bookshelf ran against the back wall with an old grandfather clock on the opposite side. There is a grey filing cabinet on the other side of the door next to the clock. A tall lamp is in the corner, offering a dimmer light compared to the ceiling lights.

Dad looks up from his desk as I walk in. He holds a piece of paper and types something on the computer.

"Zander…" he grumbles and looks back down, barely sparing me a glance.

"You have time to talk for a minute?" I ask, walking in and taking a seat in one of the vacant chairs in front of his desk.

Dad's eyes flash gold, letting me know his wolf is present, most likely already pissed off because I didn't wait for permission to sit. Sometimes it feels as though Leo is more in control than dad. It wouldn't be surprising if he was. Ever since mum passed, he's never been the same. Neither of us have, I suppose.

"If it's about Grace, Daniel already informed me of the situation," he says, still tapping away at his computer, not bothering to ask for any information, not bothering to look at me.

"Ahh, no, it's not about that," I confirm, fidgeting with the hem of my shirt. I can still scent Ashleigh on me, which has helped me calm down a fair bit, but I was still so wound up, I might as well get this over with. "I found my mate," I announce, staring straight at him, so he knows I'm serious.

He stops typing and looks at me this time, his face expressionless as the room fills with silence, fucking silence. Does he really not have anything to fucking say to me? After all these years of doing wrong, this is at least the one good thing I thought he'd be somewhat happy or at least proud of.

"Fated or chosen?" he asks after a few minutes of tense silence. The room is beginning to feel so small and claustrophobic that I nearly didn't hear what he asked.

"Fated", I mumble.

He nods and starts typing again.

Sighing, I stand and turn around to exit the room without saying anything further.

"You should bring Ashleigh around so she can start to meet the pack members and be familiar with the area."

I look up, completely stunned. I thought we were pretty good at hiding our relationship, I only told one person, Danni, and I don't think he would have told Dad.

"The energy company called when you tried to set up the old cottage. They needed permission to change things in the switch box before turning the electricity on. After they did, I went out there to check on things a few days after and saw you with her," he continues, answering my silent questions while still tapping away at the computer.

A sickening feeling falls into the pit of my stomach, "You knew the whole time?" I asked … confused as fuck as to why he would allow me to move Grace in if he knew about Ashleigh. Why the fuck didn't he say anything or want help at all?

“Yes,” he confirms, still so focused on his computer and paperwork, as if it's not a big fucking deal. He's just confirmed he has known I've had a mate this whole time.

“Why didn’t you say anything?” I demanded, folding my arms across my chest defensively.

“Wasn't my place to say anything, and you had to be responsible for your mistakes with Grace. Although I have to say, I was impressed with Ashleigh. I’m surprised she didn’t rip off Grace’s head, when we had the meeting, I was half expecting to call Samuel to say his daughter challenged our Luna,” he said, pausing for a minute.

I honestly think this is the longest we have gone without yelling at each other. I don’t know if I’m more stunned about that or the fact he already knew about Ashleigh.

“I thought you would have been pissed off because she’s from Liverpool,” I say honestly.

“It doesn't matter to me where she’s from. This pack hasn’t had a Luna for nearly fifteen years. Ultimately, as long as you treat her well enough, the issues between out packs shouldn’t matter. I was trying to make the transition more comfortable for the both of you for when you wanted to announce your relationship,” dad says, shuffling things around on his desk, looking about as uncomfortable as I at this moment.

A small pain burns through as he mentions mum. It'll always be hard to talk about her. I think this is the only time he has spoken of her since her death. Even now, it isn’t a direct conversation about mum. I don’t think we have ever had this much conversation, let alone him somewhat approving of my mate and a small heart-to-heart about mum.

I nod slowly, trying to hide the fact that I was uncomfortable talking about mum. I don’t want him to think I am weak at the memories.

“I know I fucked up, but I’m trying to make it better,” I grumble, not wanting him to know the extent of our problems. Dad nods, continuing to tap away.

“Anyways, thanks. I’m going to head out, but I’ll be around tomorrow with Ashleigh.” I wave, making my way towards the door to head back.

As I walked out of the office, a huge weight is lifted off me. I can honestly say I was not expecting that reaction from dad. I guess that explains why he wanted to meet with Liverpool. Although I’m not sure if he was happy about it or just accepted the fact that I found my mate. I hope things with Ashleigh’s family went a lot better tonight.

Chapter 52 - ASHLEIGH

Heart racing, nerves pile up as I sit in my car in front of the packhouse. I know Ollie and mum already know about Zander, but I was honestly more nervous telling dad and uncle.

I don't know how they would react. Would they be happy for us? Or still so angry over the issues between our packs?

I know we had a rocky start, but I also know that I wasn't going to reject him.

I still cared so much for him, and he has tried to show how much he cares over the last few days. And I agree that we could do more if we could be more open with our relationship with our family and pack members. Some might hate it, and others might be excited about it, but Zander and I were always meant to be together in the end.

I still haven't forgiven him for what happened, but he has explained, owned up to his mistake and is trying to make things better between us. So, I'll keep an open mind and allow him to try and make things right.

I take a deep breath as I open the door and head into the packhouse . Most of the lights are on, giving a welcoming vibe. The chatter grows louder as I open the door. Everyone is sitting around the table, waiting for dinner to be served.

Tonight is Ollie and Auntie Sarah's turn to cook. Brent is on patrol and will have some leftovers later, so he won't be home until about 10 pm.

Ollie looks up from where he is standing next to dad and uncle just in front of the kitchen, flashing me a grin as I head towards them. His smile falters as I move closer to the rest of the family.

Everyone else is already seated ... uncle at the head of the table, as usual, dad next to him on the left with Mum, and auntie next to uncle on the right, everyone else around them chatting about their week.

Ollie frowns, most likely feeling my nerves through our link.

'You, okay?' He links quickly enough for no one else to notice our silent conversation.

'I'm telling them tonight,' I confirm, pulling out the spare seat and sitting down. I see his eyes widen as he understands my meaning.

'You sure? I'll be with you one hundred percent, but I need to know you want him to be your mate.'

'Ollie... he's my mate. As hard as the start has been, he is still my mate,' I sigh. While I understand my cousin's worry, he doesn't need to be so macho all the time.

He nods in understanding before continuing to hand around the food.

Everyone's laughing and chatting around the dinner table for a good half an hour before someone notices I haven't been very talkative tonight.

"How have you been lately, Ash?" Alex looks over to me and asks. It has been a while since I have seen him and Meghan, so it's nice to sit around and chat with them for a little bit.

I hesitate before answering his question. Do I just go right ahead and tell them all or wait a little bit longer?

'*Just tell them. They will be glad we found our mate,'* Kia encourages excitedly for the possibility of bringing Zander here in the future.

"Things have been going well, umm... I have some news to share with everyone." I say, taking in a deep breath before continuing.

There are still a few murmurs around the table as I build up the courage to tell them about Zander. While I won't tell them the extent of things, it is still nerve-racking telling them about him in general.

"I found my mate," I breathe, looks of excitement flashing over everyone's faces as I confirm.

"Who, when how ..." So many different questions surround me as everyone jumps in, excited to know for more details. I look around and see Ollie's concerned face and mum's excitement, and I can tell she's nervous but excited at the same time.

"Firstly, start with who," Uncle's voice rings over the chatter, loud enough to hush everyone.

This is the part I was nervous about telling them.

"Zander Blackwood," I say confidently, looking right at my uncle, letting him know I have chosen him, that he is my mate. I'm met with tense silence and the uncomfortable stares of my family.

"Blackwood," My uncle confirms with a steady gaze, his expression is blank, but his command radiates through the room, almost suffocating me. I can tell he is pissed off.

I stand firm as Kia pushes forward to take some of the hit. Now, of all times, is not the time we submit. I need to stand firm on this for Zander and me.

Mum, dad, Alex, and Meghan have all submitted, baring their necks and casting eyes away. I had a feeling he would be mad, but not this mad.

Ollie is looking at Uncle David nervously, not sure what he is going to do next. I can feel his worry through our link. Auntie just sits there, watching her mate, not wanting to anger him further.

My confidence wavers a little as he assesses me, watching me carefully like I'm now a traitor instead of a part of his family. I know because Zander and I have already mated, I hold some of his power through Kia, and when we mate and mark fully, I will hold the full power of an Alpha female.

I nod slowly, darting my eyes around, watching carefully what he is going to do next.

"I hereby strip you of your title. You will no longer be a part of this family. I will not banish you and turn you rogue for the sake of your parents, but you will no longer be allowed on pack lands until deemed otherwise."

As soon as Uncle finishes the exile, excruciating pain moves through me as my link with Ollie and the pack is severed. I can see surprise form on Ollie and mum's faces as he stands to leave the table. I don't think any of us expected him to go this far, especially without any proof or knowledge.

"You think that little of me, uncle?" I whisper as I try to control the pain. I know Kia is holding a lot of it, but right now I still feel the fresh wound cutting deep. How could he just do that without asking any questions?

His golden eyes snap up to mine, and I see his wolf, King, completely in control.

"No, but I will not be responsible for starting a war against Charwood. They have not had a Luna in over a decade, and I will not put the lives of my members in danger."

Tears sting my eyes as he moves around the table. I can feel his anger radiating through as he leaves the room.

Everyone around me sits in silence. I can feel the rage rolling from Ollie. I know he is furious with uncle, just jumping to conclusions without proof that I had done anything wrong or that anything bad would happen.

"Ash, it'll be alright. I'll speak with him." Ollie reaches out and tries to comfort me, even though I know he is feeling the same amount of pain I am right now.

I shake my head and get up to leave. I can't be around here anymore. I don't want to experience the repercussions of what could happen if I was still on pack lands.

"Forget it, Ollie. It's done," I say, turning to leave. I wanted to say goodbye to mum and dad, but they got up and followed uncle into his office along with auntie.

I could hear shouting coming from everyone in the office by the time I reached the front door. I didn't want them to argue with my uncle for me, but I also didn't want to walk into that room and have something worse happen.

"Bye, Ollie," I whisper as I run out the door shifting into Kia, heading to the only place I knew where I would be safe right now. I know Zander might not be back just yet, but at least it is somewhere I could go tonight instead of roaming around.

~

It took longer getting to the cottage than expected. Kia wanted to go for a longer run, so I allowed her, just not on Liverpool.

It was nice to be out in the moonlight. The feeling of being free flowed through me.

If uncle had let me explain, just let me tell him that Zander and I were happy with how things were going, and we would transition me to his pack after we finished school, this would have gone a very different way. But, no. He was so worked up with the hate between our two packs and the possibility that it would lead to war he just outright exiled me like a traitor.

I tried to think of how to make this better, of how to help the situation, but I keep on coming up blank. I knew things were going to the strained between our families, but never to this extent. What would that mean if we ended up having pups together?

Would mum be able to come and see me? Would I still be able to see Brent and Ollie?

How is it that Ollie seemed so okay with Zander and me, but Uncle wasn't? As I run, more confusing questions flow through, and I am left with fewer answers.

By the time I arrive at the cottage, the pain of the exile had numbed to a dull ache. By tomorrow I wouldn't feel anything. There aren't any lights on when I arrive, and I could feel Zander's presence through our bond, so he might just be resting or asleep.

"Zander," I called out as I changed back to my human form, opening the back door and entering the cottage.

I hear shuffling around upstairs. Before long, he's downstairs looking a bit ragged, just wearing his boxers like he's just woken up.

Right now, I'm not exactly thinking straight, my mind is still foggy, and a dull burn runs through my chest as I try to heal, but I don't miss how he stops suddenly in the lounge, running his eyes over my body, sucking in a sharp breath as his eyes change to dark lust and a hint of gold flashes through letting me know Jace is present.

I look down and feel my cheeks flush with embarrassment. I completely forgot about being naked. I just walked in without even bothering about it.

Seeing my discomfort, Zander grabs the blanket from the lounge and hands it to me as he moves closer.

"Sweetheart, are you okay? What happened?" He asks as I cover myself with the blanket.

I know he has seen me naked before, but it is still too soon for us to be intimate again, despite how much my body screams to claim him right now. I still need to take some time to heal, so I appreciate him giving me that option instead of just making a move.

Zander looks at me, concerned, waiting for answers as I wrap the blanket around me and fold the top part of it down to try and help hold it up.

“Uncle exiled me,” I whisper as a huge wave of emotions comes crashing through me. Everything I've been holding in these last few hours hits me like a ton of bricks.

I fall sobbing into his arms at the realisation of not belonging to my pack anymore, of not having any links to my friends or family. Uncle cut all ties from everyone, and I wouldn't even be able to use the family link anymore.

“What?” he asks sharply, stroking my hair softly. His arms fold around me, holding me until I'm ready to give more details of this awful night. He plays with the ends of my curls on the back, just softly fiddling with them.

“I told them tonight around dinner. He didn't even ask for any information, he didn't ask for anything. He just asked if it was you. He stripped me of my title and banished me from the pack lands. I can't even link mum or Brent anymore,” I mumble in his chest, trying to focus on our bond and his scent to take the pain away.

He tightens his arms around me in comfort, giving me a small kiss on my head as I try to calm down. “Everything will be all right, sweetheart”, he assures, giving me another kiss and brushing my hair away so he can see my face. “We will figure it out together, okay.”

I nod numbly, just wanting to feel some sort of peace or something so I can move past all of this and be ok again.

“Why don't you run upstairs and have a shower? I can make something for you to eat. I assume you have been running for a while and are starving?”

“Yeah, that would be great, thank you,” I smile gratefully.

Zander turns and heads to the kitchen. I grab his arm and pulling him back for a kiss. Sparks of our bond dance along our skin as we intertwine. I slam my lips against his. I've wanted nothing more than to feel his lips move against mine these last few weeks. He's been amazing lately, and I think he deserves at least one.

One of his hands makes it to my hair, grabbing it roughly as he deepens the kiss further. Right now, I'm half-expecting him to pick me up and carry me to the lounge or bedroom, but instead, he pulls out of the kiss, leaving us both breathless as he rests his forehead against mine with his eyes closed, trying to regain control.

“If we don't stop now, I won't be able to control myself or Jace,” he mumbles, letting go of my hair and taking a step back, putting space between us.

“Ok.” I whisper, slightly disappointed yet, for the most part, a little relieved. It was definitely the bond, and Kia pushed me to do that. While I wanted to kiss him, I was grateful he didn't take it further.

I head upstairs to try and wash away my unsettled feelings about my family because right now all I wanted to focus on is Zander downstairs and wanting to help me. He was here for us and in reality, that is all that mattered.

Chapter 53 - OLIVER

Excruciating pain shoots through me as my link with Ashleigh is broken … as my Beta and my family. I will never be able to contact her that way again.

I can see everyone is shocked at what dad has done. Fuck, so am I. Hell, I'm fucking furious he did this without talking to me first. He was the one who insisted that we do the binding early so we can create better bonds. Ashleigh is my best friend and there is no one else who I trust more. I can't, for the life of me, understand why dad has taken such drastic measures.

Zander and I have always butt heads and we always will. We are both Alpha males, and we will do everything to protect our packs and our kind. There haven't been any issues or problems with our packs for years, sometimes small things here and there, but nothing to this level.

I hear the parents yelling and arguing in the main office as Ash heads out the front door. I'm sure Brent felt the link snap as well and will have questions when he gets home. I'm slightly surprised he hasn't linked me yet to ask what was wrong.

I turn to the table and see Alex and Meghan still there. Meghan has gotten up to start clearing the food away. There is no way anyone else is coming back to finish whatever was left over on their plates tonight.

I walk down the hall to the office. I'm fucking pissed off. Dad did this without any reason. When I walk in, they are at each other's throats, and Uncle is trying to hold Auntie Kylie back from ripping into dad.

Dad is beside his desk with only an armchair separating him and Kylie. Mum is behind the desk, just observing. I know she gets concerned when King can be like this. There is paper scattered around everywhere. A tall lamp is broken against the wall like someone has threw it but the bookshelf is still standing tall, thankfully.

"I don't have to answer to you, Kylie," King snarls in command, making her and uncle submit.

I can tell Uncle Robert is furious with Dad for what he did to Ashleigh. Fuck it, so am I, but these two never go against each other, they have always been a united front as Alpha and Beta. Tonight, I think that has changed.

"If you won't answer Kylie, then answer me," I demand, feeling my command flowing through. At this point, I am so fucking pissed off that I didn't give a shit that I was challenging Dad.

King can be a fucking asshole sometimes, and when he's in control, no one really likes to deal with him, I at least thought his family meant something to him, but clearly, from tonight, it didn't.

"Why the fuck did you exile Ash? Why did you cut our link? She was my fucking Beta!" I can feel Ace push forward as I ask. The pain for both of us is unbearable. I know he has taken most of the hit and is just as angry and wound up about the whole thing as I am.

At least if it were a natural transfer, there wouldn't have been any pain or issues. She would have just had a pack transfer. But dad removed her from our link and severed all ties, making things worse for both of us. Now I'm left without a Beta, and this empty void in my chest.

King being entirely in control right now, I can see mum standing behind him trying not to interfere, but of all times, this is where we needed her voice of reason.

"Watch it, boy," he snarls, trying to make me submit to him. I can feel beads of sweat start forming on my brow as I fight him. Everyone else in the room is cowering, most likely in pain. Even mum has submitted to him at this point.

"You wanted Ashleigh and me to link early to build trust and foundation in our leadership. You just cut all ties with her without any proof. You do not get to make that choice without me agreeing to it," Ace snarls back.

"Do you even understand the damage and pain you have caused us?" Ace continues. "Not only to me but also to her parents. We won't even have the family link because of what you have done."

"I have my reasons, and none of you will question me," King roars, looking around at us. I can see Kylie and Robert furious that he has shut them down.

"Trust me when I say this, brother, you had better get your shit together, or you will no longer have a Beta just like your son," Uncle Robert snarls back.

I can see Uncle Robert trying to fight his wolf for control, he knows better than to go up against King right now, but someone just harmed his pup. I wouldn't blame him for wanting to rip into dad.

Seeing I won't get my fucking answers tonight, I turn back around and head out the door slamming it behind me before more yelling and arguing starts. It's between uncle and dad. Out of everyone there, he would be the one to take dad.

I make my way to Ash's room. I needed to get some clothes and things for school. I would assume she has gone to Blackwood, but she would need something for next week at least.

I gathered the essentials. The last thing I ever wanted to do was go through my cousin's panty drawer. Fuck, if they were any other girl, I would have been all for it, but this is just fucking weird.

Assuming she didn't take her phone with her, I had to message the one person I didn't fucking want to. Sighing heavily before asking a favour to the one person I probably shouldn't be talking to right now, especially with King being so fucking stupid.

I opened Blackwood's contact, hoping she was already with him by now.

Oliver: Is Ash with you?

Zander: Yea, What the fuck happened?

Oliver: Address, and I'll explain.

Zander: Ya, no. I ain't giving that fucking info out.

Oliver: I have some of her clothes and school things. I'll drop them off along with her car and phone.

Zander: Fuck that, forget it. I'll buy her stuff this weekend.

Oliver: You won't be able to get stuff in time for school. You know how she gets when she misses class.

I waited for what seemed like forever, pacing in my bedroom for Blackwood to give me an answer. I know I was going against my pack right now. If I did this, I could potentially be exiled the same way. King had no fucking proof that anything ever happened with Zander and Ashleigh.

There have been attacks everywhere lately, small ones, one wouldn't think so significant, but there has been a pattern. We believe the person or persons are looking for someone and for King to exile Ash like that at a time like these pisses me off even more. One of the advisors told me this is similar to what happened last time, which was when Blackwood's mother was killed. I need to talk to Blackwood to make sure she could be joined into his pack so she would at least have a link with someone.

Zander: Fine, but if you bring anyone else, I'll be fucking pissed off and won't hesitate to kill them. 202 Gilbert Ave, Landon 2265

The last thing I pack is a few hundred dollars in cash I keep around just in case of an emergency like this, I know Blackwood will want to buy her stuff, but at least she would have something of her own. I grabbed the keys to her car and headed out.

"Where are you headed off to, man?" Brent calls out as I get into Ash's car. Fuck, I was hoping that no one would notice me going.

He walks up to the car, standing next to the driver's side as I slam the door shut, winding the window down as the engine roars to life.

"Just headed out," I mumble. It's not that I don't trust Brent. I just don't want him to be involved with this. We need at least one person to be able to take leadership if we all fell out.

"What happened at dinner? Why is Reid all weird and pacing, and why do I have this pain," he rambles on and on, not even worrying about my dismissiveness. I guess his wolf hasn't told him his sister was exiled because she found her mate.

"Look, I have to head out for a few hours. When I get back, I'll explain, okay?" I say, trying to get out of this situation before someone else finds me delivering stuff to Ashleigh.

"Ok, sure. Umm... where is Ash? How come you have her car?" he continues asking questions.

For fuck's sake, Brent is like a brother to me but these damn questions. "Look, we can talk when I get back, okay? I just have to head out."

I wave a dismissive hand before rolling the car in reverse, slamming on the pedal and heading into the location Blackwood gave me.

Thankfully the drive didn't take too long. At this time of night, there was hardly any traffic. I pulled up to this little old cottage on the outskirt of the city. It stood in a secluded area with woods surrounding it well enough covered for a shifter to live here.

Dragging the bag out of the car with her laptop, phone, and a few other things, I don't even bother knocking on the door. I know they both are here. One, because Blackwood's car is parked in the driveway, and two, I can scent them both.

I see Blackwood cooking in the kitchen as I close the door behind me, he looks up with silver eyes, and on high alert, I can feel his command radiating through the room.

"Put your fucking wolf away," I snap, rolling my eyes.

'Can't blame him,' Ace mumbles. He has a point, his Luna has just been exiled from our pack, and she doesn't have a link with anyone right now. Of course, he's on edge.

"Fuck off," he snaps back, continuing to cook what seemed like an omelette.

I take a minute to look around. It seems nice enough. A little woodfire heater is roaring away, dividing the kitchen and living room. The stairs leads up to bedrooms, I assume, and the kitchen seems to be working well enough, judging by how he is turning on the gas and starts cooking. A few small lamps are turned on around the place, offering a friendly soft welcome.

"Here's everything. It should be okay enough for the week or longer," I say, putting the bag on the lounge and the laptop, keys, and phone.

"Thanks, I'll take her shopping on the weekend or something," Blackwood says, concentrating on cooking rather than our conversation.

"Ollie?" I hear her voice close to me as I turn around. Ashleigh's standing halfway down the stairs in trackpants and an oversized t-shirt. I pull a face because I don't want to fucking know what these two have been doing here. I get she might not have any clothes, but jeez.

"Hey, Ash," I force a smile.

'Be happy she found her mate,' Ace says.

Even though he dislikes Blackwood, he understands the mate bond better than I do. I'm still in two mindsets about the whole mate thing. Ace doesn't like that I didn't wait for my mate, but I'm also not a total man whore like I know Blackwood has been in the past.

"You shouldn't be here. You could get in serious trouble, especially with uncle being how he is." She frantically shakes her head, walking closer to me, trying to push me out the door.

“It's fine, I can handle Dad. I just wanted to bring you some clothes and other things, so you didn’t have to dress well… like that.” I gesture toward her as I do.

Her cheeks heat up in embarrassment when she looks down and realises the shirt is a few sizes too big. A low growl came from the kitchen as we continued our conversation. I guess her mate didn’t like my relationship with my cousin. I smirk, enjoying the fact I’m pissing him off.

Chuckling to myself, I grab the bag and bring it to her. “Here, this should be enough for a few days. I also bought your phone, laptop, and car,” I continue gesturing towards the lounge where I put the rest of the stuff. “I’m not sure what your plans were, but you might want to consider joining Blackwood’s pack, especially with what’s been happening lately.”

Her eyes widen in understanding as I try to explain without giving too much sensitive information. I only found this stuff out today, I was going to bring Brent and Ash up to speed tonight after dinner, but clearly, that wasn’t going to happen.

“Uncle’s that mad,” she whispers, sadly looking down at her phone and things.

Shit, shit, make it better… Blackwood looks up from the kitchen and walks over to her, seeing she’s upset. Bringing her into an embrace, kissing her softly, trying to comfort her. I try so fucking hard not to make a face or gagging sounds with him being so… loving?? Blackwood is never this affectionate or caring with the other women he was with, but I’m glad to see he has changed his ways with her.

“No, I just found stuff out today. I was going to share with you tonight before everything went to shit, and well, honestly, it's not safe for you to be without a pack right now. You don’t have to do the whole Luna thing, and it's just so that you have a link with him and his Beta,” I try to explain.

“We will figure it out,” Blackwood says, planting another kiss on her head, trying to comfort her while she just looks so miserable.

“I don’t even have my family link anymore, and I won’t ever be able to link you or Mum or Dad again. That's what hurt the most,” she says.

A slight burn shoots through me at the realisation of that fact. I’ll never be able to link her again until I make Alpha, and even then, I’m not sure if it’s possible to get the family link back. I nod slowly, trying not to upset her or make anything worse again.

“Anyways, I’m glad you have somewhere to be tonight. I should head off, though, the parents were arguing when I left, and I don’t exactly want to be at the start of another one when I get home.” I move toward the door heading out.

“Ollie, thank you. You know you didn’t have to do this so thank you,” she says, leaning in and giving me a tight hug.

“You know I didn’t have a say in the whole thing, right? I didn’t care you two were together. I wouldn’t have done that. Honestly, I would have tried to look at some peace deal instead.” I had to make sure that she knew I would have welcomed it and would have seen it as an opportunity to have our packs working together instead of against each other.

“I know. You have shown that to me tonight,” Ashleigh smiles as she moves back to Blackwood.

I nod, letting out a breath of air I didn’t realise I was holding. I didn’t want her to come out of this thinking I hated her.

“Keep in touch. I’ll see you around school, and send me a message if you need anything, okay?” I say before heading out the door.

Unfortunately, I know this will probably be the last time for a while before I see her again. I won’t be allowed to be around her at school or anywhere else. This was goodbye for us until things settled down and dad could accept them together. I just hoped she knew this, too, and she did by the looks of things.

Ashleigh nods one more time before giving me another quick hug. “Thanks, Ollie,” she whispers before I head out the door, shifting into Ace.

Chapter 54 - ASHLEIGH

My senses are in overdrive as I feel the warm sun streaming through our bedroom window. His scent engulfed me as tingles danced along my skin. I hear his deep breathing next to me as one of his arms slung over, pulling me close to his hard chest.

Last night was hard. I had the worst night's sleep, tossing and turning until I couldn't take it anymore. I wanted Zander to hold me close to tell me everything was going to be okay, that this weird emptiness won't last forever.

I wondered if this is what it felt like to become a rogue or if it is worse. At least I don't have the scent of a rogue. I just didn't have the links and connections to the pack anymore. It's like I'm in limbo. I am just waiting. Usually, when one is stripped of a title a new one is given or one becomes an Omega. Uncle didn't even do that for me, so now I'm stuck in limbo unless I renounce my allegiance to my pack and turn rogue until I move into Zander's Pack.

In the Liverpool pack, there are a few ranks and titles:

First, in command: The Alpha and Luna. They are leaders of the pack, equal to both, and can be overturned by death or a challenge or passed down to an heir. The Alpha is usually the strongest in the pack. They will protect everyone by all means necessary.

The Luna is the mother of the pack. She is caring, loving, and sweet-natured and can usually help control the Alpha if anything they were ever to lose control. Alpha and Luna don't necessarily need to be male and female, sometimes, the roles can be reversed, and for same-sex couples, it just depends on the birthright or who wins the challenge, if one is ever presented.

Second, in command: Beta, The Beta is the most trusted person to the Alpha. They can form a link from the first shift if you know who the two heirs are. The link helps build trust and friendship between the two. A Beta is usually the more calculating and logical, ensuring the Alpha hasn't missed any areas when making an important decision.

Third, in command: Gamma, they are the Luna's Guard and are chosen by the Luna when the Alpha and Luna are appointed the pack's leaders. If a Gamma dies in combat protecting the Luna, another is appointed to the position should the Luna not choose to keep the bloodline, or if there are no Gamma heirs, The Gamma is a Luna's most trusted person in the pack. They also hold a link with the Luna, similar to the Alpha and Beta.

Advisors: Help with the command officers. They would look more at delegation and logical tactics if anything were to go wrong within our pack. They also help with processes and procedures for when a lockdown is happening or if anything needs changing in the pack.

Command Officers: Are the ones who train the warriors and lead the patrol runs. They report to the Beta and let them know what is happening within the pack.

Accountants: Help with our finances and keep Alpha, Luna, and Beta informed about all the businesses they have. Alpha and Beta will make the final decisions for the businesses, but the accountants will help with the everyday records and accounts where required.

Workers: Help with the everyday roles. They have positions similar to humans: lawyer, doctor, teacher, etc. they can be whatever they want. If you weren't born into an heir bloodline, you would typically become a worker and be placed into society like an everyday person. However, you would still have to abide by pack rules, and if you wanted, you could move up the ranks and prove you are worthy of a higher title.

Warrior: Are along the same level as a worker. When we leave high school, or whichever schooling we choose to finish, we can do a trial and see if we are fit enough or worthy enough to become a pack warrior. These trials are held at the end of every year. They sleep, eat, and live together in the village built on the main crossroads between our packs. They are the ones who train every day and do regular border patrols. They also get called out to smaller packs and help with training and protection if needed.

Omega's: Help around with the children and duties of the housing. In some packs, they are classed as maids and treated very poorly, but in Liverpool, they are classed as workers and have stable wages so they can still live a decent life.

The title doesn't matter in Liverpool, but I know some packs take their titles too seriously.

Obviously, we require respect for and understanding within the different titles, but we also make sure everyone is loved and cared for.

Over the years, the smaller packs have been eliminated and merged with the bigger packs and a lot of the time, in these smaller packs Omega is used as an insult. We have tried over the years to create an environment where everyone is equal. That's why mum and auntie set up the cooking schedule and made us do our chores so we could learn to appreciate what we had rather than take it for granted and not look down on what others don't have.

During the night, I tossed and turned, wondering why Uncle didn't demote me to a different role, why he left me feeling like this. I have never known anyone not to have a title within their pack, and they usually just go rogue. I guess maybe if I didn't have a choice to go into Zander's pack, I would choose rogue over this uneasiness. It felt horrible.

I suppose that's why a lot of them struggle without a pack. A wolf needs their pack. They depend on each other and the link. I haven't heard anything from Kia since. I just hope she is recovering okay and Jace is helping her.

It was as though Zander felt my uneasiness during the night. As soon as I got up to go and ask him to come into the same room, he immediately complied with no questions asked and no funny business throughout the night either, which was probably the hardest for him.

Still, I appreciated it so much. With everything else going on, I didn't know how I would feel if we were to have sex again. I'd rather be in the right headspace before moving forward.

I feel him moving next to me as I lay there listening to his breathing, feeling our bond, letting it guide me out of this crappy feeling. Waking up next to him for the first time since our issues felt so surreal. I hated the time we lost together, but at the same time, I know it brought us closer. The circumstances were crappy, and it was an experience I hope we never have to go through again. At least, if it were ever to emerge again, I hoped he would feel like he could come to me, and I would hope I could provide the support he needed.

This week alone, our bond has been stronger. I can feel it become stronger as I increasingly accept more of him every day. I accepted him before, but the hurt outweighed the love, and now, I think I'm ready to forgive him.

I just wanted to see how my family would react and how this weekend went, then maybe I would let him mark me. I was never going to reject him. I just needed some time, and for him to show me that he wanted this, that he wanted us together.

It was never like this before. It is almost as though the thought of losing our bond scared him so much that he needed a kick up the ass to realise the importance of it.

I feel him stirring next to me, waking slowly, "Good morning, sweetheart", he rasps deeply, pulling me in closer, kissing the side of my neck where he will one day mark me.

I go to say good morning back, but my words turn into needy moans at the movement of his kisses. My moans seem to encourage him further. As his hands move under my top, attaching to my breasts, he roughly grabs my nipples and plays with them while sucking my neck. My body reacts as my head falls on his shoulder behind me for support. All of my concerns and worries I had earlier instantly left me as he pleasures me.

One of his hands slowly moves to my sensitive area, and my legs automatically spread for him, desperately wanting more. I'm panting and moaning more and more as he teases me. "Are you enjoying this, sweetheart?" he grumbles into my neck, pinching my nipple and flicking my clit at the same time.

My body tenses, my toes curl, my back arches as I reach my climax, my wet juices spill around his fingers as he moves deeper and deeper with each motion. At this point, I can barely say anything back to him, let alone think straight.

My mind is full of lust and desire for everything Kia and I want him to be doing to us. I can feel his member behind me as I lean into him. I so desperately want more. I don't even care at this point. All the stupid reasons I had before having long vanished from my mind.

"More, Zander, please…" I manage to pant as he removes his hand from me, lifting it to his mouth and sucking my juices clean from each finger, one by one. A devilish smile creeps on his face as I watch him. A part of me hopes I don't sound too desperate, but right now, I honestly don't care.

"Your wish is my command," he declares before grabbing my chin and pulling me into a deep and desperate kiss. He pulls back and slides down my body ripping off my top and little shorts I put on when I went to bed, "Won't be needing those anymore," he says.

He sucks on my nipple one more time before making his way down lower, kissing every inch of my skin, leaving tingles erupting in flames everywhere. He kisses my hips before diving into my entrance. I let out a gasp as he latches on, sucking up the remainder of my juices, his tongue doing wonders to my clit, licking and sucking. I feel my eyes roll back in response to him, my body quivering at his touch.

I just need more. I want more. "Zander…I need…" I moan, unable to say anything further.

"Not yet, sweetheart. I'm not done teasing you."

"I don't know how I was so fucking stupid," I hear him mumble softly against my skin. A little pain shoots through at the memory, but I try to forget about it quickly not to ruin this moment. As soon as those thoughts came, they left almost immediately as he continues to tease me.

He moves back up slowly and kisses me on the lips. As he does, I feel the tip of him hard against my entrance, ready to push in.

Taking a few deep breaths before he plunges in, I scream his name as he starts pounding inside me, each movement deeper and deeper. I'm chanting his name like a prayer as he lifts my legs, wrapping them around his waist, getting a better grip.

After a few hard, rough pumps, I'm shaking in his arms. My body is about to go limp after the fresh assault he's just given me. He groans and I feel him release his seed inside me.

Our skin shines in the morning sun with a thin layer of sweat as he slides down next to me, both of us panting and gasping for air. It takes a few minutes for us before we catch our breaths.

"Well, good morning to you, too," I giggle, leaning across and giving him another kiss.

He pulls me in deeper with the kiss before letting me go, "How are you feeling today?" he asks, playing with a lock of my hair, propping himself up on one shoulder, facing me.

"Hmm, I'm a lot better than last night. I'm glad Ollie could come and see me, even if it was a short visit. I don't know what Monday will bring, and mum or Brent haven't even tried to contact me yet," I say sadly. I try not to think about the loss of my family and try to focus on Zander and our bond because right now, he is all I can focus on before I break down and become a total mess.

He nods in understanding,

"Would you like to come back to my pack today and see what it's like?" he asks, tilting his head and studying my expression.

He has been so supportive since everything happened last night, and I am so grateful that I had him to lean on right now.

"Sure, it would be nice to meet everyone," I smile in response.

When we were there for the meeting, I was curious to see around the pack, but obviously, Zander couldn't show me around at the time.

"Wait, how did everything go with your dad last night? I'm so sorry, with my disaster of an evening, I didn't even think to ask," I say, grabbing his arm as he moves out of bed, pulling up a pair of trackpants.

Guilt washes over me. I didn't even ask. Things could have gone just as badly with his dad.

Zander shrugs, "he was fine with it, I guess. He already knew," he mumbles the last bit, rubbing the back of his neck, looking a bit guilty.

I frown. How did his dad already know? I thought he hadn't told anyone yet. He must have seen my confused face before jumping into an explanation. "The electric company called Dad for approval of something. His name and contact details were still on file when I set it up. I didn't realise when I called them. Came here to check it out and he saw us together," he says while slipping on a tee.

"Ohh, okay then," I say, trying not to sound so confused over everything.

"It'll be okay." He reaches for me, gives me a kiss, sensing my uneasiness and nerves. "I'll cook something if you want to have a shower,"

Before I could respond, he was already out the door and down the stairs starting to get things ready. I sigh to myself before making my way to the bathroom. At least Zander's family seems to be okay with the two of us, and I suppose that is a good thing. Hopefully, Ollie can talk some sense into uncle, and maybe I'll be allowed to visit mum and dad and some friends in the future.

Going to a new pack as a Luna can be a challenge in itself. I wouldn't know anyone, and I wouldn't know who to trust. I hoped maybe I could still see my friends at school and maybe my family, but I also know the rules. I also doubt uncle would change his mind over the weekend.

I wonder what Zanders pack is going to be like? We had never really been on the grounds until the other day, and before then, all other meetings were on at council or other packs. I looked forward to seeing what my future home would be like.

Chapter 55 - ZANDER

My body instantly yearned for her as I left our room. Guilt consumes me as I remember what a total fuckwit I was before. I'll remind her daily how much I love her and show her what she means to me. I won't ever put that doubt in her mind again.

Never have I felt so fucking scared when I thought I was losing her. Now I just need to erase those memories and shower her with love and affection and pray that she will forgive me.

Jace is pleasantly satisfied with this morning's romp festivities and is eager to jump in the shower with her, but I thought maybe she would like some alone time before we head out to my pack territory.

Soon my pack will start the morning rounds with training and patrol runs. I am going to drive her around and show her what we did. From what Ashleigh told me, both she and Oliver participated in training and patrol.

Even if she is Luna, I'm sure she would be eager to see our facilities. Although, I wonder how she would react when she notices not many women trains, if any at all.

I hope she is okay with that. It's just how we have always been. In a larger pack, women haven't needed to train. They know the basics, to defend themselves if there is ever an attack, and get yearly training if they help look after any vulnerable people. Beyond that, it's never been a big priority for us. We always have guards or police around all the time and haven't had any issues in the last fifteen years.

Dad hasn't told me anything about what Oliver mentioned last night about some of the attacks. I hope it was an isolated thing and nothing to do with shifters, but I suppose these days, it's harder to tell. Then again, dad barely shares anything with me regarding pack business. He keeps that all between him and Jake.

I don't know how he expects me to run the pack if he isn't going to be showing me anything before my initiation. I have done the Alpha Training, I have found my mate, and until I 'finish school' there isn't anything else holding me back from claiming my birthright.

Part of me wants dad to keep it for a few more years until Ashleigh and I have settled down and are ready. Maybe we will travel for a bit, let her see the world and travel to America and Europe to meet some of our allies. But I also know she wants to go to Uni. I doubt we would be able to travel much until she finishes school.

By the time we had both had breakfast, we are ready to head out. I could feel her nerves. I try to send calming feelings to her through Jace, but that hasn't settled her so far.

The more we connect, the stronger our bond would build, and after this morning, it felt so much stronger than it has in the last few weeks. It almost feels complete. I wanted to mark her this morning. Fuck, I nearly did at one point, but thankfully I was able to pull Jace back and he allowed it this time.

Bringing her to the pack unmarked has him uneasy. He doesn't want others sniffing around her, and honestly, I don't blame him. I felt a little agitated about it, but I can't force it on her and nor will I. She should have that choice, and until she forgives me, I won't be able to forgive myself for what I did. I won't be at ease until we figure everything out.

At least she will have my scent on her. That is the only thing keeping me sane right now, knowing that others will know she is mine.

I keep glancing over at her to try and spark up a conversation, but between her nerves and my own, the car is in uncomfortable silence. I flick on the radio and try to find a decent station before giving up and plugging in my music through Spotify on my phone.

The beat of Everybody Talks by Neon Trees flows through the car. Subconsciously my hands start tapping against the steering wheel to the music as I softly sing the words.

I feel her gaze on me as I'm driving before she asks, "you like Neon Trees?" I glance back at her to see her astonished face darting towards the stereo and back to me again.

Shrugging, I say, "Yeah, they aren't too bad. My phone has a random shuffle. I can pick and choose some music, but this one was a good one. It suggested a while back."

I used to hate the way my phone would sometimes randomly shuffle some of the music, but I've gotten some good beats from them, so I can't complain if they have broadened my horizon in music.

She smiles and starts singing along to the chorus.

"It started with a whisper

And that was when I kissed her

And then she made my lips hurt."

I chuckle, joining in with her singing. Before long, the uneasiness lifts, and it seems to have relaxed our nerves for the time being. It's nice to know that we have similar tastes in music. I'll forever be taking note of her favourite songs so I can hear her sweet voice.

I feel her tense as I pull up to my border. I reach across and give her hand a comforting squeeze. I know she's not technically from Liverpool anymore. However, the patrol team will be able to scent her arrival and will still be on edge, given that everyone knew who she was because she was the Liverpool Beta heir.

I linked Sal, letting him know it was just me and a visitor passing through, so he didn't have to worry about checking in. No doubt he was going to confirm my story with dad. He has to or dad will be pissed if I just show up at the packhouse with her unannounced.

The further we move into my territory, the more uneasy she becomes. I hope this place will grow on her. I would hate for her to always be this unsettled. It wouldn't be fair to her or our pack seeing their Luna stressed and worried all the time.

Pulling up to the front of the house she just sits there nervously fidgeting, something I've noticed the last few days when she gets nervous, she fidgets with something, either her hair, or something on her clothes, or her jewellery if she is wearing anything.

I smile to myself and take note to buy her a necklace or something that will help calm her nerves. I don't want her constantly feeling uneasy. This will be her home, too.

I slam the car door shut before running around to the passenger side and letting her out. I can feel her anxiety has almost doubled since we pulled up. I've never felt her this nervous before. I pull her in for a quick kiss trying to let the bond work its magic and help her calm down.

"Everything will be alright," I whisper gently, pecking another kiss on her forehead before bringing her into an embrace, resting my chin on her head as she holds me tightly. I don't know what's wrong, I don't want to push her to tell me, but hopefully if she knows I'm here for her.

'She's nervous about meeting the pack as Luna and officially meeting your father as your mate,' Jace mumbles feeling his annoyance through me as though it's the most obvious thing in the fucking world.

I roll my eyes at his comment because part of me feels so fucking stupid, of course she's going to be fucking nervous, but she has nothing to worry about. I swear dad already likes her more than me judging from how he reacted last night. And the pack, well they will be ecstatic having another Luna.

"Come on, it'll be ok. Everyone will love you. You were born to be Luna." I tried to encourage her and started leading her toward the packhouse.

Chapter 56 - ASHLEIGH

I psyched myself way too much by the time we arrived in front of the packhouse. Zander tried to help calm me down, but my nerves got the best of me in the end. I kept replaying everything that happened last night, and one thing stuck out, the supposed reason why uncle banished me from the pack.

Charwood hadn't had a Luna for over a decade. So, of course, naturally, I was worried about so many different things. With such a high expectation, my brain went in overloaded.

What if the pack doesn't like me?

What if his father didn't like me?

What if more of his exes show up and try to challenge me?

Would they accept me because I was from Liverpool and not a part of their pack?

So many possibilities swirl around my head. I panicked and froze until Zander opened the car door and brought me into a tight hug, kissing me gently, trying to reassure me. Every time he does something like this, he surprises me, making my heart ache for him and making me fall in love with him all over again.

We walk up the steps of the packhouse , I'm half-expecting him to stop and knock for some reason, but he walks right into the foyer and calls out, "hello, is anyone around?" and we're met with an eerie silence, as he waits for about five seconds for someone to respond.

I would have waited a little bit longer for a response, but my mate is impatient and doesn't like to hang around too long.

"Of course not. What was I fucking thinking?" he grumbles to himself as he looks at his watch on his left wrist and grumbles something about being late for training.

"Come on. I'll show you the training grounds if you like?" He grabs my hand before I can protest or say anything, drags me back out the door, and lifts me into the car, not waiting another second.

"We have two main training grounds, one about ten minutes from the packhouse . That is usually where most of the training is held and is also linked with a lot of the walking tracks, and the barracks are also connected to this ground. Our warriors sleep, eat, and train together, as well as do overseas missions and interstate missions when our allies need any type of help. The other training is on the other side of our territory. This one has the field, a gym, and an Olympic indoor pool that we use year-round. The warriors are split into two-week, on-off rotations between the two grounds: Richie coordinates that side of things. This also lines up with patrol runs. Richie allocates one or two command officers to each platoon, ranging from twenty to at least thirty-five warriors each cycle." Zander starts rambling, explaining how things work here as he drives.

I sit there watching my mate's sudden weird behaviour. He's driving like a lunatic, and I've never seen him this worked up about anything. We will have an accident if he doesn't relax and calm down. Maybe he's just as nervous as I am.

I know things with his father are always tense, and I couldn't feel anything through our bond. It seems he has blocked our link, so Kia or I can't feel him. I know he could feel my anxiety earlier, but right now, I couldn't feel anything from him, not even frustration or pressure, just almost empty.

I nod, listening to his chatter, "Do you have many warriors who train daily?" I ask curiously, hoping if I respond, he'll loosen up a bit.

In Liverpool, they ranged from eighty to a hundred per session and held at least five sessions a day, two in the morning, one mid-day, one in the afternoon and another in the evening. It's all scattered around to meet everyone's schedule. Some people work two jobs. Liverpool tries to give them enough pay to maintain a comfortable lifestyle.

Still, it's tricky when little ones come along, so some of our families take two jobs to keep going. We try to support our pack members where we can by providing them with free education and a sustainable lifestyle.

Once a member has found their mate, they can choose a location where they would like to raise their family. The pack members help build the home; we cover the cost and give them a comfortable lifestyle. We only ask for respect and loyalty and to give one hundred percent into whatever field of business they choose.

A warrior would typically select a house to live in and decide if they want to stay at the barracks with their family or in their home, whichever suited them. If both partners were a part of the team, they would usually set up in the bunkers. We have small apartment blocks to hold a family of 4 people until they decide to move to their home if they wish.

Ollie and I always tried to do at least two sessions a day, one in the morning and another in the evening after school.

"We have a hundred fifty to two hundred members each session, and each training field holds these sessions. Richie and Sal coordinate between the two; we must sign up or confirm we are attending beforehand, so they know how many to expect. We have about four to five sessions a day, so around ten sessions total between the two grounds, and we train at least over a thousand warriors daily. It's compulsory to do at least one training session a day if you are a warrior. Regular pack members can join if they would like to but they need to let Richie know," Zander confirms, eyes laser-focused on the road, not even giving me a glance or a look as he's talking.

Something is up with him. I don't know why he's being all funky about this. I hope he didn't regret letting me visit the pack today.

"Wow, that's a lot of people training every day. Ollie and I did at least two sessions a day. It would be interesting to see what you guys do," I smile, remembering the times we used to race around the territory before training, getting all pumped up and excited before the sessions.

It's nice to have someone on the same level as me regarding fighting techniques. We are similar but different, and I had only managed to take him down twice since we started training properly with the warriors when we got our wolves at sixteen.

I've lost count of how many times I've landed on my ass, but lately, I have gotten a lot better, so naturally, I was sad when I knew I wouldn't be able to join Ollie anymore.

When we were younger, we would prepare daily by running and keeping fit so our bodies would accept our wolves. We didn't start training until we were in high school and had our wolves. Since we got into such a routine, it's just become a part of our lifestyle.

Zander finally glances at me with worried eyes and a hint of guilt. I cross my arms over my chest. Today I wore simple clothes, jeans, sneakers, and a nice tee with black and white polka-dots, so not a bad outfit if we wanted to join the training. The jeans might be a bit tricky, but I do have spare clothes in the back so I can change into tights if needed.

"What's wrong?" I ask as we pull up to a large lush green field with a massive building off to the left. A driveway led to a large open parking area underneath the building.

Glass windows wrapped around the entire exterior of the building except for the back, where it had a wall of dull bricks lined up to the roof. You could see a fully equipped gym looking out to the field and a grand staircase leading towards the pool.

A lot of people in the training field are already chatting, waiting for training to start. Honestly, it was lucky we found a car spot where we did. I look around, taking in my new space, and it was beautiful. These grounds alone were a lot bigger than the ones I used to. We don't even have a pool attached to our training grounds; you would have to go to another rec centre.

Looking around, I noticed that most of the people there were men. I turn to Zander, who is still sitting there nervously looking at me, waiting to say something more even though I had already asked him a question.

"Want to tell me what's going on?" I ask, tilting my head a little, darting my eyes to the field and back to Zander again.

My face formed into a confused frown as I wait for Zander to come clean on why he was all squirrely and flustered. Now don't get me wrong, I don't mind who is here or who I meet first, but I pray that he isn't about to tell me that I can't do training like I usually do because, by the looks of things, there isn't a single woman on site. I don't know what to expect but I really, really hope I am wrong in what I am thinking right now.

"Umm... so, we do things a little differently around here," He mumbles, rubbing the back of his neck, darting his eyes around, not meeting mine. I wait for him to continue before jumping in. I can feel Kia all excited about the prospect of being around other people and training.

He sighs before finally blurting, "Women don't usually train."

He almost cringes as Kia bubbles to the surface. I am one hundred per cent sure she is showing in my eyes right now, and I try to hold her back because she is just as pissed off as I am.

With what happened to his mother, you would think that he or his father would encourage everybody to participate in training because I sure hope he knows I'm not going to be the type of Luna that sits back and holds tea parties at the packhouse .

I want to be involved in everything, from Patrol runs to pack business to the hospitals and children. It's already like what I did before as Beta. I helped auntie and mum all the time.

"By choice or direction?" I grind out. I don't know what to think or expect what they want me to do as Luna, but the first thing will be to change that stupid rule.

Zander shrugs, "it's always how it has been that way for as long as I can remember. No one has ever brought it up, but the people who look after the vulnerable and children get basic training, but that's about it."

"So, will we be joining it today?" I ask, trying to calm Kia down and not letting her show as much, I know it's not technically his fault, but it still rubs me the wrong way.

"I can ask. I'm sure Richie will be fine with it, and I'll have to let them know you are my mate," he says, carefully watching me for any reaction.

I nod and quickly grab my tights from the back seat, slip them on, and throw my jeans in the back as Zander links Richie, letting him know we are joining the training today.

I'm glad I didn't have to persuade him too much for that. After all, this pent-up energy, I need an outlet. Hopefully, I'll be able to spar against someone, and he's not so funky about that.

A few minutes later, we are walking out to the training field. There must be at least a full house this morning with about 200 people. I can see a tall bulkier gentleman standing in front in a singlet top and loose shorts, which is what most of the guys around here are wearing.

All of them are huge, with enormous muscles and toned legs. Some of the younger ones are off to the back, roughing each other up, while the older ones are standing around chatting.

A few of them notice Zander walking towards whom I assume is Richie, and others start eyeing me … some with curious looks, and a few of them have their wolves peeking through, which I would only assume because I still scent like Liverpool.

I wait off to the side as Zander speaks to the man in front. All these unnecessary stares start to make me uncomfortable. I shift back and forth on my feet, waiting a little longer before turning and making my way towards Zander when a familiar voice calls out and stops me in my tracks.

"I'm glad he finally came to his senses and got his head out of his ass."

I whip back around and breathe a sigh of relief. “Daniel?”

Daniel walks up, flanked by two guys of similar age and height. I’ve seen the shaggy blonde one before, he’s nearly always hanging around with Zander at school, but the other one, I don’t think I’ve seen as much, if at all. I try to remember if he was at Chloe’s party, but honestly, that night is such a blur for me.

Daniel grabs me and brings me into a hug surprising me with such affection, I try and wriggle out of it quickly to not cause a scene, but I know my efforts have failed when I hear a growl behind me and stomping towards us.

I’m pulled away from Daniel and back into Zander with such force that I nearly stumble and have to grab onto his arm for support.

“Relax, bro, I was just saying, hello,” he says with his hands up in surrender and neck bared in submission. I can feel Jace’s possessiveness rolling off in waves. I steal a peek over Daniel's shoulder, and most of the people standing around us have silenced and submitted. The two guys behind him have their necks bared and eyes cast down.

“Jace, it's okay. He was saying hello,” I whisper, lifting a hand to him and leaning into him, trying to calm the tension using our bond. His golden eyes snap down to mine, and I can see him and Zander fighting for control as his eyes flicker.

“Mine,” he snarls towards Daniel before relinquishing control to Zander.

Well, there goes my chances of potentially sparring with anyone this morning. If he is already like that with his Beta, there is no way he would let me spar against a random.

Chapter 57 - ZANDER

'You're welcome,' Danni links me, smirking as I pull Ashleigh in a tight grip trying to regain control. Thankfully, our bond and her scent are the only things helping me not to lose my shit right now.

'For what? Pissing off my wolf in front of everyone?' I snap back.

And, of course, he rolls his eyes but still has his hands up in surrender as Jace glares at him.

The fucking little twat knows too much. I swear I wouldn't put up with him if he weren't my Beta or best friend. Don't get me wrong, he knows how to push my boundaries, and no one else can pull the same shit he does. Even Eric won't, and we have known each other since we were in diapers. But without Danni, I'd be a lost cause. I honestly don't think there is anyone who could replace him.

"Jace, it's ok, he was just saying hello," Ashleigh whispers, bringing her hand to my chin, softly stroking me and leaning in closer, trying to get Jace to give me back control.

If only she knew how much of an ass Danni can be. That's one of the things I love about her. She is always so trusting and has no clue of the hold she has over us. Jace was already smitten with her as soon as he found out we were mates, and me, well, I'm just fucking crazy about her. I'll be damned if anyone else is going to put their scent on her. Beta or not, I don't give a shit.

"Mine," Jace snarls at Danni before giving me back complete control.

'Jeez, couldn't control yourself, huh?' I ask him.

'You didn't like it either. My mate. No one touches what's mine,' Jace mumbles back, curling up in the back of my mind, sulking and glaring at me.

'Alpha, would you like to do the introductions before we begin?' Richie's voice rings through my mind.

I look around, and almost everyone is still silent. A few whispers have started up again as people observe our interaction. Most would assume she is my new flavour for the month. I haven't ever been this possessive with anyone or shown up at training with anyone. A part of me hopes maybe we can do introductions later, but that wouldn't exactly be fair to Ashleigh she deserves respect as Luna, and they deserve to know that I have found my Luna.

'Let's do something quickly now, if you don't mind,' I sigh, scrubbing a hand over my face and trying not to look frustrated with this ordeal.

'The stage is yours, then Alpha,' He nods, and I quickly bring Ashleigh to the front with me.

Addressing my pack has always come naturally to me, but at this moment, finding what to say is a slight struggle. Half these blokes knew the stuff I got up to, so you can't blame them for being curious and a little overprotective of their own children, some of whom I have grown up with.

Silence passes over the pack, waiting for me to speak as we stand in front of the crowd. I can tell she's nervous being beside me, but she doesn't falter, she stands next to me, smiling warmly at everyone. Danni, Eric, and Billy move to the side, scanning the crowd and making sure everyone is well-behaved.

"I would like to introduce to you my mate, Ashleigh Steward," I voiced to the crowd.

They all start whooping and cheering that the pack has a Luna. I can see happiness exploding from everyone as I explain who she is to me.

“We will be around the pack grounds the next few days. However, I would like to invite everyone over to the packhouse tomorrow night for proper introductions and an extended meet and greet.”

Now, this part I haven't exactly told her about or anyone for that matter, so I'm hoping this is something Danni can pull out of thin air for me to get everything set for tomorrow. I know it doesn't give me much time, but I would like most of the pack to meet her before we head back to school on Monday. That way, there would be a few familiar faces around the school should she ever need anything. I can guarantee that anyone from my pack would protect her with their life should anything happen.

Yes, we went to the same school, but I don’t think she knew anyone from my pack. We kept tabs on the heirs and ranked members but no one else, so I hope she can meet Amber and a few of my other friends so she is more comfortable walking into the school grounds.

I don’t exactly know Liverpool's plans for any changes like this. Everything moved so quickly that I’m hoping dad can bring her into the fold so she can at least have a link with the pack.

I nod over to Richie to let him know he can begin training. I just wanted a quick introduction today, nothing too fancy, so she isn’t so overwhelmed. Richie moves back to the front of the crowd and starts giving directions on what he wants everyone to do this morning.

I can still feel Ashleigh’s nerves as I pull her off to the side with Danni and the guys.

“Umm, does anyone know about this little shindig you’re spontaneously throwing?” Danni asks, looking between us both with a raised eyebrow.

I give him one of my best ‘fuck you’ smirks so he knows that this is all him. He groans at the realisation that he is the one who has to put everything together in a short amount of time and pulls out his phone, tapping away frantically as the other two move toward the group to begin training.

Danni comes back a few minutes later looking less freaked, “I have some Omega’s coming tomorrow afternoon to set up things. It shouldn’t take too long. They will bring food for everyone and drinks ready by 4.00 pm,” he confirms before rubbing his hands together putting on a smirk wiggling his eyebrows at Ashleigh. “So, what ya say, Beta on Beta? We can finally see who will win?”

Ashleigh looks up at me, questioning if it's alright. I can feel Jace push forward possessively, and I know he is showing in my eyes right now. My arm latches around her waist in a tight grip. He’s really fucking pushing it today. I didn’t miss the innuendo he’s spelling out there.

I force down the growl that starts to push up in my throat. I didn’t want to say no to her if she wanted to train, but what I would give if it were anyone but Danni.

“Will you three be joining us today?” Richie calls out, “We have an odd number if someone would like to team up with Derek?”

Derek is in his mid-thirties and has a mate and two kids. He has been with the unit since he was eighteen and his son is just a year younger than Danni. He’s not a bad bloke, a little hot-headed at times, but he’s a good bloke to have on the squad. He is nearly the same height and build as me, but I am stronger, given the Alpha blood running through my veins.

Before I could answer, Ashleigh jumped at the chance. “Sure, Captain, I’ll be happy to.” She smiles at them both and starts walking towards them.

I tense as she jumps in so quickly. He’s probably been training since she was born, and I know they are uncomfortable with the choice as I see them glance at each other. Derek looks down in submission as she moves closer to them. I know I didn’t want her sparring against Danni before, but, fuck, he’s looking like the better choice right now.

“You boys continue chatting. I’ll be over here,” she waves dismissively at us both and moves over to Richie, who looks at me with a silent question asking if it’s okay to proceed.

If I don’t let her spar, I’ll get an earful of it right here. She’ll be pissed off if I pull her back and say no, but I have to trust her, right? She was training to be the Beta of Liverpool. I know she participated in regular training, so I shouldn't worry that she won't be able to handle herself.

I let out a frustrated sigh and nod to Richie, letting him know it was okay to proceed. He gives me a weird look, shrugs, and starts explaining what we are doing this session.

I turn back to Danni, glaring at him. He’s in for a few rounds this morning, aggravating my wolf like that. What the fuck does he think he’s doing?

“Hey man, come on, I was just being friendly, you know me,” he tries to defend himself, putting his hands back up and slowly shifting back as I stalk toward him.

“That’s just the fucking problem, isn’t it? I do know you. Touch her like that again and I will give you a beating you won't be able to come out of,” I snarl, feeling Jace’s voice overlap with mine as he bares his neck.

“Duly noted. It won’t happen again, Alpha,” he says. I can see the sincerity in his eyes, and he knows he fucked up, especially when Jace is this on edge.

Lowering his hands slowly, he sighs, “Wanna start then? Offense or defense?”

“Defense,” I grunt, crouching down as he starts circling me.

I try not to be distracted as I hear Ashleigh taunt Derek behind me. I zero in on Danni and try to focus.

ASHLEIGH

I knew Jace and Zander would have a problem with me sparring against anyone today, especially Daniel, with how he greeted me, so I was hoping maybe a mated male would help lessen the tension. It seems not as I hear them still bickering over everything.

Rolling my eyes at their petty stupidity, I head toward Derek and Richie. I saw the look they shared as I move toward them. I’m not stupid. This is what always happens. They think that I’m weak, but that’s fine. Over the years, I have learnt to use that to my advantage.

Right now, I am already assessing this bloke as he stands there. He has a few scars that aren’t normal for a shifter, so I know he has been in battle, probably multiple times. Each scar tells a story that most likely still haunts him.

He leans a lot on his right side, meaning he may still have an injury that hasn't recovered properly. Even with shifter healing, some things aren't always fixable, another link to his scars and battle experience.

Richie's glance at Zander carried a silent question. They already doubt my abilities. Even when I was training in my pack, some members who didn't know who I was, would give me the same look of pity, guilt, and uncertainty. They always assume they would hurt me, that I was fragile, and that Ollie wouldn't always be there to help me. Little did they know he was the one I trained with every day. If we didn't have training with our members, we would sneak off and train on our own.

When I was younger, he caught on to what was happening between the pack members and me and saw the toll it was taking on me. Instead of showing me the same pitying look, he was determined to help me, to show me that my size and abilities are useful as a Beta.

He spent the evenings and mornings teaching me new techniques and training me to be as strong as him and men like Derek so that I would overthrow them just as easily when the time came. I admit that having Alpha and Beta blood may have given me some advantage, but I still trained every day to make sure I was the best person to be by his side when we took on leadership.

Once Richie explains what he wants us to do today, we both nod and start circling each other. My favourite thing to do is taunt the wolf within. This would make them lose control and get all stupid and flustered, especially if they didn't have as much control over their wolf, to begin with.

As Derek starts circling me, I can tell he's hesitant to make the first move. Don't get me wrong, hitting women is always wrong, in my opinion; however, when you are in training or a life and death-situation, manners be damned.

I keep circling him until he gets impatient, which doesn't take too long. Of course, this bloke is a total hothead. After about the eighth circle, his nostrils flare in frustration, and bronze rims show through his eyes as his wolf peeks through.

Bingo.

He launches at me quickly on the left, trying to tackle me, but he tumbles down as I jump out of the way on the opposite side, giving him a little kick in the ribs as I moved past.

"Come on, tough guy, like being hit by a girl?" I taunt him, laughing. I see his wolf flicker through again as he pushes himself off the ground getting back into position.

A low growl rises as his eyes darken, zeroing in on me with determination. Perfect, this is exactly where I want him.

I give him a smug smirk as he tries again. I can see he is using his wolf strength as his eyes show a more prominent bronze rim. I haven't even tapped into Kia yet. She's biting at the bit, wanting to be let out, but I won't if I can help it. Maybe one day but not today.

Derek launches at me again, but this time, I underestimated him. He does a double take as he goes to the left but moves back quickly to the right as I move, trying to dodge him. This time I'm not so lucky. Instead of pinning me down to finish the round, he yanks my arm and spins me around quickly, with my back facing his chest and his arm in a chokehold. Thankfully, he didn't dislocate my shoulder. If he had applied more force, maybe he would have.

His arm wrapped around my throat, almost choking me as I struggled to get free. This guy has taken sparring to a whole new level. I see Zander stop sparring with Daniel and make his way over. He is royally pissed off right now. I can't imagine him seeing me in this position as a good thing, but he needs to learn I'm a big girl and I can take care of myself.

I shake my head at Zander, making him skid to a halt and stop advancing. Daniel is next to him with a smug grin like he knows what I will do next. My hands reach up to his arm around my neck as I try to tug at it for a release. I can feel my airflow tighten even more as he applies more pressure.

"Nice try, princess, but I think I won this round," he growls.

I roll my eyes at his stupidity, he flexes a little bit, loosening his grip, waiting for my next move, but before he can do anything, I bring my left heel and slam into his left knee. Surprised by my action, he cries out in pain, releasing his chokehold on me and dropping one knee to the ground. I spin back around and aim for a punch right in the middle of his face. His body slumps down to the ground with a thud, completely blacking him out as I stand back up slowly, trying to catch my breath. Within a second, Zander is by my side, checking if I'm alright.

"What the fuck happened!" he demanded as he checked me over for any scratches and bruises.

"I'm sorry it was my fault. I taunted his wolf, and things escalated a bit more than I thought," I say apologetically. Zander looks between us before sighing and scrubbing a hand over his face.

"Nice going, Luna, that was awesome," Daniel grins as he comes up next to Zander before bending down to see how Derek is. "He'll be alright, just knocked out, but damn, you have a swing on you, if you can knock out Derek like that."

I just smiled at the comment. I knew Zander was already agitated with everything; I didn't want to make things worse by responding with something stupid back.

Zander pulled me in close and buried his head in my hair, inhaling my scent. "I should kill him for doing that," he grumbled. I look up at him to see Jace is in control, his eyes raging in fury.

"It wasn't his fault, Jace. I knew what I was doing and handled it. I mean, I didn't even need to use Kia." I tried to reason with Zander to get Derek out of all of this.

It was true. It wasn't his fault I taunted him to piss off his wolf. I knew better. I was about to say more when we were disrupted by clapping hands off the sidelines.

I look over and see Alpha Wyatt and Beta Jake.

Shit, I hope I'm not in too much trouble.

Chapter 58 - ASHLEIGH

Shit, Shit, Shit.

I am in so much trouble. I look between Zander and his father standing on the sidelines. One would think they are linking, but their eyes are not glazed, and they are just staring at each other. Even Beta Jake looks a little uncomfortable, shifting around at their gaze.

Their wolves flicker through, showing a rim of gold in their eyes, dominance radiating from both men. A few of the warriors were curiously watching. Most try to ignore what was happening, but it was hard to ignore two Alphas fighting for dominance.

Neither man has moved from their position. I can see Daniel's eyes cast down in submission, hands in his pockets, and looking at the grass as if it's the most exciting thing in the world. Beta Jake is looking between them as I am, slightly confused, but I'm sure he's more aware of what is going on than me.

I frown in confusion. What did I miss? I know Zander didn't have the best relationship with his father, but this type of play for dominance and power is a bit over the top for father and son.

I take a deep breath and try to break the tension. After all, I am his mate, right? This is what I'm here to do ... be by his side and be there for him. Taking a step forward, I muster up the courage to say something.

"Alpha Wyatt, Beta Jake, it's a pleasure to see you both again," I say confidently, giving them a warm smile.

Zander tenses beside me, tightening his grip around my waist, not wanting me to move. My comment seems to have snapped Alpha Wyatt out of whatever battle he was in with his son as he looks over at me and gives me a tense smile.

"Ashleigh, likewise, I hope you have had a proactive morning," his eyes flicker behind me to Derek and then back to Zander with a frustrated look. "When someone contacted me saying the Luna knocked out one of my top warriors, I had to come and see what all the fuss was about."

Shit, was it really about that or that I, a woman, joined in with training today.

"Derek was just showing some different techniques," I explain quickly. I didn't want him punished for what happened. I know Alpha Wyatt only saw the ending, but he might think differently if he had seen the start. I was partly at fault for allowing that to happen, and I will gladly explain exactly what happened. If this is anything like Liverpool, gossip will spread like wildfire.

I hear a groan and turn slightly to see Derek trying to get up. Daniel rushes over to give him some water and helps him sit up. "Easy big fella. We need to get you checked out at the clinic before you do anything else," he says softly, trying to help him sit up straight.

I approach Daniel and Derek to help them, but once again, I am blocked by my paranoid mate. Zander gives me a hard look saying, 'I don't think so' and shakes his head slightly.

'It's because his father is here,' Kia explains. *'I don't believe we were allowed to be here in the first place, so tread carefully, please,'* she begs.

"We stopped by the packhouse , but no one was there, so I wanted to show Ashleigh around some of the grounds," Zander grinds out, bringing me closer to him.

Alpha Wyatt nods in confirmation. "We were on our morning checks."

He is a man of few words. Even in the meeting, I had with Ollie. He wasn't this tense. I feel sad for Zander. If this was his life growing up … no one to talk to, no father figure to guide him through life … living up to the expectations of being the Alpha's son and the perfect pact member.

"Anyways, we should get going now," Zander says, dropping his arm from my waist and tugging on my hand, leading me away from the training area back to the parking lot as Alpha Wyatt watches us.

"I don't understand," I start to say, trying to unravel the entire interaction we just had.

"Not yet, sweetheart," Zander shakes his head before opening the passenger door for me to climb in.

We sit in silence as we aimlessly drive around. At least, it seems aimless to me. Maybe he was taking me somewhere, but he hasn't said anything about where we were going or about what happened earlier. Zander pulls up at a little corner store on the other side of town. I've never been out this far out before. I suppose that is to be expected, considering we are still on Charwood territory.

"I'll be back in two minutes," he grumbles, putting a hand on mine as I go to unbuckle my seatbelt.

I let out a frustrated sigh as he closed the car door and walked into the corner shop.

It was a nice enough area, with a few residential houses lined up along the street. They all seemed to be relatively new and well-kept. Some children were running up and down one of the side streets across the road from where we are parked.

The bell chimes from the corner shop as Zander walks back out. He is followed by an elderly lady who gives him a tight hug and a peck on his cheek. I would normally feel a surge of jealousy and burning in my heart, but considering the action wasn't of lustful nature, I felt none of that. He grinned back at the older woman and waved as he walked toward the car carrying a few plastic bags that seemed to be filled with groceries.

Part of me feels hurt that he won't to talk to me, but I also know the struggle with his dad runs deeper than I would ever know, so I'll give him time and hope that he might open up to me.

~

ZANDER

My father can be a right prick sometimes. No, wait, all the fucking time. I needed to get her out of this place right now. I know he hates it when I do regular training, but the fact that I openly disobeyed a direct order from him …of course, he is going to be fucking pissed off.

I know she wants to help Derek, it is in her nature to do that, but with Dad around, there is no fucking way I am going to risk any more than I already have.

"I don't understand," she starts saying.

"Not yet, sweetheart," I say quickly, trying to get her into the car as soon as possible.

I don't want to unravel my complicated relationship with my father in the middle of a parking lot. This conversation needs to be somewhere private. I know she wants to talk, and I can feel her wanting to speak to me.

Every now and then, she glances over, waiting for me to say something. Maybe I am being a dick, but right now, my mind is a mess, and all I can think of is getting her out of there before Dad loses his shit and scares her completely.

They say he's a feared Alpha, but honestly, he's just an asshole who doesn't know how to deal with things correctly. He scares and intimidates people, which is probably why we haven't had any issues in the last decade. But that doesn't mean it is the right way of doing things.

I can honestly say that I hate being around the man, and I hate being around the house. That's mostly why I was out chasing pussy every night, so I didn't have to be at home amongst the dullness that should be the life of the pack.

I walk into the corner store and am greeted by May. She has been like a grandmother figure to me for as long as I can remember. She wouldn't put up with my shit and is one of the few people who will ever get away with giving me shit. Occasionally, she would let allow me to crash in one of her spare rooms.

I offered her a job a while back to be a part of the packhouse permanently, but she didn't want to leave her house and corner store that has been passed down through her family for generations. When I went away to Alpha training, it was hard for me to keep in touch with her. I'm just glad I have been able to see her since I got back.

Maybe I should have gone to her with my problems about Grace and Ashleigh, to begin with. She definitely would have slapped some sense into me, but I don't exactly share that type of information with her.

Part of me always wondered if she helped me because I was the Alpha's son. But then I see her with other kids of different ages, and I realise she just has a beautiful heart and is sweet-natured. When I was ten years old all she saw was a kid who needed guidance and some direction.

"Are you going to introduce me to your beautiful mate?" she asks, handing me a couple of bags of food that I asked her to gather for me quickly. This woman has always been able to read me like a book. I consider it for a little bit, but I know Ashleigh wants to talk, and introducing her to May right now might complicate things.

"What are you doing tomorrow night? Are you free to come over to the packhouse? I want her to meet a few people then if that's okay?" I ask, as I place the money on the counter.

I always try to give her extra, especially lately since her mate passed away. It's been harder on her than she is willing to let on, but she holds on, and I'll forever be grateful for this woman in my life.

"Of course, I'll be over tomorrow afternoon," she smiles at me warmly and brings me in for a tight hug. I welcome it with open arms. It's like she could sense my frustration.

I make my way back to the car and can see Ashleigh looking back at me with a small smile, possibly even more confused than before. I need to let everything out and give it to her straight, and we couldn't have a decent relationship if I keep things from her.

Chapter 59 - ZANDER

I try to figure out the best way to start. We sit in the car silently ... Ashleigh not even trying to start a conversation since we left training. I don't really blame her. I haven't exactly been fun to speak with either, but just her presence alone is calming me down. Part of me hoped she would say something to try and ease the tension, but I know she won't until I do.

I drive a little further out of the city until we arrive at the place I had in mind. I used to go here all the time with mum and dad. It feels right to bring her here. Maybe one day we can have that same tradition, coming out here every other weekend.

The lake is exactly as I remember it. It is about the size of a football field, with shrubs and trees protecting it. I drive through the small clearing that is big enough for a car to fit through.

Not many people know about this place, I have never sensed anyone before, so it's nice this little paradise has been kept peaceful and pure all these years. She would be the first person I would ever share this place with. Ashleigh's scent lingering in the car reminds me of this place, freshwater and forest wood. I'll forever feel peace when she is around.

She looks around, observing the new area I have brought her to, I feel somewhat guilty we haven't been able to go on many dates, so I hope I can make that up in the future now that everyone knows she is mine. For now, this is what we have been doing lately, I love the wildlife scenery, but I want to show her off to everyone.

"What is this place?" she asks curiously as I lead her towards the little sitting area, we built out of fallen trees and stumps. A few logs were lying on the side facing the waterfront, with a little sandy bay area offering a way into the water as the water laps against the dark sand, rolling through the lake.

"We used to come out here nearly every weekend when mum was alive," I reply, trying not to dull the mood.

As though she senses my uneasiness, she nods and continues to follow me down the path until we reach the seating area. I moved next to the smaller logs, placing the blanket out I had in the back of the car. I've kept one in the back of my car in case we wanted to do something like this.

Ashleigh sits on the other side of the seating area, a bit too far for my liking, so I reach out and pull her onto my lap. She makes a little "humph" noise before she settles down, leaning against me.

"Want to explain what happened back there, or do I have to pry it out of you?" She finally asks after about five minutes of me just holding her and tugging on one of her loose curls, trying to keep Jace down and calm. He's been fucking restless after that interaction with dad and Derek, and is out for blood, so what I need right now is to hold her close.

I sigh heavily before explaining because she deserves the truth. Even if dad has accepted her as my mate, he is still the current alpha and a fucking asshole.

"Dad likes things done a certain way, and one of those ways is me not training until I finish school. We have enough patrol and warriors around that I don't need to be as involved as one would normally be." I start explaining.

Honestly, I fucking hate it. I think we should all be training before we get our wolves, so our bodies are prepared, and what the fuck happens if dad dies and I have to take on leadership? Anyone can challenge me. Anyone can have the upper hand because of his stupidity.

"Have you asked him why? I'm sure he would give you a valid reason for his concern?" She starts asking questions I've asked a thousand times.

"Honestly, sweetheart, I've stopped asking. In the end, I just ask Richie if I could join, and he usually allows it. Richie is my aunt's mate who happens to be my dad's sister. Even she has tried to reason with him, but it falls on deaf ears."

I sigh. We've had many arguments about me training and joining the patrol team. Ultimately, I try my best and pray he doesn't catch wind of what I'm doing. There have been a few times when I thought he was going to kick me out or lose his shit on me completely. But even then, he huffs and puffs, and we don't talk for three months or longer.

"I'm sorry you had to become a part of it all. Frankly, I didn't think he would be that mad," I say. I hate that she has to see his bad side. At least maybe then she knows what she's in for, a quiet packhouse with no one around, compared to what she had back at Liverpool.

She turns slightly so she can face me, reaches up and pulls me in for a kiss. God, I love this girl. Being open with her is surprisingly a lot easier than I thought.

"Zander, you are my mate. Your family is my family. I hope I don't get you into trouble later because that wouldn't be fair."

I sigh with happiness. I'm just glad she isn't angry at me for ending the training early.

"I love you so fucking much," I mumble into her hair as I wrap my arms around her. As soon as I say those words, I freak out. I've never felt love for anyone before, let alone said it.

Jace has been hounding me for ages to tell her, I know she told me a few weeks back, but I didn't know how she felt after all this shit went down, and honestly, I was fucking terrified that she didn't love me anymore.

"I love you, too," she whispers before leaning into a deep kiss.

I feel everything … her frustrations, her annoyance … but the one thing I feel the most is her love. It is like the bond has strengthened, like there isn't a wall up anymore. I can only imagine what it would feel like once I mark her, and I can't fucking wait.

~

We haven't sat at the dining room table for years. It was a tradition mum used to keep, but that stopped altogether after she passed. So, imagine my surprise when Ashleigh and I got home to a cooked meal and table set all nice and fancy. Now here we all are, sitting around the dining table in tense silence for the last fifteen minutes.

Danni is next to me on one side and Ashleigh on the other. Dad is across from me between Ellie and Jake.

Tension is so thick you could cut it with a knife, and no one has said a word since we started eating. I wasn't fucking game enough to say anything until dad did. I know how that would pan out If I spoke up first. I could see silent conversations between dad and Jake. Their eyes would glaze over every time one was talking. Ellie sometimes joined in now and then, only making Danni, Ashleigh, and I shift uncomfortably every few minutes.

The only thing keeping me sane right now was Ashleigh being here. I just wanted to come in and say goodbye, then take off again back to our little cottage for another night of peaceful happiness. But of course, Ellie coaxed me into staying for dinner. Now I wish I hadn't agreed.

Dad suddenly slams his fist down, making everyone jump in their seats and looks at both Ellie and Jake. Leo's Aura blazes through, making everyone cower except for Ashleigh and me.

Gotta say, Ashleigh didn't even break a sweat with dad. So fucking proud of her! After all the shit she has been through in the last two months, I'm so fucking thankful she didn't give up on me.

It was clear the conversation was about the three of us. Out of all of us, I was the one who would have to deal with this shit later. Honestly, I'd rather do it with Ashleigh here so she can help calm me.

"What's going on?" I ask and look directly at Dad and shift my gaze between him and Jake. Ashleigh puts a hand on my knee, helping me stay calm and keeping Jace at bay for now.

"Nothing," Dad growls and starts eating dinner again. Jake rolls his eyes but continues to eat.

"Clearly, you have something on your mind, so why don't you spit it out already," I grind out.

I can feel Ashleigh squeeze my thigh telling me to calm down, but honestly, if this is about earlier this morning, I'm still pissed.

"Some information came to light, and we need to sort it all out," Jake responds, earning another snarl from dad. "He deserves to know, Wyatt. He's old enough now."

That last part caught my attention. "Know what?" I ask, zeroing in on Jake. I am owed so many fucking explanations it's now beyond a joke.

Jake tries to ignore dad and begins to tell me what they were discussing, "There have been a few issues around lately," Jake starts slowly.

"I said enough, Beta. I will not have my son end up like his mother!" Dad yells, slamming down his knife.

My anger builds up even more. I need answers. In fact, I fucking demand answers if it has to do with mum. I'm so sick of being on the sidelines.

"What does this have to do with mum? You can't continue to keep me in the dark like this. Now that I've found my mate, I'll be able to claim the title of Alpha at the end of the year. As your fucking son and future Alpha, I can't believe that I'm not allowed to patrol, train, or fucking anything to do with this pack." I snarl back, venting all my frustrations over the years.

Even though we've had our fights, I've never been allowed to express how angry I have been with him. We never have a conversation unless we are at each other's throats.

I want to be a part of my pack. I want to help out as Ashleigh and Oliver did with Liverpool. No wonder my pack members think I'm a little shit who doesn't do anything because, frankly, my fucking father is an asshole who thinks he knows best and doesn't allow me to. But, of course, no one else sees that except me.

"Alpha, if I may … maybe if it is explained why we aren't allowed to do things a certain way, it will help us understand everything a bit more," Ashleigh says softly, trying to take the heat off me.

My eyes snap over to her as she watches how dad will react to her comment. If anyone can get Dad to an understanding, it's this girl right here.

I see his mind churning as he contemplates Ashleigh's words. He sighs before taking a swig of his drink.

"A few months before your mother's death, there were disappearances … children, women, our elders, basically anyone vulnerable," dad starts to explain carefully, closing his eyes. The memories are still painful to this day.

He continues, "we stationed patrols everywhere, but the disappearances still kept happening. Back then women were included in patrol and training. At some point, the kidnappers figured out which women were mated to our male warriors and would take them. The men would go crazy, and many took matters into their own hands."

He sighs. "To be honest, I couldn't blame them. We had no leads for weeks and the situation was getting worse. That was when we decided not to allow women to run patrol and training, in case the pack was being observed. We couldn't risk them being targeted and making our men fall when they lose their mate."

My memories surrounding mum's death are foggy at best - I barely remember a thing. I think I blocked most of it out because of the pain.

I only remember we stopped going to the cottage, visiting grandma, and going out during the evenings. The kids started to have warriors around when we were in the playgrounds and school, but we never found out why. It just happened one day.

"We never found them. For all we know, they could still be alive somewhere locked up. We never found out who did it or who was capable of doing it. It was always a clean job, no scent around, no evidence. The only reason we knew people were missing was that someone would report them missing. One evening they took your mother."

He sighs and scrubs his hand over his face. I know he is trying to cover the pain because, fuck, it hurts me, too. I think this is the most he has ever spoken to me without yelling or being an asshole … just having somewhat of a decent conversation.

"I thought mum was killed by rogues," I frown in confusion, looking between them all.

"That's what we told everyone," dad says with a sigh. "The truth is we don't know who or what it was. We know she was taken when she was out running one afternoon and then just reappeared at our border three days later, dead. There was no sign of how she died - no bruises, puncture marks, bites, or anything. They did a full workup on her but found nothing wrong. She was perfectly healthy. The doctors said that she shouldn't have died, but she did."

"If you don't mind me asking, Alpha, did you feel the bond break when she passed?" Ashleigh asked curiously.

Dad hesitated before answering, I hope Ashleigh didn't step on any boundaries by asking this question, but I was curious to know where she was going with this.

"It was faint, it wasn't an excruciating pain like I was always told. But the next full moon, after she was buried, that's when I felt it. So did other members who lost their mates, but we never recovered their bodies. I knew then we would never see them again. As for the children, we have no idea if they are alive still or not."

Ashleigh nodded, clearly thinking. I can see her eyes glaze as she talks to Kia.

"From some studies I remember, witches can create a sacrifice to break or weaken a bond for a brief period. I believe because you were a ranked wolf, you still felt the bond with your mate. The next full moon cycle is significant because the moon goddess gifts us with our mates. It can break through whatever spell the witches cast. They have always tried to keep wolves out of the moonlight. It helps strengthen us. That's why many packs form links and ceremonies on a full moon. It helps bind the Alpha and Luna's strength at the moon's peak," Ashleigh explained.

"The pain you and your pack members experienced was the final snap of losing one's mate. Usually, that happens as soon as the mate dies. Due to the nature of it, I would say someone is working with the witches," Ashleigh finishes.

"We have always had peace with the witches. We've never had any problems with the covens," Jake frowns.

Ashleigh shrugs, "they could have been forced to do it, taken their members until they help. Oliver mentioned something the other day about the disappearances happening again. Am I right to assume this has started back up?"

"Yes, it's not that we don't want you to train, but with what happened last time, we just don't know who to trust. At the moment, we are trying to check out all our pack members, but we have well over 800 pack members, so it is going to take some time. We need to make sure every member is safe and well," dad says, looking at me.

"I never meant for things to escalate, Zander. I only thought what I was doing was best to keep you out of harm's way, especially if we didn't know what was going on in the pack. Things settled down for a while, but it's gotten worse this year alone. It's like they are looking for someone or something. It's not just this pack they are targeting. It's everyone."

I sit silently, going over all the information I've just been told. After all these years, after all our fights and arguments, I feel the strain unravel and let go. Maybe now we can finally have a father-and-son relationship. I didn't have to worry about any implications as I did before.

I feel the energy from Jace, wanting to fight to keep my members safe. I want to train. I want to patrol. I want to figure out what the fuck is going on. I want to be the fucking alpha I was born to be and protect the ones I love, and I won't rest until the son of a bitch who killed my mother is dead.

Chapter 60 - ASHELIGH

Soft music fills the air as people stand around chatting. Daniel and the Omegas did a fantastic job putting this together for an event that only took half a day to set up.

The pack gathering was already in full swing when we arrived from touring the territory. The sun was already starting to set and lots of people were coming and going, enjoying themselves and having a good time.

I met many people who are here tonight and a lot more when visiting the different sites today. It was nice to see many of the established buildings and businesses they have up and running; it's a fantastic set-up. I understand why Charwood is the largest and strongest pack in the country.

I probably haven't met all of the pack yet, but I have met all the pack elders and advisers that helped make some of the decisions. They seem like friendly people, and I look forward to working with them.

I watch my mate from the kitchen mingling and talking with his pack members as I fix myself a drink and sit back and look around my new home. It feels weird that this will now be where I live. I feel sad that Ollie and Brent won't be able to come here and visit. Maybe one day that will change but not anytime soon. I hope I could still see the girls, but for now, I have to chat and make new friends, which isn't a problem. I worry a little about Zander's past and I don't exactly know who to trust among the women.

Yesterday, after all the information his father gave him, he was silent the whole way home. In the evening, I knew he just wanted to process everything. He didn't need me to ask him repeatedly if he was alright, especially when I knew he wasn't, so I just tried to be there for him.

Now, seeing him around his pack members, it's like he switched from worrying about everything to just getting the job done and being there for them. Honestly, I'm proud of him for how he handled last night. It would have been so hard for him to get all that information and not be able to do anything about it.

I didn't blame him for wanting to listen and taking it all in, and I didn't blame him for being silent while he mulled over everything. It's how he copes. Unfortunately, I learnt that the hard way. I hope he knows I am here for him if he wants to talk so he doesn't have to go through it alone. But then I realize that is what he is used to … doing things on his own so it will be hard for him to just stop doing that.

"I'm so happy he found you," a gentle voice echoes through, snapping me out of my thoughts.

I turn around and see a younger girl standing next to me. She's not much older than me, with shoulder-length dark brown hair, standing around the same height as me, her hair flowing all around her, loosely kept with a bright red headband, matching red shoes and a blood orange handbag. Her dress draped around her, fitting her nicely, falling to her knees. The red and orange checks against the black stood out with her soft creme skin.

"Umm... thank you?" I stammer, darting my eyes back to Zander to see if he noticed my new interaction.

"Ohh... I'm sorry, where are my manners? I'm Amber," she smiles and pulls me in for a tight hug, half-choking me. "I was furious when he came home with that girl Grace. That's one of my rules: never get too involved with someone, especially if you know you have a mate out there. It only leads to heartbreak." Amber starts rambling as she lets me go.

"Jeez, Amber, don't bombard her. She's only been here for a day," Daniel sighs, standing next to me, and pouring himself a drink.

I roll my eyes at his comment, "Come on, Daniel, you should know by now I don't scare that easily, especially after recent events."

"And you, Luna, should know I don't go by Daniel. Only my parents call me that and when I get into trouble. Danni is fine," he laughs back, waving a dismissive hand at me.

"Yo, you guys want anything?" he calls out to two guys walking up to the kitchen, who I recognise from yesterday's training sessions.

"Beer is fine," the blonde scruffy-looking guy said. Today he's looking a bit sulky, and the dark-haired guy is still wearing a stiff poker face.

"We all know what they get up to, and it's always trouble," Amber whispers to me, giggling as the boys walk up.

"I heard that," Danni grumbles, passing the cold beer to his friends.

As we stand around chatting, I notice the blonde one actively trying to get Amber's attention each time. She ignores him or gives him short answers to his questions. I wondered if something is going on between them. The other guy is chatting with Danni, his expression still blank. I catch him watching me now and then. Each time he does, Kia perks up at the back of my mind and pace back and forth uneasily. She won't say what's wrong, only that she has this uneasy feeling about him.

"Eric, seriously, we have been through this before." Amber huffs at the blonde.

"Come on, just one date?" Eric counters. "No hooking up unless you say so. Let's go to the movies or something."

"Are you two still going on about that?" Danni asks, turning his attention to them.

"Yes, well, your friend here is persistent, especially now that Zander knows we hooked up," Amber says, folding her arms across her chest with a frustrated sigh.

Danni laughed, “dude, you need to let it go. Zander nearly beat you after finding out. I don’t know why you would put yourself through that again.”

I’m so confused right now, and it seems to have shown on my face as I listen to their conversation.

“Amber and Eric hooked up a few months ago and hid it from everyone,” Danni explained, seeing my confused look. Obviously, I understood that part. I just wanted to know what it had to do with Zander being pissed off.

“And I thought I made it clear my cousin was off limits,” I hear him say over the conversations between everyone, making his way toward us.

“You never said that just that you were annoyed with it,” Eric protested. “Besides, we are all adults here. She can choose who she wants to go out with, right?” Eric says, looking around at everyone.

Whatever happened before, Zander clearly wasn't too impressed about it, so I am staying right out of that situation. He comes over to me and wraps his arms around my waist and pulls me in for a hug before bringing me into a deep kiss.

I am a little surprised, considering he's been a bit all over the place since last night, but I’m glad he hadn’t completely forgotten about me. I was beginning to miss him.

“Hi,” I giggle when he breaks away from me, his friends have gone back to their conversations, giving us some privacy.

“Hey, sweetheart,” he whispers, resting his forehead against mine, closing his eyes and breathing my scent in. “Would you like to come with me for a bit? I want to introduce you to someone,” he says before taking my hand and leading me over to the sunken lounge, where I recognise the older lady we saw yesterday.

“May,” Zander calls out to her as we approach the elderly lady. “I would like to introduce my mate, Ashleigh,” he says proudly, bringing me closer to his side.

“Hello, May,” I smile warmly at her, “It's a pleasure to meet you, thank you for your groceries yesterday. We really appreciate it,” I say politely.

This lady had a tremendous influence on Zander's life as a motherly or a grandmotherly figure to him, and I hoped we would get to see her more in the future. She smiles at the both of us and brings in Zander for a warm hug.

“Dear boy, I think you have grown again. Your father remodelled the last time I was here,” she chuckles, tapping him on the head as she releases him. “Welcome to the pack, dearie.”

She smiles at me, taking my free hand and rubbing it, reminding me of my grandmother's gesture as she started chatting to us about her corner store and what she wanted to do with it. I make a mental note to speak with Zander about helping her remodel it, and I don’t think she should have to do that herself, especially with how many times she has helped Zander over the years.

It was a lovely evening getting to know some of the members. Zander said they would make an official announcement in a few weeks and bring me into pack leadership. I'm glad I could get to know some of his school friends, so I wouldn't be entirely alone tomorrow when we headed back to school.

It was pleasant to see Zander acting like his old self for a while, and I hoped he didn't go down a revenge-seeking rabbit hole alone. He's not alone, but I don't want to be the first to bring anything up, and he needs to be able to contemplate it by himself.

The drive back to the cottage was nice. Zander explained his friend circle and how long he had known them all. I was curious about Billy, but I didn't want to pry too much into something that could be nothing. Kia's been fine except for that one instance, so, for now, I'll just be brushing it off as a one-time thing.

"Thank you," he says as we pull up to the cottage. We'd been listening to some of his music the rest of the way back, and it was nice to calm my crazy brain before tomorrow started.

I turn and look at him in confusion. I'm not exactly sure what I am being thanked for.

He sighs before turning off the car, "I know I've been a bit out of it since last night. I'm sorry, I didn't mean to ignore you or anything. I just needed to wrap my head around it. Thank you for not bugging me about it or asking me if I'm ok a thousand times. I don't exactly know what to do from here." he confesses, scrubbing a hand over his tired face.

"I'm here for you, Zander. I'll always be here for you, but remember, your father hasn't given up on finding out who did this. It'll just take time," I try to encourage him. I hope he knows he may never get the answers he wants. It'll forever be hard not knowing, but at least he will know he's done the best he can be.

"As for what comes next, we can ask if we can do private training, maybe just the three of us, if your father is worried about someone being on the inside. We need to be prepared if there have already been some attacks. Then maybe we can also start some research into witches and different things on scents and mate bonds," I say, listing everything I had planned in helping him figure this out. After all, he hasn't been the only one thinking all of this over.

Other members from other packs are also being taken. All this information needs to be brought to the council before they even consider looking into it. They won't put people on it unless there is evidence of a more significant issue, and I'm hoping it might get enough attention because there is a pattern and other packs involved.

He smiles and grabs onto my hand, kissing the back of my knuckles, "Have I mentioned how much I love you?"

"Hmm… no, not today, I don't think," I giggle, batting my eyelashes at him.

He growls playfully and yanks me over to his side of the car, making me sit on his lap, straddling him, and pulling me into a deep kiss. "I love you," he says between kisses, making his way down to my neck, making my entire body explode with fireworks.

I want him now more than ever. "Zander," I moan, frustrated with him for not giving me more. "I... need... more..." I manage to pant out as he massages my breast with one hand and my ass with the other, all while his lips kiss my neck roughly. I am already dripping wet, trying so hard not to lean back and sound the car horn, I want him right here, but my consciousness kicks in when I see lights flicker on with the neighbours a few doors down.

"Let's go inside," I whisper to him before reaching out and unlocking the car door.

Before I could wriggle off him, he picks me up, climbs out of the car and carries me towards the house. I wrap my legs around him tightly.

"I'm not letting you go," he mumbles into my neck, tightening his grip around me. I feel his dick, hard as a rock, through his jeans and excitement pulsed through me at the thought of it being inside me. I want him, all of him, forever.

His strong arms carry me upstairs as his lips travel all over my neck while he fumbles with my jeans and shirt, trying to get everything off quickly. He throws me onto the bed and stares at me for about ten seconds as I sit in a wild mess. I see Jace push through a few times, wanting to take control, and I could feel Kia move forward, wanting to respond to her mate as Zander's eyes turned a darker shade than usual.

He rips off his shirt and strips down to his boxers within seconds and makes his way back toward me. Almost animalistic, my arousal is thick in the air, his eyes dark with hunger as he prowls toward me.

"Off," he demands and tugs at my jeans, sending another shudder through my body. I quickly pull off my jeans and shirt before receiving another deep kiss, hungry with desire.

I feel his urgency as he continues feeling his way around to my entrance with his fingers. I gasp as he plunges three fingers deep inside me, feeling all of me.

"Already so wet for me," he growls. He pounds inside so hard I feel my eyes roll to the back of my head.

I scream his name in ecstasy as I hold onto the sheets, my entire body on fire as I reach my first orgasm. I want all of him fully, "Zander, all of you," I beg, "Give me all of you, mark me, make me yours forever."

He moves over me, kicking off his boxes and presenting me with his rock-hard cock. He lines up at my entrance before plunging into me. I scream out his name as he pounds inside me. This side of him, I haven't seen before. It's desperate. It's hunger. It's raw. It's all him.

"Tell me you're mine," he growls in my ear. His pounding slows down as he gives me little kisses along the base of my neck, where he'll mark me, making my entire body shiver in excitement. "Tell me you're mine, sweetheart," he growls again, overlapping with Jace's voice, still moving his cock deep inside me.

"I'm yours, always yours," I pant out, not wanting the motion to stop. I scream as I feel a sharp pain on the side of my neck. I feel Kia move forward, offering her canines wanting to mark Zander in return.

"And I'm yours forever," he growls. My entire body dissolves into a shuddering mess as I reach my climax while Kia bites down on Zander's neck, giving him his own release inside me.

We're both a panting mess as I hear his voice ring through my mind. 'So fucking sexy. All mine, forever,' he lays there looking at me in awe playing with one of my curls.

'I can hear you,' I giggle back, kissing him.

He shrugs in response, 'fine by me, sweetheart.'

'*Just letting you know, his thoughts are always in the gutter',* Jace chuckles.

'Ohh, Hi, Jace,' I smile as Jace and Kia start talking to each other.

'Offt, this is going to be hard to concentrate with,' I sigh, snuggling onto Zander.

'It'll be all right after a little while. They will quiet down,' he responds while stroking my hair as I lean into him. My entire body is so exhausted. I feel absolutely full of love and devotion from Zander, I feel everything from him, a little bit of worry and nerves, but the love and adoration outweigh everything. I couldn't wait to see what this new stage of our life would bring.

Chapter 61 - OLIVER

It was a challenging weekend. I barely went home, I had about 20 missed calls from mum and frantic messages from Kylie to know where Ashleigh was. Neither Robert nor Kylie got to say goodbye to their daughter. Now they couldn't reach her via the pack link or family link. It was a fucked-up situation just because Blackwood was her mate.

I don't even know how to begin to explain things to Brent when he got home. He walked into a house of chaos after his patrol run that night. As much as those two niggle and bicker, they were siblings. He looked up to Ashleigh as his sister and the pack's Beta. He respects her and appreciates her guidance. Now, I don't even know what their relationship will be like.

After seeing Ashleigh the other night with Blackwood, I knew she made the right choice. She had to be with her mate. She was his Luna and rejecting him wasn't an option for either of them. It was nice to see that they loved each other. However, I made a promise to myself and our family ... if he hurts her in any way, I'll kill the son of a bitch without hesitation.

That night I got home to a silent house. The food was already packed away and I thankfully couldn't hear any arguing anymore. I can hear a few heartbeats, which I'm assuming are mum, Brent, Alex, and Meghan. I have no idea where dad, Kylie, and Robert are. I just hoped they aren't somewhere killing each other.

It was hard to have the conversation with Brent, I didn't want to tell him the details of how I gave Ashleigh her stuff, but he also needed to know what happened. I remember him just sitting there, stunned. I wasn't sure if it was the part about who her mate was or what dad did. Maybe a bit of both. He just got up and paced around his room with a confused look.

I know the questions he was asking himself, his mind spinning round and round.

What does this mean for him?

Will he still be able to join the Navy?

Will he still be allowed to go away and do what he wants?

Honestly, I want him to be here with me running the pack, but I also know he never wanted that pressure. We always assumed it would be Ashleigh standing with me in pack leadership, so ultimately, the decision is his. I won't force him.

I'll just need to find a new Beta; someone I can trust. With all this shit going on, trust is a fickle thing.

So, after all, the crazy this weekend piled on us, neither of us wanted to go to school today. We still had to keep up appearances, especially if Ashleigh walks in with Blackwood.

There are a few confused people around training and the packhouse. Some even asked why their wolves were uncomfortable and where Ashleigh was, but hopefully, that will pass once Brent steps into place as the new Beta.

I'll give Brent time to adjust and decide what he wants to do. I'm just glad dad didn't force him to create a link with me like he did with Ashleigh and me. We all knew something like this could happen and this was the consequence, but he didn't care.

As for the questions on Ashleigh, dad has been locked up in his office all weekend or out on a run. No one has seen him since the dinner.

Here we are, sitting in the school's parking lot, waiting for someone to make the first move. Ace is on edge and I'm sure Reid is, too.

I scan the parking lot and spot Blackwood's car in the front row. I don't see Ashleigh's anywhere, so they must have come together.

Glancing over to Brent, I asked him, "Are you ready for this?"

"Guess I'm going to have to be even if I'm not, right?" he sighs, looking over at me.

"She'll always be our family. It'll be alright," I try to reassure him.

"Zander Blackwood is her fucking mate. Charwood and Liverpool have been enemies since before we were born. Do you think things won't be different?" Brent spits.

I see Reid flash through as he expresses what he thinks. After a weekend of not talking to anyone, not even me, everything had bottled up, making him increasingly agitated.

"I never said it wouldn't, but this will be a new beginning for both our packs. Blackwood and I will be the new leaders. Once the others are out, they won't have a say in anything anymore. Things will change for the better," I say, clasping him on the shoulder, trying to get him to see what new opportunities we can do with this. Trying to show him that we could have a relationship between Liverpool and Charwood. One that has been needed for a long time.

"You don't think the elders won't vote against it? You don't think the council will have a say as the two largest packs forge an alliance? I'll bet nearly every single pack member in Liverpool will vote against it. There is too much hate, and Ashleigh becoming their Luna won't change that hate, especially for the elders. If anything, they will see her as a traitor." He shakes his head angrily and moves to get out of the car as he pushes my hand off his shoulder.

"Brent," I start to say, but he cuts me off.

"Look, I know you want me to step up and become Beta, but I still need time to think, if that's ok?" He asks as he stands there lingering in the doorway.

I see so many emotions flash across his face - the pain of missing his sister, the frustrations with the reality of new responsibilities, and just pure exhaustion. So, I won't give him any flack this morning for disrespecting me as his Alpha, but the kid needs to learn to control his emotions.

"Yeah, no worries," I sigh, giving him a chin flick as he slams the car door shut and walks towards the school gates.

'Should have told him off a little bit,' Ace mumbles.

'If he's like that again, I will, but I'll let it go for now. He's just trying to process,' I sigh, scrubbing a hand over my face, preparing myself for the shit show that's about to happen.

'We need to start looking at other candidates if he doesn't want to be Beta. Even Reid can't change his mind right now. He's already set in his ways,' Ace says.

'Who would be your first pick?' I ask curiously as I get out of the car and walk toward the steps while some of the kids greet me good morning, parting way and letting me through the hustle and bustle of the school.

I don't mind being recognised as Alpha, it has its perks, but the downside is you have no idea who to trust. You would think, being Alpha, you would trust your pack, and don't get me wrong, I trust them to do what's right. At the end of the day, they are always going to look out for themselves.

'Theo Evans is a nice guy, and comes from a decent family,' Ace suggests. 'His training has been impeccable lately, and he was always decent towards our family and Ashleigh. He finished school last year, so there is no huge age gap. I see him with Alex now and then, so they already seem friendly,'

The guy's not a bad choice. Still, I don't know him well enough, so I'll put his name aside for now and see what other prospects we have before getting into that, and hopefully, Brent will decide positively soon.

The school seems like the usual hustle and bustle today, I haven't received any panicked links about Ashleigh yet, so I'm just bracing myself. As I round one of the corners where our lockers are, I hear Brent's voice echo through the hallways.

"It's true then? Why didn't you say anything? Couldn't you have given us a heads up before everything went to shit," he demands.

I see him standing in front of Ash with his arms folded across his chest and a scowl on his face, as he sees the mark on her shoulder.

Today she's wearing casual jeans and a light shirt that shows off her mark. I guess they are going loud and proud. No point holding back anymore since our families already know. I don't blame them. It would have been hard to try and figure out everything.

"Come on, Brent, what was I supposed to say, 'oh, by the way, Zander Blackwood is my mate.' You and I both know that wouldn't have gone down well," she sighs, trying to get him to see sense. "Besides, Zander and I needed to work through stuff before everyone else found out."

"You mean the fact that he fucks anything with a pulse and a pussy," Brent grumbles as his wolf, Reid, peeks through.

"Brent!" Ashleigh gasps, clearly hurt by her brother's words.

"All right, that's enough. You need to apologise now, Brent," I order as I walk up to them before things escalate further.

There were a few gasps from some onlookers as they overheard the conversation playing out but thankfully, they keep walking instead of lingering in the hall listening more to the discussion. They both stand there staring at each other, clearly hurt, but Brent shouldn't have taken it that far. It was uncalled for.

"It's fucking true, and you know it," he snaps back at me.

"Ollie, can you give us a minute?" Ash asks, looking at me, I try to read what she's trying to tell me, but her face is blank and not giving away any emotion. Reading my cousins was never difficult in the past as they always showed their emotions. Today, however, I sense nothing from Ashleigh. Nevertheless, I nod and walk over to the pillar surrounded by the glass windows letting all the warm sun through.

'*I told you, should have kicked his ass in line,*' Ace mumbles as he paces back and forth restlessly.

I roll my eyes, observing the area. As I do, I see Blackwood and his Beta, Daniel walking towards me from the other direction while Ashleigh and Brent are in a whispering argument.

I try and glance over every so often in case I need to step in because now, it's not just about siblings, it's about two different packs, and if he crosses that line again, especially with Blackwood in earshot, I won't be able to do much to protect him.

"Blackwood, Richmond," I greet them with a nod.

They both nod back and slow down to a stop next to me. Their eyes glaze over as they talk to each other, clearly not wanting me in their conversation. Daniel gives me another nod before continuing to walk past Ashleigh and Brent toward the back classrooms.

"Rough morning?" Blackwood asks, looking over at Ashleigh and Brent, still half-yelling and half-whispering at each other.

"Rough weekend," I sigh in response, watching them closely as Brent gets increasingly agitated. Honestly, I don't understand what the big fucking deal is. She's with her mate and happy. What else is there to it? I mean, yeah, I know a little bit why he's pissed off because she hid it all from everyone, but that doesn't excuse his behaviour.

'He's exhausted and emotional. He's going to be saying and doing a lot of stupid things today. Don't forget he had a plan, and him being Beta wasn't in those plans,' Ace sighs.

'Doesn't give him the right to be a dickhead,' I respond, still watching Brent closely.

I see Ashleigh nearly in tears as he storms toward Blackwood and me and shoves Blackwood into the pillar catching him a bit off guard.

"If you ever hurt my sister," he snarls, with Reid nearly in complete control at this point, "I'll snap your fucking neck."

Blackwood grabs his wrist as Brent goes to shove him again and leans in close, and says dangerously. "I will dismiss the fact that you just threatened me because I understand the situation, but if you ever upset her again without understanding the whole thing, being her brother won't protect you."

I could feel his aura pulsing as his eyes flickered between gold and brown. He is pissed off, and so is his wolf, and they could feel Ashleigh upset as well, which didn't help things at all.

"I mentioned it to Oliver, and I'll mention it again. I'm not the one keeping Ashleigh away from her family. Your fucking Alpha is. However, I'm still willing to let her see her family on my pack grounds. But, if there is any danger, and if you ever make her upset in any way, that privilege will be rescinded. Do we understand each other, Brent?"

Both are breathing heavily, challenging each other before Brent relinquishes control and grinds out, "Yes..." clenching his hands into tight fists, his jaw tight.

I know he isn't over it, and he won't be over it because Brent holds a fucking grudge. You would think having the weekend would help him process, but it seems to have made things worse.

"Go home, Brent. Cool off for today," I command, stepping forward and pushing him off Blackwood and holding my grip on his shoulder, so Brent wouldn't launch into a fistfight.

"What, are you serious?" he asks, looking at me, pissed off and shocked.

"You aren't in the right headspace today. I should have realised that before allowing you to come here. You need to go home and cool off and apologise to your sister for being a fucking dickhead. Blackwood is her mate. Accept that fact already. She's happy, and he treats her well, be fucking happy that she has a mate who cares for her," I say bluntly, moving him slightly toward the school gates.

Looking between us all, he huffs and heads back towards the parking lot. He stops when he is standing close to Ashleigh. She hasn't moved from her position where their conversation was, a bit astonished at what her brother is capable of.

He grabs her and pulls her in for a tight hug, completely surprising us all, and says, "I'm sorry. I'm glad you're happy. I just didn't get to say goodbye." He quickly pulls away and walks toward the school gates before shifting and running back home.

Chapter 62 - ZANDER

Ashleigh's emotions are heightened by a thousand after marking her. I feel everything - happiness, frustration, sadness ... It was a rollercoaster of a night, trying to navigate everything. Out of all her emotions, happiness and joy were what I feel the most. I am so fucking grateful that she is happy to be with us.

After the incident this morning with her brother, Jace was more aware of what was happening. He is unsettled that her family's drama saddens our mate, and I promise I will get to the bottom of it for her. I only want what is best for her and, at the same time, to have a relationship with her family. I want to work together and fix it. Oliver seems to be on board with an alliance, we just have to convince everyone else.

Thankfully, the day is easy going; I have a few classes without her, but those are in the afternoon. Lunchtime rolled around quickly, and everyone gushes around her, trying to get information on what happened and how we found out we were mates.

I know she is a private person, and I can feel her being overwhelmed with everything as all the girls come up to her and say congratulations. At the same time, I didn't want the rumours going around school about Grace and that problem. We were able to nip that in the bud pretty quickly, and nothing got out. My friends just laugh at me and call me pussy whipped, but they haven't found their mate yet. One day they will understand.

I reluctantly say goodbye to Ash as she goes off to her last class on the other side of the school. I had half a mind to put someone else from Charwood in her class, but I know the kids in Liverpool still respect her, so there shouldn't be any problems.

Jace has been agitated since this morning, but I am glad I could now link her and feel her more than before. I'll have to ask dad to bring her into the pack now that we are mated, so she can access everyone if she is ever in trouble.

On days like today, I would be more than happy to have physical activity, but with Jace stressed out as he is, he's giving me a fucking headache. The class is mixed with Riverview and Liverpool kids, and I am the highest rank by far. We were all standing around chatting and waiting for our teacher to arrive. He's taking longer than usual, but that just gives us more time to relax and do fuck all.

The class is on the top football field below the library and across from the art classrooms. A brick staircase in front of us provides decent seating when needed. The hedges all around the field are lush and green from all the rain and well-kept by the groundskeepers.

I spent half my time here and on the basketball courts when I was younger. It never changes. It was a nice thing to come back to something familiar.

Some guys are mucking around and being stupid at the oval when I smell a foul stench that reeks of garbage. Normally I would jump into action, but this is fucking human land, so it's anyone's game and rogues are technically allowed here. The school has protocols in place, but sometimes that isn't enough.

I turn to the others and call out, "Oy! Stop being dickheads for a minute, and link Oliver and Bobby now!"

They stop what they're doing and look at me like I've grown three heads. They didn't smell anything yet. It's only faint, but I know something is in the air. I start to move toward the stairs, toward the other entrance of the school, where the stench is coming from, and I heighten my other senses. It's eerily quiet and calm, I can hear the other classes going on in the other buildings, and beyond the chatter, I can just make out the soft patter of paws.

I bend down and put my hand on the dirt, hoping to get something from mother nature. This little trick was something I was taught back in Alpha training. It had helped me a few times when we were in our animal form and hunting. I've connected with Jace's strength to see what else he can pull through. I feel Jace's aura pulse as he completely takes over.

'Rogues,' Jace growls and starts to move toward where they are coming from.

`We have to tell the school, put it in lockdown before they get here, protect our mate and the pack,' I try to reason with him and gain back control before he goes all shit crazy. I don't want her to become any type of target. I know she can defend herself; she has more than proven that yesterday, but things are much harder with our school in neutral territory.

'Danni, what's the class looking like at the moment?' I call through our link. I know he has AP maths and is probably as bored as anything.

'Doing fuck all, listening to this old brute talking and not making any fucking sense,' he grumbles back.

Before I can link back to him, a medium grey wolf launches over the hedge, followed by others of all different sizes and colours. There must be at least fifty coming from different directions, straight toward us on the field.

I shift into Jace as quickly as I can and link out to my pack members, 'Rogues on the school grounds, go into immediate lockdown now!'

I don't even wait for anyone to respond before shutting off the link and linking Danni separately.

'Danni, make sure Ashleigh is safe. Take Eric with you.'

'Yes, Alpha,' he responds immediately, with his aura radiating through. He's in full Beta mode, and I need to trust that he will take care of her until I get there.

Snarls and snapping sound's ring around me as the others shift and start striking back. I see a large light brown wolf heading toward us, who I recognise as Oliver. He looks at me and sends a slight nod before jumping into action.

Two wolves attack my hind legs, and as a third one tries to get the jump on me, I kill it instantly as it tries to go for my neck. I spin around quickly, biting down on the neck of one of them, killing it instantly and stalking towards the second before pouncing and knocking it out.

Jace is not happy being so far away from our mate. We are both pissed and all we could think of is keeping her and our pack safe.

An alarm rings through the school, warning everyone of danger and to go into lockdown. I hear yelling and screaming as more wolves storm the school, and students scramble to try and get to safety.

More staff members and students from other packs and my own file out to help. I feel a link snap letting me know that someone from my pack died. I look around frantically to see if anyone from my pack is injured, but so far, it's just the other side that is dropping. These wolves were small and ragged and knew next to nothing about fighting. They were sloppy and slow, but to have this many, going against a school that they most likely knew had Alpha heirs in, was not a good sign.

The fighting on the field doesn't last long as more people participate and finish what the rogues started. Fifteen died by my teeth and claws, and I knew Oliver probably killed just as many rogues. The metallic scent of blood assaults me as I look around at the horror of what just happened, the fresh-cut grass is now smeared with blood.

Oliver and I shift back to our human forms just as everyone does. I approach Oliver when I suddenly feel a sharp pain radiating through my body, making me fall to my knee.

'Mate,' Jace whined, trying to push forward and take control to find Ashleigh.

'Ashleigh, sweetheart, please tell me you're okay,' I plead through our link, opening our bond back up. I closed it before hoping she wouldn't feel any pain from when the other wolves attacked me. I don't get a response from Ashleigh and start panicking.

"Blackwood, what the fuck happened?" Oliver starts. I shake my head at him quickly before linking Danni to find out where Ashleigh is.

'Danni, where is she?' I call out, frustrated I couldn't feel Ashleigh or Kia, and neither responded to me. Jace was two seconds from going crazy and storming the school to find her.

'Alpha, you need to get here, now,' he responds urgently before cutting the link.

"I need to find Ashleigh," I tell Oliver as I pull all my energy and sprint across the grounds to where I knew she should be.

It only takes me a few minutes to find them, I see her naked form collapsed in front of a building in a pool of blood. Eric is a few feet away from her in the same state, and Danni doesn't look much better. He's bleeding badly from a gash on his arm and many scratches. He looks fucking distraught as he hovers over her in a protective state.

My heart fucking shatters as I see her, and I try to understand why the fuck she was out here instead of in the classrooms with the others. I fall to my knees in front of her body and pick up her head softly, resting it against my knees, holding her like my life depends on it. Jace retreats to the depths of my mind to try and help heal both of them using our bond.

"What the fuck happened?" I growled at Danni, I know it wasn't his fault, but he was supposed to be protecting her.

"She heard your link and saw the rogues going for the kids who haven't shifted yet. They got to one of them. Tyler Gidding was only fifteen and was going to shift next month. She saved them, Zander, I didn't even think about the non-shifters, but she did. That was her focus, protecting the younger kids," Danni says, his body shaking as he tries to control his wolf. I can see his eyes flickering. His wolf wants out, wanting blood for the damage they have done.

"I don't know how they knew the layout. It was like they had an actual goal, and they knew where they were going. They've been here before, some of them were stronger than us. It was hard to get to her, they all came at her when they realised, she was trying to stop them from getting to the kids. Eric and I tried to help but we were too late. After she collapsed, they went for him before I got there." Danni sighs, scrubbing his hand over his face in defeat before placing it back on his bloodied shoulder.

I just sit there staring at her beautiful face. Her curls are covered in blood and dirt. She should be nearly healed by now as I am close to her and with shifter healing, yet her body still had scratches all over, barely healing.

I can barely hear her heartbeat, she's nowhere near as warm as she usually is. The gash on the side of her head hasn't started to heal and she still has bite marks all over her legs.

"Zander, let them look at her," Oliver calls out. I look up and see two paramedics standing there with a trolley to put her on. I stand up slowly with her in my arms and I place her gently on the trolley as the paramedics rush to look at her.

"We will take her to Oakwill hospital," one of them says.

"No, take her to Charwood," I commanded. I know they are both human, but she is my Luna and I want our pack doctors to be the ones to look at her.

"Sir, Charwood is a 20-minute drive at best. Oakwill is much closer," he responds, looking between Oliver and I uneasily.

"I said, take my mate to my pack hospital. This is not up for debate," I repeat, with Jace's aura pushing forward, their eyes widened as they sense the command behind it.

"Zander, even Liverpool is closer," Oliver says as he tries to help, tossing me a pair of shorts.

"And you think your father will allow that? I won't have my mate sent anywhere else except to my pack." I snap back. "Take my Gamma, too, he was also badly injured. Ensure that both of them are looked at immediately."

Oliver sighs when he knows he's beat. He fucking knows his father won't allow her to be back on Liverpool territory, and he won't allow me to be close to her either, Charwood is our best option.

A second ambulance appears, and two paramedics appear quickly and attend to Eric. They put him on a trolley before loading him into the ambulance. I hear sirens roar past as they go in the direction of Charwood.

"I need to go and meet them there. Can you look after this here?" I ask Oliver as I move toward the car park. I need to be close to her, the further away she gets the harder it will be for Jace to help with healing.

"Yeah, no worries, I'll take care of it and let you know. I'll get Bobby up to speed as well. Send me the address and I'll come and check on you guys after," Oliver says looking between Danni and I. Danni is now slumped against the brick wall, eyes closed, resting his shoulder against it so it's not causing him any pain.

"Yep, I'll let my warriors know that you are coming, so you should be able to pass through without any issues. Danni let's go bud, we need to get that looked at," I call out to him as I walk up offering a hand to help him up. I wrap my arm around his waist helping him balance, as he gets up, he loses his footing and half collapses on the grass.

"Danni, Danni, look at me," I call out, slapping him softly on the face trying to wake him up, as I drop down meeting him at eye level. He looks at me with glassy eyes. I can barely hear his heartbeat as it slows down, and his temperature isn't anywhere where it should be for a shifter.

"Come on, brother, we need to get you to a hospital quickly."

I pull him up again leaning all of his weight on me so he can try to use his legs. I don't know what the fuck happened to my pack, but the fact that my two best friends and Luna were the ones who got affected the most, worries me.

None of us even considered the non-shifters, that's why we have protocols in place. Sometimes they fail, like today, and I want to get to the bottom of this because losing a pack member is never easy. But losing my mate, I don't think I will ever be able to recover from that.

Chapter 63 - ASHLEIGH

I feel a sense of loss when Zander isn't by my side. I suppose that's why they allow mates to be in the same classes, so our wolves don't go crazy on us.

I had a crappy feeling for the rest of the day after this morning's conversation with Brent. I was already feeling bad that I was upset with him only a few weeks ago about hiding the same thing from Ollie and me, and yet here I am doing the exact same thing to him. No wonder he's so upset. At least Ollie and mum already had time to accept Zander and me being mates.

Some girls at lunchtime came up and congratulated us, but all I could see was jealousy and frustration in most of them. It hurt that they weren't actually happy. They probably just wanted him because of his title or maybe because they were ex-lovers or a number of other reasons. I don't have the courage to ask Zander how many he's been with at school ... I'm sure it's a lot. I won't dwell on that fact because he is my present and future.

So, after everything that happened this morning, I am going crazy inside. With a quick kiss goodbye, and an 'I love you', he ran out to the football field to attend his sports class. I barely focused all afternoon when I realized that Zander wouldn't be joining us for our last class.

I had Bio, which I usually love, but I guess lately I've been so focused on Zander that it is hard to focus on class. I sit there trying very hard not to link him every few minutes to ask how he is doing. I know he could probably feel my frustration and unease, but I don't want to appear too clingy. I need to get my independence back somehow.

Zanders' voice rang through as he announced that rogues are on school grounds. I assume Ollie let Liverpool know of the immediate danger, as the kids in the class start to panic and pack up their things.

Schoolwork will have to wait, the safety of everyone in school will have to come first. Mr. Trevor is human, so he still has no clue what is going on. Some of the kids try to leave the classroom, but I know that it would be the worst thing for them to do. They are safer staying in here. I may not be Liverpool's Beta anymore, but they still listened out of respect for my old title and the fact I am now Charwood's Luna.

After quickly talking them out of leaving and helping set up barricades in the room, I leave to help out Zander and the others. No one else in the class had any sort of training in this except for me, so it wasn't worth risking their lives.

I shift quickly into Kia and make my way to where I know Zander is until I see about ten wolves headed to where the younger kids have their classes.

The school is split up into different sections, for classrooms as well as year groups. The science labs are above the drama classrooms, while geography and history classrooms are in the opposite building,

With everyone going into lockdown, there appears to be no one else in sight. Oh, how wrong I was, as I see a young boy making his way to the classrooms, unaware of the rogues nearby.

'He's a non-shifter or can't scent them yet,' Kia mumbles.

As we watch in horror, four rogues sprint toward the boy without hesitation and rip him to shreds. They didn't even give me a chance to save or help him. His screams vanish as quickly as they came, and the snarls from the rogues stop as soon as they are satisfied.

Anger surges through us as we watch, our minds made up as Kia's feet carry us toward the rogues. At this moment, I wish more than anything that I have a pack link. I know it is probably stupid of me to do this alone, but I will not let them hurt anyone else. They are clearly out for blood, and I am going to do whatever it takes to stop them.

I try calling out to Zander, but it seems he blocked us while he was under attack. I understand why he didn't want me to feel his emotions or him getting hurt but I still wish I could link someone.

I have never killed anyone before. Ollie and I were supposed to go to advanced training after graduation but in the meantime, we have been training to fight in both human and wolf forms … we know where best to attack and how best to avoid getting hurt.

These wolves are out for blood. They want nothing more than to kill and hurt innocents. Zander says they are rogues, but I couldn't smell anything from them. These wolves are larger, and the way they move seems like they know how to hunt together like they are talking to each other as a pack.

I stalk them quietly and focus on the two smaller wolves at the back. I try to stay upwind so that they will not be able to scent me. The rogues are focused on finding the best entrance to the school, and the two lean wolves trail behind.

I see my chance and jump on one of them, biting its neck immediately. It howled in pain and dropped to the ground. I launch at the second one attacking its neck and front legs. The wolves at the front was alerted to my attack and start charging, snapping, and scratching at me from different directions.

We fight as hard as we can. I relinquish complete control to Kia so she could use all her strength. I try to link Zander again, so he knows what is happening, but I could still hear them attacking up in the oval and nothing from him.

Two more wolves drop down as Kia continues to fight. She tries to get us out of the circle they caged us in, but the bigger ones stop us each time, snapping at our legs. Kia howls in pain as one of them latch on, biting down hard. The one in front lunges and bites into my neck. I slowly lose feeling as the pain radiates through my body, where the teeth dig into my flesh. Just as I am about to collapse, I see two wolves running towards me to try and help.

'I'm sorry. I love you,' I whisper through our link one more time as I fall to the ground.

I have no idea if he can hear me, but I need him to know I am sorry for leaving him. I hope he knows I did it to save the others.

Chapter 64 - ZANDER

The putrid scent of antiseptic assaults my nose as I pace in the hospital's emergency room, waiting for the doctor to tell me why my Luna, Beta, and Gamma are in the state they are in.

I burst through the doors earlier to find Ashleigh, only to be kicked out, so the hospital staff had space to work on her. I hope they are helping her. I can't lose her. Her bloodstains on my skin from holding her close have now dried as I didn't want to wash away her scent. It was the only thing keeping me sane right now.

Oliver comes flying down the hall with Brent hot on his heels. I sent him and her parents a message as soon as I arrived, and Danni was checked in. He looked so pale when we got to the hospital, and it fucking killed me the state they were all in.

I hate the smell of hospitals ... The smell of disinfectant stings my nose, making my eyes water. I fight Jace for control, trying not to let him take over and go on a rampage. Hospitals always bring back bad memories, so the smell alone makes me uneasy.

"What's the update!?" Oliver demands, as he stops before me, bristling with his eyes flashing. It seems I'm not the only one about to lose my shit. Both of them look pissed and ready to kill something or someone. Honestly, I probably look just the same.

"No update yet. They are still working on her and the others."

I sigh. I'm still only wearing the loose pants Oliver gave me back at the school, and I didn't miss some of the looks I was getting from the females. Before Ashleigh, I would have gone for it, but now it pisses me off because they can all see my mark and know I am mated.

"What was it like back there?" I asked curiously. Part of me wanted to stay and tend to my pack, but I needed to be close to my Luna.

"An absolute shitfest," Oliver replies as he scrubs a hand over his face. "Council members just arrived as I left. They were going through a roll call to make sure no one else died or was injured during the attack. They found two rogues still scouting around the school and have taken them into custody."

Brent looks fucking devastated as he stands between us. I can see the gears in his head turning, I know he blames himself just as much as I did.

"It's not your fault," I tell him, clasping a supportive hand on his shoulder.

"I should have been there, it's not fair they are in such a mess," Brent mumbles, head down and a hand rubbing the back of his neck in frustration.

I shake my head, "Both my Beta and Gamma were there, and look what happened to them. You could have been in the same place or worse."

I look at both of them. We may have hated each other before, but the fact we all love Ashleigh and will do anything for her has brought us a little bit closer.

Brent just nods and continues to observe the area. He's on high alert, since he is on 'enemy land'. He moves over to one of the empty chairs and slumps down into it resting his head against the wall.

"Did the council say anything before you left?" I ask Oliver.

"No, not really. They just wanted to know how many were lost, as far as I know. I lost two, and Riverview lost one." He sighs.

"Shit, I thought it was just us who lost one," I sighed. No parent should have to go through the loss of a child. The family link alone fucking hurts just as much as the pack link. I feel for Oliver. At least I only had the one link snap, not two and I pray there isn't any more.

"We're your two non-shifters, too?" I ask.

He nods, with a haunted look on his face.

"Shit, the kids didn't even have a chance," I mumble. Cowards! They went after the vulnerable.

"Did anyone see the rogues they caught?" I asked.

"No, they just whisked them away without saying a fucking thing to anyone, had the council witch bind their mouths shut until they arrive in council territory," he said.

"Fuck, we really won't get a hold on them now will we?" I sigh.

Oliver shakes his head and moves toward Brent. It's been a fucking rough day on all of us, especially the families who lost the kids, I had to get Ellie to contact Tyler's family and I'll go around to visit them later on to pay my respects and see if they need any help with planning his funeral.

It felt like hours passed by as we watched the hospital fill with more people. Come evening patients entered with small problems while others had dislocated arms or cut legs. A part of me is curious about how those happened. It distracts me slightly from what is happening just a few doors down.

I am about to completely lose my shit when a doctor who I recognize was looking after Ashleigh walks toward us with a concerned look. My heart hammers in my chest, I can feel Jace rise in concern for our mate, I know it is taking everything for him to stay put just as it is for me.

Jace's aura spills in full force as the doctor stops in front of us. He bares his neck and submits, while sweating bullets. "Alpha," he greets me with a shaky voice.

"You better have good news doctor," Jace snarls, not even caring that everyone around us stopped what they were doing and was submitting to him.

'Settle down bud, he's the one helping them,' I sigh, fighting for control. I know he is upset, and so am I but he doesn't need to be a dick to our pack members who are trying to help our mate.

"Follow me to my office please. We will have privacy and it will be easier to talk," Dr. West gestures toward the double doors that lead out of the emergency room and towards a hallway going to his office.

His office is clean and slick, just like the rest of the hospital. It has a big double wooden desk and an office chair, with two chairs in front, and another along the side wall. Filing cabinets run along the back wall and a tall lamp offers some light in the corner next to a double window that overlooks the car park.

"Please, take a seat," he gestures towards the seats. Oliver and I move forward and slump down into them and Brent takes the one against the wall.

“May I know how our Luna, Beta, and Gamma ended up in the state they were in when they arrived?” he asks, looking between Oliver and me as he bends down and pulls a folder from the bottom drawer of his desk and starts flicking through it.

“There was an attack at school … rogues. They stopped the ones on the lower part of the school, we were up at the top in a different place. By the time we got to them Eric and Ashleigh were unconscious and Danni passed out on the way here.” I reply. I don’t know the exact details of what happened down there … even Danni couldn’t tell me much by the time we got to him.

Dr West nods and scribbles information in the folder. He switches to the clipboard he was carrying earlier and flicks through the paperwork attached to it. “I wish I had better news but … based on the blood test results and their symptoms I believe they all received a large dose of wolfsbane plus some other type of poison. This made them weak and explains why they aren’t healing properly.”

“Daniel’s dose is about half what Eric and our Luna received,” he explains. “We were able to flush out as much as we could, but they will still need a few days here in the hospital and time to recover. For now, do either of them have any allergies we should know of?” he continues.

“Not that I’m aware of, no,” I say, looking at Oliver for confirmation. Honestly, I don’t think I’ve ever asked Ashleigh if she has had any allergies, as far as I knew she didn't.

Oliver just shakes his head listening to the conversation. It seems both he and Brent are still dumbfounded by the wolfsbane and poison.

“Doctor, Daniel mentioned that the rogues who attacked them had no scent. How is this possible?” Oliver asked.

Dr. West looks taken back, “Are you sure?” he asks with a shaky voice, not as clear and precise as he was before.

We both nod. “We couldn’t sense them at all. It was like they all just vanished. They also seem different from the ones we fought, they were bigger and stronger,” I explain further.

“Witchcraft is involved. It may be more dangerous than we realize,” he mumbles as he stands and pulls out a red velvet book from one of the filing cabinets and starts flicking through the pages.

“Fuck,” Oliver hisses, I look over to him and raise a questioning eyebrow.

Mum mentioned a long time ago that Liverpool heirs had a hybrid bloodline … part-witch, part-wolf. We assumed it died out in the last few generations since none of the offspring have shown signs of magic, that we are aware of. These days, it isn’t unusual to have hybrid bloodlines, mostly because it was a lot easier to find your mate, and a lot of people are now more accepting of the supernatural world. Human-wolf hybrids are more common than part-witch or part-vampire.

Oliver just shakes his head and sighs, “I don’t like to deal with Eleanor Badrot and her coven unless I really have to. She’s a bitch to deal with and always collects on her debts. She only ever helps if she has something to gain.”

“Classic witch then,” I chuckle. “We may have no other choice though,” I sigh.

Our pack lost all contact with the witches when Dad banished them years ago. In fact, I don’t think I have ever really seen any before except for the two council members.

Oliver sighs and nods, he doesn't like the idea much but if it'll help figure out what is going on, I will pay whatever debt they want, especially if it was going to help my mate and pack.

"Can we go and see them?" I ask Dr. West. Jace and I are on edge. Even though Ashleigh is in the same building, we were antsy with not being able to be close to her. We need to be with our mate.

"Yes, I will take you to Luna Ashleigh first, the others are across the hall from her," he nods as he stands and leads the way out of his office and through the hospital to their rooms.

It wasn't long until we arrived at her room, I could smell her scent, filtering through to the hallways. Even though I was in the same building as her, it was frustratingly annoying that I couldn't be close to her.

"Before you leave, I would like to take some blood samples from the three of you to check if there are any traces of poison or wolfsbane," the doctor says. "Just to make sure. We want to play it safe to avoid any issues later on," he goes on to explain.

My eyes are fixated on the door in front of me. All I want right now is to hold my mate, I don't give a fuck about anything else.

Out of the corner of my eye I see Oliver and Brent shifting uneasily on their feet and looking at each other with concern.

"I understand both of you are from Liverpool, but please keep in mind doctor-patient confidentiality also exists in pack lands. I only wish to ensure everyone is protected, even more so if witchcraft is involved in this mess." Dr. West continues to make his case to reassure them.

"We can discuss this later, doctor. I'll stop by once we are all done," I didn't want them uneasy, more than they already probably are. "Now, can I please see my mate?"

"Yes, Alpha, my apologies," he nods and opens the door behind him. "Please be mindful that she hasn't healed much, so it may be a scary sight," he warns, closing the door behind us as we walk in.

The room is big enough for a single bed, two chairs, and a small sink and mirror are next to the bed for easy access. Another door leads to a walk-in bathroom with a shower, toilet and sink. A large window is on the other side covered by sheer curtains to block the glaring sunset.

I push past the curtain wrapped around her bed, and my eyes land on her fragile body. They dressed Ashleigh in a light blue hospital gown that hangs off her body. A dressing is on the side of her neck, and bandages are wrapped around her arm. Her hair is a frazzled mess, with blood from the battle still matted in it.

'Mate,' Jace whines and pushes forward, wanting to hold her.

"Fuck", I sigh, dropping to my knees at the side of her bed. Her scent engulfs me as I pull back strands of her hair that cover her face.

"We need information … I'll give whatever the witches want, but this stops now. I can't lose her, and I won't lose any more pack members. We can't go on like this."

I don't give a shit if Liverpool were our enemies, that was the past. Right now, we need to build an alliance against this, it's bigger than all of us and unless we know how to stop it, working together is the only option.

"I agree, I'll see if we can find them as they always move around. I'll have my trackers try and track them down," Oliver says. "I'll forward any information I find and send you updates."

My mind reels with so many possibilities of what this is, and what it could be. We don't know much yet, but hopefully we will find something out soon.

Chapter 65 - ASHLEIGH

The pain that radiated throughout my body is now gone. I can't feel anything ... I can't see anything. Instead, I find myself alone in this pitch-black void.

'Kia, Kia', I try to call out to her, hoping she will help me pull out of this. Once again, I'm left with emptiness.

My mind spirals, thinking of all the possibilities, the "what ifs", and trying to figure out what just happened. I'm numb; it feels like nothing exists anymore. If this is death, it is a horrible place to be … a black void with nothing by me and my hazy, uncertain thoughts. I miss them … Zander, my family, my friends. The idea of never seeing them again scares me.

I feel like I've been floating around in this void for hours when suddenly I smell this odd yet familiar scent. It is a sweet, floral scent making my mind spin, trying to remember what it reminded me of. I try to move in the void to get closer to the scent. I need to get closer.

A strong pull snaps me out of the darkness as the scent becomes overwhelmingly powerful, and pain immediately fills my body. A horrible beeping sound fills my ears, and I hear a familiar voice I recognize. I try to move my hands, but the heavy weight of the anaesthetic doesn't allow me to move. I try to move my head from side to side, but even the slightest movement causes me to groan in pain.

"Come on, sweetheart, come back to me," I hear him plead. Sparks move through my body as he holds my hand and tugs on one of my hair curls, softly brushing a finger across my face.

I try to speak again, but my throat is dry and scratchy, barely letting me say anything.

"Here, love, have some water." He places a straw against my lips. I carefully sip as the cold-water trickles down, providing some relief to my throat.

"That's it. Can you open your eyes, sweetheart?" He asks softly. I slowly open my eyes, and I see him … my mate.

His hand is intertwined with mine sending fireworks through my body. Every fiber of my being aches for him. He looks like an absolute mess, like he hasn't slept in days. His dark hair is messy and flopped all over the place, his hazel eyes have dark rings around them, and his clothes are unkempt. Even looking like this, I want nothing more than to reach out and pull him in for a kiss, just to be close to him.

I look around the room … the blinds are closed, so it is dark except for the light from a nearby lamp. Near the lamp is the small pull-out bed that is unmade and smells strongly of Zander. To my left are a tap and basin. There are two doors. One, I assume, leads to the corridor. I can see the monitors next to me flashing and beeping, really starting to frustrate me.

"Oh, thank fuck," he sighs, still holding my hand tightly and moving the other through his hair. "How are you feeling?" He asks softly, stroking my face.

I allow myself to lean into him, yearning for his touch, giving in to what my body wants. "I feel like crap," I sigh, but my voice comes out in a croak.

"You gave us all a scare, sweetheart, you were out for three days," he whispers.

I could feel through our bond how terrified he was of losing me. He wasn't sure he would be able to live with himself. I frown. Three days is a long time for shifters. Considering we have fast healing. I should have woken up on the same day, more so because we were marked and mated.

"Why so long?" I ask curiously, yawning.

He chuckles at me, amused by how tired I am even after three days of sleep.

"Doctor West can explain more in the morning. I'll let him know you woke up tonight. For now, just get some more rest. Do you need more painkillers? I can ask the nurse to bring some," he asks, placing a soft kiss on my forehead.

"Hmm, how long till morning? Maybe just something to get me through the rest of the night?" I whisper, not wanting to strain my voice anymore.

Zander nods as his eyes glaze over, requesting the nurse to come in.

Moments later a young woman dressed in light blue scrubs enters the room. Her dark hair is pulled back into a ponytail. In one hand she is holding a clipboard and in another, she has a small cup with some pills.

"Hello Luna," she greets me with a smile. "Welcome back. I'm Natalia, one of the night nurses who has been looking after you. Here are some painkillers, hopefully, they will be able to help you rest until we can give you something stronger later on," she softly says passing me the medication, looking between Zander and me before moving along the machines making them finally stop beeping.

Jealousy runs through me at the thought that he has been around them the last three days. She looks at Zander, but he has his eyes trained on me the entire time, not even paying her any attention, just holding my hand tightly and letting his love and affection flow through our bond.

"Let me know if you need anything else. Doctor West will be around first thing this morning to check on you," she bows her head and walks out of the room.

"No need to be jealous, love," he whispers against my neck as he leans in, giving me a kiss on my mark, allowing my body to relax completely.

I roll my eyes taking the tablets, despite how much it hurts lifting my arms. "I wasn't jealous," I mumble as I feel the heat of embarrassment flush on my cheeks.

After a few minutes, the tablets have helped my body relax, and I fall into a deep sleep, the worry of missing Kia fills me. I didn't tell Zander but I'm sure he has already figured it out since there has been nothing but silence through our link. Even Jace hasn't said anything which worried me a little, I hoped he hasn't also lost his wolf because of me.

~

It didn't feel like I was asleep for long before I feel him trying to wake me softly, shaking me as the sparks fly through my body. I smell him before I see him, smiling as the familiar scent of wildflowers and honey flow through, but another odd smell, someone else was in the room with us.

My eyes quickly snap open, alert to my surroundings. I see Zander standing at the foot of my bed with an older gentleman. He is dressed in a collared long-sleeved light blue checked shirt and dark navy dress pants. A lanyard is draped on his neck, and he is holding the same clipboard the nurse was holding last night. His deep blue eyes hold concern as he watches me carefully, observing me.

I start to panic, and Zander moves closer to me, sensing my unease. “It’s alright, sweetheart, this is Doctor West. He has been looking after you and monitoring your symptoms the last few days,” he says softly before kissing my forehead.

“Doctor,” I manage to choke out, giving him a small smile in acknowledgment.

“Good morning, Luna. My apologies for coming this early, but I wanted to see how you feel before my first round of surgery this morning.” Doctor West quickly explains, moving through the notes on the clipboard. “I see they gave you some tablets last night when you woke. How are you feeling this morning?” He asks, looking at me.

“Good, actually, a lot better than last night when I first woke up. There isn’t as much pain anymore. I mostly feel heavy and weak,” I try to explain this weird feeling moving through my body. I look up at Zander to see how he is. I wonder if he felt the effects of everything through our bond.

“Yes, that would be the effects of the wolfsbane and poison wearing off. We tried to flush out as much as we could so it wouldn’t affect your wolf or our Alpha, but there is still some left in your system that we couldn’t get out,” Doctor West explains further.

“Do you remember much more of the events that happened? Maybe that can help us understand how it entered your system in the first place,” he asks, looking between Zander and me.

I try to recall what happened that day. It feels so long ago, yet it was only three days. My mind is hazy, and the exhaustion is making it harder for me to remember. “I remember seeing them moving towards the school buildings, and them killing the boy before I moved on them. It sort of goes a bit hazy from there,” I try to explain as much as I could.

“It’s alright. This is to be expected. You have a concussion and lost a lot of blood. It may take your memories a few days to return,” he explains. I hope I didn’t lose any memories, but considering the events that happened, it's a very high possibility.

Before he leaves, Doctor West does a routine check up and lets the nurse know to provide more pain reliever every couple of hours if I need it. He then lets me know I can head home with Zander at the end of the day if everything feels back to normal.

Zander climbs onto the bed with me and wraps his arms around me, pulling me against his chest, and holding me close. “I have never been so scared before in my life,” he whispers, breathing in my scent, and placing another kiss on my mark, making my entire body shiver. “The thought of losing you, I don’t know if I would ever recover from that.”

“I’m sorry. I know I should have waited, but when they killed that boy, I knew they were going to do the same to others if I didn’t try to do something. I couldn’t let that happen.” I try to explain why I had to, why it was a part of who I am, growing up being Beta and even more being Luna and wanting to protect everyone, not just my own pack members.

“I know. That's why I love you so much. You don’t run. You stay and help fight. Just promise me you won’t do it again,” he asks. I can hear the pain in his voice as he holds me close to him.

I know it was probably something he didn't want to ask, but I can't ever promise that just like I can't ever ask him to not fight for them, because he always will.

"I can't promise that, Zander. If someone is going to hurt the innocent people of our pack, do you really want me just to sit back and do nothing? Especially since I have been training as a Beta and am more than capable of trying to stop them myself."

I turn slightly to face him, and I see the pain etched all over his face. I never want to hurt him, but I won't be one of those Lunas who sits back and does nothing. He should know that by now.

He lets out a frustrated sigh, knowing I'm not going to back down.

'We just missed you, little mate,' Jace's gravelly voice rings through my head, and I see him peeking through Zanders' eyes.

I lean in and give him a deep kiss, I feel his desperation and frustration, but most of all I feel his love for me. Everything combined in the last few days has had him nearly losing his mind.

"I love you," I whisper, breaking out of the kiss.

"I love you too, sweetheart," he says, pulling me in closer to him. The tingles of our bond dance along my skin as I relax, and I drift off to a peaceful sleep.

A soft knock at the door wakes me. Zander is still holding me tightly, in the same position as before, his soft snores filling the room.

Mum's head pops in, and she looks around before spotting me on the bed. "Ohh, hun," she says, rushing into the room before standing next to my bed, bending over, and examining me.

Zander is suddenly jolted awake by her arrival but quickly relaxes when he realizes who it is.

"I'll, um, give you guys some space to talk," he mumbles before releasing me and manoeuvring his body from mine. As he moves away from the bed, she grabs him and pulls him in for a tight hug.

"Thank you for saving my daughter," she sighs, releasing him.

I can feel overwhelming happiness come from him as he tries to regain composure.

"I love her. No thanks are needed," he says, looking back at me with a small smile, before leaving the room.

"Oh baby, how are you feeling?" mum asks. "When Zander called, Oliver had already filled us in. We were so worried. Your father was furious because the school didn't even call us to tell us you were in the hospital," mum says quickly as she brings me in for a hug and starts fiddling with my sheets, making sure everything is tucked in nicely.

"I'm okay, ma, a lot better now than last night." I sigh. "How is dad? Is he around, too?" I look towards the door hoping he would walk through. I was half surprised that Brent and Ollie didn't come with her.

"No, I'm sorry, darling. The council is still trying to figure out what happened. Despite the captured rogues that they cold interview they are being dicks and not letting us do anything," mum says watching me as she sits down in the chair next to the bed.

"It's okay. Thank you for being here now. I'm sure it was uncomfortable considering the circumstances," I say.

It was nice to be able to be in this room and have her around. I wonder where Zander went, but I could still feel he is close, giving us some privacy to talk like he said.

I've missed mum. Everything that has happened in the last few days has been such a roller coaster of emotions I almost don't know how to deal with it. But I am so glad I had Zander, and he was willing to allow my family into his territory despite the issues.

Mum pauses to take a deep breath then speaks, "I'm sorry your uncle treated you that way. If I had known, I would have tried to talk to him before you told him."

"It's okay, mum," I am quick to reassure her. "I expected some sort of problem, but obviously not to that extent. I'm just glad Charwood accepted me. His father mentioned he will hold a ceremony in the next few weeks, but that might be moved forward considering the circumstances."

I believe that everything is okay because, despite everything that happened, Zander and I are more than okay. We have marked each other and are fully mated.

We are starting to build a future together. I was more than happy being beside my mate. I need him, and he needs me.

Chapter 66 - ZANDER

The last few weeks have been crazy. With Ashleigh's recovery, our exams finally ending, and graduation just around the corner … It has just been a whirlwind of activities.

I was so fucking proud of my girl when she announced that she got accepted into all the universities she applied to. Now she just has to choose her major and decide which one to go to.

Personally, I admit that I am running pretty low on energy just dealing with Ashley's anxiety and dad showing me the ropes of running the pack. Don't get me wrong, I love my girl, but sometimes, feeling her anxiety through our bond can hit me like a tidal wave and completely throw me off for the entire day. As Danni has learnt, whatever she is feeling, I feel it tenfold.

Today we finally had a meeting with the council. We tried to have one immediately, but they kept changing it and blocking us. It was their fifth time adjusting the schedule, and even then, they called everyone this morning and said today was open only for an hour if we wanted to take the spot or wait another month.

God damn fucking politics, I hate them, but even Dad says some rules must be held on both sides, or the relationship just won't work. Ha. Some fucking relationship, they barely keep to their side of the deal.

As Alphas, we have 100% autonomy in how we run our pack. But things get murky when dealing with humans and their laws. I considered becoming a lawyer so that I could be sure we are always on the right side of it. Thankfully, I don't have to, as that is what the pack advisers are there for, among other things...

Everyone in the car is tense as we drive to the city, where the council building is.

Ashleigh is a nervous wreck. I can't blame her after everything she's been through and not having any answers. Her nightmares have been taking a toll on both of us. She still wakes up crying and shaking some nights, and I feel fucking useless not to be able to help her in any way. I just want her to feel safe again. Some nights she holds me tightly until she drifts off to sleep, and I'm able to feel like I've helped her in some part.

She has a theory that the people who have been taking the pack members are the ones who stormed the school. We both feel responsible for what happened. It fucking kills me to see her distress. I feel guilty all the time, but I try to mask that from her. I don't want her to feel any worse than she already does.

Dad pulls up to a grand old building lined with sandstone and massive steps leading to huge double doors. This is where we hold all of the hearings and the majority of where the offices and council people are.

Ashleigh fidgets next to me. Her nerves are all over the place and being back in neutral territory makes her more anxious than she likes to admit. She struggled the first few weeks going back to school but wanted to push through. I wouldn't know she was nervous if it wasn't for our bond. She puts on a brave front for everyone else.

Frustration, annoyance, and a hint of anger always bubble not too far from the surface these days. It's hard to keep a tight lid on all these emotions when my mate and pack are attacked, and no one has any fucking answers.

I hope this council meeting isn't as useless as they usually are, because if I don't get the answers I'm looking for, I might just snap, and no one wants that. I don't know how dad went for so long without answers. One hit on our pack on neutral ground, and I'm a goner, and all my training went out the window. I'm always pissed off, and I'm not sure if it's just because of my mate's emotions.

We walk up the stairs of the grand building, only to stop a few feet away from Ashleigh's old pack leaders. Her mother, father, brother, Oliver and uncle, the Alpha, are all standing around and talking in strained whispers. From this distance, we can only hear the muffled voices, but they stop talking, and her uncle and father tense as we all walk in.

She hasn't seen her father since that day, and her mother regularly visits our old cottage, but they worry that if her father visits, things will escalate further with her uncle than it already has.

He gives her a small smile and tries to hide his emotions, but I can see his love for her and how much he misses her. Her mum just smiles at her warmly. Brent and Oliver are standing next to them, unsure of what to do. Oliver gives me a slight nod in recognition as we pass by, and Brent just shuffles around awkwardly. Her uncle just stands there with a deadpan look showing no emotion whatsoever.

I feel her uneasiness grow as we pass them. I pull her in close to me, wrapping my arm around her and planting a kiss on her head and whisper, "I love you. You know that, right?"

Ashleigh blinks up at me and smiles, "I know. I love you, too,"

The receptionist tells dad we will be in room 88. We walk down the corridor until we come to the room that we were assigned to. I begin to wonder why Liverpool hadn't entered, but I get my answer when the Westfield Alpha, Alpha Benjamin and the chief council Jones walk out, still in deep discussion about something.

My body stiffens, and I feel my anger surge to the surface. Westfield didn't lose anyone that day. Neither Lachlan nor Samantha was injured. I don't even remember seeing them on the battlefield at all. All of their pack were already on the other side of the school, away from the attack, when it happened. The others kept on brushing it off as a coincidence, but personally, I don't fucking believe in coincidences.

They both suddenly stop talking and look up at us with surprised faces. I don't know why they are fucking surprised. We had this meeting booked. Jace starts pacing in my mind, itching to get out. He's been more and more on edge lately, just as much as I have been.

"Alpha Wyatt, is there something I can help you with?" Chief Council Jones says, looking between all of us.

Dad looks at him with a deadpan expression, I can tell he's just as frustrated as I am, but after years of practice, he can hold a good poker face.

"We received a call saying the meeting had been moved to this morning," dad responds, just as Oliver and his family walk up.

Chief Council Jones looks back at Alpha Benjamin with a concerned look before looking back at Dad. "I'm sorry, but you were misinformed," he says, with a slight tremor, just as Bobby and Jax from Riverview show up with their Alpha and Beta. All are looking just as confused as the rest of us.

"Well, considering we are all here, I highly doubt that" Dad grinds out.

I see the people passing by watching us all curiously, probably wondering why each leader from the four largest packs in the country is talking to the Chief Council.

"Look, Chief Council Jones, with all due respect, this meeting has been pushed back for weeks now. We need to discuss the next steps and what to tell our packs of new protocols." Ashleigh's father steps forward and speaks.

Jones looks at his watch and sighs, giving Alpha Benjamin another weird look before deciding, "Fine, but make it quick. I have another meeting in an hour."

'Have your wits about you, be observant and don't take everything at face value,' Dad warns through the mind link as we all file into the boardroom.

'I don't like this,' Jace mumbles as I take a seat between Dad and Ashleigh. She puts a hand on my thigh, and I allow our bond to relax me, drinking in her scent.

'Are *both of you always this paranoid?'* Kia chimes in, seeming to be completely at ease. '*They can't do anything with so many Alphas in one room,'* she sighs.

'Or that's just their plan all along.' Jace mumbles as he stays alert but retreats to the back of my mind, still aware of our surroundings.

'And that's why we all left two people with a rank back at the pack, so if anything does happen, they will still have a leader.' Kia responds.

I quickly block out Kia and Ash to have a private conversation with Jace, 'Why are you being so weird lately? You're also very possessive for some reason.'

He just mumbles, '*you will find out later,'* before curling up and sending me a glare.

The board room is large with a tan and black colour scheme that gives off a luxurious feel. A huge table is in the middle, a projector board at the back wall and a computer off to the side. There are leather seats all around, offering comfortable seating for people to sit at.

"Right, let's get to business then," Jones sighs as he sits at the head of the table.

"Our people captured two rogues that tried to escape the school that day. The families who lost the children will be reimbursed and provided with funding for the funeral. For any children who are struggling with what happened, the school will provide the necessary assistance to help them through this tough time. The school will implement a new protocol to safeguard against something like this happening again. It will soon be reviewed and will be confirmed by the end of the year. Are there any questions?" Jones rambles hurriedly.

I look at the others. Lachlan and Samantha look so bored they look like they are about to fall asleep. Bobby and Jax seem to be mind-linking with each other and are in deep conversation. I can feel the anger and frustration coming from them. Even Oliver has a confused frown. I guess this wasn't what he was expecting to be discussed at this meeting. And frankly, it wasn't exactly what I was expecting either. I was expecting more information in regard to what's been happening with the disappearances lately, hoping that will have some sort of link between the attack.

"Can we interrogate the rogues?" I ask after a few moments of silence.

Everyone snaps their eyes at me, and Dad's eyes dance in amusement. Like he knows something is going to start.

Jones shakes his head, "I don't think that is necessary. They aren't saying anything to us. I doubt you will get anything."

I fought back my snarl in frustration. They attacked my Luna, Beta, and Gamma. Out of everyone in the room, I think we deserve a shot at talking to the rogues. I can feel Jace push forward in frustration, and I know he is in my eyes when I see Oliver smirk over at me, raising an eyebrow.

"What of the recent attacks on our packs?" Oliver asks as everyone's attention turns to him.

"What of them?" Jones asks. His bored expression matches Westfields.

"Well... do you have any leads?" Oliver grinds out, crossing his arms across his chest, looking pissed.

"No, we haven't had anything back from our investigation, and our scout reports still come back negative. Obviously, with no evidence to support any type of theory, we would ask you to please keep the chatter amongst your pack members to a minimum." Jones says, looking between us all.

"How do you expect us to stop them from talking about it when their families are disappearing, and they aren't getting any answers? You won't even give us anything to help them through a time like this," Ashleigh speaks up, surprising me entirely.

I can feel her anger and frustration through our bond. I sling my arm across the back of her chair and draw tiny circles on her back to try and let the bond effect flow through.

"You would do well to listen and only speak when spoken to, pup," Jones growls back at her, his eyes flashing with his wolf pushing forward.

As soon as those words leave his mouth, a snarl rips through mine. I know Jace is out at full force when I see Danni and some of the others flinch away and turn white.

"She is my Luna. Show her the same respect you would show me," Jace snarls.

"Everybody out," he hisses, his eyes blazing with fury as he eyes Jones. I can feel the full force of his aura pulsing around. He was fucking pissed.

'Jace, it's ok,' Ashleigh whispers through our link, rubbing my arm, trying to calm me down, but even then, the bond won't help Jace's fury now. He's too far gone.

'They do not get away with this shit… and I am so fucking tired of this,' he growls back.

She sighs, and I watch as she, dad and the others start to file out of the room. Her mother looks back at me, concerned, giving me a small smile, but honestly, I just didn't give a fuck. No one treats her like that, and fucking gets away with it. No one.

Oliver is still sitting back in his chair, smirking, with his arms folded across his chest and puts his feet up on the table, looking so fucking relaxed.

"Are you leaving?" Jace asks, and I can tell he's still furious but has toned it down with Oliver, considering the last few weeks we have both been through shit and somewhat working together to sort this stuff out.

"Nah, I'll just stay and make sure you don't kill the fucker," he chuckles, nodding toward Jones, who is still seated at the head of the table. Jones is white as a sheet, shaking violently, I can sense his wolf wanting to come forward, but with both Oliver and me here, he didn't fucking stand a chance.

I nod. It would be good to have him listening in. I don't even try to fight Jace for control on this because, honestly, I felt the same fucking way as he did. He lets the walls down, and I find my way up as he allows me to share control with him.

Jace's aura still whips around us, as Oliver looking pretty fucking smug about the whole thing, not even bothered by my power.

"So ... as my mate asked, what is the most recent update," Jace growls, eyes flashing directly at Jones.

~Ashleigh.

I've never seen Zander or Jace so mad. I can feel their fury hit me all the way from the boardroom. I wanted to stay, but I knew he needed to do this. Zander holds so much guilt for what happened. I just hope he doesn't kill Jones to get the answers.

As everyone flies out, I look around for Ollie, but I can't see him anywhere.

"Oliver stayed with Zander, just to make sure nothing happens to him or Jones," mum whispers as they walk past.

I nod and smile inwardly. I know those two may hate each other, but I'm glad they are working together to try and move through this.

"I don't think I have ever seen Zander so pissed off," Danni mutters, talking with Beta Jake and Alpha Wyatt.

"I did tell him to keep his cool with Jones. I just hope he doesn't kill him for disrespecting Ashleigh," Alpha Wyatt sighs. "Jones is a disrespectful mutt who made it into the council through blackmail and by having friends in high places."

"Then why did you allow him to be by himself?" Jake asks, looking frustrated with everything, "You know we have been trying to get this meeting for weeks now."

Alpha Wyatt shrugs. "Zander has undergone Alpha training, and he needs to learn how to handle the politics of council meetings. I'm just surprised that everyone else followed."

"Ashleigh," I hear my name being called, and I spin around to see dad walking towards me. I put on my best smile and move to give him a hug, but he shakes his head. "Not here, sweetie," he mumbles softly as he moves closer.

“Alpha Wyatt,” dad greets him with a nod, “Would you mind if I talk to my daughter for a moment?”

Wyatt nods and moves the others off to the side as dad makes his way over to me.

“Hi, sweetie, I’ve missed you,” he whispers, bringing me into a deep hug as I embrace his familiar scent.

“Hi, daddy,” I whisper back, I try not to let my emotions get the better of me, but the last few weeks have been hard not being able to talk to him or go through our usual routine. I am thankful that mum takes the time to come and see me at the cottage. I hope that uncle will one day see the pain he is causing his family and realize that it’s just not worth it anymore.

“I want you to know that I am so proud of you and what you have accomplished these last few weeks. Oliver said you got into all the universities you applied for and that you have been taking on a lot more leadership roles in Zander’s pack lately.” Dad says as he moves us further away from where uncle and mum are to give us some privacy.

I give a small nod, I wasn’t sure where Ollie got that info from, but I would assume Zander has been keeping him up to date with a lot of different things considering they meet every few weeks to make sure everything is running smoothly between both packs.

I am thankful that, finally, they are able to come to some sort of an agreement to protect all packs; they aren’t including Westfield in any information yet because Zander is just paranoid lately. But I am proud of the way Zander and Ollie have stepped up in their roles. I just hoped uncle didn’t punish Ollie later.

Moments later, the doors fly open, and I see my furious-looking mate marches out with Ollie hot on his heels, in fits of laughter, trying to contain himself. Concern washes over me as I see the two men walking towards us.

“Robert,” Zander nods at dad as he slips next to me, wraps his arms around me and pulls me close, breathing in my scent to help him relax.

“Zander, did you get what you wanted from Jones?” dad asks, looking between the two.

Zander's scowling face tells me everything. I can feel his anger as he tries to control himself.

“Jones didn’t say much, but the things he did say were interesting,” Ollie mumbled.

“Which was?” dad asks again, looking between them both.

“Gave us some names that might be able to help us get more information on the rogues, he also gave us a contact to help locate the witches. It's been a few weeks and my trackers still haven't come up with anything,” Ollie sighs, scrubbing a hand over his face.

I didn’t pay attention before, but as I look closer all three of them look exhausted. Running on next to no sleep and training every single day, I know Ollie isn’t looking after himself now his routine is all out of place, and everything is going on with uncle.

“Ollie, when was the last time you had a good sleep?” I ask my stubborn cousin.

He shares a look with Zander before answering me. “Few weeks, since you left, I guess,” he shrugs and says nonchalantly.

“Ollie, you can’t do that to yourself…” I start, I know things at home haven’t been great, but he needs to at least look after himself, he can’t run himself to the ground.

“Love, leave him be…” Zander sighs, giving me a small kiss, “We should get going, we have shit to do now that Jones is being a fucking princess and won’t give us any more information.”

Ollie nods in confirmation, “I’ll message or call with any updates, let me know if anything arises on your end.”

Zander nods and grabs my hand leading me back towards the others who have now made their way out. I stop suddenly, realizing this may be the last time for a while I get to see my father.

I pull out of Zander’s grasp and quickly run back to dad, giving him one last hug goodbye.

“Love you, daddy,” I whisper, inhaling in the familiar scent one more time. I hope things can sort out soon with David, because I miss my family. I still see mum and Ollie all the time, but I miss dad, I miss being able to see them whenever I want to without all these stupid rules in place.

“Love you, too, sweetie. Be safe, and stick with Zander until this all settles down,” he says, before letting go and giving me a kiss goodbye.

Epilogue - ASHLEIGH

After everything that life has thrown at me this year, I was so proud and excited to finish school and go to one of the best universities in the country to study psychology. Graduation went beautifully; I was so happy mum and dad both came and saw me give my valedictorian speech, and despite everything I was glad they supported me.

It was a huge honour to be the school's valedictorian this year. It put a little bit of pressure on me, having to write a speech, but it wasn't anything I couldn't handle.

The dinner was beautiful, something they held yearly to send off the seniors after stressful exams. I appreciated saying thank you and goodbye to everyone, I hoped I would still see them in the future, but no one can make any promises.

I had one more fabulous night with my girls, Chloe and Skyla and I was filled with laughter and love. Our friendship won't ever change, no matter what pack we are in. Thankfully, Zander has accepted that.

I'm glad I chose psychology. I wanted to choose something that would help with our pack so that when our members would come and seek help, I would know the proper counsel to help them if they didn't feel like speaking to anyone else about certain things.

I was so giddy with excitement when I got accepted that Zander didn't know what to do with me.

He has been quiet the last little bit of the trip. I glance over at him as we drive through the streets of our pack that has started to become familiar to me. I don't even know where we are going, but I can feel his nervousness rolling off him in waves.

This afternoon when he got home, he said, "wear something nice and comfy. We're going out tonight." So here I am in the passenger seat of his car wearing nice jeans, a flowing floral top, and slip-on sandals. I did my hair all nice and loose and put a little makeup on, just how he likes it. He looks handsome in dark black jeans and a navy button-up top.

I sit here wondering what could be making him so nervous. He's been acting a little weird all week, blocking me from some of his emotions and thoughts now and then, but I just put it down to stress and being thrown into learning more about the pack and how it is run.

Since finishing school, his dad has helped us transition into our roles full-time and figure out everything. We are holding my Luna ceremony next month at the full moon, and everyone is going to be there. It'll be an amazing event. I couldn't wait to meet the rest of Zander's pack. Wyatt suggested we invite some Alphas and Beta from other packs to mark the special occasion.

"Zander, babe, you've been driving me crazy, what's going on?" I finally ask him, getting sick of the silence and his stress levels.

"Huh?" He asks, turning to me and blinking out of his daze.

"Why are you a nervous wreck right now?" I ask as I reach out and touch him, offering relief through our bond.

"It's nothing, I promise," he gives me a sexy smile, mischief dancing in his eyes as he looks at me...

"Am I allowed to know where we are going?" I sigh,

"All in good time, sweetheart," he chuckles. I am at least happy he isn't too stressed tonight, just nervous.

Soon Zander pulls up at the familiar little cottage that we both have grown so fond of. I smile at the memories we both shared here. I miss the days we could escape and just be peaceful here. While it is a good thing that Zander is more involved with the pack now, I do miss the connection we had back when things were simpler.

He helps me out of the car as we make our way toward the front. I frown as I see little rose petals and daisies lining the door.

"What's going on?" I ask curiously as he unlocks the door leading me inside.

The cottage was transformed into something completely magical: a string of fairy lights climbs along the staircase rails, and little floating tea lights are placed around the living room with rose petals and daisies.

It's beautiful. I gape in awe as I looked around. Did he do all this for me? Why?

My heart is thundering in my chest as I try to understand what's happening. Kia has slipped into the back of my mind not offering any assistance. Even Jace is quiet.

I turn around to ask Zander what is going on, only to find him down on one knee, holding a little box in his hands.

"What are you…." I trail off as he begins to talk.

"Ashleigh Kylie Steward, you are the best thing that has ever happened to me. I know our start was rocky, but I only hope to make a better future for us both. I love you so much, sweetheart, and I can't wait to be by your side for the rest of my life. Will you marry me?"

I blink at him, flustered. It wasn't the conventional thing for wolves to get married. Once we found our mates, we would just move in with our significant other, and that was it. You would have some sort of celebration but never anything huge like a wedding.

"Yes... yes... yes..." I squeal, jumping up in his arms and bringing him closer into a deep kiss.

He picks me up as I wrap my legs around him for support as carries me toward the bedroom.

~

We quietly enjoy each other's company as we lie in bed in tangled sheets. I trace a finger on his naked chest while Zander plays with my hair. Moments like these are rare, nowadays, with everything we need to do. Finally, we have peaceful bliss.

"I have one more thing to give you," he mumbles before reaching across the bedside table. I sit up slightly to face him, and he pulls out the little blue velvet box I once owned. My heart thunders in my chest, and tears threaten to fall.

The one little item I had fallen in love with weeks ago sat in his hands as he held it out to me. I believe wholeheartedly that I made the right choice at the time, giving it back, but I missed wearing this little item that meant so much to me.

"Now that you are going to be my wife and mate, will you also be my Luna?" he whispers, looking at me with so many emotions. I could feel everything through our bond. I love him more than anything in this world; I know he already knew the answer. But I still appreciated him asking me.

I nodded vigorously, unable to speak, with happy tears streaming down my face. He breaks out into a big grin before bringing me into another smouldering kiss.

Epilogue - ZANDER

I stand at the end of the aisle in front of a room full of hundreds of people, the majority of whom I know. I know most of my pack and most of the Alphas and Betas who accepted today's invitation.

Dad made a point of inviting nearly everyone to Ash's Luna ceremony. Guess he was finally over all of the grudges and is ready for a new beginning.

Jace is bouncing around in my head, anticipation to finally see her. Danni is next to me, buzzing with excitement. This kid, it feels like he's always a ball of happiness. He and Eric adore Ash, and I couldn't have chosen anyone better to help protect her and be by our side in leadership.

Her family are here except for her uncle and aunt. I'm glad her mother and father were able to come today. I could feel how happy she was through our bond. She was fucking ecstatic when they arrived this morning.

Oliver and Brent are sitting next to Kylie in the front. Brent looks a little uneasy, but Oliver doesn't seem to mind anymore. He's been back here a few times and has met several different people working with us to get stuff sorted out between our packs.

It's funny to think that we once hated each other's guts. Now we can somewhat have a decent conversation and be in the same room without ripping each other's heads off. Things might not yet be resolved with her family, but I hope that one day they will be. After all, both of our packs can benefit from an alliance. Oliver seems more than willing to join up, it's just his father that is in the way at the moment, and maybe with time, things will turn around, but for now, we just have to let it all settle down and give him time to come around.

My palms are all clammy, and my body feels numb. I'm excited, don't get me wrong. But I never thought we would have been able to pull off this thing in a month.

With Ashleigh's Luna ceremony happening, Ellie suggested why not combine the wedding and Luna ceremony, so with not seeing my mate the last 24 hours mind and body are a mess from missing her too much.

"Breath, son, there's no need to be nervous," dad tries to reassure me by clasping a hand on my shoulder.

"Who says I'm nervous?" I mumble back. He raises a questioning eyebrow and chuckles. He's right, though, I feel fucking giddy. I keep on fidgeting, and no doubt he can smell the nerves rolling off me.

The soft music of Ed Sheeran's 'Perfect' starts playing, and the doors open as Chloe and then Skyla starts to walk down the aisle in white sequin dresses.

My heart thunders in my chest as I wait for her. Everyone stands as she walks toward me.

Thump. Thump. Thump. Shit, I think I forgot how to breathe.

She looks like a fucking vision as she comes into view … everything melts away, and it's just her. A royal blue dress with a full skirt and a low-cut neckline, it's simple but elegant at the same time. Clutching a bouquet of white wild daisies. Her hair is long, and half done up in the hairpiece I gave her.

I don't even want her to make it down the aisle. I just want to throw her over my shoulder and have my way with her.

I unconsciously take a step forward before Danni puts a hand on my shoulder, stopping me from moving further.

"She's coming to you, man," he laughs softly.

Her father holds her tightly as he walks down the aisle with her, helping her not to fall over.

Her scent engulfs all around me as she stands next to me. She leans in and gives her father a quick hug and a kiss before passing him the bouquet.

"Hi," she whispers, smiling softly at me.

"Hi, sweetheart, you look fucking amazing," I whisper back as I rake my eyes over her beautiful body. All I want to do at this moment is pull her close and give her a kiss. She looks fucking stunning.

The music quiets, and Dad clears his voice before starting, drawing everyone's attention. Usually, the ceremony is done by a council member or pack elder but as the pack's Alpha, dad is more than happy to officiate. There are also several council members and elders here today to witness today's ceremony.

"Today we are gathered for a very special occasion. My son has found his mate!" dad's voice rings through the room, smiling at Ashleigh and me.

I wasn't expecting the eruption of cheers and happiness that came from my pack and her family beaming at us as dad waits a few moments for it to quickly die down before starting again.

"As his mate, she must accept her place in this pack and vow to fulfil her duties." Dad continues, smiling at us.

Over the last few weeks, they have grown closer. I am so thankful that dad put aside his old grudge against her previous pack and accepted her. In doing so also becoming another father figure as he shows her the ropes to what her new role will be.

"Ashleigh Kylie Steward, do you willingly accept your duty as Luna to this pack, and it's Alpha as your mate?"

Ashleigh nods confidently as a smile breaks out over her face "I do."

"Do you swear allegiance and loyalty to this pack and willingly take on the responsibilities as Luna?"

Her eyes meet mine as I give her hands a tight squeeze in reassurance. She is more than ready for the role she was born for. "I do."

"Do you swear to put the needs and safety of our pack members first and foremost above anything else and treat them with the love and care as you would your own child?"

Again, her response is, "I do."

Each time she responds with more and more certainty, our bond flows through us with love and affection, and I couldn't be prouder of her.

Jake passes dad a small dagger placed on a black cloth, “Having sworn your allegiance to Charwood pack, now for the blood tie and pack link.” Dad gets the blade first and slits it across his hand, making a cut.

Ashleigh releases one of her hands from mine and holds it out in front of dad, offering her own blood as a sacrifice. Dad pulls the blade across her hand, making the same identical cut as his before grabbing her hand in his and joining her to the pack. Their blood mixes as he holds her hand.

I feel the surge of power pour over me and our pack members for something that we haven’t had in years. A missing piece that we never knew was so important.

With a proud smile, dad releases her hand and turns to the front, “Before we come to the end of this ceremony, I have one more announcement.” I whip back around to face him. He didn’t tell me anything else was happening. Panic starts to set in as I think of all the possibilities that could happen.

“These last few months Zander and Ashleigh have stepped up to their role more than I could have ever imagined. Therefore today, I have made the decision to step back from my role as Alpha and pass the title to my son and his mate.”

Wait… What!?

I stare at dad, my mouth opening and closing like a fish out of water. I’m sure I look like a fucking idiot right now. Way to announce something and not give me a heads up.

‘*You deserve it, son, now more than ever. I am so proud of who you have become. I’ll help transition the next few months, but from here on out, you are the Alpha of this pack*,’ he says through our link.

So many emotions flow through me, and I’m in complete shock that dad was so willing to pass it to me. I was honestly thinking I had to wait a few more years.

Before I knew what was happening, dad held out his hand to grasp mine and to make a similar cut to his and Ashleigh’s holding our hands together, he binds our blood and speaks.

“I, Alpha Wyatt Dane Blackwood of Charwood pack, hereby relinquish my title as Alpha and pass it to my son, Zander Wyatt Blackwood,”

My mind is still trying to comprehend as I hear him say these words, I don't even know how to process this.

‘*You have to accept the title, son. Trust me, you are more than ready.*’ Dad encourages through our link.

“I, Zander Wyatt Blackwood, hereby accept the title of Alpha for Charwood pack.”

“Do you swear to protect your pack first and foremost before anything else?”

I nod slowly. “I do.”

“Do you swear allegiance and loyalty to this pack and willingly take on the responsibilities as Alpha?”

As my mind and body begin to accept that this is actually happening, I nod confidently.

“I do.”

"Do you swear to uphold the rules and traditions of this pack?"

Again, I nod, "I do."

Dad breaks out with a huge smile as he releases my hand and turns back to face the crowd.
I feel the surge of power move through me, as I say the final vow, linking me completely to the pack as Alpha.

"Ladies and gentlemen, I am proud to announce your new Alpha and Luna of Charwood, Alpha Zander Blackwood and Luna Ashleigh Blackwood."

If I thought the cheers before were loud, I was wrong, the room exploded with cheers and congratulatory happiness.

Everyone stands and claps as I pull Ashleigh in for a deep kiss, something I've been wanting to do since I laid eyes on her.

I grab her hand, and she happily follows me back out of the hall. I spin her around before bringing her into another kiss.

Bonus

Grace

I lay on the hotel's disgusting bed, looking up at the cracked pink paint, watching every scrap as it peels off, falling from the ceiling. The dimly lit light flickers through the room as I try to focus on the walls around me.

“Happy birthday to me, happy birthday to me,” I softly sing as tears stream down my face.

How did everything get so fucked up? I had a foolproof plan that would have worked if he didn’t find his fucking mate. Who would have guessed Ashleigh Steward was my boyfriend's mate?

I honestly thought it would be me. I’m an Alpha's daughter; I had a higher possibility. We had a magnetic attraction from the start, and everyone back home said we were perfect together. Dad is obsessed with Zander. But then, all he ever wants is power and money. Charwood, being the biggest pack in the country, has both.

‘We should go out. I saw a bar when we walked past here,’ my wolf Talia says encouragingly, pushing forward hopefully.

‘We need to stay hidden, Talia,’ I scolded, ‘we don’t want them or dad to find us.’

Talia whimpers and curls up at the memories of home. They used to be happy memories, but since mum passed away, giving birth to my baby brother, dad turned feral. With my brother, Drake, watching his every move, he has become even more aggressive.

Dad's mistress, Denice, is just as money hungry and doesn’t give a shit about anyone either. As they say, “I learned from the best”.

All I wanted was Zander. He was everything to me. I loved him more than anything, despite what my father wanted and what they wanted, but I couldn’t tell him. They warned me; told me people were watching, and they were right. I have the scars to prove it.

When Zander broke things off with me, I was devastated, especially when I found out that it was because he found his mate.

That day that we went to the clinic for the ultrasound, the pure rage was on Zander’s face when he found out the truth. I didn’t even get a chance to explain. I knew that if I didn’t get out of Charwood's territory quickly, his wolf Jace would surely kill me.

That day my phone rang nonstop with people demanding to know what was happening, and I couldn’t tell them. I didn’t know. I’d never seen Zander so angry in my life.

‘Let's go. You’ve been moping about Zander for a few weeks. We need to shape up and ship out,’ Talia says. ‘But first, we need money. This is the last hotel we can pay for with the cash we had.’

I sniffle, wiping away my pathetic tears because I know she is right. Our last few hundred dollars could only get us this dinghy room for the weekend, and tonight is our last night.

I flick on the TV as I start to get ready. It is only 8 pm, so it's not too late to go out. It probably is a slow night, but being my birthday, I hoped that would benefit me.

In breaking news, Summervale College was attacked by rogue shifters earlier today. Three students remain in critical care, and four have lost their lives. Charwood's, Luna Ashleigh Blackwood, Beta Daniel Richmond, and Gamma Eric Stephens are all in ICU facing life-threatening injuries. We wish them a full recovery and will follow this story closely with further updates.

I freeze as I hear the news report. They actually went through with it. After everything, I couldn't believe they did it.

I am so glad I changed my phone number and deleted the other numbers from my phone so that they couldn't track it. I couldn't be linked back to anything. I can't ever go back. It will be my mission to never be found by them, only to be dragged back to that hell hole.

I look at myself in the mirror as I brush my hair. Sadly, it needs a good cut and clean. The hair dye I used a few weeks ago has started to fade, and my brown roots are starting to show.

I wish I could use my credit cards more than anything, but since I haven't reported in, I know they will be waiting for me to slip up. I know they are looking for me. I got as much cash out as I could at the first point, then stopped using them so they can't find me.

They told me to contact them twice a week. If I missed a scheduled update, they sent someone to punish me.

This isn't the first time I've missed an update. I hope they would forget or just not send anyone, but they always come. I moved my fingers along my last 'punishment' on the right side of my hip. The skin healed quickly despite the red-hot iron bar they pressed against it, leaving me with a jagged scar. They remembered to use silver so that the scar would always be there as a reminder that they owned me. I tried to plead with them, explaining that I was doing what they asked, but each time they ignored me and didn't care because they wanted information.

I collapse on the shower flow and sob for what feels like hours. The alarm on my phone buzzes loudly. I look at it and see that only ten minutes has passed and a reminder that there is something I needed to do tonight.

I get up from the shower floor and put on my best top and a skirt with my favourite high heels and get ready to go out for the night.

The bar is only a few blocks down. Even in heels, it is a short enough walk.

Muffled music could be heard from behind the door. A few people waiting around the front, which is surprising for a Monday.

The two bouncers out the front are in black tees and dark pants. One of them looks me up and down with lust-filled eyes and a smirk on his lips. The other just looked at me and remained expressionless.

By their scent, I could tell that they are both humans. Not wanting to give away that I am a shifter, I flash a sweet smile as they part for me to enter.

It is a cosy bar for one that is on the side street and not open to heavy traffic flow. I walk in and look around. It has an open floor plan, with tables and chairs scattered and a pool table off to the side. Along the back wall is the bar with bartenders serving drinks. The shelves are lined with liquor bottles illuminated by lights.

There aren't too many people out tonight, mostly all humans. The shifters who were here earlier have since left, as their scent is faint. Sighing, I move to the bar. I hope I can get something for free. If not, I'll have to use my last fifteen dollars to get at least something decent to eat.

"What can I get ya," the bartender asks in a gravelly voice. His eyes directly go to my boobs as I push them out, making them look more presentable.

"Mojito," I say with a sweet smile, batting my eyelashes.

"Comin' up," he nods, giving my boobs one last glance. "So, what's a fine young lady like yourself doing around these parts of town?" he asks, giving me a creepy smile while making the drink.

I shrug and twirl my hair, "oh, you know, just visiting some friends."

He chuckles at my response while passing me the drink. "On the house," he smirks as his eyes dart to my boobs once more.

I lean forward and give him a little peck on the cheek with a sweet "thanks". I turn around and walk to one of the tables in the corner.

As I look around, a strong scent of cinnamon and mint hits me so suddenly I'm in a complete daze.

'Mate, mate', Tahlia jumps around excitedly.

'What!?!?' I panic. If he's here, he's not a shifter. There aren't any shifters around.

I frantically look around to see who the scent belongs to, and as I do, my eyes land on the most beautiful man I have ever seen. He's sitting along the back wall in a booth, buried deep in books and paperwork, with a few beers pushed to the side on the end of the table.

His hair is pitch black. His jaw is covered in short stubble, and his glasses keep slipping down his nose every few seconds as he moves through his work, so distracted by it that he doesn't even notice his surroundings. His long-sleeved shirt is wrinkled and pushed up his arms, and his tie is loose, like he's pulled at it trying to get it loose after a rough day of work.

My heart skips a few beats. He's beautiful. I wonder how I can go over and speak to him. I've never been shy about approaching people, but now, at this moment, I am terrified of speaking to my mate.

I slowly walk over to him, and as I do, his scent amplifies by a thousand. My body is buzzing like it's on fire, and Tahlia is so excited, jumping around in my mind like a crazy person making it harder for me to concentrate.

I put on my best smile and tried to get as much courage as possible to say something to him,

"Hi, I'm Grace," I say, trying not to let my voice come out like a squeak.

At first, I don't think he hears me and just continues moving through his paperwork, but after the most intense five seconds of my life, he looks up. Blue, his eyes filled with the most beautiful colour of deep blue I have ever seen in my life. I suck in a sharp breath as he looks at me.

He frowns, opens his mouth slowly and says, "Elijah," his rough voice weakens my knees.

Get a grip, Grace… I murmur to myself, only to have Talia snicker at me in the background. His name is as beautiful as he is. I want to move closer and jump in his arms, covering him with kisses, but I hold myself back. I don't know how much he knows about shifters.

By now, everyone knows about shifters, but some people choose not to accept or believe or have some sort of hatred towards us, so I have to tread very lightly here and see what his beliefs are before I reveal our bond.

Tahlia whimpers at the thought of our mate not wanting us. No one else ever wanted us, but the thought of our mate not wanting us and being a different species only makes things harder.

Elijah is the first to snap out of our staring contest and moves back to his paperwork and books, shuffling everything around on the table in some organised mess.

"Mind if I join you?" I ask, sliding myself down into the booth opposite him.

He looks back up. His eyes hold no emotion, but frustration is etched on his face. He gives a quick nod before grabbing his beer and taking a swig.

** **Elijah** **

Work is stressful. Being a university professor has its challenges. Talking to people every single day and not having a break can be hard, so I like to go to my local bar and do the paperwork there.

Benny, the barkeeper, is my best friend and owns the pub, so drinks and food are half off. It's a decent enough place to remain hidden but has the ambience.

When this girl, Grace, walks up to me and introduces herself, I feel this weird pull toward her. I don't know how to explain it, but suddenly it's like nothing else matters, and all I want is her.

I didn't even feel this much pull with my most recent girlfriend. We were together for three years, but six months ago, she decided to end it, telling me that she was now bored and had enough of life with me. She packed up her stuff in our apartment and moved out that same day.

I drank my sorrows away for the first two months. After that, Benny helped me get my shit together again. The one person who I wanted to settle down with was bored of me. If only she knew the truth, she might not have been so bored…

"So, what are you doing?" Grace asks curiously, looking between all my paperwork sprawled across the table.

"Grading papers," I grumble. My mind is in such a fog with her around. Something else had to be at play here. She smells of sweet strawberries and mint. Every time she leans closer to me, I can smell it, making my body tingle all over.

"You teach?" she asks, looking at me cocking her head slightly, observing my every movement.

"Yes, history and philosophy," I sigh, moving through one of the papers.

I feel her mood instantly change. From the corner of my eye, I see her expression change to one of worry as she shifts uncomfortably in the seat opposite me. Something flashes in her eyes so quickly that I almost don't see it.

Fuck, fuck! is she what I think she is?

A vampire's eyes don't change like that. Their eyes only change when they drink blood. Witch's eyes do change colour but only when casting a spell. As for werewolves, it isn't just the eyes. When the animal moves forward, it can take control and its entire body shifts from human to wolf.

So, If she shows her eyes again… I'll be able to determine which one she is … witch or wolf. But why is she interested in me? Hardly anyone ever speaks to me when I am sitting here, they know not to approach me.

Grace looks curiously at the papers and starts reaching for them. I guess to see what I was grading them on. I get agitated and quickly move my hand down on hers, stopping her movements.

She jumps up in fright and pulls away her hand, but not before I feel an eruption of sparks surge through me. Her eyes turn silver, and I can see her wolf peeking through, interested in what's going on.

"Sorry, I didn't mean to hurt you. It's an organized mess. I have the different piles so I can grade them later and know what marks to put down." I explain softly, confused by the sparks.

Think, damn it… think… What do the sparks mean with the wolves? And then it hits me like a freight train. The pull, the sparks, the scent.

"How old are you?" I ask her. I need to be one hundred per cent sure I have this right before making any assumptions.

"Umm... I just turned eighteen today," she mumbles, looking away. Suddenly her surroundings are more interesting than me as she looks around the room fiddling with her fingernails.

"So old enough to find a mate," I state bluntly.

She looks back at me, shocked.

"Yes," she whispers sadly. "I understand if you don't want me, but all I ask … can you please reject me tomorrow … I don't want it to taint my birthday."

I sit there, completely stunned. I couldn't believe this girl is my mate. The moon goddess is surely playing a sick joke on both of us.

"Where are you staying?" I ask. I need to know she was safe here.

"The motel on the corner," she mumbles while looking down at her hands, as her face flushes with embarrassment.

"What are you running from?" I ask curiously.

You only go to that motel if you need something cheap. Her hair was half done, she had only half applied her makeup, and her outfit was all over the place. She was running from something or someone.

She shifts around in her seat, clearly uncomfortable with my question.

"Look, I just want to know what I'm getting myself into," I tell her before grabbing one of her hands and squeezing it tightly to give her some reassurance. If we are both running, I'd like to know what she is running from so we can make plans for when we need to move next.

The sparks of the bond fly through me, jolting my entire body to life, making me want nothing more than her.

She looks up at me with hope shining in her eyes, her beautiful brown eyes. Fuck she's gorgeous! The more I stay around her, the more I just want to be in her presence.

She opens her mouth to say something but hesitates when she looks down at my hand. I release hers and move mine back towards me.

"You're one of them…" she whispers quietly, panicking and trembling as she pushes away from the table, trying to get out.

I frown, looking at the back of my wrist. I used to have an old tattoo there but got it removed a long time ago. Right now, it is nothing more than a scar.

How the fuck does she know what that symbol means? Unless …

Before I even get a chance to process what happened, Grace has already sprinted toward the door, wanting out. I scramble quickly out of the booth, following her. I don't know what she knows, but I am nothing like them. That's why I left. She needs to understand that.

"Grace, let me explain," I call out to her, fuck, she's fast, but I'm gaining on her. She nearly reaches her hotel, and she spins around to face me.

"No, I am not going back to them. You can't make me," she shrieks as her wolf pushes forward with full force and slams her fist into my chest. Making me stumble a little and grunt in pain.

I snatch her wrist and spin her around to hold her. If the mate bond is as powerful as all the books I have read, I pray this will calm her down so she will listen as I talk.

"I'm not one of them anymore. I left, and I ran. I couldn't be part of something so disgusting. I will never let them hurt you. Do you understand me?" I hold her close. Her eyes swimming with tears, she looks up staring into mine.

"You were still one of them," she whispers. I can still feel her shaking violently, and her wolf pushing forward as she struggles to break free.

"Years and years ago, when I was a kid, I needed quick cash. I never knew what happened behind closed doors. But when I moved up the ranks and found out the truth, I got out and have been running ever since. I use the knowledge I have of the supernatural now to teach kids. I swear to you, I will not let them hurt you,"

I watch the tears streaming down her face, as she breaks down completely falling into my chest crying.

I made a silent promise to her and to myself … no one will ever find us; we will never be a part of that again.

Pack Information

Charwood Pack

Alpha Wyatt Blackwood

Luna Molly Blackwood deceased

Alpha Heir Zander Blackwood (Son)

Beta Jake Richmond

Beta Female Ellie Richmond

Beta Heir Daniel Richmond (Son)

Liverpool Pack

Alpha David Steward (Brother)

Luna Sarah Steward

Alpha Heir Oliver Steward (Son)

Beta Robert Steward (Brother)

Beta Female Kylie Steward

Beta Heir Ashleigh Steward (Daughter)

Beta Heir Brent Steward (Son)

Riverview Pack

Alpha Lucas Enderson

Luna Lyla Enderson

Alpha Heir Bobby Enderson (Son)

Beta Cillian Sommers

(Mother unknown)

Beta Heir Jax Sommers (Son)

Westfield Pack

Alpha Ethan Kings

Luna Kira Kings

Alpha Heir Lachlan Kings (Son)

Beta Gregory Brown deceased

Beta Female Ally Brown deceased

Beta Heir Samantha Brown (Daughter)

Acknowledgements

Thank you to my fabulous partner has who helped me through the late nights and, going through some of my ridiculous plots while trying to make sense of everything. Thank you for supporting me during our hard times. I am forever grateful to you.

I thank you immensely my fabulous editor, Penny Tan, I would not have been able to do this without you, your tips and tricks have helped made me a better writer. Thank you for putting up with my crazy hours and pushing through my shocking spelling.

https://www.instagram.com/slvrdlphn/

Thank you to Central covers for the amazing artwork.

https://www.instagram.com/centralcovers_/

Lastly but not least, Thank you to the lovely ladies who have supported me through this crazy journey, without your support and able to vent to you all about our crazy experiences I would have not been able to complete what I have.

Your support and kind words have been something that helps me push through the hard and crazy days. I will be forever grateful to you for showing me what you can do when you follow your dreams and create something so incredible.

C.J. Primer   Stacy Rush   Saree Bee

Moonlight Muse   Author Bryant

Author Note:

To my lovely supporter,

Thank you for purchasing and reading my story, I hope you enjoyed it as much as I enjoyed creating it. While Alpha Zander is a Happily Ever After romance shifter novel, a lot of questions will be answered in Alpha Oliver.

I apologize if this is frustrating to you as a reader, however I hope you will understand as you read Alpha Oliver to why this was done.

I hope you enjoyed my world, I have very much enjoyed creating it.

The Alpha Series:

Alpha Zander: Book 1 of the Alpha Series

Alpha Oliver: Book 2 of the Alpha Series

Alpha Narissa: Book 3 of the Alpha Series

Please follow my social accounts for updates, inspiration ideas and announcements to more of my works.

https://www.instagram.com/authorv_turner/

Printed in Great Britain
by Amazon

20395610R00169